"I get the feeling we're completely lost," Adon mumbled as he pushed through a tangle of vines into a small clearing.

"Impossible," Kelemvor said gruffly. "There is but one road, and it leads only to Castle Kilgrave."

"But we may have gone off the road hours ago," Adon whined. "Who can tell?"

The forest, silent until now, suddenly shrieked to life. Kelemvor stood beside Midnight, Caitlan, and Adon, watching as a group of bizarre creatures erupted from the trees. He heard a low growl and turned to see a pair of yellow dogs, each bearing three heads and eight spidery legs, creeping up on them from behind. The dogs separated and maneuvered to attack.

"Adon! Midnight! Back-to-back formation with me. We have to protect Caitlan!" The cleric and the mage responded instantly, helping the fighter form a triangle with the young girl in the center.

Midnight prepared to unleash a spell and prayed that the magical chaos in the Realms wouldn't affect it. She attempted to conjure a decastave—a pole of force—using a fallen branch. As the first of the dogs leaped at her, she completed the incantation.

Nothing happened.

For an instant Midnight smelled the fetid breath of the middle head of the creature, and three sets of jaws opened wide to rend her flesh.

THE AVATAR TRILOGY

FANTASY ADVENTURE

SHADOWDALE

by Richard Awlinson

**Cover Art by
JEFF EASLEY**

TSR Inc.

SHADOWDALE

Distributed to the book trade in the United States by Random House, Inc., and in Canada by Random House of Canada, Ltd.

Distributed in the United Kingdom by TSR Ltd.

Distributed to the toy and hobby trade by regional distributors.

FORGOTTEN REALMS is a trademark owned by TSR, Inc. The TSR logo is a trademark owned by TSR, Inc.

First Printing: April, 1989
Printed in the United States of America.
Library of Congress Catalog Card Number: 88-51723

9 8 7 6

ISBN: 0-88038-730-0

All characters in this book are fictitious. Any resemblance to actual persons, living or dead, is purely coincidental.

TSR, Inc.
P.O. Box 756
Lake Geneva,
WI 53147 U.S.A.

TSR Ltd.
120 Church End, Cherry Hinton
Cambridge CB1 3LB
United Kingdom

For their kindness and support,
this book is dedicated to:
Anna, Frank, Patricia, Gregory, Laura, Marie,
Millie, Bill, Christine, Martin, Michele, Tom, Lee,
Joan, Allison, Larry, Jim, Mary, and Alice.

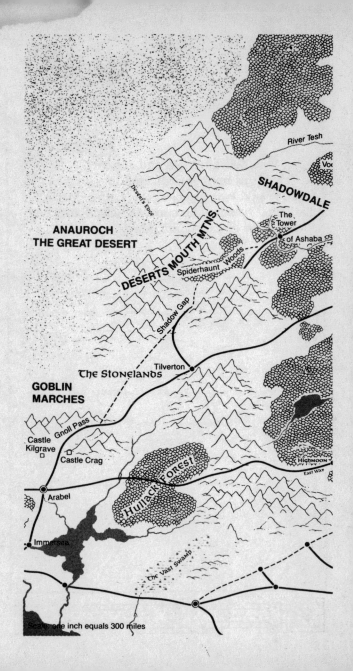

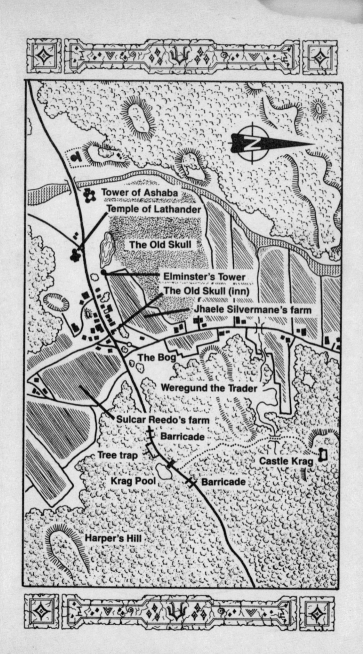

Tower of Ashaba
Temple of Lathander
The Old Skull
Elminster's Tower
The Old Skull (inn)
Jhaele Silvermane's farm
The Bog
Weregund the Trader
Sulcar Reedo's farm
Barricade
Tree trap
Castle Krag
Krag Pool
Barricade
Harper's Hill

Prologue

Helm, He of the Unsleeping Eyes, God of Guardians, stood vigilant, watching his fellow gods. The assemblage was complete. Every god, demigod, and elemental was in attendance. The walls of the great pantheon that hosted the gods had long ago vanished, but the windows remained, hanging on the empty air, and through them Helm looked out onto a universe crumbling into decay. The pantheon, with its many unfinished altars, was located in the heart of the cancerous decay; it had been constructed on an isle that was only large enough to house the meeting place of the gods.

A path made of crumbling gray stepping stones floated outward across the sea of decay to a destination that lay beyond the vision of the gods. It was the only avenue of escape from the pantheon, but none of the gods had been foolish enough to take the first step upon those craggy stones, fearing the path might lead them to a place even more terrifying than this one.

The air around the isle was a white canvas dotted with ebon stars. Streaks of light, so bright that even the eyes of a god could not look into them for long, burned into the ivory tapestry. The streaks formed runes, and Helm shuddered as he read them.

All that has been, is gone. All we have known, all we have believed, is a lie. The time of the gods is at an end.

Then the runes vanished. Helm wondered if one of the summoned gods had sent the cryptic message in an effort to frighten the others, but dismissed the idea. He knew that the runes had been sent by a power greater than any of the gods around him.

Helm listened to the dull roar of thunder as mammoth gray clouds with veins of black lightning rolled in and shadows fell across the pantheon. The pure white sky was obscured by the clouds, and the stepping stones that drifted outward from the pantheon crumbled and fell away into the vast sea of decay.

Helm had been the first to be summoned. One moment he was in his temple, ruminating over his recent failings as guardian to Lord Ao. The next moment he was standing alone in the pantheon. Soon his fellow gods began to appear. The gods had seemed disoriented, weakened by the journey to this place that was apart from all that was known.

The summons had come wearing the face and form of that which each of the gods feared most. To Mystra, Goddess of Magic, it appeared as a harbinger of magical chaos. To the beautiful Sune Firehair, Goddess of Love and Beauty, it appeared as a haggard, cancer-ridden creature, crying out against its fate while delivering Sune to hers. To the Black Lord, Bane, the summons came in the guise of absolute love and understanding, its light searing his essence as it carried him from his kingdom.

Helm had only to shift his gaze slightly to see Lord Bane, Lady Mystra, and Lord Myrkul in a heated discussion that climaxed with Mystra storming off to seek more appropriate company. Glancing in another direction, Helm saw Llira, Goddess of Joy, wearing a slightly worried expression, wringing her hands without thought, then catching herself and staring down at her hands in horror. Standing beside her, Ilmater, God of Suffering, could not contain a steady stream of laughter as he danced in place, whispering knowing comments to no one in particular.

As Helm studied the faces of the gods, a small group of deities who had not been affected so traumatically by the summons surrounded him. The God of Guardians tried to ignore the pleas of these gods, whose dignity apparently no longer mattered to them, as they whined and clawed at him for more information.

"My home was destroyed! My temple in the Planes was shattered!" God after god repeated the complaint, but Helm was deaf to their words.

"Ao has issued a summons. All will be made clear in time," Helm told each of them, but he soon grew tired of repeating himself and eventually warned the small group of gods away. Change was coming. Of that there could be no doubt, Helm concluded as he pondered the will of his immortal liege, Ao.

Ao's will had been so great that he rose from the swirling

mist of Chaos at the beginning of time and set about to create a balance between the forces of Law and Chaos. From this balance came life: first with the creation of the gods in the heavens, then with the mortals in the Realms. Ao, Maker of All Things, had chosen Helm to be his right hand. And Helm knew that it was the power of Ao that brought the gods to this place of madness and confusion.

As Helm stood quietly in thought, Talos, God of Storms, surged forward. "An end to the trickery, I say! If our lord wishes to make a point, let him speak, let his wisdom fill our bankrupt hearts and empty minds!" Talos said "wisdom" with as much contempt as he could muster, but the others were not convinced. His fear was as evident as theirs.

The challenge of Talos was not met, and all who stood within arm's reach of the God of Storms moved away from him. In the silence that followed Talos's outburst there was an answer more unnerving than any proclamation; in the silence was heard the finality of Ao's judgement. It was then that the gods understood that their fate, whatever it would be, had been sealed long before this summoning. That terrible silence filled the great hall, but it was soon shattered.

"Keepers of the Balance, I address you one and all!"

It was Ao's voice, and in that voice was heard the power of a being so great that the gods fell to their knees in response. Lord Bane alone managed to place only one knee on the pantheon's cold floor.

"Most noble was your heritage! Yours was the power to stave off the ever-present threat of imbalance between Law and Chaos, and yet you chose to act like children, resorting to petty thievery in your quest for power. . . ."

Bane suddenly wondered if the being who had given the gods life long ago had called his creations to this place to undo his mistake and begin anew.

"Extinction may be your future yet, Bane," Ao proclaimed, as if the Black Lord's thoughts had been spoken aloud. *"But do not let it concern you, for that fate would be most merciful compared to what shall soon befall you—and the other gods that betrayed my trust."*

It was Helm who then stepped forward. "Lord Ao, the tablets were in my keeping, let it be—"

"Silence, Helm, lest you suffer a fate such as theirs."

Helm turned and faced the assemblage of gods. "You should know your crime, at least. The Tablets of Fate have been stolen."

A beam of light erupted from the darkness and enveloped the God of Guardians. Wisps of white flame encircled Helm's wrists and ankles, and he was lifted up an unknowable distance, almost beyond the senses of the other gods, who gasped as they watched. Helm, who had never been borne off his feet before, grit his teeth helplessly as he stared into a patch of darkness greater than any darkness ever seen, a darkness that lived and sought to consume, a darkness that was the anger of Lord Ao.

"Stand you with your fellows and not your liege, good Helm?"

Through gritted teeth, the god responded. "Aye."

Suddenly Helm was cast down, his descent too quick and too brutal to be tracked by the senses of the other gods. Bloodied and bruised by the impact, Helm struggled to rise and again face his lord, but the task was beyond him. His fellow gods made no move to help him, nor did they meet his imploring eyes as he fell, face down, to the stone floor of the pantheon.

Occasional flashes of light revealed black bands of energy that moved ever closer to the gods.

"No longer will you sit in your crystal towers, looking down upon the Realms as if they had been created simply to amuse you."

"Exile," Bane murmured breathlessly.

"Aye," said Lord Myrkul, God of the Dead, a chill finding the core of even his lifeless soul.

"No longer will you ignore the very purpose for which you were given life! You shall know your transgressions and remember them for all time. You have sinned against your liege and you will be punished."

Bane felt the coils of darkness approach.

"The thief!" Mystra shouted. "Let us discover the identity of the thief for you and return the tablets!"

Tyr, God of Justice, raised his arms imploringly. "Let us not pay in kind for the foolishness of but one of our brethren, Lord Ao!" Darkness, like the lash of a whip, slashed across Tyr's face, and he fell back, screaming and clutching at his now useless eyes.

"You see nothing but the salvation of your own skins!"

The gods were silent, and the dark bands darted between them, drawing the gods closer to each other, as if herding them together to create a single target for Ao's wrath. The gods cried out—some in fear, some in pain. They were not accustomed to such treatment.

"Cowards. The theft of the tablets was the final affront. You will return them to me. But first, you will pay the price for a millennium of disappointment."

Bane stood his ground against the bands of energy, and suddenly the biting strands of darkness erupted into blinding flames of cold blue light that seared him. He turned from the light and caught a glimpse of Mystra as she, too, held her ground, a slight smile etched across her features. Then the bands caught Bane, and his world became pain such as only a god could imagine or endure.

After an eternity of torment, all the gods were caught in the dark bands of power and drawn tightly together. Only then did the deities find movement and thought once again possible.

And fear. This they knew intimately.

Finally, Lord Talos managed to speak. His voice was weak and hoarse, his words escaping in frightened gasps. "Is it over? Could that have been all?"

Suddenly the pantheon seemed to vanish and the gods, still bound together, found themselves staring full into the face of what frightened each the most—chaos, pain, love, life, ignorance. And each god saw his or her own destruction there, as well.

"That was but a taste of my anger. Now drink deep from the goblet of a true god's rage!"

A sound was heard then unlike any other.

The gods screamed.

Mystra struggled to retain some vestige of control as she found herself plummeting through a fantastic vortex that defied reality. She suffered unbearable pain as godhood was ripped from her. But the Goddess of Magic was not alone in her torments. All the gods, save Helm, were cast from the heavens.

After a time, Mystra awoke in the Realms. She was startled to find that her form had been reduced to its primal essence. Her body was little more than a glowing mass of blue-white light.

"You will take an avatar." Ao's voice resounded in her mind. *"You will possess the body of a mortal and live as a human. Then perhaps you will appreciate what you once took for granted."*

Then she was alone.

The fallen goddess hovered for a moment as Lord Ao's words turned over and over in her mind. If she had to take an avatar, possess a body of flesh and blood, then Ao really did intend on keeping the gods out of the Planes. Though Mystra had suspected Ao would punish his servants for their failings—and she had even planned for the event by secreting a shard of her power in the Realms—the goddess simply couldn't comprehend the loss of her status, the loss of her beautiful palace in the heavens.

Mystra looked around and came as close to shuddering as she could in her formless state. The land around her would be quite attractive to mortals: rolling hills stretched out around the Goddess of Magic, and an ancient, crumbling castle dominated the horizon to the west. Yes, most humans would find this scene peaceful, Mystra thought, but it is a repulsive eyesore when compared to my home.

Nirvana, the plane of ultimate Law, held Mystra's domain. It was a perfectly regimented, infinite area where light and darkness, hot and cold, were ideally balanced. Unlike the chaotic landscape of the Realms, Nirvana was structured like the insides of a huge clock, with equal, ordered gears meeting in ideal junctions. On each of these gears rested the realm of one of the lawful gods that inhabited the plane. Of course Mystra saw her realm as the most beautiful in Nirvana, in all the Planes, in fact.

The Goddess of Magic studied the ruined castle for a moment, then silently cursed Ao. Even when that ruin was newly built, it was but a closet in my home, Mystra thought bitterly, and the image of her magnificent shimmering palace came unbidden to her mind. The castle that filled her realm was built of pure magical energy, drawn directly from the weave of magic that surrounded Faerun. Like everything else in Nirvana, the palace was perfectly structured and eternal. Its towers were all the exact same height, its windows the same dimensions. Even the magic-woven bricks that made up the castle were identical to one another. And in the center of Mystra's home stood her library, which contained every book and scroll, listing every spell ever known in the world, and some that had not yet been discovered.

Mystra turned her gaze to the dark storm clouds that filled the sky. "I will have my home again, Ao," she said softly. "And I will have it soon."

As the Goddess of Magic stared at the roiling clouds, she caught a glimpse of something glowing in the air. When she tried to focus on the beam that seemed to hang from the clouds, she felt dizzy. I'm still addled from Ao's attack, she thought, and tried again to see what was flickering from the sky to the ground near the ruined castle. In a moment, her vision cleared and she recognized the wavering image before her.

A Celestial Stairway.

The stairway, which changed its shape continually as Mystra watched it, was a common path for the gods to travel between their homes in the Planes and the Realms. Though Mystra had rarely used the bridges to Faerun, she knew that there were many of them throughout the Realms and that they led to a nexus in the heavens. The nexus, in turn, led to all of the gods' homes.

The stairway changed from a long wooden spiral to a beautiful marble ladder as Mystra, still bleary-eyed, watched it. Then the goddess suddenly realized why it was so hard for her to focus on the Celestial Stairway: It was only visible to gods or mortals of very great power. She was now neither.

That realization spurred the fallen goddess to action, and she set about to recover the shard of power she had hidden with one of her faithful in the Realms in the hours before Ao's summons. Mystra started to cast a spell to locate her cache of power. Even in her nebulous form, the Goddess of Magic easily completed the complicated gestures and spoke the incantation necessary for the spell. But when she was done casting, nothing happened.

"No!" Mystra cried, and her voice echoed over the hills. "You cannot rob me of my art, Ao. I will not stand for this!"

The goddess tried to cast the spell again. A pillar of green energy erupted from the ground and moved quickly to engulf Mystra. She screamed as the energy struck her insubstantial form. Bolts of green light shot through the misty blue-white cloud that was the Goddess of Magic, causing Mystra to scream in pain. Her vision rested on the black clouds swirling around the glowing Celestial Stairway in the seconds before she lost all consciousness.

At the top of the stairway, at the nexus of the Planes, Lord Helm, God of Guardians, watched as Mystra was knocked unconscious by the misfired spell. Helm was still bruised and bloodied from Ao's wrath, but unlike the other gods, he still retained the form he usually took in the Planes: A huge, armored warrior, with unblinking eyes painted on his steel gauntlets.

Helm's eyes were clear, but they reflected his sadness as he turned and looked up at the pulsating black cloud that hung over him. "What of my punishment, Lord Ao?"

There was silence for a time. When Ao spoke, Helm nodded slowly. The answer to his question was not unexpected.

❦ 1 ❦

Awakenings

In Zhentil Keep, the heaviest rainfall the city had suffered in almost a year engulfed the narrow streets, but Trannus Kialton did not notice. Nothing could disturb his slumber. The shutters of the small rented room he shared with the beautiful but lonely Angelique Cantaran, wife of the most wealthy importer of spices for the city, quaked unnoticed against the forces that raged outside. Only a cool breeze that seemed to suddenly acquire form and coalesce in the darkness threatened to wake him, and then only when it had already floated across the room to the sleeping man and vanished between his partly opened lips.

Thunder roared, and Trannus dreamed of a darksome place where only the cries of the dying brought warmth to the resident lord, who was himself a shadowy figure on a throne made of jewel-encrusted skulls. Fiery red vapors flitted in and out of the skulls' eye sockets, then vanished within the opening and closing jaws of other skulls that seemed to scream even now, long after their agonies should have ended.

The figure on the throne of skulls was too large to be a man, yet it had a vaguely human appearance. What garments it wore were black on black, with only the occasional streak of red to break the monotony. On its right hand, the creature wore a jewel-encrusted gauntlet, streaked with blood that would never wash off.

The room surrounding the throne was enshrouded by bluish mists. Although there seemed to be no walls, no ceilings or floors, there was a sense of oppression that smothered those unfortunate enough to be delivered to the hellish room before their final moments of life elapsed and they looked upon the true face of the hideous creature on the throne.

Yet now the fearsome being seemed content to sit alone, staring down into a golden chalice filled with the tears of his enemies. The lord of this terrible place, the god Bane, suddenly looked up at the dreamer and raised his cup in a toast.

Trannus woke with a start, gasping for air. It was as if he had been so engrossed in the dream that he had forgotten to breathe. Madness, he thought, and yet his hands and feet were numb, and he had to climb out of bed to stamp full sensation back into his tingling limbs. He felt a sudden urge to dress, and the cold touch of leather soon fell upon his skin. Angelique stirred, reaching out to him with a grin.

"Trannus," she called, unsatisfied with only the warmth his body had left upon the silken sheets as a companion. She reached up and brushed the hair from her eyes. "You're dressed," she said, as if trying to convince herself of that fact and fathom a reason at the same time.

"I must go," he said simply, although he had no idea of his destination. All he felt was an urgent need to be free of the confines of the building.

"Hurry back," she said, settling into the comforting embrace of the feather-soft mattress, her dreamy expression echoing her confidence that he would return. Trannus looked at her and was suddenly taken with the knowledge that he would never see her again. He closed the door behind him as he left.

Outside, the heavy rain soaked him to the skin, and in flashes of lightning the streets of the city were revealed to him. He appeared to be alone, but he knew better than to trust appearances. The streets of Zhentil Keep were never truly deserted; they simply bore the illusion with the practiced grace only cutthroats and thieves could have taught them. In Zhentil Keep, the shadows lived and breathed, and monsters chattered in sharp, high-pitched tones from their dark hiding places. Strangely, he was left alone and allowed passage through the dangerous labyrinth as if the way had been cleared before him by a herald none would dare stand against.

Throughout his journey, Trannus thought of the dream. He imagined the streets were slick with the blood of his enemies, and the rain that fell caressed him like the tears of their widows. Lightning struck and loosed a section of a wall nearby, and debris crashed to the ground around him. And still the cleric traveled on, oblivious to everything except the siren call that gave strength to his weary legs, purpose to his sodden brain, and desire to his deadened heart. Trannus only wondered why he, a lowly priest in the servitude of Bane, had been given this vision, blessed with this desire.

Ahead lay the Temple of Bane, and Trannus stopped for a moment, mesmerized by the sight. The Dark Temple was a silhouette against the night sky, its imposing towers jutting upward like black serrated blades waiting to impale an unsuspecting enemy. Even when lightning flashed and the world was cast in sharp light, the temple was black, revealing not a single crevice in its granite facade. Rumors abounded that the temple had been constructed in Acheron, Bane's dark dimension, then brought to Zhentil Keep, stone by stone, a river of blood and suffering the glue that cemented the temple together.

Trannus was surprised to find no guard stalking the temple's perimeters. Then he heard the drunken laughter of the guard and his companion as it drifted toward him from the shadows. The sound filled him with a rage that was echoed by the storm's fury.

Trannus looked up, and through the rain he could see heavy clouds race across the sky, moving impossibly in directions counter to one another. Suddenly the sky exploded and the great white clouds parted as streaks of black lightning issued forth. The heavens were on fire, the stars struck from view. Huge spheres of flame were hurtled from the sky, and one fireball came sailing down, ever closer, and grew to horrible proportions as Trannus realized it was headed for the temple.

There was no time to shout out a warning before the sphere struck the Dark Temple. Trannus was rooted to the spot, and he watched as the granite spires glowed reddish yellow, then sank into a molten heap. Bits of debris sailed to each side of him, but he was left unharmed. Then the cleric watched as the walls collapsed inward and the Dark Temple glowed red, the blood and torment of its past victims seemingly taking form and bubbling over as brick, metal, and glass were reduced to glowing ash and slag in a matter of seconds.

In the end, there was nothing but a flaming ruin where once there had stood a temple. Trannus moved forward, toward the wreckage of the temple, and wondered if he were still dreaming. The steaming, molten slag beneath his feet did not burn him, and the raging fires that filled his sight merely crackled and died away as he approached, allowing him a pathway to the center of the disaster. The flames reformed and resumed their dance once he had passed.

From the partially standing walls, Trannus knew that he was close to the throne room of his lord, and he stopped as the object of his quest rose up before him. The black throne of Bane had been left untouched. Soft, white mists drifted toward Trannus, and phantom shapes gently encircled the priest's wrists as he was led forward without force until he stood directly before the throne. It was a throne only a giant could have rested in comfortably, and beside it sat a replica, this one constructed for the use of a man.

The jewel-encrusted gauntlet from Trannus's dream rested upon the smaller throne.

Trannus smiled, and for the first time, his heart knew joy, his spirit release. This was his destiny. He would rule an empire of darkness. His dreams of power had been rewarded.

Dutifully he picked up the gauntlet and felt tremors of power surge through him. One of the jewels suddenly became a single red eye that flashed open, then followed the movements of the priest, although Trannus was blissfully unaware of the trespass upon his private ceremony.

Arcane rivulets of gold and silver flowed down from the gauntlet when Trannus gingerly slipped it on, and a biting pain pierced his arm as an evil fire corrupted his bloodstream. A darkness closed over the cleric's wildly beating heart, and his blood became ice that flowed to his brain and washed away any traces of the man's former consciousness. The words "my lord" escaped from Trannus's lips as his soul was exiled from his body in a puff of white mist.

The Black Lord looked out through frail human eyes and felt a sudden weakness. He clutched the black throne for support and his mind, now pitifully limited to human understanding, reeled as he attempted to comprehend the changes taking a human avatar had wrought. No longer could he see beyond the mortal veil, and read or influence the moment and manner of his followers' deaths. No longer could he see beyond lies and hapless circumstance, or bore heavily into a man's soul and know the truth only found in the lower consciousness. And no longer could he witness a near infinite number of occurrences simultaneously, commenting and acting upon them in perfect concert as he occupied his mind with other pursuits.

"Ao, what have you done?" Bane cried, and felt the soft stone of the throne crumble beneath his powerful fingers. He struggled to maintain control of his rage. The others would come soon, the hundreds of other worshipers upon whom he had visited the dream, and Bane would have to be prepared.

The God of Strife sat upon the small black throne, attempting to ignore its counterpart that had once been his. My followers will look upon me and see only a human form, he thought, one of their kind gone mad with claims of visitations and possession by their god. They will put this body to death, once they finish torturing it for information on who truly leveled this temple.

The Black Lord knew then that he had to appear more than human in order to inspire his worshipers. He recalled the visage he had given himself in the dream and set about making it flesh. From contact with his followers, Bane knew that a treasure room was located somewhere beneath the temple, and he formed the image of a jade circlet and delivered a spell that would transport the object to his waiting hand. A moment later, armed with the circlet, he began to recite a shape change spell, his movements perfect and graceful, just as the spell required.

He began with the eyes, setting the orbs aflame within the

human's skull. The skin surrounding the avatar's eyes could not accept the strain, so Bane altered the pale flesh until it became black and charred, then leathery with flaps that partially revealed secret hidden ruinations. The skull itself then grew sharp spikes that jutted from the blackened flesh, and the visage realigned itself to the most bestial configurations imaginable while still remaining human.

Bane's hands became talons capable of rending flesh and bone or shattering steel. It became painful to wear the gauntlet, but Bane knew he had no choice if he wished to impress his worshipers. And he could already hear the plodding footfalls of his priests, soldiers, and mages as they made their way through the ruins toward the shattered throne room.

Bane sensed that something was wrong with the spell. He was certain he had performed the casting perfectly, yet the force that moved through him, effecting the changes he desired, had built up momentum and would not subside, despite his mental commands. The air surrounding him felt as if it had solidified, and would soon crush the life from him. He knew a moment of pure human panic and sought to end the spell. Instead, Bane found his new form dressed in black leathers and caked with unholy reddish blood.

The Black Lord shattered the circlet in an attempt to negate the spell, which had moved completely beyond his control. Instead of regaining his human form, Bane found that the effects of the spell had not vanished and he retained the monstrous form he had created.

Bane did not have time to ponder the spell's curious behavior. The first of his flock appeared, armed and ready to destroy the desecrater of the Dark Temple. The Black Lord didn't even give his follower a chance to speak before he stood upon the throne and spoke.

"Kneel before your god," Bane said simply, and held the sacred gauntlet up over the hideously grim head of his avatar. The cleric instantly recognized the artifact and did as he was told, a shocked expression on his face. As more worshipers rushed into the ruined temple, they did the same.

Bane looked into the fearful faces of his followers and held back the laughter that raged within him.

* * * * *

Midnight closed her eyes and felt the morning sun wash over her, gentle fingers of warmth caressing her face. It was in these simple moments when a remembrance of life's tender side overtook the magic-user and she was able to luxuriate in blissful forgetfulness of the trials she had recently faced. For close to twenty-five summers, Midnight had walked the Realms, and there was, she believed, little left that held the power to surprise her. Experience should have taught her better, she knew, especially since her current circumstances were, at the very least, quite unusual.

She had woken in a strange bed, in a place she could not remember coming to. Outside the window she saw a small clearing with a thick forest beyond. Wherever she was, she had not reached her destination: the walled city of Arabel, in northern Cormyr.

Her clothes, armaments, and books had been neatly piled upon a beautifully crafted dresser at the far side of the handsomely adorned room, as if whoever had handled them wanted Midnight's possessions in plain sight. Even her daggers were left within reach. Stranger still, Midnight found herself dressed in a beautiful nightgown made of fine silks, the color of a winter's first frost, white with traces of pale blue.

The young woman immediately examined her books, and was relieved to find them intact. She then went to the window and opened it, letting in the fresh air. Opening the window took some effort, as if it had been sealed off and left untouched for years. Yet the room itself was immaculate and had obviously been cleaned recently.

Turning from the window, Midnight caught sight of a gold-framed mirror, and the image that confronted her from the glass was startling.

Midnight's waist-length hair had been washed and brushed with meticulous care. Upon her cheeks she saw the artificial, yet subtle blush of a young maiden. Her lips were unusually crimson, and someone had placed an ever so delicate hint of chartreuse above her eyes. Even the carefully maintained tone of her shapely body had softened.

In contrast to the sweaty, disheveled adventurer who had fought an unearthly storm on her way to Arabel the previous night, the woman whose reflection the mirror presented was almost a goddess who could beguile followers with her unnatural allure.

Midnight reached to her throat, and beneath the gown she felt the cold steel of the pendant.

She removed the gown and moved closer to the mirror to examine the pendant more closely. It was a blue and white star, with strands of energy that darted across the surface like tiny streaks of lightning. And as she turned the pendant over to examine its back, she felt a slight tug at the skin on her neck.

The pendant's chain was grafted to her skin.

Casting a simple spell upon the star to detect magic took all of her concentration, but the results of the spell were staggering. A violent blast of light erupted from the pendant and lit up the entire room. The simple piece of jewelry contained a power so great that it left Midnight weak in the knees, with the room slowly spinning about her.

Turning to the bed, Midnight made her way back to the feather-soft mattress and lay upon it before she collapsed. Fingers clutching at the sheets, she squeezed her eyes shut until the dizziness she felt had passed, then she turned over onto her back, and looked at the room once more. Her thoughts drifted back to the incidents of the previous month.

Midnight had joined the Company of the Lynx under the command of Knorrel Talbot less than three weeks ago, in Immersea. Talbot had learned of the death of a great wyrm on the shores of Wyvernwater. Unknown to the valiant heroes who brought the aged dragon low, this particular wyrm had attacked a diplomatic envoy crossing the desert, Anauroch.

From the tale of the sole survivor, the dragon had swallowed the visiting diplomats whole, consuming the vast riches the men had carried with them as gifts for the rulers of Cormyr. Talbot wanted to find the dragon's remains, and retrieve a number of magically sealed pouches the wyrm had swallowed. It was a filthy job, certainly, but also a very lucrative one.

The quest had been successful, and the task of unsealing the pouches had fallen to Midnight. It took her the better part of a day to gently undo the many-layered wards the wizards had placed upon the items. When she finally removed the magical traps, the company was saddened to learn that the contents of the pouches were nothing more than what Talbot interpreted as treaties and promises of trade.

Midnight stayed with the company as Talbot paid their salaries from the gold he had amassed on a previous quest. But it wasn't until that evening that Midnight learned of Talbot's secret agenda.

She had just been relieved of watch duty by Goulart, a burly man who rarely spoke, and was settling into a deep slumber, when the sound of raised voices alerted her. The voices died away instantly, and Midnight feigned sleep as she prepared to defend herself. After a time, the voices resumed, and this time Midnight recognized Talbot's voice. She cast a spell of clairaudience to eavesdrop on the conversation, and learned that their mission had not been a failure after all.

Upon the scrolls were the true names of many of the Red Wizards of Thay. The information on the documents had been collected by various spies in the employ of King Azoun as insurance against the growing threat of the eastern empire. With the information found on the parchments, the Red Wizards could be destroyed.

Midnight had been the last member of the company to be recruited, and for good reason. Parys and Bartholeme Guin, twin brothers, were the company's true magic-users. They had refused to be involved in the opening of the pouches, fearing the superior magic of the far-off empire that had sealed them. They forced Talbot to hire another magic-user for the task, with the intent of slaying the new member of the company when the job was done.

Talbot, however, wanted to tell Midnight the truth and give her the opportunity to join them as they sought the enemies of the Red Wizards and auctioned the parchments to the highest bidder. As the men argued, Midnight used her magic to steal the valuable parchments and make good her escape.

Midnight traveled north from the camp on Calanter's Way, worried over the odd behavior of her mount. Traveling at night had never bothered the beast before; its blood-red mane had risen with the winds even in the darkest hours of morning. Yet, that night, the horse refused to break its slow, measured pace as they traversed the final length of the seemingly deserted road that led to the walled city of Arabel and sanctuary.

"We have to make the city tonight," Midnight whispered sweetly, having already tried ranting, raving, kicking, and screaming to motivate the horse into action. After a time, Midnight became worried that the company would catch up with her. There was no one in view on the open road, however, nor were there any woods close to the road that could hide an ambush.

Midnight felt the stolen parchments in her cape. Talbot and his men would be after her for these. Although she had not read the inscriptions, she fully realized the power the parchments held; power to rock far-away empires.

Midnight's mount reared up, but there was nothing within range of Midnight's senses to warrant the beast's alarm. Then she noticed the stars. Many were blacking out, then reappearing in huge clusters. Even as Midnight raised an arm to protect herself, the brothers Guin appeared, riding the air itself as they attacked front and rear. The darkness flanking Midnight expelled Talbot and the rest of his men as they charged.

Midnight fought well, but she was hopelessly outnumbered. Only her ownership of the parchments kept the others from killing her outright. And when she was knocked from her mount, Midnight beseeched the goddess Mystra for assistance.

I will save you, my daughter, a voice said, revealing itself to Midnight alone. *But only if you will keep safe my sacred trust.*

"Yes, Mystra!" Midnight screamed. "Anything you ask!"

A great, blue-white ball of fire suddenly burst from the darkness, traveling at incredible speeds. It struck Midnight and her foes, enveloping them in a blinding inferno. Midnight felt as if her soul was being torn apart; she was certain she would die. Then the night closed in.

When Midnight woke, the road before her was burned, and the entire Company of the Lynx was dead. The parchments were destroyed. Her mount was gone. And a strange, beautiful blue-white pendant hung around Midnight's tanned neck.

Mystra's trust.

Dazed, the magic-user continued on foot. She was only vaguely aware of the intense storm that raged around her. Though it was night, the road before her was lit as bright as highsun, and she walked toward Arabel until she collapsed of exhaustion.

Midnight remembered nothing from the time she collapsed on the road until she woke in the strange room where she now found herself. She fingered the pendant unconsciously, then set about clothing herself. The star was obviously a reminder of the favor that had been granted her by Mystra, Midnight decided. But why was it grafted to her skin?

Midnight shook her head.

"I suppose I'll have wait for an answer to that question," the magic-user said sorrowfully. There would be answers, in time. She was certain of that. Whether or not she would care for them was another matter.

Midnight was anxious to examine her new surroundings, so she quickly finished gathering her belongings. As she bent over her pack, stuffing her spell book in with her clothes, a slight rush of air warned her that she was not alone in the unfamiliar bedchambers; an instant later she felt hands at her back.

"Milady," a soft voice said, and Midnight turned to face the source of the gentle summoning. A young girl dressed in a pink and white gown stood before her, looking for all the world like a delicate rose blossoming with every movement. Her face was framed with shoulder-length hair, and the expression worn upon her attractive features was that of a frightened child.

"Milady," the girl began again. "Are you well?"

"Yes, I'm fine. Quite a storm last night," Midnight said, attempting to allay the girl's fears with pleasantries.

"Storm?" the girl said, her voice barely a whisper.

"Aye," Midnight said. "Surely you're aware of the storm this land suffered last night?" Midnight's tone was stern. She did not wish to stoke the furnace of the child's fears, but neither would she be mocked by feigned ignorance.

The girl drew a breath. "There was no storm last night."

Midnight looked at the girl, shocked to find the truth in her eyes. The magic-user looked back to the window and hung her head, her waist-length raven-black hair falling forward, obscuring her face. "What is this place?" Midnight said at last.

"This is our home. My father and I live here, milady, and you are our guest."

Midnight sighed. At least she didn't seem to be in any danger. "I am Midnight of Deepingdale. I woke to find myself dressed as a fine lady, yet I am merely a traveler, and I do not remember coming to your home," Midnight said. "What is your name?"

"Annalee!" a voice cried from behind Midnight. The girl shuddered and drew into herself as she turned to the doorway, where stood a tall, wiry man with thin brown locks and a rough growth of beard. He was dressed in what appeared to be a soft brown frock, belted with thick leather. Gold lace adorned the open folds of his collar and the wide expanses of his cuffs.

Annalee floated past Midnight and left the room, the scent of some exotic perfume gracing the air with her sudden passing.

"Perhaps you would be so kind as to tell me what this place is and how I came to be here. All I remember is the wicked storm we suffered last night," Midnight said.

The man's eyes shot open wide and his hands flew to his mouth; he could not mask his surprise.

"Oh, how extraordinary," he said as he sank to the edge of the bed. "What is your name, beautiful wayfarer?"

Midnight suddenly wished she understood the proper etiquette to accept a compliment gracefully. Because she did not, she merely looked away and studied the floor as she dutifully recited her name and place of origin.

"And your name?" Midnight said. The weakness she had felt earlier was returning, and she was forced to sit on the edge of the bed.

"I am Brehnan Mueller. I am a widower, as you might have guessed. My daughter and I live in this cottage, here in the forest to the west of Calantar's Way." Brehnan looked about the room with sadness in his eyes. "My wife became ill. She was brought to this, our guest room, where she died. You were the very first person to lay upon this bed in almost a decade."

"How did I get here?"

"First, how do you feel?" Brehnan said.

"Sore. Tired. Almost . . . dazed."

Brehnan nodded. "You say there was a storm last night?"

"Aye."

"A great storm did shake the Realms," Brehnan said. "Meteors split the sky and laid waste to temples all across the Realms. Did you know this?"

Midnight shook her head. "I knew of the storm, but not the destruction."

The magic-user felt the skin of her face grow tight. She looked toward the window once more. Suddenly the images before her came sharply into focus. "But the ground is dry. There are no traces of such a storm."

"The storm was two weeks ago, Midnight. Annalee's prize stallion had become frightened by the storm, and bolted. I caught up with the horse past the woods, near the road, and it was there I found you, your skin glowing with a luminescence that all but blinded me. Your hands clutched at the pendant that hung from your neck. Even when I brought you here, it was all I could do to pry your fingers from the object. And I could not remove the pendant.

"At first I worried that the bed we sit upon now would be your final place of rest, but gradually your strength returned, and I could sense the process of healing as it transpired, day by day. Now you are well."

"Why did you help me?" Midnight said, absently. The weakness she felt was passing, but she still felt dizzy.

"I am a cleric of Tymora, Goddess of Luck. I have seen

miracles. Miracles such as the one that surely touched you, fair lady."

Midnight turned to look at the cleric, hardly prepared for his next words, or for the fervor with which his words were delivered.

"The gods walk the Realms, dear Midnight! Tymora herself can be seen between highsunfeast and eveningfeast in fair Arabel. Of course, there is a slight donation to the church that must be made for the privilege. Still, isn't the sight of a god worth a few gold pieces? And her temple must be rebuilt, you see."

"Of course," Midnight said. "Gods . . . and gold . . . and two weeks gone . . ." She saw that the room had started spinning again.

Suddenly there was a noise from outside the window. Midnight looked out and saw that Annalee was leading a horse across the clearing. The horse looked to the window, and Midnight gasped. The creature in Annalee's care had two heads.

"Of course, there have been a few changes since the gods came to the Realms," Brehnan said. Then his tone became reproachful. "You haven't tried to use any *magic* yet, have you?"

"Why?"

"Magic has become . . . unstable, since the gods came to the Realms. You'd best not throw any spells unless your life depends on it."

Midnight heard Annalee call each of the horse's heads by a different name, and almost laughed. The room was spinning wildly now, and the magic-user knew why—it was the spell she had thrown. She tried to stand, and fell back onto the bed. Startled, Brehnan called Midnight's name and tried to grab her arm.

"Wait. You aren't well enough to go anywhere. Besides, the roads aren't safe."

But Midnight had already stumbled to her feet and was heading for the door. "I'm sorry. I have to get to Arabel," the magic-user said as she rushed out of the room. "Perhaps someone there can tell me what's been going on in Faerun these past few days!"

Brehnan watched as Midnight headed toward the road and shook his head. "No, milady, I doubt that anyone—short of perhaps the great sage Elminster himself—could explain the happenings in the Realms to you these days."

❧ 2 ❧

The Summoning

Kelemvor walked through the streets of Arabel, the great walls that protected it from invasions time and again somehow always in view. Although he would never admit it, the walls made him edgy, their vaunted promise of security little more than the bars of a cage to the warrior.

The sounds of the hustle and bustle of a typical day in the merchant city as highsun approached filled his ears, and Kelemvor studied the faces of those he passed. The people had survived recent hardships, but survival was not enough if the spirit of a people had been shattered.

Kelemvor heard the sounds of a brawl, though he could not see the fight. The warrior could hear shouting and the sound of blows falling against mail—a common enough occurrence these days. Yet perhaps the display was nothing more than a carefully laid trap to gain the attention of a lone traveler for the purpose of laying open his head and taking his purse.

Such occurrences were also common these days.

The sounds died down, as presumably did their makers. Kelemvor surveyed the street and saw that no one else was responding to the brawl. It seemed that he was the only one who heard it. That meant the sounds could have come from anywhere. Kelemvor's senses were marvelously acute, and this was not always for the best.

Still, the robbery, if it had been that at all, was nothing unusual. In some ways, Kelemvor was relieved by the fact that the fight was only a mundane occurrence, for little in Arabel—or the entire Realms—seemed commonplace anymore. Everything was unusual, and even magic was untrustworthy since the time of Arrival, as that day was becoming known. Kelemvor thought of the changes to the Realms he had personally witnessed in the past two weeks.

On the night the gods entered the Realms, a close ally of Kelemvor lay wounded in his quarters after a skirmish with a wandering band of goblins. The soldier—and the cleric who attended the soldier—perished in the flames of a fireball that erupted from nowhere when the cleric attempted to ply his healing magic. Kelemvor and the other onlookers were shocked; never before had they seen such a bizarre occurrence. Days later, after the survivors of the destruction of Tymora's temple regrouped, the goddess herself leading them, the church officially disavowed any responsibility for the actions of the cleric, and branded him a heretic for bringing forth the wrath of the gods.

Yet this incident was only the first of many strange happenings that would plague Arabel.

The local butcher had run screaming from his shop one morning, as the carcasses he had kept on ice were now suddenly alive, and hungry for revenge against their slayers.

Kelemvor himself stood by as a mage, attempting a simple spell of levitation, found that the spell was no longer under his control. His assent went unchecked, and the fighter watched as the dwindling form of the screaming magic-user vanished into the clouds. The mage was never seen again.

Over a week ago, Kelemvor and two other members of the guard had been summoned to attempt to free a magic-user who had called a blinding sphere of light into existence and then found himself trapped within the globe. Whether he had summoned the sphere by accident or design was not known. The incident took place in front of the Black Mask Tavern, and the members of the guard had been called to control the crowds of people who had gathered to watch as yet another pair of magic-users attempted to help their brother. The sphere did not falter until a week later, when the trapped mage died of thirst.

Kelemvor noted sourly that business at the Black Mask Tavern had never been better than it was for that week. And, from all Kelemvor had heard from the travelers who sought the great walled city for protection, it seemed that all the Realms—not just Arabel—were in chaos. He turned his thoughts away from that path and set his sights instead on the here and now.

The warrior's right shoulder ached, and despite the ointments and salves that had been applied to his wounds, the pain had not lessened in days. Usually, his condition could have been cured by a few healing spells, but Kelemvor did not trust any magic after what he had seen. Still, despite the common mistrust of magic, many prophets, clerics, and sages proclaimed a new age, a time of miracles. Many would-be prophets suddenly climbed out from beneath an avalanche of well-deserved anonymity, all claiming personal contact with the gods who walked the Realms.

A particularly fervent old man had sworn that Oghma, God of Knowledge and Invention, had assumed the form of Pretti, his cat, and spoke with him on matters of the greatest urgency.

And while no one believed the old man, it was commonly accepted that the woman who had walked out of flames left in the wake of the destruction of Arabel's own Temple of Tymora was indeed the goddess in human form. Standing in the midst of the flames, the woman had displayed the power to unite the minds of hundreds of her followers for the briefest of instants, allowing them to share in sights only a god could have witnessed.

Kelemvor had paid the price of admission to look upon the face of the goddess, and had seen nothing remarkable. As he was not a follower of Tymora, he did not bother to ask the goddess to heal his wound. He was fairly certain she would have charged extra if he had.

Besides, the pain would make it difficult for Kelemvor to forget that Ronglath Knightsbridge had wounded his pride more than his body when he buried a spiked mace deep in his flesh. They had battled high atop the main lookout tower, where Knightsbridge had been posted. During the battle, Kelemvor had been sent hurtling over the walls of the city toward certain death.

But he did not die.

Kelemvor was not even seriously injured by the fall.

The warrior paused in his contemplations and caught his

reflection in the glass of the House of Gelzunduth, a merchant of questionable repute. Kelemvor looked past his image, to the odd collection of items displayed in the window. It was rumored that behind the carefully maintained facade of buying and selling hand-crafted jewelry, costume weapons, and rare volumes of forgotten lore, Gelzunduth trafficked in forged charters and other false documents, as well as information concerning the movements of the guard throughout the city. Numerous attempts by unmarked agents of the guard to entrap the sly Gelzunduth in any of these practices had failed.

Just before Kelemvor turned away from the window, the sight of his own reflection once again caught his gaze. The warrior studied his face: piercing, almost luminescent green eyes, set deep against a darkly tanned face consisting of a strong brow, straight nose, and practically square jaw. His face was framed by a wild mane of ebon hair with only a few streaks of gray to reveal that he had walked the Realms for over thirty summers. In the places where his bare skin was not protected by his clothing, it was plain that his chest and arms were covered by thick black hair. He wore chain mail and leathers, and carried a sword half the length of his body in a sheath slung behind his back.

"Ho, guardsman!"

Kelemvor turned and regarded the slip of a girl who had challenged him. She was no more than fifteen, and her delicate features appeared to have paid the price for the hardships and worries she had obviously recently undertaken. Her hair was blond and cut short in a boyish style, the strands matted to her scalp by her sweat. The clothes worn by the girl were somewhat better than rags, and she could have easily been mistaken for a beggar. The girl seemed weak, although she smiled bravely and attempted to move with a confidence her body no longer seemed ready to indulge.

"What business have you with me, child?" Kelemvor said.

"My name is Caitlan Moonsong," the girl said, her voice cracking slightly. "And I've traveled a long way to find you."

"Go on."

"I have need of a swordsman," she said. "For a quest of the

utmost urgency."

"There will be a reward for my efforts?" Kelemvor said.

"A great reward," Caitlan promised.

The warrior scowled. The girl looked as if she might die from starvation at any moment. Less than a city street away was the Hungry Man Inn, so Kelemvor took the girl by the shoulder and guided her toward the inn.

"Where are we going?" Caitlan said.

"You need a hearty meal in your gut, do you not? Surely you already knew that Zehla of the Hungry Man Inn provides to those in need." Kelemvor stopped, a touch of worry moving across his hard-set features. When he spoke, his words were measured, his tone cold and harsh. "Tell me you did not need me to inform you of this."

"Certainly not," the girl said. Kelemvor did not move. His worry did not ebb. "I did not need you to tell me of this. You did me no favor."

"That's right," he said, and resumed the journey to the inn.

Caitlan allowed herself to be led, puzzled by the odd exchange that had just taken place. "You seem troubled."

"These are troubling times," Kelemvor said.

"Perhaps if you were to discuss . . ."

But then they were before the Hungry Man, and Kelemvor was ushering the girl inside. It was a quiet time of the day, and few patrons had arrived for highsunfeast. Those who were foolish enough to stare at Kelemvor and the girl were given a look that froze the blood in their veins and caused them to look away instantly.

"A bit young for your tastes, Kel," a familiar voice said. "But I suspect you have honorable intentions."

Coming from anyone else the remark would have brought violence, but coming from the elderly woman who now approached, it caused a thin smile to etch its way across Kelemvor's lips. "I fear the waif may collapse at any second."

The woman, Zehla, touched Kelemvor on the shoulder and looked at the girl. "A scrawny thing indeed," she said. "I have just the thing to put some meat back on those paltry bones. A moment and all will be ready."

Caitlan Moonsong watched as the old woman left, then

looked back to Kelemvor. The fighter's attentions seemed to have drifted once more to the thoughts that had been troubling him. Caitlan knew it was important that she choose her champion well, and so she dug into her pocket and removed a blood-red gem she had been saving. She hid the gem in the palm of her hand as she reached over and covered Kelemvor's hand with hers. There was a flash of pure red light and Caitlan felt the gem cut into her flesh at the same moment it scratched the hand of the fighter.

Kelemvor leaped up from the table, drawing back and away from the girl. His sword had left its scabbard and was poised over his head when the voice of Zehla rang out.

"Kelemvor, stay your hand! She means you no harm!" The old woman stood a few tables away, Caitlan's meal in her hands.

"Your past is open to me," Caitlan said softly, and Kelemvor looked down at the girl, shocked from his rage by her words. Caitlan held the glowing red stone in her open palms, and she spoke as if she had been possessed. Slowly Kelemvor lowered his sword. "You were on a mission filled with endless days and nights of waiting and deception. Myrmeen Lhal, ruler of Arabel, feared that a traitor lay in her midst. She assigned Evon Stralana, the minister of defense, the task of soliciting mercenaries to infiltrate the city's guard and attempt to ferret out the traitor."

Zehla set the tray down before Caitlan, but the girl didn't even glance at the food. It was as if her voice had been consumed by the words she'd spoken.

"What sorcery is this?" Kelemvor said to Zehla.

"I don't know," the old woman said.

"Then why did you stop me?" Kelemvor said, worried that the girl might still prove to be a danger.

Zehla's brow wrinkled. "In case you have forgotten, blood has never been spilled in my establishment. While I'm alive, it never will be. Besides, she's just a child."

Kelemvor frowned and listened as Caitlan spoke again.

"The minister of defense approached you and a man named Cyric. You were newly arrived in town and the sole survivors of a failed attempt to retrieve an artifact known as the Ring of Winter. The traitor was feared to be in the employ of those plotting the economic collapse of Arabel through the sabotage of trade routes, and the overall discrediting of Arabel as a vital city in the Realms.

"With the help of Cyric and one other, you found the traitor, but he made good his escape and now the city is blanketed in fear and distrust. For this you blame yourself. Now you toil as a common guardsman, allowing your talent for adventure to languish unfulfilled."

The stone ceased to glow, and it now looked like a common garden stone. Caitlan caught her breath.

Kelemvor thought of the ice creature that stood guard over the Ring of Winter. He did nothing as the creature literally froze the blood of his companions, their screams ending abruptly as ice filled their throats. Their deaths had purchased the time Kelemvor and Cyric needed to escape. It had been Kelemvor who had first learned of the ring, and organized the party to retrieve the object, although he had deferred leadership to another.

"My 'talent' for adventure," Kelemvor said with contempt. "Men have died because of my so-called talent. Good men."

"Men die every day, Kelemvor. Is it not preferable to die with your pockets lined with gold—or at least in that pursuit?"

Kelemvor leaned back in his chair. "You are a magic-user? This is how you see into my innermost thoughts?"

Caitlan shook her head. "I am no magic-user. This stone . . . this gem was a gift. It was the only bit of magic I possessed. Now it is spent. I am defenseless and at your mercy, good Kelemvor. I apologize for my actions, but I had to know that you were an honorable man."

The fighter replaced his sword and took his seat. "Your food is getting cold," he said.

Caitlan ignored the food, although her hunger was apparent. "I am here to make you an offer, Kelemvor. An offer of adventure and danger, of riches beyond belief and excitement such as you have craved these many weeks. Would you like to hear what I propose?"

"What else do you know about me?" Kelemvor said. "What else did your gem tell you?"

"What else is there to know?" Caitlan said.

"You did not answer my question."

"You did not answer mine."

Kelemvor smiled. "Tell me of your quest."

* * * * *

Adon smiled fearlessly, despite the presence of the four armed guards who surrounded him and led him through the great citadel of Arabel. They passed all the sights that Adon had familiarized himself with during his last visit to the citadel—the opulent halls filled with activity, the gaily colored glass windows through which precious light had filtered, warming his face. The splendor of the citadel was a shocking contrast to the squalor Adon had witnessed in the streets. The cleric ran his hand over his face, as if fearful that the filth he was thinking about had somehow rubbed off, marring his pristine appearance.

Sune Firehair, the goddess he had been a faithful cleric to for most of his young life, had blessed him with what he considered the smoothest, most fair skin of any in the Realms. He had been accused of vanity from time to time, and he shrugged off such accusations. Those who did not worship Sune could not be expected to understand that, although he gave thanks regularly, he was in charge of the care and keeping of the precious gifts the goddess had granted him. He had fought to preserve her good name and reputation, and never suffered so much as a scratch to mar his features. And in this he *knew* he was blessed.

Now that the gods had come to the Realms, Adon felt it was merely a matter of time before he crossed paths with Sune. Had he learned her whereabouts, he would have already gone off in search of her. As it was, Arabel, with its constant flow of merchants all heavily equipped with wagging tongues and unquenchable thirsts, was the best place to wait until more information came his way.

Of course, in the Temple of Sune, there had been some dissension. Two clerics had left the temple under questionable circumstances. Others were distraught over what they claimed was the abandonment of Sune—a fact heralded by the silence of the goddess to their prayers. Of course, since the time of Arrival, only the clerics of Tymora had successfully achieved clerical magic, and that was attributed to the proximity of their god-made-flesh. And it seemed that if a cleric was more than a mile from his god, his spells did not function.

Naturally, healing potions or magical objects that copied the effects of healing magic were now sold at a premium, though they, too, were untrustworthy. Local alchemists were forced to hire private guards to protect their wares and their person.

Adon had adjusted better than most to the chaos in the Realms. He knew that all things concerning the gods occurred for a reason. A true follower should have the patience and good sense to wait for enlightenment, rather than allow his imagination to run rampant. Adon's faith was unwavering, and for that he had been rewarded. The fact that the fair Myrmeen Lhal, ruler of Arabel, had requested his presence, was proof that he was blessed.

Life was good.

The group passed through a corridor that Adon was unfamiliar with and he attempted to pause as they passed a mirror, but the guards nudged him on. Somewhat annoyed, he complied.

One of the guards was a woman with dark skin and almost black eyes. It pleased Adon that women had been allowed into the ranks so easily. "Find a city ruled by a woman and you will find true equality and fairness throughout the land," had been his motto. He smiled to the guardswoman, and knew that his choice of the city of Arabel as his new home had truly been a wise one.

"What honor am I to be awarded for my part in bringing down the foul villain Knightsbridge? Have no fear, if you tell, I'll say nothing and seem completely surprised. But the suspense is almost more than I can bear!"

One of the guards snickered, but that was the only response Adon received. The cleric's recompense for his work for the city had been slight, and he had petitioned the minister of defense on the matter. Now Myrmeen Lhal had personally intervened, and Adon could guess why.

Adon's role in bringing down the conspiracy was to seduce the mistress of one of the suspected conspirators, a woman who was rumored to talk in her sleep. Adon performed admirably, but his reward was almost a week in the company of guardsmen, watching the movements of two mercenaries the minister of defense had recruited for the Knightsbridge matter.

The battle with the traitor, when it finally occurred, was brief and startlingly without conclusion. Knightsbridge had escaped, although Adon himself had discovered the whereabouts of the conspirator's war room and a personal ledger that held information that could only be interpreted as the key points of the conspirator's attack against Arabel.

Adon turned from his memories back to the present. They were traveling downward, ever downward, to a dirty, dusty section of the fortress that Adon had heard of, yet never visited before.

"You're quite certain our lady requested to meet me here, and not, perhaps, in the royal chambers?"

The guards remained silent.

Light had suddenly become a precious commodity, and the cleric heard the sound of scurrying rats from somewhere down the hallway. Behind them he heard the sound of massive doors swinging shut. The echo was deafening in the midst of the corridor's silence.

The guards had taken flaming torches from the walls, and the heat from the torch behind Adon was making him uncomfortable.

The only sounds now were the footfalls of the group as they plunged ahead. And though the broad shoulders of the guard before him blocked Adon's view of what lay ahead, he had a fair idea.

A dungeon! Adon shouted in the relative safety of his own head. These buffoons have led me to a dungeon!

Then Adon felt the hands of the guards on him, and before he could react, he was thrown forward. His lean yet muscular body absorbed most of the fall as he rolled and sprang into a fighting position just in time to hear a steel door swing shut. The lessons Adon had suffered through on the art of self defense would have come in handy had he realized the situation earlier.

He cursed himself for surrendering his war hammer so

easily and, just for a moment, cursed his own vanity that had clouded his reason. These rogues were loyal to Knightsbridge! The cleric was sure that his compatriots, Kelemvor and Cyric, would soon be joining him.

We were fools, Adon thought. How could we have believed the threat to be over simply because one man had been driven off?

There was no light in the room, as Adon dusted off his fine clothing. He had worn his favorite silks and carried a handkerchief laced with gold—in case the lady became overwhelmed with tears when he accepted her proposal and became royal consort. His boots were shined, and even the tiniest glint of light reflected off them, despite the filth he had been forced to walk through.

"I'm a fool," Adon said to the darkness.

"So I'm told," a woman's voice answered behind him. "But we all have our weak points." Then Adon heard the striking of flint and a torch was lit, revealing the bearer of the light, a beautiful dark-haired woman.

Myrmeen Lhal.

Her eyes caught the reflection of the flames, and the flickers of fire seemed to dance just to celebrate her beauty. She wore a dark cloak, parted at the waist, and Adon stared at the fullness of her proud bosom that heaved in its chain mail dress.

Adon opened his arms and walked forward to his love, a warrior woman who had the courage and the wisdom to control a kingdom.

Life was better than good.

"Stand your ground unless you relish the idea of leaving here as naught but a stuck pig."

Adon held his ground. "Milady, I—"

"Do me the honor," Myrmeen said angrily, "of limiting your answers to 'yes, milady' or 'no, milady.' "

The ruler of Arabel moved forward and the cleric felt the cold tip of a blade pressed against his stomach.

"Yes, milady," Adon said, then was silent.

Myrmeen moved back and studied his face. "You are fair," she said, though she was in truth being kind. The cleric's mouth was a trifle large, his nose a shade from perfect, and his jaw was far too angular to be considered particularly pleasing. Still, there was a boyish, mischievous quality that lurked behind his far too innocent to be believed eyes, and a soul that sought adventure, both in service to his goddess and to many of the fair ladies of Arabel—if rumors were to be believed.

Adon allowed himself a smile that quickly vanished as the knife point found a new home somewhat lower. "A fair face, coupled with a healthy, serviceable body . . ."

Serviceable? Adon began to wonder.

"And an ego the size of my kingdom!"

Adon drew back as Myrmeen shouted at him, her torch held dangerously close to his face. The cleric felt sweat form on his brow.

"Is this not so?"

The cleric swallowed. "Yes, milady."

"And was it not you who spent all of yestereve bragging that you would bed me before this month was out?"

Adon stayed silent.

"No matter. I already know it to be so. Now listen here, foolish man. When and if I choose to take a lover is my business and mine alone! It has been, and shall ever be!"

Adon wondered if his eyebrows were being singed.

"I received word from Lord Tessaril Winter of Evening-star about you even before I allowed you residence in Arabel. I even considered your talents valuable in the gathering of information through private intrigues, and at that you have proven yourself useful."

The cleric thought of Tessaril Winter's milky white shoulders and her soft, perfumed neck, and prepared himself to die.

"But when you turn your vile imaginings against Myrmeen of Arabel there can be only one fit punishment!"

Adon closed his eyes and awaited the worst.

"Exile," she said. "By highsun tomorrow you are to be gone from my city. Do not force me to send my guards after you. Their tender mercies would not leave you with reason to give thanks."

Adon opened his eyes just in time to see Myrmeen's back as she carried herself from the cell in the most regal, haughty display of contempt Adon had ever seen. He admired her grace as she signaled and two guards fell in beside her, the remaining pair advancing on Adon. He admired her great courage, wisdom, and forgiveness at giving him the option of leaving the walled city instead of simply ordering the guards to slit his throat.

However, as the two guards approached him, forcing him deeper into the cell instead of allowing him to take his leave of it, his admiration dimmed just a bit. He knew that whatever mischief they planned, he dared not fight back. Even if he defeated the two guards in this dungeon, there was little chance he would make it to the gates of the city, let alone beyond them. Even if he did, he would be a fugitive, not an exile, and his actions would bring disgrace and possible retribution upon the church.

"Please don't mar my face!" he cried and the guards began to laugh.

"This way," one of them said as they grabbed Adon's arm and dragged him from the cell.

*　*　*　*　*

Cyric made his way back to his room at the Night Wolf Inn with a weariness in his soul. Although he had made the decision that his days of thieving were long behind him, he continued to think like a thief, to move and act like a thief. Only in the heat of battle, when his full concentration was needed to ensure his survival, was he able to resist the pull of his former life.

Even now, with evening closing in, Cyric took the dimly lit back stairs to his room, and only a truly keen observer would be able to detect any sounds made by the short-haired, lean shadow of a man who gracefully moved forward to the second floor landing.

Recent events had been distressing. He had come to Arabel to begin anew, and yet it had become necessary to utilize his skills as a thief to uncover the evidence against Knightsbridge. Now his days were spent enacting the simple duties of a guardsmen, the mindless tedium a relentlessly depressing recompense for his troubles. The bounty originally promised by Evon Stralana had been halved because of Knightsbridge's escape.

Stralana had approached Cyric and Kelemvor because they were outsiders, newly arrived in town and probably unknown to the traitors. Although Cyric had no real intention of joining the guardsmen of Arabel, Stralana made this a stipulation. Stralana insisted on the authenticity of a signed contract to prove that Cyric was a guardsman and to allay the suspicions of their quarry, who was believed to have infiltrated the guard. Yet the contract Cyric had signed as part of his subterfuge turned out to be binding. And when the crisis struck, Stralana held Cyric to the terms of the contract. Arabel needed all the guards they could muster.

Many of the city's defenses, once made strong by magic, were no longer trustworthy, and the city had gone so far as to draft civilians into temporary duty. Cyric believed in a good axe or knife, the strength of his arm, and the strength of his wits and skills to get him out of trouble. Those who relied solely on the power of magic had become rare in recent weeks.

The presence of the "gods" in the Realms was also distressing to Cyric. On a dare from Kelemvor, his fellow unfortunate in the Knightsbridge fiasco, Cyric had visited the ruined Temple of Tymora, and paid the price to bask in the presence of Arabel's newly seated resident deity. Although Cyric had promised himself to view this event with an open, optimistic eye, the "goddess" saw right through him.

"You do not believe in me," Tymora said, her tone devoid of feeling.

"I believe in the evidence of my senses," Cyric said bluntly. "If you are a goddess, what need do you have of my gold?"

The goddess regarded him in an aloof manner, then looked away and raised one of her finely manicured hands to indicate the audience was ended. Cyric picked the pockets of three of Tymora's clerics on the way out and gave the money to a mission for the poor that afternoon.

Most disturbing of all to Cyric, there were hundreds of signs that not all was right in the Realms. And Cyric had witnessed his share of odd events since the night of Arrival.

One night he was summoned to a feasthall named the Gentle Smile, where he was forced to protect a cleric of Lathander who was on his way back to Tantras. The cleric had innocently attempted a spell to purify a rancid piece of meat he had been served, and although the spell had no effect, mass hysteria had broken out amongst the other diners who feared that the cleric had somehow poisoned all the food in the hall with his "unblessed magic."

One afternoon, at an outdoor marketplace, two magic-users became entangled in an argument that led to a battle in which magic was loosed. By the look of surprise on the faces of both mages, their spells had not acted in the manner that had been expected—one of the magic-users was carried off by an invisible servant, and the other watched helplessly as a blanket of webs fell from the sky, encompassing the length of the market. The strong, sticky strands attached themselves to everyone and everything in sight. Almost all of the merchandise in the marketplace was ruined, and because the webs were highly flammable, Cyric and his fellow guardsmen spent the better part of two days hacking away at the unusually strong webs in an effort to free the innocents who had been trapped.

Cyric broke from his reverie as he rounded a corridor. A young couple started as he surprised them. They fumbled with the key to their room and Cyric passed them by, recognizing the young man as the son of a guardsman who spoke endlessly of the trials his son put him through. The girl with the young man must have been the "harlot" the boy's father had forbidden him to see.

Cyric pretended he hadn't recognized the boy, although he had registered the waves of fear that emanated from the young man. Cyric envied their strong feelings. Nothing in his life had stirred his emotions, for better or worse, in quite some time.

Come around, man, Cyric thought. This is the life you've chosen.

Or the life fate has chosen for you, he quickly added.

He entered his room by thrusting his weight against the door, causing it to swing open wide and slam against the wall. Someone in another room pounded on the wall in response to the noise.

No one behind the door, else they would have been caught by its flight, Cyric thought as he entered quickly. He kicked the door shut at the same time he rolled onto his bed, prepared to withdraw his short sword, ready to fend off any intruders who might be clinging to the ceiling, preparing to drop down on him.

But there was no one.

He bounded from the bed and kicked in the door to the closet, listening for the shout of surprise that would erupt when an unseen attacker suddenly realized Cyric had rebuilt the door to collapse inward.

And still there was no one.

Cyric contemplated the task of resetting the door and decided it could wait until after dinner. He checked on the weaponry he had secreted in the recesses of the closet; his hand axe, daggers, bow, arrows, and cloak of displacement had not been touched. He checked the hair he had attached to the window frame and saw that it had not been broken. Finally, he relaxed slightly.

Then Cyric noticed the shape, roughly the size of a man, that suddenly appeared outside the window. The window imploded and Cyric flung himself backward, attempting to avoid the flurry of razor-sharp glass fragments that rained into the room.

Cyric heard his assailant drop down into the room before the last of the shattered glass fell. He imagined his opponent only moments before, waiting in the room above Cyric's, listening for the sounds of the former thief's arrival. Cyric cursed himself for adopting a routine; it was obvious the assailant must have been watching Cyric for days.

A slight rush of air at his right alerted Cyric to danger as he rose. He moved to the left, barely avoiding a knife thrust to his back. Without turning, Cyric crashed his elbow into the face of his foe, then dove across the bed to the opposite side of the room. His short sword was in his hand before he landed, facing the direction of the shattered window.

There was no one in the room. Through the destroyed window frame, Cyric observed the rope his attacker had used. It swung back and forth like a pendulum, entering the room, then exiting again. Yet the man who had used it was nowhere to be found.

A rush of air again alerted Cyric, and he moved quickly. In the wall beside him he saw a dagger materialize.

Invisibility, Cyric noted calmly. Yet something was wrong. Invisibility only protected its user until he attacked. In this case, his adversary had become invisible *as* he attacked.

Cyric knew he had very little chance of survival. Still, a grin wider than any he had known in recent times spread across Cyric's face.

The thief moved quickly, cutting an area before him with his blade at all times, connecting with nothing but air, shifting direction constantly. With his free hand, Cyric picked up stray items in the room and tossed them in random directions, waiting to hear something hit the unseen assassin.

The edge of the bedspread pulled slightly, and a thread from it rose up into the air, seemingly attached to nothing, yet obviously hooked to the clothing of the invisible enemy. Cyric turned his back on his attacker and moved away, then suddenly fell into a crouch.

The attacker's thrust was high, and Cyric quickly reached up and felt his fingers tighten on a human arm. He rose up and threw the man over his shoulder with ease and heard a knife skitter across the floor, then saw it materialize.

Cyric brought his knee down over his attacker's throat and slid his blade in beside it.

"Show yourself," Cyric commanded.

"Have to wait," a muffled voice said.

"What?"

"Have to wait for the spell to fade. Takes a bit once I've stopped attacking. Anything to do with magic works a bit strangely these days, you know. If it works at all."

Cyric frowned. Despite the fact that the voice was muffled, it had a familiar ring to it.

A moment later, the spell faded and the man was revealed. His face was wrapped in some type of fabric that seemed to have been reinforced by steel mesh, and most of his leathers had been similarly enshrouded. The only other noticable detail was the blue gemstone that sat in a ring upon his finger. Cyric unwrapped the fabric from the man's face with his free hand.

"Marek," Cyric said in a whisper. "After all these years."

Cyric stared into the older man's eyes and Marek began to laugh—a hearty, good natured roar. "Always the ill-tempered student, Cyric. Even to your mentor."

Cyric tightened his grip, and Marek looked to the ceiling. "Young fool," he said hoarsely. "If my intent had been to take your life, your last breath would have been drawn days ago. I merely wished to prove to myself that you still possessed the skills I taught you, that you were yet worthy of my attention." Marek grimaced. "An old man's folly, if you will. You might well have killed me in my foolishness."

"Why should I believe *you*, the master of lies?"

Marek let out a dispassionate wheeze. "Believe what you like. The Thieves' Guild wishes you back where you belong, back with your own kind."

Cyric attempted to hide his reaction, but he could not quell the smile that crossed his lips and betrayed him to Marek.

"You have had these thoughts as well," Marek said, pleased. "I have observed you, good Cyric. The life you lead isn't worthy of a dog."

"It's a life," Cyric said.

"Not for one with your gift. You were shown the way, and you elevated it to undreamed-of heights."

Cyric's smile broadened. "Once the lies begin it is as a dam bursting, is that it? I was a *fair* thief. My absence was noticed by few. This is only a point of pride for you. In fact, I would wager the Guild knows nothing of this visit."

Marek grimaced. "How long can this charade last?"

"That depends," Cyric said, and pressed the blade tightly against his former mentor's throat.

Marek looked down at the knife. "Will you kill me, then?"

"What?" Cyric grinned. "And waste the sharp edge of my blade on such as you? Nay, I believe Arabel will have use for your talents. I may even reap a decent commission in the process."

"I'll expose you!"

"I'll be gone," Cyric said. "And no one will believe you, nor care to find me even if they do. Our kind is rarely in demand once our secrets are out."

"Others will come," Marek said. "Sell me into slavery and others will come."

"Then you would prefer I kill you?"

"Yes."

"All the more reason not to," Cyric said and rose up and away from Marek, the game at an end.

"I taught you too well," Marek said, then stood to face his former student. "The Guild *would* take you back, Cyric. Even though you didn't even try to take my ring." Marek winked. "Stole it from a sorcerer, along with a cache of items I don't pretend to understand."

There was a knock at the door. "Yes?" Cyric shouted, taking his eyes from Marek for only a heartbeat. Cyric heard the sound of glass crunching. When he looked back, Marek was nowhere to be seen. Cyric rushed to the window and caught sight of Marek on the street below. The older man seemed to dare Cyric to follow him.

The knock at the door was repeated.

"A summons from Kelemvor and Adon to meet at the Pride of Arabel Inn at your earliest convenience."

"And your name?"

"Tensyl Durmond, of Iardon's Hirelings."

"Hold for but a moment, good Tensyl, and I will have a gold piece for you."

"Join us," Marek called from the street. "Else your petty little life among the hard-working will be shattered in a fortnight. I'm not above exposing you to get what I want, Cyric. Remember this."

"I'll remember," Cyric said softly, then turned his back and went to the door. "I *always* remember."

Cyric opened the door to the boy, ignoring the gaping expression of surprise on Tensyl's face as he saw the shattered window and the clear signs of a recent battle in the small room.

❧ 3 ❧

Convergence

Midnight's head cleared quickly after she left the farm, and she got a ride into Arabel with a small caravan, which was a common sight on the road to the city, even in times of trouble. Still, none of the travelers she met could tell her anything new about the events of the past two weeks, though all had stories of magic gone mad or the unrest in nature. Once the caravan reached the city, Midnight went off in search of her own answers.

She spent the day wandering the streets of Arabel, attempting to verify Brehnan's tales of the gods and the odd state of magic in the Realms. Midnight knew that she could spend as much time as she wanted in the search for answers, as she still had the handsomely filled purse she had earned with the Company of the Lynx. If she was prudent, the gold would last her at least three months.

Early in her search, Midnight found The Lady's House, the Temple of Tymora, and paid her admission to look upon the face of the goddess. When her gaze met with Tymora's, some strange emotion stirred within Midnight, and she suddenly knew, beyond any doubt, that this woman was the goddess-made-flesh. There was a feeling of affinity between them, as if on some primal level they shared a great secret or truth, although Midnight had no idea what this might be. Yet the most disturbing part of the exchange was the look the goddess gave Midnight just before the magic-user took her leave.

A look of fear.

Midnight hurried from the temple and spent the rest of the day exploring the city. She did not find a temple to the goddess Mystra, and when she finally braved a local tavern, her inquiries as to the whereabouts of the Goddess of Magic were met with blank stares or shrugs. It seemed not all of the gods had made spectacular entrances on the night of Arrival, as Tymora certainly had. In fact, some gods had not yet appeared at all.

Eventually, Midnight's wanderings brought her to the Pride of Arabel Inn, just in time for eveningfeast. She stood on the doorstep and watched a gigantic black raven that circled like a vulture in the semi-darkness. Then she looked away from the creature and went inside. Taking a table near the back, Midnight ordered a tankard of her favorite beer and a hearty meal.

After a time, a small party of adventurers caught her attention, and although they were seated at the other end of the immense taproom, their conversation one of many in the rapidly filling inn, Midnight found her eyes drawn to the burly fighter and his companions again and again. Finally, she left her table and moved to the far end of the bar, where she could hear their words quite clearly.

*　*　*　*　*

"The walls live and breathe," Caitlan Moonsong said. "They say no walls truly have ears? These do!"

"And this is to encourage us?" Adon said.

Kelemvor leaned back, downed his ale, and let out a belch. Adon glared at him. The Pride of Arabel was an expensive inn, and one in which a certain decorum had to be maintained. Visiting noblemen sometimes stayed at the inn if rooms became scarce at the palace, and visiting traders and merchants of only the highest rank could afford the prices at the Pride.

For bringing down the Knightsbridge conspiracy, Kelemvor, Cyric, and Adon had a standing offer to visit the inn whenever they so desired, free of charge. Although they had indulged separately, this was the first time they had visited the inn together.

As the adventurers sat, listening to Caitlan's story, Adon noticed a pretty serving girl looking over and smiling at him.

The girl seemed familiar, but the cleric couldn't place her.

"It's not possible for a fortress to be alive," Cyric noted.

"This one is! The walls can close in on you. The corridors can shape themselves just out of your sight to put you in a maze in which you'll starve and die. The dust itself is enough to kill you—it has the power to solidify into daggers that can pierce your heart or a fierce warrior who never knows fatigue or exhaustion."

Ah, then how did you escape, little one? Cyric wondered, a smile playing across his shadowed features. He sat with his back to the wall, another hard-earned lesson from his days of thieving, and one quite reasonably applied now, considering the battle with Marek had occurred less than an hour earlier.

It was clear to Cyric that Caitlan wasn't telling them everything, and for that reason alone the thief maintained his silence and covered his advancing smile with a gloved hand.

"Tell me again why we should risk life and limb simply to help you and this mere girl who promises great riches yet wears nothing but rags?" Adon said to Kelemvor.

Cyric noticed that the cleric seemed anxious—so anxious, in fact, that he flinched every time the doors of the inn admitted a new customer. The cleric had been acting strangely ever since he arrived in answer to Kelemvor's summons, and he was now in a mood that made him unfit for human company. The effect was disconcerting.

"Expecting someone?" Cyric said to the nervous cleric. Adon simply grimaced.

"Certainly there's a risk," Kelemvor said finally. "But what else is life, if not a series of risks? I don't know if I speak for the two of you, but I cannot bear the thought of spending another day locked within these maddening walls."

"And my lady is trapped within that unholy place, a prisoner for all time unless you three can rescue her!" Caitlan had become increasingly pale as she spoke, and beads of sweat had appeared on her forehead.

Adon looked away and saw that the serving girl who had smiled at him was drawing closer. She was petite, with flaming red hair that reminded him of Sune herself. She carried a tray filled with drinks and stopped at the table nearby.

Suddenly he remembered their conversation from two nights before, when he met her as a fellow patron at the High Moon Inn. Adon liked the company at that inn, and the girl's wages were too low for her to think of indulging herself in the fineries of the Pride of Arabel.

"Adon," she said, taking in his full measure.

He could not remember her name. "My dear."

A moment later Adon was on the floor, the impact of the serving tray still ringing in his ears. "Fine advice you gave me, you lout! Demand equal pay! Fair treatment as a person and not merely a serving wench to be ogled at and fondled by the rich drunkards in their fancy clothes who pass through these doors!"

Adon attempted to shake some sense into his rattled brain and failed. Yes, the words certainly sounded like his. . . .

"The conversation was not a success?" the cleric said quietly.

The serving girl trembled with rage. "I lost my place in line to become the next fine lady of the inn, wife to the inn-keeper. A life of luxury thrown away because of you!"

She threw down the tray and Adon was careful this time to avoid it. The serving girl stormed off and Adon regarded his companions.

"How soon can we leave?" Adon said, then accepted Cyric's helping hand.

"Well met," Cyric said, his smile hidden no longer.

"We must take into account more than our haste to take flight and our desire for adventure," Kelemvor said. "Even though magic is untrustworthy, we should bring a mage along on this journey."

Cyric frowned. "Yes, I suppose you're right. But who?"

After a moment, Adon said, "What about Lord Aldophus? He is a sage of great repute, and firm friends with King Azoun."

"'Curious happenstances abound—and all burning Hell breaks loose,'" Cyric said quietly, repeating the phrase Aldophus coined, a phrase whose meaning had taken on a new, somewhat darker significance than the sage had intended when first he uttered those words.

"Aldophus is a dabbler in the physical sciences." All heads

turned to stare at the dark-haired woman who stood before the adventurers. "I doubt heartily the practice of divining the qualities of base metals and simple dirt will be of much help where the lot of you intend to tread."

Kelemvor sneered. "I suppose you could do better?"

The woman raised an eyebrow and Kelemvor studied her face. Her eyes were a deep and fathomless black, with flecks of scarlet that danced within. Her skin was deeply tanned, and he guessed she was from the South. Her lips were full and as red as blood, and a cool smile had etched itself upon her intriguing face, which was itself framed by long black hair that had been braided.

She was tall for a woman, slightly taller than Kelemvor, and she wore a cloak that allowed only a glimpse at a beautiful blue-white star pendant she wore beneath. Her clothing was a deep violet in color, and two large books, bound together by a leather strap, had been slung over her shoulder.

This is man's business, Kelemvor thought, and she's interfering. He started to tell her that, but cried out as his tankard split apart and a dragon made of bluish white fire with a wingspan the size of a man suddenly leaped into existence with a roar that seized the attention of all the inn's guests. The dragon opened its jaws and revealed its fangs, which appeared as sharp as daggers. Then the creature reared up and rushed forward with the sole intent, Kelemvor was certain, of snapping off his head, thus ending the bloodline of the Lyonsbanes.

The swiftness and fury of the monster prevented Kelemvor from drawing his sword in time, and the dragon could easily have killed the fighter in an instant. But, suddenly, the creature stopped, let out an unearthly belch, and vanished completely.

Kelemvor's seat was in pieces on the floor beneath him, and he sat, legs spread, sword before him, heart racing, eyes darting back and forth, when the woman grinned and let out a yawn. Kelemvor looked up sharply.

"Do better?" she said, repeating the fighter's snide comment. "I suppose I could at that." Then she pulled up a chair. "I am Midnight of Deepingdale."

Swords found their sheaths, axes their proper places, bolts were removed from crossbows, and a general calm fell over the inn.

"A mere illusion! We need a magic-user, not an illusionist!" But Kelemvor's throaty laugh was cut short by the sight of the table where the fire dragon had appeared: the heavy oak had been scorched.

Such control of magic was startling, especially from a woman, Kelemvor thought. Perhaps it was an accident.

Kelemvor used his sword for leverage and rose to his feet. Before the thought to return his sword to its sheath occurred to him, an all too familiar voice rang out.

"Nay! My eyes must deceive me! Surely it is not Kelemvor the Mighty come to grace this poor inn with his magnificent presence!"

Kelemvor rose, sword at the fore, and looked for the laughing face of the mercenary, Thurbrand. And Kelemvor saw that he was not alone. Two square tables had been pushed together to accommodate Thurbrand's party, which consisted of seven men and three women, none of whom would ever be confused with a regular patron of the Pride of Arabel without a heady amount of imagination. The men had the look of combat veterans, despite their apparent youth. One man, an albino, reached for his dagger. Thurbrand gestured for the albino to remain at ease. A beautiful woman with short, blond hair sat beside Thurbrand, riveted to the mercenary's every word and gesture. A girl with short, brown hair sat at the other end of the table, keeping to herself, eyeing Kelemvor suspiciously.

Kelemvor stared into the all too familiar emerald eyes of Thurbrand and found them as deceptive and hypnotizing as they always had been to him. Kelemvor grimaced.

"And here I thought the dogs were kept to the kennel," Kelemvor spat out. "The keeper must surely be chastised!"

Thurbrand shook his head and smiled as he regarded his companions. The look he gave them made it clear they were not to interfere, no matter what might occur. "Kelemvor!" he said, as if uttering the name was a trial in itself. "Surely the gods could not be so cruel!"

Kelemvor glared at the onlookers from the other tables

and one by one they averted their unwelcome stares. "You're getting old," Kelemvor said, his volume greatly reduced.

Thurbrand was just past thirty summers, scarcely older than Kelemvor himself, and yet the ravishes of age had truly begun to prey upon the fighter. Thurbrand's hair, golden and fine, had gone to thinning, and was worn unusually long in an effort to cover huge patches of bald scalp. Thurbrand was obviously self-conscious about this, and he constantly patted his hair and cajoled it with fingers to keep it in place over the bald spots.

Lines had formed on Thurbrand's forehead and around his eyes since Kelemvor had seen him last, and the manner in which he held himself, even when seated, suggested the slouch of a fatted businessman, not the conditioned posture of the finely honed warrior Kelemvor had shared a few wild adventures with in years past, before a disagreement—the subject of which was long forgotten by either man—had caused them to part ways. Still, Thurbrand's face was red from too much sun, and his arms were as well-defined and powerful as Kelemvor's.

"Old? Thurbrand of the Stonelands, old? Gaze into your own mirror once in a while, you lumbering wreck. And has no one told you that civilized men do not draw weapons unless they have a use for them?"

"I pity the man who mistakes either of us for civilized," Kelemvor said, and sheathed his sword.

"Kel," Thurbrand said. "You'll shatter the frail bonds of my ruse. I'm a regular guest in this establishment. A respected agent of arms and experienced talent to wield them. Speaking of that, I may have a little job that you—"

"Enough!" Kelemvor said.

Thurbrand shook his head in a mockery of despair. "Ah, well. At least you know where to find me."

"I wouldn't know that unless I had eyes in the back of my head," Kelemvor said, and turned his back on Thurbrand.

Kelemvor found a new chair waiting, and spied a serving boy darting into the kitchen with the pieces of the shattered chair tucked beneath his arms. Midnight sat confidently between Cyric and Adon. Caitlan sat in silence, her gaze riveted to the magic-user's pendant, which now rested outside Midnight's cloak. The girl looked as if she might faint. Her skin was white and her hands were trembling.

"We were discussing the proper route, and the proper share of the booty for someone of my expertise," Midnight said confidently, and Kelemvor felt every hair on his body prickle. "My suggestion is—"

"Get up," Kelemvor said simply.

"You need me," Midnight said incredulously as she reluctantly complied.

"Aye," Kelemvor said. "Just as I need my throat cut in my sleep. Begone!"

Suddenly Caitlan stood up, her mouth moving as if she were about to cry out. She clutched at her throat and fell across the table.

Kelemvor looked down at the girl with panic in his eyes. "My reward," he whispered. When he looked up, he realized the others were waiting for him to tell them what to do. "Adon!" Kelemvor said harshly. "Don't just stand there. You're a cleric. See what ails the child and heal her!"

Adon shook his head and held his hands open at his sides. "I cannot. With the gods in the Realms, our spells do not function unless we're near them. Surely you know this."

Kelemvor swore with disgust when he saw that Caitlan was shivering, despite the warmth of the room. "Then get a blanket or something to keep her warm."

Midnight moved forward. "My cloak," she said, and reached for the clasp by her throat.

Kelemvor looked up sharply. "You are not a part of this."

A serving girl appeared with a spare tablecloth. "I overheard," she said as she helped Kelemvor wrap the girl in the tablecloth, then backed away as the fighter hefted the unconscious girl in his arms.

Kelemvor looked into the faces of his companions. "Go with the magic-user or come with me," he said simply. Adon and Cyric looked at one another, then at Kelemvor. They didn't even look at Midnight.

"As you wish," the magic-user said coldly. Kelemvor and his companions filed past her, and she watched as Adon held open the door for the others, then made his own exit.

Midnight turned, almost colliding with a serving girl whose slight form was capped with an uneasy smile. The girl played nervously with her apron. "Say your peace," Midnight snapped.

"Your bill, milady."

Midnight looked over to her original table, where the meal she had ordered had long since become cold. It hardly mattered. She had lost her appetite. Midnight followed the girl to the bar and paid the innkeeper.

"Are there any rooms available?" Midnight said.

The innkeeper handed Midnight her change. "No, milady. We are full up. Perhaps the Scarlet Spear? It is nearby . . ."

Midnight took the directions from the man and gave him a gold piece for his trouble. Before the man could even put words to his surprise at such an extravagant tip, Midnight was already halfway to the door.

As Midnight passed through the doors of the inn and greeted the biting chill of the thin night air, a dark figure rose up from a purposefully neglected table. There was little, it seemed, a fistful of gold could not purchase in Arabel—the right to sit undisturbed in a poorly lit corner of an inn the very least of what was available. The blackened pits of the stranger's eyes seemed aflame with images of the adventurers. He grinned from ear to ear, then merged with the shadows and was gone before anyone was aware he had ever arrived.

*　*　*　*　*

Caitlan was slung over Kelemvor's horse as he rode through the night, Cyric and Adon riding close behind. Soon, they arrived at the Hungry Man Inn, and Cyric helped Kelemvor as he lowered the girl to Adon's waiting arms. The fighter leaped from his mount and ran for the door to the inn without bothering to tether his horse.

"Should we follow?" Adon said.

"Give him a moment," Cyric said, and soon Kelemvor emerged from the inn, barking orders to take the girl around back.

They were met at the rear entrance by an old woman who

carried a lantern and gestured frantically for them to get inside. Kelemvor seemed subdued in the woman's presence.

"Zehla, this is Cyric, a fellow guardsman, and Adon of Sune," Kelemvor said.

The old woman shook her head. "Time enough for pleasantries later. Follow me."

Moments later they stood by Zehla's side, in a room she had always reserved for emergencies, watching the fever-plagued motions of Caitlan Moonsong. As beads of sweat formed on the girl's brow, Zehla wiped her forehead with a wet towel.

"She's ill, possibly dying, Kel," Zehla said, her wizened features and the lines of her face speaking volumes on her authority on pain and suffering.

Kelemvor realized Caitlan had become conscious: she was trying to say something. He bent low that he might hear her words.

"Save her" The girl's voice was weak and ragged. "Save my mistress."

"Rest," Kelemvor said simply, brushing the girl's hair from her eyes. Then Caitlan suddenly grabbed his massive hand with an iron grip that made the fighter flinch.

"She can *cure* you," Caitlan said, then her muscles relaxed as she sank back on the bed.

"Zehla!" Kelemvor cried, but the old woman was already there. Kelemvor looked to the others. If they heard the girl's promise, they gave no sign. His secret was safe.

"She's alive," Zehla pronounced. "For now."

The old woman turned to Cyric and Adon, and asked them to leave the room so that she and Kelemvor might speak privately. Both men looked to Kelemvor for confirmation, but he was staring down at the girl, lost in his own concerns. They left without further prompting, and Zehla closed the door behind them.

"My reward," Kelemvor said, gesturing at the girl. "If she dies, I will be cheated of my reward."

Zehla moved toward him. "Is that your only concern?"

Kelemvor looked away from the girl and turned his back on the old woman.

"Riches can be counted in more than gold, good Kel.

There are people who help others simply for the pleasure it gives them to do so, and the knowledge that they have made a difference in the world. Hired arms are cheap and plentiful in comparison. You would do well to think on this."

"You think I don't know that? I think of that every day! But, remember, I'm no wide-eyed youth, no child for you to lecture. I have no choice but to follow the path that's been laid out for me."

Zehla went to him, touching his arm. "But why, Kel? Can you not tell me why?"

Kelemvor's shoulders fell as the anger that had raced through him evaporated. "I cannot."

Zehla shook her head and walked past the fighter. She then moved a chair out of the way, and pulled at a floorboard that came away in her hands without effort, revealing a small box that had been hidden in the tiny space. Zehla pulled out the box, then used the bed as support as she dragged herself to her feet.

"Help me," Zehla said as she set the box beside Caitlan. Kelemvor hesitated. Zehla's features turned cold. "Come, we must protect your investment."

Kelemvor moved forward, watching as Zehla opened the box and a series of multi-colored flasks were exposed. "Healing potions," Kelemvor said.

"Of course. That's why you came here, instead of taking her to one of the temples, isn't it?"

"Aye," Kelemvor said. "Clerical magic can't be trusted. I told Adon to cure her earlier, without thinking, as if it were still the time before Arrival. Of course, he couldn't. I feared the worshipers of Tymora would turn her away, as she was not one of their own, or force us to bring her back in the morning. By then she might have died."

"Having her drink this might be just as deadly as not treating her at all," Zehla said as she held up a vial. "*All* magic is unstable."

Kelemvor sighed and looked down at Caitlan, who was still shivering. "But we really have no choice, do we?"

Zehla took the lid off the flask and raised the girl's head. Kelemvor assisted her and they coaxed the unconscious girl to drink.

"So you came to me for my healing potions."

"I knew that if you didn't have the potions, you'd know where to get them," Kelemvor said. "The black market, if necessary. These items go at a premium." The flask was empty and Kelemvor allowed Caitlan's head to sink into the soft pillows. "Now what?"

"Now we wait," Zehla said. "Unless we've poisoned her, it will probably be morning before we see any results."

"If the potion works, will she be fit to ride with us?" Kelemvor said anxiously.

"She will live," Zehla said. "We will see about the rest."

Kelemvor reached for his gold, but Zehla stayed his hand.

"Unlike you, Kel, I need no reward other than the knowledge I have saved a life." Zehla motioned to the opened box. A half dozen flasks lay untouched. "Put those away," she said, and left the room.

Kelemvor stood for long moments, staring at the girl and the flasks, Zehla's words weighing heavily upon him. When the fighter finally emerged from Caitlan's room, he found Cyric and Adon waiting for him.

Zehla had already informed them of Caitlan's improving condition, and they wished to discuss their next move. Kelemvor, however, was in no mood for discussion. He left the inn, his comrades in tow, and waited until they had taken to their mounts and were well away from the inn before he let loose a string of orders that surprised Cyric and quelled some of the former thief's earlier doubts about Kelemvor's abilities.

"The boy you mentioned earlier, Cyric. The one you saw at the inn, with the girl: the one whose father is a guardsman. Pay the boy a visit and convince him to serve as a distraction at highsun tomorrow, when his father is guarding the north gate. If he objects, threaten to expose his liaisons with the girl. And tell him to maintain his silence after we're gone, as you have friends in the city who will expose him in your absence. Do this under the cover of night, then get some rest and gather your belongings. We will meet at the Hungry Man at first light.

"Adon, I want you to visit a man named Gelzunduth. I'll give you directions. Cyric and I will need false identifications that will hold up under scrutiny. That fat old buzzard is a master at creating bogus documents. We will also need a false charter." Kelemvor threw a bag of gold pieces to Adon. "That should more than cover your expenses. With your innocent face, you should have no problem convincing that pig to go along. If he refuses, come to my room at the Hungry Man. If I'm not there, wait for me, and I'll go back there with you. I've a debt to settle with that man, anyway."

Adon seemed confused. "Neither of you stay at the barracks, with the other guards?"

Kelemvor looked to Cyric.

"Part of our reward for bringing down the traitor," Cyric said. "The independence was welcome."

Adon frowned. "False documents? That's hardly legal."

Kelemvor pulled up the reigns and brought his mount to an abrupt halt. He glared at Adon. "You can't heal. You can't throw spells. You're *adequate* in a fight. Buying false documents shouldn't be too much to ask, all things considered."

Adon hung his head and took the directions Kelemvor offered, then rode off toward Gelzunduth's house.

"What will you do?" Cyric asked.

Kelemvor almost laughed. "Try to find a competent magic-user who's *not* a woman."

The fighter rode off into the night, leaving Cyric to pursue his own task, and ponder his own questions.

* * * * *

The streets of Arabel were deserted, and Midnight wondered briefly if a curfew had been in effect. She had wandered from the course the serving girl at the Pride of Arabel had laid out for her, and soon found herself lost. Midnight knew that this was for the better, as it gave her time to calm down before she found herself in the company of others at the Scarlet Spear.

Midnight touched the pendant—Mystra's trust—as she thought of the blue flame dragon that had materialized at the Pride of Arabel. She had tried to throw a simple spell of levitation to impress Kelemvor, but somehow the spell had been altered. And though Midnight had remained visibly calm, and claimed credit for the dragon as if it was what she had intended to create, she had been terrified.

The magic-user touched the pendant once more. Perhaps it had something to do with the dragon. Then again, perhaps it was only the unstable nature of magic that caused the dragon to appear.

Unable to decide the real source of the misfired spell, Midnight turned her attention to finding the Scarlet Spear.

Then, in the street ahead of her, Midnight saw a horse, and a man called out to her. It was Thurbrand, the mercenary who had challenged Kelemvor at the inn.

"Fair daffodil!"

"I am known as Midnight," she said as the man approached. There was no one else on the street. The name he called her brought a slight tinge of amusement to Midnight, despite the cries of her better nature to beware the smiling man before her.

"I am *no one's* 'fair daffodil.' "

"Then there is no justice in this world," Thurbrand said, his green eyes picking up the light from the brilliant moon overhead.

"What do you want, Dragon Eyes?"

"Ah, I see Kelemvor's tender mercies have not left you unscarred," Thurbrand said softly. "He has that effect on many who wish to embrace his friendship. He has suffered much, Lady Midnight, and he inflicts that suffering on all those around him."

"Just 'Midnight,'" the magic-user said as she felt a sudden chill and pulled her cloak tight about her shoulders.

Thurbrand smiled and brushed a strand of hair that had revealed a bare spot back in place. "Come, I offer a place to rest for the night, and company who will appreciate one as lovely and capable as yourself."

Thurbrand turned and walked in the direction of his horse. "Perhaps we can discuss business as well."

Either Midnight's eyes deceived her, or the horse Thurbrand walked toward was adorned with a blood-red mane; a horse that was the very image of the one she had been separated from outside the city of Arabel. Heart racing, Midnight watched as Thurbrand stopped and looked over his shoulder. Midnight sauntered to his side, smiling as a plan began to form in her mind. Perhaps Thurbrand would be able to assist Midnight in proving to that overbearing fool Kelemvor that she was not a woman to be trifled with, although Thurbrand himself would not have cared for the direction her thoughts had taken.

"More specifically, the business that scoundrel Kelemvor did not have the sense to employ you for. There is much I would like to know."

Midnight frowned and cast a forget spell upon Thurbrand. There was a soft, blue-white flash at the base of his skull and Thurbrand cocked his head in annoyance, swatting at the back of his neck. "Damn bugs," he said sharply. "Now, what were we talking about?"

"I don't remember."

"Strange," Thurbrand said as he mounted the ebony stallion, then looked to Midnight who held out her hand. Midnight leaped, sinking her boot into the fighter's hand, almost dragging him off the mount as she settled comfortably on it herself.

"Strange?" she said.

"I can't seem to remember either." Thurbrand shrugged. "I suppose it was of no matter."

"Aye," Midnight said, and she gave the mount a gentle kick. Then she held on tightly as the riders suddenly found themselves in motion, racing through the night. "I suppose you're right. Lovely mount you've got."

"Purchased him just last week. Somewhat unruly, but fearless in battle."

Midnight grinned and patted the flank of the horse. "Takes after his master, I would guess."

Thurbrand laughed and rested his gloved hand on Midnight's bare knee, then removed it as the horse shot forward, forcing him to hold the horse's reins or risk falling.

Midnight wondered if she knew a spell to make the man keep his paws to himself, and his head on his own pillow in the dead of night. In truth, it didn't matter. If Midnight chose not to entertain company this evening and if her magic failed her, she still had her knife.

A knife always worked.

Midnight smiled to herself and relaxed slightly. Kelemvor wouldn't turn her away after he saw what she was going to do to Thurbrand.

* * * * *

Kelemvor returned from his fruitless quest angry and tired. He found Adon mysteriously bunked out on the floor, and roused the man long enough to find that all had gone according to plan: Gelzunduth had provided the false documents. Once Kelemvor had the papers, Adon crawled back to his bed of crumpled blankets on the floor and immediately fell asleep.

The fighter wanted to know how the mission had gone and, more importantly, why Adon was not spending the night in the temple, but he was relieved Adon hadn't volunteered an explanation. A vivid memory of an evening spent on watch, listening to the cleric endlessly praise his goddess, and himself for that matter, was enough to keep Kelemvor from asking for an explanation of even the simplest matter: Adon would invariably turn the conversation into a chance to praise Sune.

Hours later, when Kelemvor was sound asleep, Adon woke from his dreamless slumber and found he could not return to sleep. The cleric had feared he would find an armed guard waiting to escort him back to the dungeon at his humble quarters in the Temple of Sune, and so he had avoided the temple completely that night. Adon was grateful to Kelemvor for his generosity in letting him stay the night, but he had learned it was unwise to voice such sentiments to the man. He would find some other way to give thanks.

Of course, Adon knew that he was being overcautious. After all, Myrmeen had given him until highsun the following day to leave Arabel. But if her mood had changed, he might have found himself on the receiving end of an assassin's sword. His experience with the serving wench at the Pride of Arabel had made him wary.

So Adon dressed in the semi-darkness, attempting to ignore the condition of the room. The cleric's quarters had always been meticulously kept; Kelemvor's room looked as if some minor disaster had swept through the place, leaving weapons, maps, dirty clothing, and bits of half-eaten dinners laying everywhere. Judging from the look of the room, Kelemvor did not allow the cleaners access under any circumstances.

Realizing he should at least try to retrieve his belongings, Adon left the inn, and nervously traveled the back streets to the Temple of Sune. Once he reached the temple, he saw no signs of any guard, so he entered and charged a fellow Sunite with the task of retrieving certain belongings from his adobe. The Sunite rumbled some less than good-natured threats, mostly concerned with battering Adon's thick skull with his flail for having disturbed his slumber. However, once his fellow cleric understood that Adon was to be taking permanent leave, he acquiesced with enthusiasm.

When the Sunite returned from the adobe, Adon checked to be sure he had packed his war hammer, as he would likely need it from the girl's description of the castle. Then Adon returned to the Hungry Man Inn, cleared a small section of the floor for his belongings, and fell into a deep sleep.

Come first light of morning, Cyric woke the slumbering pair with news that his mission had also proceeded smoothly. Kelemvor immediately dressed and went to check on Caitlan's condition. He was pleasantly surprised to find her sitting up, attacking the breakfast that Zehla had only just brought.

"Kelemvor!" Caitlan cried when she saw the fighter. "When do we leave?"

Zehla gave Kelemvor a warning glance.

"As soon as you are able. And—"

"Is Midnight with you? I have such questions for her," Caitlan said. "She's a wonder, don't you think? So beautiful and intelligent and talented—"

"She won't be coming with us," Kelemvor said, noting the distressing effect his words had on Caitlan. The girl turned pale before his eyes.

"She *has* to come with us," Caitlan said.

"There are other magic-users—"

"It's my quest," Caitlan said, her true age showing for the

first time. "You take Midnight or you don't go at all!"

Kelemvor rubbed his forehead. "You don't understand. Zehla, explain to her that a woman is not appropriate for a mission of this type."

Zehla rose from the bed and crossed her arms. "And a child is?"

Kelemvor realized he had been defeated, and gave in with a sigh. His quest for a magic-user the previous evening had been futile. The few mages who had shown any interest in the adventure were enthusiastic, but quite incompetent. One mage even burned himself out of house and home in an attempt to prove his worth.

"I suppose I could try to find her," Kelemvor said. "But Arabel is a large city. It may take more time than we have."

Caitlan looked away. "Then we'll wait."

"What about your lady?" Kelemvor said suspiciously, and again his words produced distressing effects.

"We'll wait just a little while," Caitlan said softly.

Zehla ushered Kelemvor out of the small room and joined him in the hallway. "I noticed the healing potions were untouched," Zehla said.

"I'm many things," Kelemvor said. "But I'm not a thief. Do you have any idea what caused her condition?"

"Exposure, exhaustion . . . her system was weak, and susceptible to any illness. It seems she'd been wandering the city for quite some time, trying to choose her champion."

Adon and Cyric had entered the hallway in time to hear this, and immediately joined the discussion.

"That's flattering," Adon said brightly. "She must have seen something special in you, Kelemvor."

"Actually, she'd become desperate. Kelemvor was simply the first likely candidate to speak to her," Zehla said. "She's a talkative little thing, once you get her going."

Kelemvor flinched slightly. What else had the girl mentioned to Zehla? Had she revealed his secret?

"We have work to do," Kelemvor said, and motioned for Cyric and Adon to follow.

Escaping unnoticed from the city would be a difficult matter. Both Kelemvor and Cyric would be expected on duty shortly after eveningfeast. Cyric may have had stealth enough to make it past anxious guards or over unclimbable walls, but the squarely built fighter with a child, a foppish cleric, and a magic-user in tow surely could not.

"Cyric, go buy clothing and whatever else you think we could use to disguise ourselves. Adon, try to find Midnight. We're going to . . . have to settle for her. I'll be here, finishing the packing and working on a plan," Kel said as soon as the three adventurers got outside.

An hour later, when Kelemvor emerged from his room, he almost collided with two of Zehla's men carrying armfuls of food. Outside, he found Cyric and Adon packing the supplies with a surprising lightness of step.

Adon grinned and nodded to the shadows of the stables, from which Midnight appeared, leading a magnificent black horse with a blazing red mane. Kelemvor's shoulders slumped in defeat, the memory of Caitlan's face and the possible loss of the gold she had promised weighing down his acid tongue.

"Do you gamble, Kel?" Midnight asked, playfully.

"It seems I am about to," he grumbled.

Midnight held out her hand. In it, she had a huge, braided tangle that resembled the head of a mop. "Courtesy of your friend, Thurbrand," Midnight said. Kelemvor recognized the strands as human hair; all the human hair, it seemed, that had been left on Thurbrand's head.

"Is he? . . ."

"Quite upset, aye."

Kelemvor smirked, despite himself. "You just mentioned gambling?"

Midnight nodded. "Consider this my stake to enter your game."

This time Kelemvor did laugh, a hearty laugh that was cut short as he noticed the disguises that peaked out from the packages that sat beside Cyric's mount. He examined the packages to find wigs, surprisingly lifelike masks, and the tattered dresses of a pair of elderly beggar women.

Caitlan appeared behind them, looking bright and healthy. She greeted Midnight as if the woman had been the answer to her prayers, then looked beyond the party, as if to a sight beyond the walls of Arabel, her expression once again turning serious.

"We must go," Caitlan said gravely. "There isn't much time."

Midnight looked to Kelemvor. "I can help Adon with the supplies, if you'd like."

Kelemvor nodded, and snatched up the packages that contained their disguises. Cyric followed him into the inn.

"What's the name of the place we're going to again?" Midnight asked.

"Castle Kilgrave," Adon said.

Midnight shrugged and removed her cloak to work more freely. Her blue-white star pendant glared in the sunlight as she placed her cloak on her mount's back.

In the shadows of the stables, a single shade broke away from the darkness, assumed the form of a raven, then burst from the stables and flew over the heads of the adventurers, flying at speeds no creature of nature could ever attain.

❦ 4 ❦

Nature Runs Wild

Bane had not been idle in the two weeks since the time of Arrival, as his worshipers now called the night he was thrown from the heavens. Almost constant activity was needed to avert his attention from his distressingly mortal state, and on the few occasions when he allowed himself to turn his attentions inward and examine the frail mortal shell that necessity had forced him to assume, the Black Lord became lost in the endless intricacies of the machine that gave him movement and voice.

Such gifts and miracles he found within the submicroscopic areas surrounding the cortex! And when he immersed his consciousness in but a single cell of the body's endless stream of blood and allowed the path of his explorations to be decided by the body itself, Bane felt a rapture that rivaled godhood itself.

It was then he understood the trap and forced himself to pull away. He placed barricades within the brain of the body he was forced to inhabit, and fortified his perceptions in an effort to train them outward, ever outward, and never again succumb to the dangers locked within his mortal frame. Bane was a god; miracles had always been boring and commonplace to him before. But now the miracles of the Planes were locked away from him, and he would have to concentrate on the task before him, so that he might one day soon reclaim the heavens and satisfy his ever-gnawing hunger for miracles and wonder in a manner that befitted a god.

During Bane's first days in Zhentil Keep, the human rulers of the city fell on their knees in his presence and placed all their assets at Bane's disposal. Bane was grateful the coup had been bloodless; he would need as much human fodder to grease the wheels of his machinations as he could get his talon-shaped grip on.

Construction of the Black Lord's new temple had begun, and soon the rubble was cleared away and makeshift walls rose to hide the intricate planning sessions Bane called. Although Lord Chess, sensing his own position as nominal ruler of Zhentil Keep at risk, offered to place himself and his staff at Bane's disposal, Bane chose to remain near his black throne. Besides, he didn't care to experience the boredom of the day to day operations of the city, so long as its occupants were loyal and ready to become sacrifices at a moment's notice.

On his third night in the Realms, Bane began to dream, and in his dreams he saw Mystra, smiling in the face of terror, laughing at Ao as the gods were delivered to their fate. Bane, the giver of nightmares, had finally fallen prey to one himself. He cursed his flesh for sharing this new weakness with him. Still, the nightmare served a purpose, and Bane once again pondered the meaning of Mystra's enigmatic farewell to the Planes.

So Bane decided he should seek out Mystra and discover why she viewed Ao's wrath so calmly.

Five days after the time of Arrival, Tempus Blackthorne, a mage of great power and importance, arrived with the news of Mystra's location in the Realms. Bane set a seal upon the doors leading to his private chamber and teleported Blackthorne and himself to Castle Kilgrave. They found Mystra outside the castle, weakened and helpless from some trauma or attack. Perhaps she had attempted a spell that had gone awry, Bane thought, and laughed at the irony.

As the Black Lord stood over her, Mystra suddenly became aware of his presence and released a single shred of her power—a modified geas spell meant for her intended avatar. The spell took the form of a bluish white falcon, soared into the night sky, and escaped. Bane ordered Blackthorne to follow the magical creature. The emissary transformed into a great black raven that took flight after the falcon, only to lose sight of it in Arabel.

When he imprisoned the goddess in the dungeon of Castle Kilgrave with mystic chains born of enchanted fires, Bane felt a wave of power rush across the room. The barren rock dungeon shook as Mystra came to her senses and tested the strength of her bonds.

And then Bane summoned a horror to keep Mystra weak and tractable.

Come, monster, I call you into this plane, as my minions have so many times before.

Bane heard a growl, deep in the back of his mind as the creature replied, *I come.*

It first appeared as a swirling red mist, spiraling like a cyclone as it rose up and sprouted hundreds of quivering, misshapen hands that cleaved the air before the goddess hungrily. An equal number of pale yellow eyes suddenly opened, and they floated all around the swirling mist, passing like ghosts through their fellows as they darted back and forth, each eye anxious to study its prey from every angle. Finally, a score of wounds tore through the mists, revealing gaping mouths that reached back into an endless succession of dark dimensions. The mouths opened and closed rapidly as a cry that could only be considered one of hunger was loosed from them.

Mystra recognized the creature: it was a *hakeashar*, a being from another plane with a voracious appetite for magic. Bane had no doubt made a pact with the monster. In return for aid in crossing into the Prime Material Plane, the monster would give the Black Lord something he valued—power. For the *hakeashar* had the ability to release some of the magic it consumed, and Bane would want that raw energy to power his plans.

Mystra considered her options. If Bane had been foolish enough to enter into a pact with the creature, known for its treacherous nature, there might be a way she could use it to her advantage.

"We have much to discuss," Bane said, the *hakeashar* hovering behind him.

"Why have you imprisoned me?" Mystra said.

"I will be happy to release you from these shackles once

you have heard me out . . . And you agree to help me complete my plan."

"Go on."

"I wish to form an alliance of the gods," Bane said. "Swear your allegiance to me and my cause, Goddess, and I will set you free."

Despite the presence of the *hakeashar,* Mystra could not hold back her laughter. "You're mad," she said.

"No," Bane said. "Merely practical." He turned to the creature. "She's yours," Bane said calmly "But remember our agreement."

Of course.

A hundred eyes turned from Bane and this time Mystra could not hold back her screams.

When it was over, the grotesque creature giggled and fed its own glowing eyes into its gaping maws, ready to sleep now that it had feasted. Mystra was surprised to find herself alive. The pain, even in her nebulous form, had been horrifying.

Bane screamed curses at the creature until it opened a few eyes and let loose a burst of bluish white fire that enshrouded the villain. After a moment, Bane literally pulsed with stolen power.

"Enough!" Bane cried, and the blue-white fires ceased.

"It was you, wasn't it?" Mystra said as she struggled sluggishly with her bonds. "You stole the Tablets of Fate. I suspected you from the beginning."

"I took them," Bane said, and the creature he had brought to this plane slumped in place, swallowed the last of its eyes and fell into a deep, silent slumber. "Along with Lord Myrkul."

"Ao will make you pay for this," she said, and Bane felt a trace of the magic that had been siphoned from her curl within him, waiting to be unleashed.

"Ao will have no power over me," the Black Lord said, his laughter filling the chamber.

Since that night, Bane had let the *hakeashar* take Mystra's power, which seemed to replenish itself like the blood cells of a human, more than a a dozen times. Each time, Bane received a fraction of that energy, according to the terms of his bargain with the creature.

Each time he was given more power, Bane prowled the corridors of New Acheron, the former Castle Kilgrave, longing for his true temple, and wishing for someone to share his triumphs with. Blackthorne was away almost constantly, either supervising matters in Zhentil Keep or searching for some sign of the magic Mystra had loosed before her capture. The handful of humans Blackthorne had conscripted to look after Bane's human needs were pitiful examples of the species, and Bane had no interest in any of them.

Today, Lord Bane stood in the massive dungeon beneath Castle Kilgrave, staring at the still water of the scrying pool he had constructed, speaking to Lord Myrkul. Much of the room—much of the castle, in fact—had been modified to suit Bane's needs, and Castle Kilgrave had undergone many changes since the god took it over as a base. The Black Lord had attempted to magically sculpt certain chambers and hallways into replicas of his Temple of Suffering in Acheron, although his efforts had met with failure much of the time. The instability of magic made it impossible, even for a god, to throw every spell accurately, and when using magic, Bane felt like an artist attempting to paint without benefit of hands. The shape of the castle was almost amusing to Bane except for its existence as a monument to his loss, and in that regard it gave no pleasure to the displaced god.

"What do you hope to achieve by draining Mystra's power?" Myrkul said impatiently. "Your mortal form can contain only so much power at a time, and the vessel must always be refilled."

"You miss the point," Bane said. "You and I formed an alliance when we stole the tablets together."

"A temporary alliance," Myrkul said. "Which has hardly proven successful. Look at what we have become. Less than gods, more than men. What place have we in the Realms, Lord Bane?"

Bane looked at the emaciated, almost skeletal face of Myrkul's avatar, then thought of his own hideous form and shuddered.

"We have our birthright," Bane said. "We are gods, no matter what trials Ao puts us through." Bane shook his head, then stopped himself as he realized it was a purely human gesture. "Myrkul, think back to why we took the Tablets of Fate."

Myrkul scratched his bony face, and Bane nearly laughed. The sight of the feared God of the Dead plagued by something so ordinary as a human itch was so pathetic it was almost funny. The God of Strife sighed at the idea and went on.

"We stole the tablets because we believed Ao drew strength from them, and without the tablets, Ao would be less inclined to interfere with our dealings."

"So we believed," Myrkul said ruefully. "We were fools to do so."

"We were right!" Bane shouted. "Think for a moment! Why has Ao not *taken* the tablets back?"

Myrkul set his bony hands at his side. "I have wondered that myself."

"I think it is because Ao cannot!" Bane said. "Perhaps he no longer has the strength. That may be why our liege exiled us from the Planes! Our plan succeeded, and Ao feared that the gods would unite, and rise up in revolt. That is why Ao has scattered us across the Realms and made us suspicious, afraid, and vulnerable to attack."

"I see," Myrkul said. "But this is only your theory."

"Supported by the facts," Bane said. "I have already captured our first pawn in this game, if you would call her that."

"Mystra?"

"With her power, all the magic in the Realms will be ours to control!" Bane laughed. He was lying, of course. If the goddess had such power, he never would have captured her so easily.

"Those gods who do not wish to go along with your plans will be enslaved or destroyed, I assume," Myrkul said suspiciously. "And you will use Mystra's power to accomplish this."

"Of course," Bane said. "But we are already allies. Why speak of such things?"

"Indeed," Myrkul said.

"Further, I believe there is power to free us from this state," Bane said. "Power Mystra has secreted somewhere in the Realms."

Myrkul nodded. "How do you plan to proceed?"

"We will discuss that later," Bane said. "For now I must deal with other, equally pressing matters."

Myrkul lowered his head, and his image faded from the scrying pool. In truth, Bane had contacted Myrkul prematurely; he had not yet decided what the next move should be.

Bane turned sharply as a black raven flew into the dungeon at a mind-boggling speed, and then became his servant, Blackthorne.

"Lord Bane, I have much to report. I believe I have located the human in Arabel that holds a gift from Mystra. She wears it as a blue-white star-shaped pendant."

Bane smiled. The pendant Blackthorne described was identical to the symbol Mystra had worn in the Planes.

"Better still," Blackthorne said, "the magic-user who wears the pendant is coming here."

* * * * *

The party left Arabel separately. Adon departed the city first, alone. Half an hour later, Midnight and Caitlan followed, leading two packhorses. Finally, at highsun, Kelemvor and Cyric, dressed as elderly beggar women, made it through the gate without incident. Then they rendezvoused a half hour's ride away, as Kelemvor had planned. The fighter insisted on burying the costumes he and Cyric had worn. Actually he wanted to burn them, but he worried that the smoke would be visible from the watchtowers in Arabel.

Now, the better part of an hour had passed since the oppressive walls of Arabel dwindled away into nothing but a faint speck marking the horizon at the heroes' backs, then vanished altogether. There was nothing in sight but the well-traveled road before them and the flat earth that stretched endlessly across the land to the east and west. The mountains of Gnoll Pass were visible in the distance to the north.

Kelemvor rode up beside Cyric and slapped him on the back. Cyric was thrown forward in his saddle by the blow and he looked at the other man warily.

"Ah, this is the life, is it not, Cyric?"

Simple pleasures for simple minds, Cyric thought, but merely responded with a grin and a healthy "Aye!" Soon Kelemvor moved on, and Cyric stopped to check the tethers that secured the packhorses attached to his mount and found everything to be in order.

After a time, Cyric set the wanderings of his fanciful imagination on another, more pleasant course, and studied the silky smooth legs of Midnight as they clung to the sides of her horse just ahead. Every now and again he caught a glimpse of her beautiful features as they contorted into a pained grimace. Adon, riding beside the magic-user, was deluging her with a constant and embarrassing stream of compliments.

Cyric wondered if the cleric was trying to seduce Midnight with his words. It didn't seem likely. It seemed, instead, that Adon preferred the din of constant conversation, even if he were the only willing participant, to the silence of the land they passed through. Perhaps Adon doesn't want to be alone with his own tedious thoughts, Cyric noted.

Ahead, Midnight had come to this same conclusion what seemed to be an eternity before. She sensed that Adon was troubled, but she found it difficult to be sympathetic as the man refused to divulge the nature of his problems. Worse still, this was the time she should have been using to conserve her energies and lose herself in meditation, but her unwanted traveling companion would not allow her a moment's peace.

Her patience reaching its end, Midnight attempted to express her desire to be left alone. Subtlety had not worked, so she tried to address the issue directly.

"Go away, Adon! Let me ride in peace!"

But even being direct did not earn Midnight a rest from Adon's endless list of compliments.

"A veritable goddess!" Adon cried.

"If you believe you can continue to sing my praises without benefit of both lungs—pray do go on."

"And modest as well!"

Midnight looked to the sky. "Mystra deliver me!"

"Ah, to bask in the warmth of one even the strongest of flames would pale beside . . ."

Finally she looked back and said to Kelemvor, "May I kill this man?"

Kelemvor shook his head, enjoying the entertainment. Caitlan rode up beside him. She seemed to find nothing amusing about the apparent dissension in the ranks; if anything, the display made her nervous.

"Nothing to worry about," Kelemvor said to the girl. "Trust me."

Caitlan nodded slowly, unable to shift her gaze away from the dark-haired magic-user and the cleric.

"Ah, with a fiery temper, matching her flaming heart!" Adon said.

"Portions of *your* anatomy will be flaming if you do not cease this instant!" Midnight cried.

And so it went, until the air grew thin, and storm clouds gathered overhead. Suddenly, the sky split with a mighty roar, and a summer shower poured warm rain upon the heroes.

Adon continued to drone on, occasionally pausing to spit out rain water, but the sounds of the storm served to muffle his voice until his words were nothing but a dull hum buried beneath the patter of the rain.

Midnight threw back her head. The gentle caress of the rain served to relax the magic-user's nerves, and as the storm grew worse, Midnight closed her eyes and gave herself over to the soothing sensations caused by the steady rainfall. She smiled, imagining strong, firm hands massaging her temples, neck, and shoulders. She pictured Kelemvor's arms; they seemed strong enough to wrestle a tree from its roots, and yet they were furnished with hands gentle enough to wipe away the tears of a child. Midnight's mount reared up and the magic-user shook herself from her daydream.

"I sent Adon back to convert Cyric to the ways of Sune," Kelemvor said with a grin, despite his notable annoyance at the constant flow of the rain. His long black hair was matted to his skull, and the gray streaks made him look as if he wore the fur of a skunk who had died of fright. Midnight felt it her duty to tell him so, and he hung his head, muttering some private oath, attempting to ignore the rain as he continued to speak.

"We have not discussed . . ." He paused and spat out a mouthful of water. "Division of duties."

Midnight nodded.

"You, being the woman, will be in charge of preparing the food and all other domestic chores."

Midnight's mount shuddered as his mistress ground her powerful legs against his flanks and dug her hands firmly into his neck.

"Being the woman?" Midnight said, biting back the spell she had studied that morning that would turn the pompous ass beside her into a species more suitable for his attitudes. Then she remembered the last time she had prepared a meal for an entire party. The lone cleric who had not partaken had to use all his healing spells on her unintentional victims.

"Caitlan can help you. We will divide the man's work amongst ourselves."

Midnight flinched, trained her eyes forward, and spat out a simple, "Aye."

"Well met!" Kelemvor said, and slapped Midnight's horse. The mount turned his head slightly, and ignored the blow that was supposed to cause him to go galloping off at a mad pace. Midnight's grip on the animal loosened and became a pleasant caress.

Kelemvor turned back to speak with the others, and Midnight strained hard to remember exactly why it had been so important to her to ride with these men.

Unconsciously, her fingers had found the surface of her pendant, and she was still stroking the blue-white star when she noticed the effects the rain were having on the flatlands surrounding them.

Patches of ground grew damp, while others hardened as

if to solid rock. Elsewhere, small fissures opened in the surface of the earth. In other places, whole areas of green grass rose up at an incredible pace, nurtured by the strange rain.

Suddenly, the soaked earth became black and charred, and trees long dead began to sprout and grow, their blackened limbs reaching out to the sky as if imploring the maker of this madness to stop at once. Small armies of worms hung from the quivering branches, growing to obscenely bloated sizes before exploding and turning into blood-red apples. Small black bugs crawled about the fruit, then revealed themselves to be tiny black eyes, which blinked wildly at the falling rain.

Beautiful saplings sprouted and grew upside-down out of the earth, their most fragile upper branches impossibly assuming the weight of the main trunk as it grew straight up. The trees were filled with gorgeous green leaves and transparent pink and golden fruit. At their crowns, the trees began to sprout a network of amber roots that reached high into the air and intertwined with the new roots/branches from its nearest neighbor. Finally, even the branches of the decaying trees reached up into the air and joined the network, their ebony strands mixing with the amber roots.

Where only moments ago there had been nothing but barren earth now stood a lush forest filled with miracles and mysteries. Above the road, the network of roots had formed a canopy of crisscrossed roots and charred tree limbs that grew tighter and more complex until the sky, which was now red, was visible only in patches and rain fell only lightly on the heroes.

Travel through the new forest, even on the road, was slow going. And soon the road itself became blocked by trees, and the heroes had to follow it on foot as best they could through the tangle of tree limbs on the ground.

"I get the feeling we're completely lost," Cyric mumbled as he pushed through a tangle of vines into a clearing.

"Impossible," Kelemvor said gruffly. "There is but one road, and it leads only to Castle Kilgrave and what lays beyond."

"But we may have gone off the road some time ago, Kel.

Who can tell?" Midnight said, stopping to help her horse over a branch and lead it into the open area.

"We may have been traveling in circles for hours," Adon whined.

The forest, silent until now, suddenly shrieked to life. Insects buzzed, speaking their secret language. The rustle of wings merged with the thumps of newly formed legs that burst from ichor-laden cocoons and took their first short, plodding steps.

But the heroes could see nothing in the gathering darkness of the forest. And through the small gaps in the canopy, Midnight and saw the blood-red sky turn black. The rain had stopped, at least momentarily.

The bonds that secured the packhorses strained as the frightened animals struggled for freedom, pulling away from Cyric and his panic-stricken mount. Then the tethers snapped, and the animals stumbled wildly away from the party and back into the forest. Cyric cursed and moved to follow the nearest horse.

"Leave them!" Kelemvor warned. The noises grew loud again, and Cyric joined the others in the clearing. As the heroes watched, the forest grew dark, and the sounds of movement in the trees got closer.

Suddenly, the shrieks of the packhorses echoed in the forest. Kelemvor drew his sword as he moved to Midnight's side. "An old ambush trick," he said. Around them the noise rose until it became a constant din. "Passed down from generations of warriors . . ."

Cyric found his cloak of displacement in one of the canvas sacks on his horse and swiftly threw it across his shoulders. His image seemed to shimmer, and a score of phantom Cyrics appeared around him—some ahead, some behind, others making slightly varied gestures, until it became impossible to tell which was the true Cyric. Each of them seemed surprised by the cloak's effects, surprised and delighted.

Kelemvor was shocked by the effects of the cloak, too. "Cyric! What's going on?"

"I don't know! The cloak has never done this before!"

In the trees, specks of light, flashes of silver and amber,

were now visible nearby and deep in the forest, as well. As the lights grew larger and the sounds even louder, Midnight guessed at their true nature.

Glaring eyes.

Chattering teeth.

The roots and vines above the heroes shuddered. The earth beneath them appeared to bleed, and Adon saw large colonies of fire ants rising from the wounds. He shouted as he accidentally stepped on a freshly excavated mound and a swarm of ants ran up his legs. He slapped at the insects and their already swollen bodies burst beneath his blows.

A tree split open near Cyric and expelled the slime-drenched, stumbling body of a white-faced, ghoulish creature, naked and covered with black veins that pulsed and rerouted themselves across its body at random. The thing's limbs bent backward and forward, and the sickening sound of bones shattering and bursting from flesh filled the air as a dozen of the abominations were jettisoned from the large blackened trees.

"Let the horses loose!" Kelemvor screamed, and the heroes let go of the animals' reins. Being well-trained and used to danger, though, the mounts didn't stray far across the clearing.

The creature before Cyric laughed as its amber eyes sunk back into its skull and emerged on its tongue. Then it swallowed them again, and they burst this time from the pale flesh of its chest. The creature moved forward, ripping its own arm from its socket to use as a weapon, and charged at Cyric, the claw-like fingers of the disembodied arm opening and closing with a fervor.

Cyric only had time to note that the creature did not bleed from its empty shoulder before it struck at one of his shadow selves. The thief spun and used his hand axe to hack at the creature.

Kelemvor stood beside Midnight, Caitlan, and Adon, watching as the white-skinned creature attacked Cyric. Then he heard a low growl and turned to see a pair of yellow dogs, each bearing three heads and eight spidery legs, creeping up on them from behind. The dogs separated and maneuvered to attack.

"Adon! Midnight! Back-to-back formation with me. We have to protect Caitlan!" The cleric and the magic-user responded instantly, helping Kelemvor form a triangle with Caitlan in the center. "Caitlan, crouch down, hands around your knees, face tucked in. Try not to look up unless you have to. Be ready to run if we fall."

Caitlan did as she was told, without question. From her vantage, close to the ground, looking out past Kelemvor's boots, she spotted more of the dogs in the forest—some waiting outside the small clearing; others attacking the white-skinned creatures. One of the spider hounds, racing close to the ground, seemed to be coming directly for Caitlan. She squeezed her eyes shut and tucked her head down, then offered a prayer to her mistress for their deliverance.

Midnight prepared to unleash a spell in their defense, and also prayed that it would not go awry. Magic missiles might not have the power to stop the beast, and Midnight didn't dare throw anything as powerful as a fireball, for fear of it backfiring and killing her friends. So she attempted to conjure a decastave—a pole of force—using a fallen branch for the spell.

The magic-user completed the spell just as the first of the dogs leaped at her.

Nothing happened.

For an instant Midnight smelled the fetid breath of the middle head of the creature, and three sets of jaws opened wide to rend her flesh. Then Adon flung himself at the dog, knocking it away before Midnight could be harmed. Adon and the spider hound struck the ground separately, the hound falling in a muddy pit, its legs bicycling in the air as it attempted to right itself.

Adon looked up and shouted. "Midnight, Caitlan, move!"

The second dog had leaped at Kelemvor. He bent low and gutted the screaming animal as it passed above him. Midnight grabbed Caitlan and scrambled out of the way as the fighter was dragged down by the weight of the dog and fell in the spot where Caitlan had crouched only seconds before.

Kelemvor rose, pulling his sword from the body of the

hound. He noticed that the other spider hound seemed to be drowning in the pool of mud. The fighter went to the beast and ran it through, ending its misery and its threat. The creature whimpered once before it died and sank into the mud.

More of the spider hounds prowled the edge of the clearing, avoiding the quick death their pack leaders had found on Kelemvor's sword, and busied themselves by attacking most of the white-skinned creatures that had emerged from the dead trees.

"Quick, Adon. Help Cyric!" Kelemvor yelled as another of the humanoid creatures moved in to attack the thief.

Midnight hissed, "If you have you some dark trick to unleash, Kel, now might be the time!"

"Never ask for what you are not prepared to receive," the fighter growled, then shook his head and braced himself as a trio of the white-skinned creatures that had avoided the dogs approached. Caitlan stood between Kelemvor and Midnight. The best they could hope for, Kelemvor knew, was to keep the creatures away from the girl for as long as possible.

A few yards away, Adon waded into the sea of quivering body parts that lay in a heap surrounding Cyric as he fought with yet another of the white-faced abominations. This one noticed Adon, ripped off its own head, and sent it flying at the young cleric. The head flew by, baring huge fangs, as Adon sidestepped and swung his hammer at a disembodied, claw-like hand poised to rip out Cyric's throat.

The hand exploded as the hammer struck, and Adon turned suddenly, the sound of mad panting and the heat of something dark and evil at his ear. The disembodied head floated in midair beside the cleric, its broad smile full of sharp teeth.

"They're not human," Cyric shouted. "Not even alive, not the way we think of it. They're plants of some sort, shaped like humans!"

The head that floated beside Adon made an odd sound, like a giggle.

Adon backed up slightly, never taking his gaze from the head, and raised his hammer. The head rushed toward the cleric, but he struck it soundly in the jaw before it had a chance to bite him. Moaning loudly, the head spun madly to the ground.

Moments later, after he dispatched the head, Adon saw that all three of the humanoids who had dared to attack Kelemvor now lay in quivering, bloodless pieces on the ground. But, another pack of the creatures was approaching Kelemvor and Midnight, and behind them, a dozen of the creatures were emerging from the forest, their razor-sharp claws twitching as they sliced at the air.

Midnight ordered her fellows to stand behind her as she attempted to find that perfect center of peace that was required for spellcasting. She began to sway, and her chanting rose above the gibbering of the approaching creatures. Suddenly there was a blinding flash of light and volleys of blue-white missiles leaped from her hands, striking at all of the humanoid creatures in sight. The tide of magic seemed endless, and even Midnight seemed startled by the effects of her spell. The darts of magical light pierced the creatures like daggers, and suddenly the monsters stopped their attack.

Then the ghoulish creatures began to wander. They looked to the sky, then to themselves, and then they fell, one by one, their flesh losing its consistency as the illusion of humanity fell away and their true nature was revealed. Roots erupted from their bodies, entering the earth, and moments later, all that was left of the creatures was a network of black and white vines.

Midnight looked down at the pendant, and watched as a few tiny streaks of lightning played across its surface, then vanished. She felt drained.

The easy prey destroyed, the spider hounds began to emerge from the forest and advance toward the heroes. There were more of the creatures than Kelemvor had realized: at least twenty of the beasts had moved into the clearing.

Suddenly, something fantastic caught Midnight's eye: a blur of movement, the size and shape of a horse and rider. Then, the quicksilver rider was upon them, circling the party with blinding speed. Midnight felt as if she were in the eye of a whirlwind. A sudden yellow flash caught her eye, and she realized the rider was Adon. But how was he able to accomplish this feat?

Midnight turned away from her speculations as she watched Adon break from the protective pattern he had formed around the adventurers and speed off toward the spider hounds. He rode through the hounds, his war hammer cutting through the unprepared horde of creatures like a sickle through wheat, and in seconds the spider hounds retreated into the woods.

Yet even though the threat was ended, Adon and his mount continued to move in a blur until they vanished into the forest. It was obvious Adon had lost control of whatever magic he was wielding.

"By Mystra, you'll be the death of me yet," Midnight said as ran off on an impossible quest to catch the cleric.

An icy cold rain started to fall and was seeping through the canopy of trees. Midnight felt a biting sensation as the tiny droplets struck her skin and the winds struggled to force her back.

Adon, heart pounding, mind racing as he held on for dear life, realized that his lungs weren't drawing air and his tenuous grip on the horse beneath him was giving way. He had given the beast a dose of his potion of speed, the single item he had withheld during Kelemvor's careful inventory of everyone's belongings. Adon knew that it was wrong to lie about such things, but he also knew that the potion had been a boon from the goddess Sune, and it would be her wisdom alone that guided his hand in its use.

However, when the spider hounds grouped to attack, and Adon received no sign from the goddess, he panicked and took matters into his own hands. He fed the potion to the horse but it was already moving before he could use more than a few drops on himself. The small vial then flew out of his hands as he held on for dear life.

Now, as the horse's speed stole the breath from his lungs and he neared unconsciousness, Adon saw a vision—a beautiful woman's face, carved from the fleeting specks of light and color that surrounded him in the vortex of speed. The woman's hands reached out and touched the sides of his face, gently pushing him this way and that, as if to fully explore the wonders Sune had bestowed upon him.

"He's not hurt too badly," Midnight said.

Adon blinked, and the illusion of motion began to fade. "I thought you were Sune," he said.

"He seems addled," Kelemvor said.

"Aye," Cyric said. "But is that anything new?"

The world abruptly came into focus, and Adon found himself staring up into the faces of his companions. They appeared to be in a forest, although Adon was certain there was nothing but flatlands along the way to the castle. Tiny flickers of scarlet radiance showed through the branches of the trees above them, although some of them appeared quite strange.

"Midnight, you—you saved me!" Adon said in amazement, a smile crossing his face.

"You fell off your horse," Midnight said. Adon's saddle and supplies were strewn about on the road beside him. Midnight realized the cleric must have been holding on to the saddle, and it was the bonds that held it in place that shattered under the strain of the horse's speed.

Horror surged through the cleric. "My face! It's not—"

"Undamaged," Cyric said wearily. "Same as always. Now give me an explanation for what we witnessed."

"I don't understand . . . ," Adon said, attempting to appear as innocent as possible.

"You rode like the wind, Adon. You seemed more a blur of motion than a rider and mount," Kelemvor said. "I thought your magics had failed you."

"I wouldn't phrase it quite that way," Adon said.

"I don't care how you would *phrase it*. What are you holding back from us?"

Midnight moved forward, and helped the cleric to his feet. "Don't be a fool, Kelemvor," she said. "It's obvious he can't explain what happened, any more than any of us can explain the madness the Realms have been infected with since the gods fell."

Kelemvor shook his head. "Shall we go?"

Adon nodded gratefully, and everyone except Midnight returned to their mounts.

"That was a mistake, Adon." Midnight spoke in hushed tones. The cleric was about to speak when Midnight cut him off. "It took me a few moments to understand. You have potions, don't you?"

Adon lowered his head. "I had one. It's gone now."

Midnight frowned. "Any other surprises?"

Adon became alarmed. "No, Midnight! I swear to Sune herself!"

"Using magic might send you to Sune faster than you'd want, Adon. In fact, you could have killed all of us."

Midnight nodded.

"Please don't tell Kelemvor what I did. He'd skin me alive!" Adon whispered.

Midnight smiled. "We can't have that," she said, and walked away from the cleric.

"Certainly not," Adon said with a bravado he did not feel. He bent down and began to gather his belongings.

"Come," Caitlan said to the cleric. "We must be off to the castle right away!"

"But we're still lost," Adon cried.

Then, as if in answer to the cleric's words, the trees began to shrivel and melt. Within seconds, the road was again clear and the rain had stopped.

"Sune be praised!" the cleric said, and rushed to join the others.

Because his horse was gone, Adon was forced to ride with Kelemvor. His initial preference had been to ride with Midnight, so they might continue their conversation from earlier that afternoon, but Midnight narrowed her eyes to slits and Adon abandoned the notion. Caitlan rode with the magic-user instead. Because both packhorses had been killed, the party was forced to carry their remaining supplies on the backs of the remaining mounts.

Midnight led her horse, which carried Caitlan, on foot until they were a mile clear of the ruination. The once living forest had already lapsed into an advanced state of decay. Midnight guessed that by morning the forest would be nothing more than the dust and dry earth it had been before their approach.

The heroes made camp beneath the stars, and ate the

food that had not been infested by ants or lost to the arcane legions that had attacked them, then rested beneath the night sky. They would go on. There were no dissenting votes.

Though he did not suggest turning back, it was clear that Cyric was worried about the strange events that had plagued them all day. Instead of discussing the battle, however, the thief gathered his blankets and went to sleep immediately after dinner.

Just before he attempted to sleep, Kelemvor watched as Caitlan sat alone, staring off at the horizon. The girl had said very little after the attack in the forest, and the fighter wondered what was going on behind her enigmatic stare. At times Caitlan appeared to be nothing more than a frightened child; at other times her intelligence and resolve reminded him of a battle-weary general. The contradiction was baffling.

Kelemvor himself had always refused the reins of command. He was uncomfortable with responsibility for anyone but himself. Why then had he accepted this quest with such unquestioning belief that he was the man to lead it? Kelemvor told himself that it had been boredom that spurred him on, causing him to accept the quest and leave Arabel. He needed adventure. He needed to leave the ordered, civilized life of the city behind. But there was another reason he chose to come.

She can cure you, Kelemvor.

The fighter knew it was better to cling to the shadow of hope than embrace the light of reality and find himself filled with despair. He could only hope Caitlan was telling the truth.

Kelemvor's thoughts continued in this vein until he fell into a deep slumber and dreamed of the hunt.

Midnight took the first watch as everyone else retired, her senses far too alert, far too *alive* to allow her to sleep or even relax.

As she sat, listening to the sounds of the night, the mage pondered Kelemvor's strange actions since the battle. At dinner, the fighter insisted that everyone help in preparing the meal. After they ate, he insisted that everyone help bury the garbage, so as not to attract scavengers. He seemed like a different man from the one she'd first met at the tavern in Arabel.

Perhaps the fighter had come to realize that Midnight was indeed a valuable part of the company, and he felt ashamed of his own poor judgement in accepting her only as a last choice, then having the bad taste to point out that fact again and again. Besides, there was one thing Midnight and he shared—a wild streak that marked them as fit for the life of wanderers and adventurers, and very little else.

Midnight spent the next four hours wrestling with her growing feelings for the fighter and her questions concerning the pendant that had been grafted to her flesh. Her thoughts led her in circles for hours, until Adon came to relieve her on the watch.

The cleric watched Midnight as she immediately fell into a deep sleep, and envied her. Still, despite the hardships and the horrors he had faced this evening, despite the foulness of the air, the stench of the dead lands that assaulted his nose, he knew the situation could be worse. At least he was in the company of stout-hearted comrades, and he was free. He didn't have to concern himself over the imminent danger of incarceration or the humiliation he would have faced had Myrmeen Lhal gone directly to his elders at the Temple of Sune.

No, he was free, and a better man for it.

On the other hand, just one silken pillow would have been welcome.

*　*　*　*　*

The bedchambers of Myrmeen Lhal were spectacularly designed, with a bowl-shaped ceiling crafted in tiers of concentric circles that spiraled upward to its center. The room was dominated by a huge round bed, a dozen feet in diameter, adorned with red silk sheets and a dozen soft gold-laced pillows. Works of art abounded; some breathtaking, others merely beautiful.

But the finest work of art, Myrmeen herself, could only be seen through icy black curtains, constantly charged by the finest illusionists of the city, that allowed her to look out on any exotic port of call with only the slightest prompt from her imagination.

Myrmeen rose from her huge bath, carved from the finest ivory by visiting artisans from far-away Shou Lung, and kept warm by jets of constantly flowing, heated water. The most exotic of oils and enchanted spices treated her skin to fiery delights pleasurable beyond the caress of even the most experienced lover. She hated to end her luxuriant session in the enchanted water, but she knew she dared not allow herself to fall asleep—not unless she wanted to find herself so lethargic by morning that she would have to postpone her duties for a week before the effects passed and she could think clearly again.

A translucent azure gown, sparkling with tiny stars, found its way to Myrmeen's hand. The gown dried her skin and set her hair in the most regal of fashions as she slipped it over her head.

The gown was the gift of a powerful—and amorous—mage who visited the city a year ago. And though the magic gown had been checked by her court magicians, Myrmeen worried that the unpredictability of magic might make it dangerous to wear, and promised herself she would do without it from now on. Of course, she had been promising herself this for almost a week.

If the gown kills me, Myrmeen thought, at least I'll look presentable for the clerics.

Suddenly she thought of Adon of Sune, and spasms of uncontrollable laughter raced through her. The poor sod was probably shaking in his boots, hiding in the most horrid of places, in fear for his life. Of course he wasn't in any real danger, but Myrmeen couldn't pass up the opportunity to take the conceited cleric down a peg or two; in fact, she had precious few chances to indulge her former talent as a trickster. She sighed and stretched upon the bed.

She was just about to ring for a page when she noticed something quite odd: the rubies of her golden chalice were missing. Myrmeen rose from the bed, her warrior's instinct dulled by years of rule, and moved too late to avoid the darkly clad man who rushed at her and slammed her back against the bed, knocking the wind from her in the process. She felt the man's weight upon her, holding her in place, as a hand closed over her mouth.

The man's face and body had been swathed in a gauze that appeared to be some sort of steel mesh. The strips over his face had been arranged to leave spaces for the man's eyes, nostrils, and mouth.

"Be still, milady. I have no wish to harm you," the man said, his voice low and throaty. Myrmeen struggled all the more fiercely. "I deliver word of the conspiracy."

Myrmeen stopped fighting, and she felt her assailant's hold lessen a degree. "How did you get in here?" she mumbled into the man's hand.

"We all have our secrets," he said. "It wouldn't do to give them up."

"You—you mentioned . . . the conspiracy," she said, her chest heaving with her imagined fear. She wondered if she should begin to sob, then thought better of it.

"The villain Knightsbridge is still at large."

Myrmeen's eyes narrowed.

"But you knew this. What *may* come as news is that all three of the agents Evon Stralana used have fled the city. Kelemvor, Adon, and the former *thief* Cyric left in disguise before highsun in the company of two strangers.

"Was it not the hands of these three that allowed Knightsbridge to fly free? Think on this, milady. That is all I have to say."

As Marek started to get up, Myrmeen rolled to the left, as if to bring her hands to her reddened face, and instead grabbed hold of the edge of the bed and delivered a kick with both legs to the stomach of the intruder. From his cry and the crack she heard, she guessed she had found the man's ribs.

"By the gods!" the thief shouted as Myrmeen delivered an open fist blow that narrowly missed his throat. He recognized the technique and grabbed her arm, realizing his mistake as she kicked sharply into his ankle, bringing a second howl of pain from his lips and causing him to release her arm before he could twist it from her shoulder. Myrmeen had been shouting the entire time, so it wasn't a surprise to

Marek when the doors to her chambers burst open and a handful of guardsmen raced in.

Marek thought first of attacking the guards, or trying to run. But when he considered how easy it would be for him to escape from the pitifully constructed dungeons of Arabel, he held up his hands and surrendered.

"Get some answers from this dog," Myrmeen said, oblivious to the stares her almost completely naked body had elicited. "Well? Are you deaf? Move!"

She stopped one of the men. "And send word that I wish to see the minister of defense in the planning room immediately!" She looked down at her torn nightgown. "When I am more properly attired."

"I told you not to complain about guard duty," one of the guards said as he dragged Marek away, and Myrmeen waited until she was once again alone in her chambers before she let out a wide smile at the words of the roguish guard. But her smile faded as quickly as it had formed when she thought of the trio who had perhaps betrayed her, and the measures she would take to ascertain if this was so.

Half an hour later, in the planning room, Myrmeen related all the information she had been given to Evon Stralana, a thin, dark-haired man with a pallid complexion. Stralana nodded gravely.

"Then I fear that worm, Gelzunduth, was telling the truth," Stralana said.

"You knew about this?" Myrmeen screamed.

"This morning, one of our men succeeded in gaining the evidence needed to arrest the forger, Gelzunduth."

"Go on."

Stralana took a breath. "Last night, Adon arrived at Gelzunduth's, and paid the forger for false identifications for men who sound suspiciously like Kelemvor and Cyric. He purchased a false charter, too. Gelzunduth knew at once what he was dealing with, and went along as cordially as he could.

"When Gelzunduth was first interrogated, he hinted that he could expose corruption in the guards. Gelzunduth felt he could use the information to bargain for his freedom or a lesser sentence. It took until a few hours ago before the pig broke and he told everything."

Myrmeen stared at the tiny flame from the lone candle that sat between Stralana and herself. When she raised her gaze, her fury over what she had been told was evident in her eyes.

"I want to know who was guarding the gates when Kelemvor and the others left Arabel. I want them brought here, and questioned. We'll deal with their punishment once we figure out which gate they left through."

Stralana nodded. "Yes, milady."

Myrmeen's hands were balled into white-knuckled fists and pressed together. She forced her hands to relax as she spoke. "Then we shall deal with Kelemvor and his party."

🌣 5 🌣

The Colonnade

Cyric, last to take the watch, gazed at the beautiful pastel pink of the early morning sky. Gentle strokes of ochre seemed to set fire to the pure white clouds that rose over the horizon. However, the thief soon noticed a wealth of heat soaking his neck. He turned, and found a second sunrise that mimicked the first to total perfection.

Off to the north and the south, other suns were rising with visible speed. Illusions or no, the effects were disconcerting. The sweltering heat from the blinding orbs caused the tiny pockets of mud in the road to dry and harden, and the earth itself began to smoke with a foul odor. Cyric roused the others before the full effect of the tremendous heat became apparent.

Kelemvor, still groggy from a miserable night's sleep, went in search of their sole tent, then cursed himself as he remembered it had been destroyed when the packhorses were killed by the creatures the day before. He ordered the others to fetch any blankets or cloaks and cover themselves at once, as the flatlands that surrounded the heroes offered little protection from the suns.

"Midnight!" Kelemvor called. "If you have any more miraculous spells to aid us, now is the time!"

Midnight ignored the sarcastic tone of Kelemvor's voice.

"Bring everyone together!" Midnight cried. "The horses as well. Then gather our water in one place."

Midnight's requests were met, and a heavy fog filled the air as the dark-haired magic-user released a minor cantrip to dampen the area. A second cantrip chilled their drinking water, ensuring it wouldn't evaporate in the heat. The blankets cloaked the adventurers in darkness and helped to decrease the intense heat from the suns. Midnight was thankful that her spells had not gone awry. She saw tiny streaks of lightning play across the surface of the pendant and felt a chill, even in the intense heat of the rising suns.

In the darkness under a blanket, Adon remembered a simple spell he knew that would allow him to endure the effects of the intense heat without injury. He wished he could pray for the spell, but he knew there would be no effect. Before and after his watch, he had prayed to Sune and attempted spells; his efforts were failures, just as they had been since the time of Arrival.

Midnight could see the suns, even through the fabric of her cloak. She watched in fascination as they converged in a dazzling array of light directly overhead. Then they were one and the heat dwindled to normal levels almost immediately. The crisis was seemingly at an end.

The heat had its effect on the adventurers, however, and even as they prepared to leave, arguments broke out over which of the suns had been real, and which direction they wanted to travel. At length they surrendered to Cyric's unfailing instincts and a semblance of normalcy was restored to the journey.

After a time, the flatlands gave way to lush, rolling hills to the east, and the imposing spires of the mountains of Gnoll Pass in the far distance. The heroes left the main road and were pleasantly surprised to find the ruins of a colonnade encircling a sparkling pool of fresh water, which Adon tested and pronounced pure. They drank greedily and replenished their canteens.

The idea of bathing had no sooner occurred to the sweat-drenched adventurers when Adon, quite unabashed, began to strip.

"Adon!" Kelemvor shouted, and the cleric froze in place, balanced on one leg, hands clutching his boot. "A woman and child are present!"

Adon lowered his foot before he fell over. "Oh. Sorry."

Midnight shook her head. The idea of bathing and refreshing herself before the final leg of their journey was not without merit, but other arrangements would have to be made.

"If the three of you wish to bathe, then I will take Caitlan and wait for you at the other end of the pool—with our backs turned," the magic-user said.

"Ah. Then we will do the same for you," said Kelemvor, already taking off his shirt.

"Aye, except you will be over the next ridge before we enter the water." Midnight took Caitlan by the hand and led her away.

Once Midnight and Caitlan were at the other end of the colonnade, Adon stripped completely and gently folded his clothing into neat piles before he made a running start and leaped into the crystalline water. He splashed about and whooped like a child as Kelemvor laughed "Well met, lad!" and stripped as well. Even Cyric entered the pool, although he seemed quite self-conscious in comparison to the others.

Midnight was surprised by Caitlan's silence as they waited for the men to finish. She enjoyed talking to the girl, yet even as she gently prodded at Caitlan for a few words, the girl remained completely silent, gazing at the horizon.

"Midnight!"

Without turning, Midnight responded. "Yes, Kelemvor?"

"Something I must tell you."

Midnight frowned, noting the playful tone in Kelemvor's voice. "It can wait."

"I might forget," Kelemvor said. "Don't worry, we're in the water."

Midnight's shoulders dropped and she looked to Caitlan. "Wait here," she said. Caitlan nodded.

Midnight rose and found Kelemvor close to her side of the pool. Adon and Cyric remained at the far end.

Midnight's occasional imaginings about Kelemvor's unclad physique turned out to be not all that far from the truth: the sight of Kelemvor's water-soaked, glistening body caused Midnight to shiver, despite herself. She could not remember the last time hands such as his touched her. Kelemvor shocked Midnight from her thoughts with a healthy splash of water as he swam up close, playfully taunting her to join him.

"You'd like that, wouldn't you?" Midnight said, folding her

arms over her chest.

"Aye," Kelemvor said, a mischievous, boyish glint in his eyes.

"That's why my clothing is remaining firmly in place until the lot of you are safely over that hill," she said, kicking at the pool and sending a splatter of water at the handsome face of the fighter. He grabbed at her ankle and missed, fell forward and struck his head on the stone edge of the pool with a heavy thud. The fighter's arms pinwheeled as he began to sink, a slight trace of blood riding the water.

"Kel!" Midnight shouted, and suddenly a whirlpool formed and a hand made of swirling, spraying water lifted Kelemvor from the pool and deposited him on a small bench. Adon raced to the man's side. Midnight brought their clothing as Kelemvor began to stir.

"He should be fine," Adon said, examining the wound. "I wouldn't suggest moving him for a little while."

"Foolish," Midnight scolded, but Kelemvor merely grinned and shook his head. Adon placed a blanket over the fighter and went to talk with Cyric, who was already completely dressed.

"Would have been worth it," the fighter said. Then concern creased his features. "You're shivering."

Midnight was, in fact, shivering uncontrollably. She hadn't tried to throw a spell to rescue Kelemvor, but she was sure that she had somehow rescued the fighter. Perhaps, the magic-user thought as she hugged herself to stop the shaking, the pendant is going to explode. After all, it was magical.

Then Midnight shouted as a second geyser of water shot up from the pool and engulfed her in a sparkling column. The mage was shocked as her clothing, all but the pendant, disentangled itself with no move from her, and pleasant jets of concentrated water washed her clean even as her clothing danced in the air, receiving the same treatment. The others could see very little of what went on inside the column, and when it was over the water was hungrily swallowed back by the pool and Midnight stood fully clothed and shining clean.

Her shivering had stopped, but Midnight was again struck

with uncertainty. Well, she concluded, whether it had been the pendant or some power in the water itself, that did all this, obviously there was no harmful magic at work.

"Nice trick," Cyric said, smiling at the magic-user. "But I'm surprised you'd trust your spells after what we've seen."

"I haven't thrown a spell since those cantrips this morning," the magic-user said. "I don't know what's causing this. It could be Caitlan for all we know."

Midnight looked over to the place where she had left the girl, and felt a momentary surge of panic when she saw that the bench was empty. Before she was able to say a word there was a splash from behind her, and Midnight turned to find Caitlan taking advantage of the sparkling pool.

Because of Kelemvor's wound, the heroes chose to make camp in the colonnade, then continue traveling to the castle in the morning. Cyric spent much of that afternoon studying the pillars and statues that surrounded the camp.

The columns were thick and smooth, and a dozen feet above the ground, beautiful stone archways reached out like earthbound rainbows from one column to another. Then stone beams led across to the next column, which again sprouted an archway, and so on.

Some of the columns had been shattered, their spires fragmenting into jagged lances at their peaks. Cracks reached downward from the broken crowns to corrupt the lengths of the pillars without mercy, and huge fragments of stone were dug deeply into the ground beside the fractured columns. Many archways were completely missing, disrupting the once-perfect symmetry of the colonnade and replacing it with a wild, unpredictable design.

The statues were of the most interest to Cyric, though almost all of the sculptures were broken in some way and many were missing their heads. Some were male, some female, but all were perfect physical specimens. The thief stood for hours, staring at one particular statue: a pair of headless lovers with their backs turned to the colonnade, their hands displaying the emotions their missing heads could not.

As darkness closed in, a strong luminescence emanated from the pool, as if its bottom had been lined with phosphorus, even though close examination proved this not to be true. The blue-white light from the water played upon the features of the travelers as they relaxed and occasionally found some topic for conversation.

Cyric related tales of ill-fated adventurers who had sought their fortunes in the legendary ruins of Myth Drannor, ignoring the warnings of the heroes who guarded that place. All his stories ended with the adventurers being killed or disappearing forever. Midnight playfully chastised the man for bringing up such depressing tales.

"Besides, how would you know what those people faced in the ruins unless you had been there with them, and somehow made it out alive?" Midnight asked.

Cyric stared at the water and said nothing. Midnight decided not to press the issue.

Adon began to extol the virtues of Sune and Kelemvor cut the cleric off by changing the subject to dreams and their fulfillment.

"Not to be depressing," Kelemvor said, directing Midnight's words back upon her, "but Cyric's tales have meaning for us all. All too often I have seen men led astray in pursuit of their dreams. Then one day they look around and recognize all the joy and wonder they have missed because they were so busy trying to get from place to place and amass their riches."

"That's pretty grim," Midnight said. "I've certainly known such men. Have you?"

"Passing acquaintances," Kelemvor said.

"I don't see what that subject has to do with us," Adon said sullenly.

"It has everything to do with us," Kelemvor said as he watched the almost hypnotic motion of the water. "What if we are killed tomorrow?"

Caitlan blanched, guessing where Kelemvor's words were leading.

"As Aldophus said, 'curious happenstances abound—and all burning hell breaks loose.' Think of what we faced yesterday. Is anything really worth the risk of facing such nightmares again? Or things that might be worse? I have sworn to go on. But I'm willing to let any of you out of your pledges," Kelemvor said as he looked at the water.

Adon stood up. "I'm insulted. Of course, I'll continue. I'm no coward, despite what you might believe."

"I never said that you were, Adon. I would not have asked you on this quest if the thought had ever entered my head." Kelemvor turned to face the others.

Midnight saw that Caitlan was trembling, and the magic-user wrapped her cloak around the girl. "My pledge is to Caitlan, as much as to you, Kel," Midnight said, hugging the frightened girl. "I will continue. There should not have been any doubt."

Cyric had retreated to the shadows, out of the light from the pool. He understood fully the game Kelemvor was running, attempting to rally the support and enthusiasm of the company by calling those very qualities into question. Yet for Cyric, Kelemvor had merely voiced the same concerns that had plagued him from the beginning of the quest.

I can walk from this, Cyric thought, and no one would move to stop me.

"Cyric?" Kelemvor called. "Where's Cyric?"

"I'm here," Cyric said, surprising himself by walking back to the others, and taking his place beside them. "I thought I heard a noise."

Kelemvor looked around suspiciously.

"But there was nothing," the thief said and knelt down in front of Caitlan, to whom he had uttered scarcely a word during their entire journey. "For what it's worth, Caitlan, you have my pledge, once again, to rescue your lady from the castle."

Cyric looked to Kelemvor. "Some believe that our lives are predestined, that we have little control over them and might as well surrender to whatever fate throws at us. Have you ever felt that way?"

"Not at all," Kelemvor said. "No one rules my destiny but me."

Cyric reached out and grasped the fighter's hand. "Then we finally agree on something," Cyric said, and smiled, although in his heart he knew that he was lying.

* * * * *

They must be close, Bane thought. He churned the waters of his scrying pool until his arm became tired. Relief spread through him as an image began to form. Yet something was interfering with his attempts to spy on Mystra's rescuers. Even when the water of the scrying pool finally became still, the image was hazy and indistinct.

Bane studied the nearly still portrait of the humans who had come to rescue Mystra. He was most interested in the woman, yet she was asleep on her side, and he could not see the pendant. He studied the others and a tide of laughter suddenly erupted from the god-made-flesh. Bane's all too human larynx rebelled against the cruel treatment it was being awarded, and the roar of Bane's laughter became a hoarse croak.

Bane stood before Mystra, who had been roused by the Black Lord's cruel laughter. "This is what you send against me?" Bane said, pointing at his scrying pool. "They are even less impressive than Blackthorne's description of them."

Mystra said nothing.

"I had thought your saviors would at least be fit to provide some sport. But these four?"

Mystra restrained herself from showing any reaction, although she suddenly felt a glimmer of hope. Only four? she thought. Then the sending worked!

When Bane captured Mystra, the goddess had used a fraction of her power to send out a modified geas spell in the form of a magical falcon. The potential avatar it would locate would be young, with immense potential—an untrained, yet great magic-user. When it located Caitlan, there was an instant of contact between Mystra and the girl, and in that instant, the goddess instructed her to find Midnight and the pendant, and gather warriors worthy of her cause.

Mystra also gave the falcon a few spells to bestow upon the one who received her calling. One had been a spell to see into the mind of another, so that a proper champion could be found. The second was a cloak against any form of magical detection. The third and final spell had not yet been utilized, Mystra sensed. A tiny flicker within her essence had signaled the release of the first two spells when they occurred; no such sensation had arrived from the casting of the third. Not yet.

Contempt stained the features of the Black Lord as he spoke again. "At least they had sense enough to leave the child behind. There would have been nothing to gain from her death, other than your further discomfort. And I truly have no wish to cause you pain, dear Mystra. Unless, of course, you leave me no choice."

Mystra had learned patience in her time as a prisoner of Lord Bane, and she practiced what she had learned with the utmost skill, even though she wished to let out a cry of thanks that her plan had succeeded up to this point. Caitlan had been protected from Bane's prying sorceries; he did not know that she was still with the party.

"I'll offer my lenience once more. Pledge yourself to my cause. Help me unite the gods against Lord Ao, so we may retake the heavens. Do this and all will be forgiven. Fail to take the opportunity I offer and I swear I will inflict the torments of the damned upon these humans who seek to free you from my grasp!"

There was a noise behind them. "Lord Bane!"

Bane turned to greet Tempus Blackthorne. The magic-user had pale, almost ivory skin, with long, jet-black hair that he wore in a tail. He wore a breastplate made of pure black steel, with a blood-red jewel the size of a man's fist in its center. He also appeared to be insubstantial, almost like a ghost.

"Urgent matters require your attention in Zhentil Keep," Blackthorne said. "Knightsbridge has been found."

"Knightsbridge?" Bane said, shaking his head.

"The conspiracy against Arabel. He was our agent."

Bane let out a deep breath. "The one that failed."

"Lord Chess wishes to execute him immediately," Blackthorne said. "Yet the man has a flawless record and he was set against impossible odds in his task."

Bane ground his taloned hands together. "This is a personal matter for you, isn't it?"

Blackthorne lowered his head. "Ronglath Knightsbridge and I were friends since childhood. His death would be a senseless waste."

Bane let out a deep breath. "Let us discuss the matter. You will take my judgment to Chess. No one will dare to question it."

Mystra watched as Bane and his emissary spoke. The God of Strife's attention was consumed by the matter that weighed so heavily upon Blackthorne, and Mystra was grateful for the respite from his constant badgering.

At least I have a chance to escape, Mystra thought. That my intended avatar has actually found the one who holds my trust is more than I could have hoped for. I will not get another chance like this.

And then I will give Lord Ao the identities of the thieves, and I will be returned to my home!

There was no time to rejoice in the moment, however. There was only time to act. Shackled as she was, Mystra knew that she could not escape her bonds. Yet her bonds—and the attentions of the *hakeashar*—had not completely kept her from saving up enough mystical energy to throw one last minor spell.

Mystra concentrated, and suddenly felt a connection with Caitlan.

Come at once! Mystra commanded, her words thundering within the skull of the girl. *Use the final spell I granted you and come at once. Do not wait for the others. They will arrive soon enough.*

Suddenly the connection was broken, and Mystra heard Bane's footsteps. Blackthorne was gone. Bane stopped in front of the goddess.

"Have you changed your mind?" Bane said. "Decided to join me after all?"

Mystra was silent.

Bane sighed. "A pity that you will be dead soon. After all, how many more times can you endure the *hakeashar*? The torments it inflicts on you as it violates your essence must be beyond belief."

Mystra did not stir.

"I will find a way to overthrow Ao with or without you, Mystra. You'd be wise to join me before I must kill you."

When the Goddess of Magic remained silent, Bane turned

from her and walked to the scrying pool, where he resumed the vigil for the guests camped right outside his castle.

* * * * *

Come at once, Mystra commanded, and Caitlan responded. Despite the words of the goddess, ordering her to leave her newfound friends behind, Caitlan was tempted to rouse Midnight or Kelemvor, and tell them of Mystra's summons. Tell them that no more time could be wasted; they had to go to the castle right away.

But Mystra's commands had to be followed to the letter, so Caitlan silently repeated the words to the spell, and was lifted into the night sky. Cyric didn't even hear her stir. And despite her exhilaration at the experience of sailing through the air, Caitlan never forgot the somber reason for her flight.

The goddess needed her.

Along with Mystra's summons, Caitlan had received a complex series of images, and by following the real life counterparts of these images she soon arrived at Castle Kilgrave and entered it undetected. Caitlan sensed a consummate evil in the place, although the dusty corridors she traveled through seemed harmless enough. Eventually the girl found the chamber where she saw the odd, glowing form of the Goddess of Magic.

Mystra did not appear the least bit human. The goddess had been shackled to the wall of the dungeon with strange, pulsating chains, and she hovered across the room from Caitlan like a ghost.

A horribly deformed man was in the chamber, as well. He stood in the center of the room, staring into an ornately carved tub that held dark, black water. Caitlan saw that his features were part human, part animal, and part demon. Turning suddenly, the deformed man glanced in the girl's direction, but she stayed hidden in the shadows. It was as if he heard her enter the dungeon or somehow sensed her presence.

The dark man turned to Mystra and smiled. "I do wish the sun would rise, so those pitiful humans could come and entertain me."

"They'll do more than entertain you, Bane," Mystra said.

Caitlan almost gasped. The deformed man was Lord Bane, God of Strife! He must have taken an avatar, like Tymora did in Arabel.

It was then that Caitlan knew what was expected of her, and she rejoiced in the knowledge of her ultimate fate. Before her, Bane shouted at the goddess, hurling vile threats against her, imploring the captive goddess to join him in some mad plan he had devised. Mystra did not respond, and Caitlan feared that the goddess's essence was dwindling, that the goddess might die. Then she shook herself from such thoughts and waited for Bane to turn away long enough for her to cross the distance that separated her from the Goddess of Magic.

Then it would be Mystra's turn to rejoice.

❧ 6 ❧

New Acheron

As the heroes crested the final hill and looked down into the valley where Castle Kilgrave lay, they saw the state of absolute disrepair the castle had fallen into. Kelemvor felt his heart sink as they rode to the ruin.

"Unless some creature got her or the ground swallowed her up, Caitlan is here somewhere," the fighter said. "But I still don't understand why she ran off."

Cyric sighed. "I've told you a dozen times this morning, Kel: I don't think she ran off. Caitlan was still asleep when I came on watch, and I didn't hear her leave."

"But that still doesn't explain where she went," Midnight said, her concern for the child evident in her voice. "Or how she got out of camp without anyone hearing her."

"With all the strange goings on," Adon said, "I wouldn't be surprised if the ground *did* swallow her up."

Kelemvor tensed. If the girl was dead, or even just gone for good, he wouldn't get his reward. A slight ripple ran through his muscles. "Get off this horse, Adon. Now!"

"But—but—"

When Kelemvor didn't even turn around to argue with him, Adon realized he'd best just walk the rest of the way to Castle Kilgrave. He didn't like sharing a mount with the fighter anyway; he sweated too much.

Kelemvor turned his attentions back to the castle. There could be no question that Castle Kilgrave had once been magnificent. The castle's design was insidiously simple, which made the place all the more intimidating. The keep was a perfect square, with gigantic cylindrical towers placed in each corner. Huge walls connected to the window-

RICHARD AWLINSON

less towers, and a massive obelisk jutted from the wall facing the heroes on one side—obviously the entrance. The entire structure had the look of bones left out in the sun to bleach.

As the heroes got closer, they saw that the castle was three stories high, and was surrounded by a moat that had dried up long ago. Whatever creeping terrors the moat once held to frighten away thieves and assassins were now reduced to fragments of misshapen bone that jutted from the rich brown earth and served as excellent grips for Cyric as he descended into the bowl-shaped crevice.

"Try to climb up to the gate," Kelemvor called to Cyric as the thief reached the bottom of the dry moat and started to climb toward the castle.

"Still stating the obvious," Cyric muttered under his breath. "That's our Kelemvor."

The drawbridge stuck partially open, and the massive chains that worked its mechanisms were rusted together, refusing to make even the slightest sound as Cyric climbed from the moat to the base of the chains and grabbed hold of them, using the huge links as hand and footholds. Cyric climbed higher then, to a crumbling ledge, and followed it to the side of the partially raised drawbridge itself. There, Cyric slid between the bridge and the wall, and dropped fifteen feet to the floor. Moments later, he forced the mechanisms to lower the drawbridge.

Kelemvor, Midnight, and Adon tied the horses to the posts that stood as sentinels before the drawbridge, and took only their weapons and some torches with them as the bridge creaked noisily to the ground before them.

"So much for stealth and subtlety," Midnight sighed. "Perhaps we should simply wait here for the owners to welcome us in, too."

Adon found the mage's comments amusing. Kelemvor did not. "Let's just get this over with," the fighter growled as he headed across the bridge. "We can still hope for some reward if we can find Caitlan or her mistress."

Cyric stood at the gate, his sword drawn, waiting for a foul guardian to rush at the heroes as they entered Castle Kilgrave. But no creature reared its ugly head. In fact, the drawbridge's loud descent seemed to attract no attention at all. "This is very odd," the thief said as the heroes joined him. "Perhaps we've found the wrong ruined castle."

Kelemvor frowned and led the way into the first, huge room of the castle. Visibility within the walls was difficult, even with the guttering torches the heroes carried. But it soon became clear that the vast main entry hall was completely empty, and the party headed down a corridor across the room from the gate.

Cyric looked into many of the small rooms they passed as the heroes made their way deeper into Castle Kilgrave. The rooms he saw were all very similar—the shattered remains of a table propped up against one wall, the broken seat of a once-regal chair laying nearby, the decaying corpse of some animal that had found its way in and starved, or became diseased before it met its death in a corner. Other rooms were completely vacant.

The corridors themselves were framed by ivory pillars trimmed with gold at intervals of every sixteen feet. The gold had mostly been scraped away. The rugs that ran through the halls were water-logged and ruined, although the patterns and materials, visible even through the grime, revealed them as once-priceless fineries. The ceilings were arched, and the details of the intricate plasterwork representations were obscured in all but a few cases. The random images visible were odd, chaotic mixes that spoke of clashes between titans, and faceless monarchs who sat upon thrones made of skulls. Not once did the plaster hold an illustration of kindness or joy.

After almost an hour of wandering and finding nothing to substantiate the child's wild story, Cyric put voice to the notion that troubled them all.

"Gold," he said sarcastically, his words echoing wildly through the deserted and shadowy corridors.

"Aye," Kelemvor said, wishing not to be reminded. A violent shudder ran through his body, and the fighter reminded himself that the quest was not over yet. He still might get his reward.

"Riches beyond imagining, adventures beyond belief," Cyric said, cracking his knuckles to relieve the boredom.

"My limbs ache," Adon said quietly.

"At least they're still attached," Kelemvor reminded him, and the cleric fell silent.

"Perhaps there are riches to be found here," Cyric said at last. "Some reward to justify our efforts, at the very least."

"Don't you think this place has been picked clean many times before?" Midnight waved her torch around. "Have you seen anything of value here so far?"

"Not yet," said the thief. "But we haven't gotten very far."

Adon was not convinced. "If Caitlan's mistress *was* held prisoner here by brigands, human or otherwise, we should stay long enough to find the body and give it a proper burial. Perhaps Caitlan is already here somewhere doing just that."

"Then the best thing to do is split up so we can cover more ground. Adon, you go with Midnight and search the lower floors. Cyric and I will search upstairs," Kel said at last. "We *must* get some reward for this journey, and I'm not leaving until we find something of value."

When they found a staircase, Kelemvor and Cyric departed to search the upper levels, hoping to find Caitlan—or at least some hidden riches in what had surely once been the royal bedchambers of the wealthy families who raised the fortress long ago.

Adon accompanied Midnight on a search of the castle's lower levels. They descended the spiral staircase, the air growing colder as they made their way beneath the ground. Just as they stepped off the final landing and moved into a small antechamber at the foot of the stairs, Adon uttered a startled cry. A wrought iron gate had descended, impaling one of his billowing sleeves and holding him in place while two other gates shot out, one at each side, their long spears threatening to end the cleric's life.

The cleric tore loose before the gates slammed into place, but he was now separated from Midnight. Adon looked at his torn sleeve, mourned it for no more than a second, and moved to help Midnight as she tested the strength of the bars from the other side of the barricade.

"Kel!" Adon yelled. "Cyric!"

Midnight knew the cleric's cries would not be heard—at

least by their friends. She turned away from the bars and was shocked to find a heavy wooden door, three times her height, blocking the way behind her. The door had not been there moments ago. Then there was a scraping at the door, and the sound of a voice crying out beyond it.

"Caitlan?" the magic-user cried. "Caitlan, is that you?"

Midnight leaned in close to the door and strained to make out the sounds more clearly. The door flew open then, revealing a long, empty hallway. The crying had stopped.

Midnight shook her head. "Adon, you wait here and I'll see where this leads."

But when she turned around, the cleric was gone.

* * * * *

Kelemvor and Cyric found the upper levels of the castle in the same state of decay as the ground floor. The only thing that seemed odd was the total lack of windows. Not a single opening had presented itself since they attained the uppermost floor, and each chamber they visited was much like the one before it, either empty or filled with broken furniture and tattered rugs.

At one point they came upon a huge chest, the lid rusted shut. Kelemvor drew his sword and shattered the lock. They both pulled at the lid, then recoiled as their efforts were rewarded by the sickening smell that accompanied their "treasure." Within the chest they found the corpses of a small army of rats. The sudden exposure to the air caused the bodies to decompose rapidly, and they melted into a disgusting pulp that dripped from their splintering skeletons.

As Cyric and Kelemvor returned to the corridor, the fighter felt his muscles tighten and pain shot all through his body. "There's nothing here!" he cried. The fighter dropped his torch and put his hands up to his face. "Get out of here, Cyric. Leave me alone!"

"What are you saying?"

"The girl must have been lying all along. Just leave my mount, take the others, and ride out," Kelemvor said.

"You can't be serious!" Cyric said.

Kelemvor turned his back on the thief. "There is no

reward to be found in this place! There is nothing! I renounce the quest."

Cyric felt something strange beneath his feet. He looked down and saw that, beneath him, the tattered rug had begun to reweave itself, its brilliant patterns spreading outward like wildfire down the hall in both directions. The rejuvenated carpet seemed to root itself into the floor; then it sped upward and covered the ceiling.

The corridor began to shake as if an earthquake was tearing through the land beneath the castle. Chunks of the wall broke free and fell on Kelemvor and Cyric, but the blows were absorbed by their armor and they protected their faces the best they could. Then the rug moved to attack them, as if giant, powerful hands were using it like a glove. The rug was clearly trying to grab the warriors and crush the life from them.

Cyric felt a sharp pain as the hands of the carpet grabbed him from behind and threatened to tear him limb from limb. He quickly slashed at the rug with his sword. "Damn you, Kel, do something!"

But the fighter was frozen, his hands still over his face. The carpet grabbed him in a dozen places.

"Caitlan lied," Kelemvor said, pale and shaking. "No reward—"

The fighter let out an unearthly scream. Then he released a catch near his shoulder and allowed his breastplate to fall. The mail beneath ripped apart, and Cyric thought he saw one of Kelemvor's ribs burst from his chest. Then Kelemvor stumbled forward into one of the the rips Cyric had created in the carpet and dashed toward the staircase, even as the flesh of his skull seemed to explode outward and something with green glowing eyes and jet-black skin emerged.

*　*　*　*　*

The Black Lord felt a smile run across his face. He had hoped to test the powers of the pendant and gauge the strength of Mystra's would-be rescuers. His hopes had been rewarded. Each member of the party had fallen into a separate trap where Bane could observe them and work his dark magics upon them, tearing their souls apart in the process.

Mystra continued to struggle against her eldritch bonds, the proximity of the pendant driving her wild.

"Soon it will be here," Bane said as he turned to the goddess. "Soon it will be mine." The God of Strife threw back his head and laughed.

Mystra's struggles ceased, and she joined Bane in his mad laughter.

"Are you insane?" the Black Lord said as he stopped laughing and moved closer to the captive goddess. "Your 'saviors' do not even know why they're here. They have no idea the power they face, and they have no loyalty to you. All they desire is gold!"

Mystra only smiled, blue-white flames crackling throughout her essence. "Not all," she said, and then was silent.

Bane stood no more than a foot away from the Goddess of Magic and stared at her ever-changing form. "The *hakeashar* will make you a little less smug," the god said, but he was afraid Mystra had hidden something from him, some other reserve of power.

The surface of the scrying pool bubbled, demanding Bane's attention.

The Dark Lord looked into the pool, and a cruel smile crossed his deformed face. "Your would-be saviors should at least be rewarded for their efforts, don't you think?" Bane tried to cast a spell on the water of the scrying pool. A burst of light erupted from his hands, and six glowing darts flew wildly around the room. The God of Strife cried out as all the magic missiles struck him at once.

"Magic has become unstable since we left the heavens," the Black Lord growled, holding his arm where the missiles had hit him. "Join me, Mystra, and we could make the art stable again."

The Goddess of Magic remained silent.

"No matter," Bane said as he started the incantation once more. "The magical chaos affects we gods far less than it does your mortal worshipers. I will eventually succeed."

Bane cast the spell again, and this time it worked. The water grew hot, set itself to boiling, then became steam and reformed into sparkling clear liquid. The images the water reflected had changed dramatically and Bane watched with interest as the stage for the next part of his plan was set. He dipped his goblet into the water and let it fill.

"They are here for gold and riches? Fine, let them have gold and riches. Let them have their heart's desire, though it may destroy them!"

* * * * *

The beast that had been Kelemvor relied on its senses as it padded through the beautiful forest. It recognized the scent of newly fallen dew, and the moist earth beneath its paws felt soft and burgeoning with life. The sunlight from above was magnificent; it warmed and comforted the beast, which stopped to lick a trace of deer's blood from one of its paws, then moved on.

The trees in the garden touched the heavens themselves, and their branches, blanketed by amber leaves, swayed gently in the breezes that caressed the soft fur of the animal, sending a tingling sensation through its body.

But something was wrong.

The panther came to a clearing. Objects its limited mind could not identify rose into view. The objects had not grown from the earth, had not fallen from the sky. They had been placed here by man, and their purpose intrigued the beast, despite its low intelligence.

Suddenly a stab of pain bore into the animal's skull, and the beast found balance and movement difficult. The panther snarled and threw back its head as something clawed at its gut from within. Then the creature let out a long, horrible wail as its rib cage expanded and burst. Finally, its head split in half and the thick, muscular arms of a man exploded from the ruined skins.

Kelemvor tested his limbs before he attempted to rise. Bits of the panther's flesh still clung to him, and he clawed at the hated reminders of the curse his bloodline had fated him to endure. For now his naked skin was smooth and hairless, although he knew it would only be a matter of minutes before the soft tufts of hair that normally covered his body once again grew into place, spreading across his skin with a will of their own.

Abandoning the quest had caused the transformation this time, Kelemvor decided. Without a reward, going on the journey with Caitlan, risking his life, had been for nothing. The curse did not approve, and the panther had been the punishment.

In the clearing, Kelemvor found his clothing and his sword. His clothing had been soaked through with blood, and the clamminess of the wet leathers against his bare flesh made him wish to strip them off once again, but he knew that would be foolish.

He did not remember coming to this place that seemed to be far removed from Castle Kilgrave. The garden looked little like the flatlands of northern Cormyr. In fact, it looked more like the setting of a tale of romance, where knights jousted for honor's sake and love always won the day.

Kelemvor knew that he was smiling, and memories long repressed flooded back. Before him the memories took flesh, as marble podiums, glazed in soft blue and pink pastels, formed from the air, and a vast library of forbidden books arranged itself. As a child in Lyonsbane Keep, Kelemvor had been denied access to the library except when an adult was present, and then he was only allowed to read military texts or histories. Fantasies, adventures, and romances were hidden on the highest shelf, where only his father could reach them.

In retrospect, Kelemvor wondered why they had been there at all. Was his father, the monstrous, mean-spirited man that he was, taken with these gentle tales? At the time Kelemvor did not think such a thing was possible. No, the books must have belonged to Kelemvor's mother, who died giving birth to him.

From the amount of dust Kelemvor had found on those forbidden books on the frequent occasions when he disobeyed his father and crept into the library in the middle of the night, arranging the chairs and tables to give him access to the wondrous tomes, Kelemvor felt secure that the books were his private treasure, that even his father, at his most cruel, could not take away. In the books he found stories of epic adventure and heroism, and tales of strange and beautiful lands he hungered to one day visit.

Hiding in the forest, after having killed his own father, Kelemvor drew strength from those tales—and hope. Some day, he would be a hero, too, instead of a beast that killed its own kin.

And now a library, its huge shelves filled with wondrous exploits of heroes whose names and adventures had become legend, grew around the fighter. A few of the books flew from the circular arena that was forming in the forest, and opened themselves to display their secret dreams to Kelemvor.

He was shocked to find his own name mentioned time and again in the tales of bravery and heroism. But the events recounted in the stories had not actually occurred. Perhaps this is prophecy, Kelemvor thought as a story in which he saved the entire Realms passed before him. No, he sighed to himself, there could be no payment high enough to satisfy the curse. And if I am not paid in full for doing something that is not in my own best interest, I become the beast.

Kelemvor was so consumed by the words he read in the floating tomes and his musings on the Lyonsbane curse that he did not notice the changes that had been wrought in his surroundings until a familiar voice called out.

"Kelemvor!"

He looked up to behold a beautiful hall that had replaced the forest. The books vanished, and hundreds of men and women stood in the hall. They were perfectly still, standing high upon platforms or pedestals. By their garb and their stance, Kelemvor was certain they were warriors. Each was bathed in a column of light, although the light had no source and melted into the darkness above their heads.

"Kelemvor! Over here, boy!" the same familiar voice called.

The fighter turned and found himself face to face with an older man whose build and stature matched his own perfectly: Burne Lyonsbane, his uncle. The man was standing on a platform, bathed in light.

"This cannot be! You're—"

"Dead?" Burne laughed. "Perhaps. Yet those who are

SHADOWDALE

remembered in the annals of history never truly die.
Instead they come to this place, this hall of heroes, where
they look down on their loved ones and wait until they are
joined by them."

Kelemvor backed away from his friend. "I am no hero,
good uncle. I have done horrible things."

"Indeed?" Burne said, raising one eyebrow. With a flour-
ish he withdrew his sword and cleaved the air beside him. A
shaft of light pierced the darkness and revealed an empty
platform. "It is your time, Kelemvor. Take your place
amongst the heroes and all will be revealed."

Kelemvor drew his sword. "This is a lie. A travesty! How
could you, of all people, betray me now? You were the one
who saved me when I was a child!"

"I can save you again," Burne said. "Listen."

"Kel!" a voice called. Kelemvor turned, and standing
beside the platform that had been reserved for him was a
red-bearded man dressed in the fineries of a warrior king.

"Torum Garr!" Kelemvor said. "But—"

"I would pay tribute to your purity and honor, Kelemvor.
If it had not been for your presence at my side during the
final battle in our war against the drow, I would have died.
You fought, despite the fact that I could pay you with nothing but my thanks. The way you often gave of yourself to
protect others, while asking for nothing in return marked
you as a true hero!"

Kelemvor's head was swimming. He tightened his grip on
his sword. In his memories, Kelemvor had turned his back
on Torum Garr, and the exiled king had died in the battle.

"Kelemvor, thanks to you I regained control of my kingdom. Yet when I offered to make you my heir, as I had no
sons, you declined the offer. I see now that you acted cor-
rectly and with honor. Your bravery has been an example
for others to emulate, and your adventures have made you
a legend. Accept at last your just reward and stand at our
side through eternity."

Another man appeared, a man who was the same age as
Kelemvor. He had wild, ebon hair, and an even wilder
expression upon his handsome features.

"Vance," Kelemvor said, his voice cold and distant.

The other man stepped down off his pedestal and embraced Kelemvor, forcing the fighter to lower his sword. Vance stood back and regarded Kelemvor. "How fare you, childhood friend? I've come to pay tribute."

Kelemvor had never even imagined what Vance would look like at this age. It had been ten years since the man had been attacked by assassins and Kelemvor had been forced to turn away from his pleas for help, his actions dictated by the curse that had always been the bane of his existence.

"You saved my life, and although the time we spent together was short, I have always treasured you as my first and closest friend. You returned for my wedding, and this time saved not only my life, but that of my wife and our unborn child. Together we discovered the identity of the one who wished me harm and we put an end to the threat. I salute you, my oldest and dearest friend!"

"This can't be right," Kelemvor said. "Vance is dead."

"Here he is alive," Burne Lyonsbane said, and Kelemvor's visitors parted to allow the older man to stand before his nephew. "Take comfort in this place. Assume your rightful position in the hall, and you will remember nothing of your former life. The ghosts that haunt you will be laid to rest, and you will spend an eternity reliving your heroic acts. What say you, Kelemvor?"

"Uncle . . . ," Kelemvor said as he raised his sword. His hands were trembling. "I have dreamed of the day when all you have promised might come true, but the time for dreams has passed."

"Is that the way you wish to see reality? Then behold," Burne said.

Suddenly the book that detailed Kelemvor's life of heroism appeared in his uncle's hands. The pages began to turn by themselves, slowly at first, then increasing in speed as it progressed. Kelemvor realized the book was being rewritten even as he watched. The tales of Kelemvor's heroism were vanishing, to be replaced by stories of his true past.

"Your dreams can become reality, Kel! Choose quickly, before the final tale is written over and your only chance to be a true hero passes you by!"

Kelemvor watched as the tale of his rescue of Vance from

the assassins was revised. He heard a scream and looked up just in time to see Vance fade away from the hall. The history in the tome was becoming true, and his chance to right the wrongs he had committed was vanishing before his eyes.

Torum Garr grasped his arm. "Choose quickly, Kelemvor! Do not let me die again!"

Kelemvor hesitated, and the chapter dealing with Torum Garr was rewritten. The red-bearded king was again slain by the drow. Kelemvor was no longer there to protect him.

Before Kelemvor, Torum Garr vanished.

"It's not too late," Burne Lyonsbane said. "It is not too late to change what you remember." The older man ground his teeth in desperation. He fixed his nephew's gaze with his own. "You remember how it ended between us, Kelemvor. Do not let it happen again! Do not turn away and let me die again!"

Kelemvor squeezed his eyes shut and hacked at the gold-bound volume before him. The binding of the book shattered, and a glowing mist flowed out. All the heroes in the hall faded into clouds of red mist. Then, the hall itself started to blur around the edges and disappear, too. In seconds, only wisps of illusion hung in the air, then they vanished as well.

Kelemvor found himself in a ruined library on the first floor of the castle. At his feet lay an aged, torn volume of children's fairy tales. Kelemvor kicked the book out of his way as he ran to the doorway.

In the hallway, the fighter saw the savaged corpse of a man—probably the deer from his dream. Kelemvor didn't notice that the dead man wore the symbol of Bane, God of Strife, as he raced for the stairway to Castle Kilgrave's dark lower levels.

*　*　*　*　*

Midnight found herself walking through an endless series of dark passageways. Adon was gone, and she could not remember how she came to these shadowy hallways. Tiny movements played at the corners of her senses, but she trained her gaze forward and ignored them. She heard something that might have been voices—sounds of anguish and horror. She ignored them, too. They were meant to distract, to lead her away from her goal. She could not allow that to happen.

The magic-user stopped before a well-lit archway. She took a breath, then moved forward into the light, which engulfed her senses as she felt an iron grip take hold of her arm.

"You're late!" an elderly woman snapped. Midnight blinked, and the details of the shining corridor that the older woman led her through at an alarming speed became shockingly clear. Midnight saw a vast hall of mirrors. Each mirror was embedded in a finely trimmed archway, with an ornately detailed bench covered in bright red leather placed before it. Candelabras were set at each side of the archways, and hundreds of chandeliers descended from the arched ceiling. Thousands of candles burned in the corridor, and Midnight recoiled as she caught sight of her own image.

"The ceremony has already begun!" the old woman hissed, shaking her head.

Midnight was dressed in a beautiful gown of sparkling diamonds and rubies, and jewelry made of imperiously set gems adorned her hands and wrists. Her hair had been thrust up and back and was held in a glorious pose by a jeweled crown.

The pendant was gone.

Weakness overtook her limbs at this discovery, and the elderly woman set Midnight down upon one of the regal benches. "Now, now, my dear, this is no time to surrender to butterflies in the stomach. You are to be awarded a great honor this day! Sunlar will be most disappointed if you keep him waiting."

Sunlar? Midnight thought. My teacher from Deepingdale?

Midnight felt the blood drain from her head as she attempted to stand. Then the world became a maddening swirl of chandeliers and glowing candles only to right itself as Midnight realized she was now sitting on a throne in a beautiful temple. A throng of robed men and women stood before her, and the opulence of the domed chamber made the corridor of mirrors seem like a tasteful example of understatement.

Sunlar entered the temple with a small group of students attending him. He was the high priest of Mystra in Deepingdale, and he had taken a personal interest in Midnight's care and training when she was younger, although he would never explain the reasons behind his actions.

Sunlar had been handsome and strong when Midnight knew him, and as he crossed the length of the throne room, Midnight saw that his features were exactly as she remembered them. His eyes were a ghostly blue-white, and his hair was brown and full, with immaculately styled waves and two locks that fell to his eyebrows, framing his chiseled features. But he was dressed in ceremonial robes that Midnight had never seen before, such fineries surely held in reserve for greeting visiting royalty.

A handful of men and women surrounded Midnight. They wore the blue-white star symbol of Mystra, and were careful to avert their gaze whenever Midnight attempted to make eye contact with one of them, as if they were not worthy of looking directly at her. Midnight was unsettled by their actions, and just before she opened her mouth to question them, Sunlar arrived before her.

"Lady Midnight," Sunlar called. "This gathering is in your honor. Yet it is in the interest of all who attend to hear your words and honor your decision."

"My . . . decision?" Midnight said, quite confused.

Sunlar seemed troubled. Despite the reverence in which Midnight and these proceedings had been held, a tide of whispers flooded the chamber. Sunlar raised his hands and there was silence.

"It is only proper that Midnight is allowed to formally hear what has been offered to her once again," Sunlar said as he turned to the hundreds of worshipers who had gathered in the temple.

Sunlar looked back to Midnight.

"This honor has not been given by the Lady of Mysteries in a long time," he said, and held out his hand to Midnight. She rose and took it. Suddenly the lights dimmed in the

RICHARD AWLINSON

chamber, and an immense blue-white star appeared above their heads, a constant flow of smaller shimmering stars circling its perimeter. There was a collective gasp from the worshipers as the glowing star revealed itself to be flat, like a coin. Then the surface of the star sparkled and changed, becoming a portal to another dimension. The light from this other realm was blinding, and Midnight could see very little of what lay beyond the gateway.

Midnight covered her eyes. "The power of the Magister?"

Sunlar smiled. "Yes, Lady Midnight, the power of the Magister." The glowing portal was spinning wildly, turning end-over-end.

"Lady Mystra, Goddess of Magic, has chosen you above all else in the Realms to become her champion—the Magister," Sunlar said.

They stood directly below the spinning portal. Midnight raised her hand and felt the tiny stars that accompanied the portal as they caressed her flesh. The sensation brought a smile to her lips. She surveyed the faces of the people who had gathered in the temple. They wore expressions of kindness and love, and a great surge of expectation could be felt emanating from them. She recognized many of the people as fellow students from her time in Deepingdale.

Midnight looked up, into the blinding light of the gateway. "You can't be serious."

Sunlar reached up and the portal descended toward them. Midnight was rooted to the spot. "Come. We will visit Mystra's domain, the magical weave that surrounds the world. Perhaps that will help you to decide."

The gateway engulfed Midnight and Sunlar, and the magic-user found herself in a realm of bizarre constructs of bluish white light that displayed themselves before her, their constantly changing patterns almost a language unto itself. There was a blinding flash, and Midnight saw that she was rising into the air. She and Sunlar passed through the walls of the temple, then rose into the air and flew beyond the clouds until Faerun was only a spinning mote of dust far below. Midnight viewed the planet for a moment, then felt a presence at her back. She turned and found herself confronting an incredible matrix of energy, a beautiful weave

🌢 118 🌢

of power that spread itself across the universe and pulsed with a fire unlike anything Midnight had ever seen.

"You can be a part of this," Sunlar said.

Midnight reached out to the weave, but stopped as she caught sight of her own hand. Her flesh had become translucent, and within the boundaries of her form, she saw a pulse of fantastic colors that mirrored the raw magical energy before her.

"This is power," Sunlar said. "Power to build worlds, to heal the sick, to destroy evil. Power to serve Mystra as she wishes you to."

Midnight was overwhelmed.

"It is within your grasp," Sunlar said. "And it is your responsibility to take it, Midnight. No one else can be Lady Mystra's champion on Faerun. No one but you."

The raven-haired mage was silent for a moment, then she said quietly, "But what does Mystra want in return for this honor?"

"Your absolute loyalty, of course. And you'll have to devote the rest of your life to fighting for Mystra's causes all across the Realms."

"Then she wants everything. I'll have no life of my own."

Sunlar smiled. "That's a small price to pay to become a goddess's most powerful representative in the world."

Sunlar faced the tiny world far below and spread his arms wide. "All this will be yours, Lady Midnight. You will be gaining the entire world as your charge. And without you, it will certainly perish."

The fabric of the universe began to tear. Vast sections of the weave unraveled before Midnight's eyes, and images of the temple and Mystra's followers could be seen beyond the rips. They were screaming, calling out for Mystra to save them. Calling for the Magister to heal the Realms.

"You must choose quickly," Sunlar said.

The holes in the universe widened. In places Midnight could no longer see the weave at all.

"You are the only one who can save the Realms, Lady Midnight, but you must decide to do it right now."

Midnight's breath became ragged. The weave seemed to call to her. She started to open her mouth to speak, to accept

RICHARD AWLINSON

her responsibility, when she heard a voice, soft but distinct, crying out with the worshipers in the temple.

"Midnight," a familiar voice cried. "I need your help to save Cyric and Adon!"

"Kel!" Midnight cried. "Sunlar, I must help him."

"Ignore his petty concerns," Sunlar said. "Better still solve his problems by helping all the Realms."

"Wait, Sunlar. I cannot forsake everything that makes up my life, everyone that I care about, on a moment's notice. I need more time!"

"That is the one thing you don't have," Sunlar said softly.

Eternity vanished. The weave was gone. Only the temple remained. Midnight looked down at her hands and saw that they were flesh and blood once again. She felt the sting of tears on her cheek and almost laughed.

One of Mystra's worshipers moved forward. It was a man, and she recognized his face.

Kelemvor.

The fighter held out his hand. "Come back," he said. "The others need you. I need you."

Sunlar grasped her shoulder and turned her to face him. "Don't listen to him. You have a duty to your goddess! You have a duty to the Realms!"

"No!" Midnight shouted as she pulled herself free from Sunlar's grasp. Mystra's followers froze in mid-motion, and Kelemvor, now dressed in his fighting gear, stood before her.

"You have dishonored yourself and your goddess," Sunlar said, his face fading into the shadows that fell upon the throne room like curtains, darkening the illusions. Then he was gone. In moments only scattered patches of illusion remained, and Midnight saw Kelemvor crawling on the floor of a room that once might have been an audience hall. A large, overturned chair that bore a striking resemblance to the throne she had sat upon lay in the corner. The musty chamber was domed, just as it had been in her illusion.

Midnight looked down and saw that the pendant was still there, still grafted to her skin.

"What's going on here? One minute I'm opening a door, the next I'm floating above the world, now I'm in a ruined throne room."

Then Midnight noticed that Kelemvor appeared wounded. She ran to his side as he collapsed, but saw that his face and body were unscarred. Still, the fighter was sweating and seemed very frightened.

"Offer me something!" he snarled, his voice low and very menacing.

"What? What are you talking about?"

Kelemvor flinched and his ribs seemed to move of their own accord. Midnight looked at him warily.

"A reward!" he said, and his flesh began to darken. "For helping to free you from the illusion and for going on with the quest. We abandoned it, Cyric and I—"

The fighter shuddered and turned away from Midnight. "Hurry!"

"A kiss," she said softly. "Your reward will be a kiss from my lips."

Kelemvor collapsed on the floor, out of breath. When he rose, his skin had returned to its natural complexion.

"What was that all about?" Midnight said.

Kelemvor shook his head. "We have to find the others."

"But I—"

"We can't possibly make it out of here alive without them," Kelemvor yelled. "So, for our own good, we have to do it *now!*"

Midnight did not move.

"We were separated," Kelemvor said. "Sent to different parts of the castle. I awoke in a library on the first floor. I followed the noise until I found you."

"Noise? Then you saw and heard—"

"Very little. I heard your voice and followed it until I found you. But we'll have more time to figure this out later. Now, help me find the others!"

Midnight followed the fighter down the darkened corridors.

*　*　*　*　*

After Kelemvor escaped through the tear in the carpet, it started to close in around Cyric, and it dwindled until it was the size of a large chest. The thief tried to slice the rug with his sword, but it was no use; the blade simply bounced off each time he struck at the trap. The carpet continued to shrink until Cyric felt it conform to the shape of his body and squeeze with such pressure that he blacked out. When he awoke, he was in one of the back alleys of Zhentil Keep, being kicked awake by a watchman, just as he had been regularly in his childhood.

"Move along," one of the Black Guard said. "Or else nothing but steel will fill your gut this day."

Cyric fended off the blows and rose to his feet.

"Stinking vagrants," the guard said, and spat at the ground near Cyric's feet. The thief moved forward to attack the man, but something reached out from the shadows behind him. Hands were pressed against Cyric's mouth, others held his arms. He fought against the pull of the hands but there was nothing he could do. He was dragged into the side alley as the watchman stood and laughed.

"Calm down, boy," an all too familiar voice said.

Cyric watched as the guard walked to the end of the alley and turned off onto the street, vanishing from sight.

The thief allowed his body to relax, and the iron grip that held him loosened. Cyric turned and faced the shadows. Even before his eyes adjusted to the darkness he knew the identity of the men before him.

One was known as Quicksal, an evil little thief who took great pleasure in killing his victims. Just as Cyric remembered it, Quicksal's fine, golden hair was unwashed, and traces of dyes of every type could be found within it, as he generally tried to disguise himself. False beards, age make up, strange accents, odd personality traits—all these were part of an ever growing repertoire that Quicksal called upon to create vivid characters for potential witnesses to remember. His face was thin and hawklike, and his fingers were extremely long. Strangely, Quicksal still appeared to be in his teens, though Cyric knew he had to be at least twenty-five years old.

The other man was Marek, and when Cyric examined the face of his mentor, he did not find the aging, hard-lined visage he had looked upon just the other night, when Marek ambushed him at the inn. This Marek was younger, and the tight, curly hair upon his head was jet-black, not the salt-and-pepper-gray it should have been. His skin had only just begun to show a hint of the wrinkles that would one day develop. His piercing blue eyes had not surrendered any of their earlier fires, and the man's large frame no longer displayed any trace of flabbiness. This was the man Cyric had studied under, had robbed and committed now unthinkable acts for without hesitation. Cyric had been an orphan, and in many ways, Marek was the only father he ever knew.

"Come with us," Marek said, and Cyric obeyed, allowing himself to be led through a set of doorways into the kitchen of an inn that Cyric did not recognize. Cyric had always allowed himself to be led, it seemed, and when they passed into the lighted hallway, Cyric noticed his own reflection in a nearby mirror. More than ten years had been taken from his face—the crow's feet were gone from around his eyes; his skin seemed more resilient, less hardened by the passage of time and the hardships he had endured.

"You're probably wondering why we're here," Marek said to the grotesquely fat cook who stood near a curtain at the other end of the kitchen.

"No, not at all," the fat man said, a broad smile holding up his blubbery cheeks. He pointed to the curtain and said, "She's right in here."

Marek grabbed Cyric by the arm and led him to the curtain. "Look," Marek said and drew open the curtains very slightly. "There's our next victim, and your ride to freedom, Cyric."

Cyric looked out. Only a few tables in the taproom were visible from his vantage, and only one of those was occupied. A handsome middle-aged woman, dressed in fine silks and carrying a purse filled to overflowing sat at the table, sipping a bowl of soup that had just been brought to her by an attractive serving girl. She stopped the girl.

"This soup is not piping hot!" the woman shrieked in a voice that made Cyric's teeth hurt. "I asked that my soup be piping hot, not merely warm!"

"But ma'am—"

The woman grasped the serving girl's hand. "See for yourself!" the woman cried, and thrust the girl's hand into the steaming bowl of soup. The girl bit back a scream, and managed to wrench her hand free without spilling the contents of the bowl upon the middle-aged woman. The flesh of the girl's hand was bright red. The soup had been scalding.

"If you cannot meet my needs, I will have to take my business elsewhere!" the woman said. She rolled her eyes. "I do wish I knew what was keeping my nephew. He was supposed to meet me here." She frowned and gestured at the soup. "Now take this away and bring me what I asked for!"

The serving girl took the bowl, bowed slightly, and turned to walk back to the kitchen, causing Cyric to draw back before he was seen.

"Relax," Marek said from behind Cyric, and the curtains parted, admitting the girl. She looked at Marek and shoved her serving tray into Cyric's waiting hands. She pressed against Marek and kissed him full on the lips. Then she pulled back, grabbed a damp cloth from the sink, and wrapped it around her hand.

"I'd like not to wait for my cut this time," she said.

Quicksal eased his blade from its sheath then slammed it back again, making a sharp scrape that caused the serving girl to smile. "I promise our benefactor won't have to wait for *hers*."

"I'll second that," Cyric said, surprising himself with the sentiment.

The serving girl winked at Marek. "You know where to find me this evening. We'll celebrate."

She took the serving tray back from Cyric and went to a boiling pot of soup in the kitchen and ladled out another serving. Then she dropped the wet cloth and headed back to the taproom with the steaming soup.

"Stay here," Marek said, and followed the girl. Cyric parted the curtains and watched as Marek spoke to the woman. Cyric dropped the curtain when Quicksal tugged on his sleeve.

"Time to go," Quicksal said, and moments later they were once again crouched in the shadows of the alley behind the inn. The doorway opened and Marek ushered the woman into the alley. She looked around, disoriented and confused.

"I don't understand," the old woman said. "You say my nephew has been beset in this alley, that he can't be moved, and—"

Understanding lit in her eyes as Quicksal pushed away from the shadows.

"You're not my auntie," Quicksal said. "But we'll take your money anyway."

The woman started to scream but Quicksal pushed her against a wall and put his hand over her mouth. He drew his knife and placed it against her throat. "Quiet now, Auntie. I wouldn't want to have to kill you right away. Besides, this is Zhentil Keep. If your screams do draw someone here, they'll only want a share of your money."

Marek grabbed the woman's purse and rifled through it. Then he nodded with a pained expression.

"Alas, this is not enough," Marek said, and motioned for Cyric to move forward. Quicksal backed away from the woman, but kept his blade extended toward her as he did.

"I have nothing else!" she cried. "Mercy!"

"I would respect your request," Marek said sadly, lowering his head. "But I cannot deny the young ones their pleasure."

Cyric drew his blade. Quicksal placed his hand on the boy's chest and snickered. "You'll never be able to kill her, Cyric. And then Marek will be stuck with you as an apprentice forever." The blond thief moved toward the woman again. "You might as well let me kill her, Marek."

"Stand away!" Cyric said, and Quicksal turned to face him.

There were tears in the woman's eyes. "Help me," she cried, her hands shaking.

"Ah, such a dilemma," Marek said. "Who shall spill this innocent blood?"

Cyric turned sharply. "There is no innocence in this world!"

Marek raised an eyebrow. "But what crime has this woman committed?"

"She hurt the girl."

Marek shrugged. "So? I've hurt her many times myself. She didn't seem to be complaining." Marek laughed. "I think Quicksal should kill the woman. After all, Cyric, you have never showed me that you're ready to be independent, and

RICHARD AWLINSON

the Thieves' Guild might not approve."

"You're lying!" Cyric shouted. With each step Quicksal took toward the woman, Cyric saw his chance for independence slipping farther away.

"A moment," Marek said, raising his hand to Quicksal, then turning to Cyric. "Does she deserve to die, just so you can have your freedom?"

"I know her. She is . . ." Cyric shook his head. "She is arrogance and vanity. Privilege and prejudice. Content to ignore the poor and the needy, ready to let us die before she would raise a hand to help. She is distant and cruel, except when her head is on the block. Then she cries for mercy, for forgiveness. I have seen her type before. She is all that I despise."

"And she has no redeeming qualities? She is not capable of love or kindness? There is no chance she might change her ways?" Marek said.

"None at all," Cyric said.

"Quite an argument," Marek said. "But I am not swayed. Quicksal, kill her."

The woman gasped and tried to run, but Quicksal was far too fast for her. She hadn't taken two steps before the blond thief was upon her and her throat was slit. The woman collapsed into the alley. Quicksal smiled. "Perhaps next time, Cyric."

Cyric looked into Quicksal's eyes and felt as if he had delved into twin pools of madness. "I deserve my freedom," Cyric growled and drew his knife.

"Then prove it to me," Marek said. "Show me your worth and I will award you your independence. I will give you safe passage from the city if you want it, and I will make the Thieves' Guild recognize you as a full member. Your life will be your own, to do with as you will."

Cyric shuddered. "Everything I've dreamed," he said absently.

"But only you can make the dream a reality," Marek said. "Now be a good boy and kill Quicksal there."

Cyric looked back to Quicksal and saw that the blond thief was now holding a sword that he did not have only seconds earlier. However, instead of readying to attack, Cyric's rival stood in a defensive posture and looked very frightened.

"Put away your knife," Quicksal said in a voice that was not his own. "Don't you recognize me?"

Cyric held his ground. "Only too well. And don't try to confuse me by disguising your voice. I know all your tricks."

Quicksal shook his head. "This isn't real!" Cyric knew he should have recognized the voice Quicksal was using but he couldn't concentrate on it. The blond thief took a step backward. "It's an illusion, Cyric. I don't know what you think you see in front of you, but it's me, Kelemvor."

Cyric struggled to place the name or the voice, but it was difficult to think.

"You've got to fight," Quicksal said.

"He's right, Cyric," Marek said softly. "You have to fight this." But Marek's voice was suddenly different, too. He sounded like a woman.

Cyric didn't move. "Something is wrong here, Marek. I don't know what kind of games you're playing with me, but I really don't care. I expect you to hold to your word." With that, Cyric lunged at Quicksal.

Quicksal sidestepped Cyric's first thrust, and surprised Cyric by retreating a few steps and assuming a defensive posture. This isn't Quicksal's style at all, Cyric thought.

"Stop this at once," Quicksal said, parrying Cyric's next thrust. Cyric moved with the force of the parry and crashed his elbow into Quicksal's face. At the same time, he tossed his blade from one hand to the other and grabbed Quicksal's wrist. Then Cyric rammed the blond thief's hand against the wall and forced him to drop his sword.

"With your death, I gain a life," Cyric cried and raised his knife to kill the blond thief.

"No, Cyric, you're killing a friend!" Marek screamed, and Cyric recognized the voice as Midnight's just before his dagger struck his opponent's shoulder. His victim wasn't Quicksal: it was Kelemvor.

As best he could, Cyric pulled back on his knife thrust. But it was too late. The dagger sunk into Kelemvor's shoulder.

Kelemvor pushed him away, and Cyric crashed to the floor, his dagger still stuck in his victim's shoulder. The fighter picked up his sword and started toward the thief. "Forgive me," Cyric whispered as the warrior raised his sword to strike.

"Kel, don't!" Midnight shouted. "He can see it's us!"

The fighter stood still, then dropped his sword. Cyric backed away and saw Midnight standing where Marek had stood only a second earlier. Then Kelemvor was beside her, blood leaking from his wounded shoulder. The fighter's face had gone white.

The alley started to fade and disappear, but the body of the woman Quicksal had killed, the woman Cyric would have murdered if he'd been given the chance, still lay face down in the dirt. A pool of blood was still spreading out from beneath her. Cyric stared at the woman until she, too, faded from sight.

"What does he see?" Kelemvor whispered. "There's nothing there." Midnight shook her head.

"I'm sorry, Kel. I thought you were someone else," Cyric said as he approached the fighter.

Kelemvor plucked the dagger from his shoulder, flinching at the incredible pain. He dropped the weapon at Cyric's feet as Midnight helped him bind up his wounded shoulder.

"We have to find Adon," Kelemvor said. "He's the only one left."

"I can guess what his temptation is," Midnight said as she finished binding Kelemvor's wound and the heroes raced for the stairs.

*　*　*　*　*

Adon had turned away from the bars that separated him from Midnight and walked a short way down the hall, just to see if there was some easy way for him to rejoin the mage on the other side of the barrier. Now he found himself staring up at an incredibly beautiful, star-filled sky.

And such a strange array of stars, too, Adon noted as he looked up at the night sky. They all appear to be moving.

Indeed the stars *were* in motion, rocketing across the sky at such speeds that many were only blurs of light. Adon closed his eyes, but the stars remained, playing their games even behind his closed lids.

Adon gazed at the stars for a long time. When next he looked around, he found himself laid out on a delicate bed of roses, and the fragrance that flooded his senses was sweet and gentle, although it caused his heart to beat faster and his head to grow numb. The pedals brushed against his fingers so lightly that he could not help but smile at the delicacy. Then it occurred to Adon. The stars weren't moving at all; he was.

He opened his eyes and gazed over the edge of his bed of flowers only to find a dozen of the most beautiful beings he had ever seen. Their hair seemed to have been set aflame, and their bodies were specimens of utter physical perfection. Adon's magnificent bed rested upon their willing shoulders.

The presence of these beings reassured Adon so much that he didn't even flinch when a wall of flames sprang up around him. His vision blurred a bit, and all he surveyed seemed to take on an amber cast, but there was no heat as the flames leaped from the red to white roses, changing them to black orchids, and finally jumped to the cleric's flesh. There was no pain, not even mild discomfort, when the fires engulfed him. There was nothing but the bright glow of love and well-being that coursed through his soul as he came to the final understanding of his own death, that must have happened long before this moment.

Strain as he might, he could remember none of what happened after he was separated from Midnight in the corridors below Castle Kilgrave. He woke upon his funeral pyre, being carried to what could only be his eternal reward.

But how did I die? Adon wondered, and the shifting, beautiful voices of his bearers filled the crackling air around him.

"One never remembers," they said. "The moment of pain is suffered by another, to spare you."

Another?

"Others such as we have become. Our purpose is to alleviate suffering. We live your death that you might be reborn into the Kingdom of Sune."

Shining crystal spires cut through the night, and Adon focused his attention on the temple before him. As it stretched across the horizon, the temple's walls were graced with stunningly beautiful crystalline designs, though no uniform pattern made the infinite palace boring or repetitious. It was as if each of Sune's followers who found rest in this place had contributed their own concepts of the boundaries and appearances that eternity should reveal. An amalgam of expectations resulted, yet some guiding hand had taken all the disparate images and incorporated them into an ordered whole, disappointing no one and creating a place of beauty that defied Adon's wildest dreams to surpass.

The entrance alone was larger than any temple Adon had seen before, and what lay beyond was a world unto itself. His bearers brought him through lands where a countless number of worshipers bathed and frolicked in pools that had been formed from their own tears of joy, and the rocks they lay upon as they luxuriated in the warmth of Sune's love for them had once been the stones of disbelief that weighted down their souls and made union with the goddess impossible. Relieved of the terrible burdens of life, they could now devote themselves totally to the preservation of order, beauty, and love by worshiping Sune.

Adon and his bearers passed through many such lands, each new vista overwhelming Adon more than the last, and Adon was surprised at his capacity to take in more and more of these spellbinding raptures until at last his bearers vanished and he found himself standing before a wrought iron gateway that shimmered and became a shower of sparkling water. He passed through it.

What lay beyond was a very small chamber in comparison to the wonders Adon had witnessed just moments before. There were no walls to this room, though, and all around it vast and intense flames leaped to the sky. Soft, billowing curtains protected the cleric's eyes from the roaring flames and set the boundaries of the room that lay in the heart of beauty's eternal fires.

"A drink?"

Adon turned and the Goddess of Beauty herself, Sune Firehair, stood before him. Glasses filled with a rich, crimson nectar waited in each of her glowing hands. As Adon took one of the glasses, he saw that his flesh started to blaze with the same amber light as Sune's flesh.

"Goddess," Adon said, and fell to his knees before her, spilling not a drop of the drink in his hand.

Sune laughed and brought him to his feet with one of her powerful hands. Adon felt his breath freeze in his lungs as she touched him, a power undreamed of flooding through his limbs as he stood before her.

Breath. I'm still alive, Adon thought, rejoicing at the knowledge.

Sune seemed to read his thoughts. "You have not died, foolish boy. Not yet. I have brought you here for the most basic of reasons: I am in love with you. You, above all my worshipers, are all that I desire."

Adon was speechless, and so he brought the chalice to his lips and felt the sweet nectar run its course through his body. "Goddess, surely I am not worthy—"

Sune smiled and disrobed before him, shedding a fiery silk robe and allowing it to fall to the floor and vanish. Adon looked down and saw rolling clouds beneath his feet.

"I am beauty," Sune said. "Touch me."

Adon walked forward, as if in a dream.

"Truth is beauty, beauty truth. Embrace me and the answers to all your unspoken questions will be made clear."

From somewhere Adon heard a voice cry out in warning, but he ignored it. Nothing could be more important than this moment. He took the goddess in his arms and brought his lips to hers.

The kiss seemed endless. But even before Adon opened his eyes, he felt Sune changing. Her gentle lips had become fierce, demanding. An endless series of sharpened pincers seemed to move from her elongating jaws, seeking to rend the flesh of the cleric's face. Her fingers had transformed into vicious snakes that latched onto his flesh as they threatened to tear him apart.

"Sune!" Adon cried.

The creature laughed as the snaking tendrils of its fingers wrapped themselves around Adon's throat. "You are not worthy of the goddess," it said. "You have sinned against her and you must be punished!"

Across the open, central courtyard of Castle Kilgrave, Midnight, Kelemvor, and Cyric stared as the cleric fell to his knees in absolute terror, driven to this position by something that only he could see.

"Goddess forgive me!" Adon cried. "I will do anything to win your forgiveness. Anything!"

"We have to get to him quickly," Midnight said.

"You will do nothing!" a thunderous voice rang out, its echoes filling the courtyard. "You will do nothing but die by the hand of Bane!"

Suddenly the trio was bombarded by illusions. In the span of a dozen heartbeats, Kelemvor was sent into the dream world of his childhood books: he lived an epic love story wherein he was a foreign prince sent to marry a lovely but heartless princess, and he forsook his very kingdom to run off with a peasant girl. Midnight saw herself as a powerful queen, saving her kingdom from poverty and want. At the same time, images of a free and unfettered life passed before Cyric's eyes, along with offers of gold and priceless artifacts. But the images of heroism and power and freedom held no sway over them. As one, the heroes charged to the center of the courtyard.

The challenges occurred more rapidly as the heroes moved on: Sunlar appeared before Midnight, daring her to a magical duel. Her entire class lined up behind the teacher, anxious to try their skills against her. Cyric faced the ice creature that stood guardian over the Ring of Winter. He watched helplessly as the monster reached out for him. Kelemvor faced the executioners who took the life of his grandfather, but now they had come for him. He looked down to find that he was now old and tired. His attempts to find a cure for his condition and salvation for his withered soul had been a failure.

But still the heroes pressed forward to the center of the courtyard and Adon's side.

Still on his knees, Adon stared as paradise tore itself apart and was reordered. The demon creature that had pretended to be the goddess had left him, but Sune's kingdom had changed. The death and punishment of its charges was now the mainstay of its existence, as robed figures enslaved and tormented Sune's faithful.

"This is a lie!" Midnight screamed as she got close to Adon.

The cleric turned, wide-eyed, and saw someone who looked just like Midnight standing beside him—but she wore the robes of the Sunites' tormentors.

"But . . . it was so beautiful!" Adon said, angry at Midnight's words.

"Look about you," Midnight said. "This is reality!"

Adon looked and saw the goddess Sune chained to a huge slab. The robed figures were lowering the slab into a river that ran scarlet with the blood of Sune's followers.

And each of the robed figures wore a pendant, exactly like Midnight's.

"The pendant!" Sune shouted. "It is the source of their power! Take it and I will be free!"

Midnight grabbed Adon by the shoulders. "Damn it, listen to me!"

"No!" Adon screamed, and before Kelemvor or Cyric could react, the cleric lunged at Midnight with a ferocity she had not expected. Adon's hand closed over Midnight's dagger, and he pulled it away from her. Feet together, Midnight kicked the cleric in the midsection, sending him flying backward, the dagger still clutched in his hand. There was a sharp crack as Adon's head struck the ground. Then the cleric lay in a heap, stunned by the blow.

Midnight began the movements and the chanting that would release a spell to dispel the magical assault. As she prayed that the spell would not go awry, the tiny fires upon the pendant crackled. There was a blinding flash of blue-white light as Midnight's spell released a maelstrom of magics that enveloped the courtyard.

* * * * *

Bane fell back, crying out as the water of the scrying pool became a scalding torrent of blood that erupted in a geyser as the pool exploded. All around Castle Kilgrave, the spells Bane had used to transform the ruins into a minor reflection of his home in the Planes were shattered by Midnight's magic.

Bane's temple, his New Acheron, was crumbling. The fantastic gateways he had opened were now closing. The corridors and chambers that so cleverly held replicas of Bane's former temple in the Planes lost their tenuous hold on reality and burned away.

In moments all that was left was the ruined remains of a mortal's castle. Bane fell forward, sobbing, and part of his mind marveled at discovering another new sensation these humans lived with every day of their short existence:

Loss.

New Acheron was gone.

When at last he turned and summoned the *hakeashar* so he could gather the power to kill Mystra's would-be rescuers, the Black Lord was shocked to find the mystical chains that held the goddess empty.

Mystra had escaped.

❧ 7 ❧

Mystra

Midnight was on her knees, recovering from the shock of her spellcasting, when Adon appeared beside her. The courtyard of Castle Kilgrave displayed no vestige of the battle that had taken place in its confines.

"It's gone," Adon said. "Sune's kingdom is gone, as if it never truly existed."

Midnight looked up at him. When she spoke, it was in a comforting tone. "I'm sure it exists somewhere, Adon. When the time comes, you will find your way there."

Adon nodded, then he and Cyric helped Midnight to her feet. A few yards away, Kelemvor coughed twice and slowly came around. "What happened?" Kelemvor said, holding his wounded shoulder.

"Something was playing games with our minds," Midnight said. "It tried to control us, set us against one another. I tried a simple dispel magic incantation and—"

"You caused that explosion?" Kelemvor said, sitting up abruptly.

"You shouldn't move," Adon said, and attempted to force the man to lay back. His efforts were futile.

"Damn it, Adon. We lost a day at the colonnade because I was flat on my back. Just leave me alone; I'll be fine!"

"Let him go, Adon," Midnight said, smiling at the fighter. "Yes, Kel, I caused the explosion—or my magic did, anyway. I gathered from what was happening to us that someone was casting a powerful illusion on all of us. I tried to dispel it, but the spell caused some kind of backlash. It seems to have stopped whoever was throwing the spell."

"The voice of Bane," Cyric said, laughing. "Probably just

some madman with delusions of godhood."

"Then I suggest we find him," Kelemvor said as he looked around. "He's got to be the one who has Caitlan's mistress captive."

"I thought you'd given up on finding her," Cyric said.

Kelemvor smiled and looked at Midnight. "I had. But I think the reward I'll get for concluding the quest will be worth toughing it out." The fighter looked at the bloody rags over his shoulder and wondered if he would be able to wield his sword with only one arm. He was able to make a loose fist with his right hand, although the process caused sparks of pain to erupt before his eyes.

Cyric simply shook his head as he went to the courtyard's entrance and looked out into the hallway. There was no sign of movement. The corridors looked much the same as they had when Cyric first examined the castle.

"We should find Caitlan's mistress and escape while we can," Cyric said as he went back into the courtyard. Kelemvor nodded in agreement, and soon the adventurers were in the hallway.

"Now what?" Kelemvor said. "Search the castle again, floor by floor?"

Midnight turned and froze, her mouth open wide.

"I don't think we'll have to," Cyric said. "Look!"

Kelemvor looked over his shoulder and saw a horrible, blood-red mass barreling down the corridor at them—the *hakeashar*. From the mist that composed the creature's form, Kelemvor saw hundreds of ten-fingered hands reaching out, clawing at the air. Disembodied yellow eyes broke from the mist, anxious to study the prey before it.

Kelemvor's shoulders slumped. "I've had about enough of this for one day," he said as he drew his sword with his one good hand. His movements weren't graceful, but he hoped the stance would be impressive enough to frighten the huge creature.

The creature let out a roar that sent a burrowing pain through the heroes' skulls. The creature had grown large, gaping mouths, that seemed to grow larger as it approached. Cyric grabbed Midnight's arm and they ran down the hall, away from the *hakeashar*.

"Perhaps you could stand a little more?" Adon said, imploringly, as he backed away, then ran.

The creature let out another roar.

"Perhaps," Kelemvor said as he broke his stance and ran, the swirling mist biting at his heels as he attempted to catch up to the others.

The heroes kept well ahead of the mist creature for a few moments, but they soon tired. By the time they'd reached the turret located two hundred yards from the courtyard, the *hakeashar* was in close pursuit. In the turret, the stairs leading to the upper levels of the castle were filled with debris, so the heroes followed the stairs down, Adon in the lead. In the darkness of the subterranean corridors, the *hakeashar* appeared as a burst of light as it exited the turret.

Midnight realized that the corridor ahead of them was blocked by rubble at the same moment the *hakeashar* caught up with the adventurers. Turning to face the creature, she shouted for her fellows to move out of the way. She was already casting a spell as the creature filled the width of the corridor and stopped, its eyes blinking wildly as Kelemvor held up his sword and Cyric put on his cloak of displacement.

Suddenly a gust of wind surged through the corridor, originating at Midnight's fingertips. The wind cut through the creature, holding it at bay for a moment. Abruptly the wind died away.

The *hakeashar* slowly moved forward, the incredible power it had sensed in Midnight's pendant drawing it's attention.

Cyric walked forward, his cloak of displacement creating a dozen phantom images of him. The many eyes of the *hakeashar* fixated on the images created by the cloak as they wildly crossed one another to alter their vantages of the illusion.

"Besides managing to confuse this thing, what good have we done?" Kelemvor whispered to Midnight. The magic-user stepped away from the fighter just as the hands of the creature shot forward and grabbed the cloak from Cyric. The images disappeared as the cloak was devoured by the *hakeashar*.

A dozen new eyes and mouths opened as the creature grew larger.

"What are you waiting for?" Kelemvor said. "Cast your spell!"

The *hakeashar* giggled, memories of feeding from the magic of the goddess flooding into its mind.

Midnight stopped, and turned to face the fighter. "Kel."

The *hakeashar* was drifting closer.

"Hack it to pieces," Midnight said.

Kelemvor tightened his grip on the sword with his one good arm.

The *hakeashar* stopped.

Over a hundred images of the hairy human moving forward, sword in hand, registered in the *hakeashar*'s brain. The beast was filled with an odd sense of curiosity. It moved five of its jaws over the human, clamped down, and was surprised that it did not receive any sustenance from the effort. The human began to laugh and a lancing pain cut through the creature as six of its eyes were shut forever in one mighty sweep of the human's sword.

* * * * *

The roars of the *hakeashar* echoed through Castle Kilgrave as the Black Lord knelt in the still water of his ruined scrying pool. Bane had summoned the creature and turned it loose in the castle to search for Mystra.

A small stone struck the puddle of water before Bane's face, causing the fallen god to look up.

A young girl he had never seen before stood in the doorway. She was smiling from ear to ear. A handful of stones that she had dislodged from the crumbling wall beside her rested comfortably in her hand.

"It's not pleasant, having your power turned against you, is it?" she said simply, and the voice was horribly familiar.

"Mystra!" Bane shouted, and lunged at the goddess-made-flesh. Mystra threw the handful of stones at the Black Lord, her voice rising as she began to cast a spell. The stones changed in midflight, becoming blue-white missiles that pierced the body of the Black Lord, sending him sprawling back to the floor of the dungeon.

Another roar sounded from the hallway, this one greater than the last. Mystra shuddered as she heard the sounds of the *hakeashar*, and Bane used the distraction to cast a spell himself. He tore a ruby from his gauntlet. Then the stone vanished and a blood-red shaft of light surged toward the Goddess of Magic.

Bane gasped as Mystra harmlessly absorbed the effects of Nezram's Ruby Ray, a spell that should have separated the goddess from her avatar. Then Bane shuddered as a red beam of light shot back at him and pierced his chest. The beam hung in the air between Mystra and Bane like a rope.

"You were foolish to try a complicated spell," Mystra said. "The magical chaos seems to have finally caught up to you." With that, Mystra grabbed the beam with both hands.

Bane felt a horrible twisting inside. The red beam glowed brightly and a pulse of energy shot from his body to Mystra. The spell had misfired and was allowing Mystra to drain off his power.

Bane struggled to retain his senses as crimson bands grew from the beam and surrounded him, tugging at his flesh as if to tear it from his bones. He felt his ribs crack, one by one, as the force of the attack suddenly reversed itself, and threatened to crush the life from him. Mystra released the beam and it shot back at Bane.

The Black Lord's chest burst open and a flood of bluish white fires exploded from him and engulfed Mystra, who held her hands out to the flow of magic and welcomed it into her. The fires changed, becoming a blazing amber, then a bright, glowing red as Bane felt the last of the energies he had taken from Mystra leave him and the first of his own depart as well.

"You imprisoned the Goddess of Magic, you fool! Now you will pay in kind for what you did to me."

Bane cried out as more of his energy left him. "Mystra! I'm—"

"Dying?" she said. "Aye, it would appear so. Do give my regards to Lord Myrkul. I don't believe he's ever had a god as one of his charges before. But you're not a god anymore, are you, Bane?"

Bane raised his hands imploringly.

"All right, Bane, I'll give you one chance to save yourself. Tell me where the Tablets of Fate are hidden, and I'll show you mercy."

"You want them for yourself?" Bane gasped as another pulse of energy left him.

"No," Mystra said. "I want to return the tablets to Lord Ao and end the madness you've caused."

There was movement in the corridor, and Mystra turned to see Kelemvor and his companions standing in the doorway.

Suddenly a spiralling black vortex appeared before the Black Lord and Tempus Blackthorne stepped from the rift his magic had created. Grasping the body of his wounded master, Blackthorne dragged Bane back into the vortex. Before Mystra could move to strike down the Black Lord and his emissary, they vanished. Mystra's spell was broken as the vortex closed, and a blast of chaotic energy threw the goddess against the wall. When she looked up, she found Kelemvor standing above her.

The fighter seemed pale. "I knew you were made of stern stuff, little one, but even I am impressed."

Mystra smiled as she felt the wild flow of power course through her.

"Caitlan," Midnight said. "Are you alright?" The magic-user leaned toward the avatar, and the star pendant flashed into view.

"The pendant. Give it to me!" Mystra cried.

Midnight stood back. "Caitlan?"

Mystra looked at Midnight once more and realized that the pendant had grafted itself to the magic-user's skin to protect itself—keep itself from being taken from her if she were asleep or injured.

"We should get the child outside," Midnight said.

"Wait a minute," Cyric said. "I want to know how she got out of camp that night, and why she left."

"Please," Adon said calmly. "We should be worried about the poor girl's mistress."

A sudden anger passed through the goddess. "I am Mystra, Goddess of Magic! The creature I fought was Bane,

God of Strife. Now give me that pendant! It's mine!"

Midnight and Adon stared at the avatar in shock. Kelemvor frowned. Cyric eyed Mystra suspiciously.

Kelemvor folded his arms. "Perhaps the battle has addled her young brains."

"Caitlan Moonsong and I have become one," Mystra said calmly. I brought her to this place and merged our souls to save us both from Lord Bane. You aided her on her journey, so you have earned our thanks."

"And a damn shade more," Kelemvor said.

"The debt will be repaid," Mystra said, and Kelemvor remembered the words of Caitlan on her sickbed.

She can cure you.

Mystra turned to Midnight. "On Calanter's Way, you entered into a pact with me. I saved your life from those who wished you harm. In return, you promised to keep safe my trust. You have done so admirably." Mystra reached out with her hand. "But now it is time to return that trust."

Midnight looked down and was shocked as she realized that the pendant hung away from her flesh. She took the pendant from around her neck and gave it to the girl, who instantly blazed with a ferocious blue-white fire.

Hanging back her head, the goddess indulged in a moment of absolute rapture as a portion of the power she had wielded in the Planes coursed through her body. As it had been before the time of Arrival, Mystra's will was again enough to bring magic into existence, and though she was still considerably weaker than she was before Ao cast her out of the heavens, Mystra was again linked to the weave of magic that surrounded Faerun. The feeling was glorious.

"Let us put some distance between ourselves and this place," Mystra said as she addressed her rescuers. "Then I will tell you all you wish to know."

Moments later, the heroes felt the warmth of sunlight as they approached the gate of Castle Kilgrave, and they were blinded for a moment as they left the dark ruins. They walked from the castle with a leaden quality to their step, as if daring the castle to throw one last barrage of madness their way. But the castle was bleak and lifeless.

Mystra looked at the sky. She could see the sparkling

Celestial Stairway as it rose toward the heavens, its aspects frequently changing. At times the goddess had a vague impression of a figure standing at the top of the stairway, but then it was gone, the image losing consistency after the briefest of instants.

The adventurers followed Mystra as she made her way toward a spot no more than five hundred feet from the entrance to the castle. Along the way, a heated argument had broken out.

"Have you taken leave of your senses?" Kelemvor shouted.

"I believe her," Midnight said.

"Aye, *you* believe her. But can your 'goddess' prove her wild claims?"

Mystra commanded the party to wait for her as she turned toward the stairway. Kelemvor stormed forward, ranting about the riches they had been promised and the goddess stared at the man, her eyes blazing with a blue-white fire.

"You have the gratitude of a goddess," Mystra said coldly. "What more could you want?"

Kelemvor remembered his encounter with the goddess Tymora, after paying admission to gaze upon her.

"I'll settle for a decent meal, clothes on my back, and enough gold to buy my own kingdom!" Kelemvor shouted. "I'd also like to be able to use my arm again!"

Suddenly Mystra cocked her head to one side. "Is that all? I assumed you wished to be made into deities."

Cyric's eyes narrowed. "Is such a thing possible?"

Mystra smiled and glowing fireballs leaped from her hands. Kelemvor almost screamed as the crackling energy of the first fireball engulfed him from head to toe, and suddenly he felt a vitality he hadn't felt in days. The flames died away and Kelemvor lifted his arm, staring at his healed limb incredulously.

The second fireball struck the ground, bringing into existence two regal mounts to replace the ones that had been lost, and two packhorses carrying restocked supplies and a fortune in gold and precious stones. Then the goddess turned and walked to the stairway. She opened her hands, spread her arms, and lowered her head, as if in meditation.

Kelemvor stood beside Midnight, and soon their argument resumed. Cyric watched without interfering, and Adon stood, silently watching the goddess before him.

"Certainly she is powerful, and her tale of bonding with her mistress may well be true," Kelemvor said.

"Then why do you deny your senses? Don't you appreciate Mystra's gifts of gratitude?" Midnight said.

"They were well earned!" Kelemvor said as he stuffed a large chunk of sweetbread in his mouth. "But a powerful mage, such as Elminster of Shadowdale, could easily perform the same feats. I have seen another of these 'gods' and I'm not sure they aren't powerful lunatics!"

Mystra looked up at the mention of Elminster, and a smile played across her face as some private reverie amused her for a moment, then she returned to her preparations.

"And so you blaspheme in their presence!" Midnight shouted.

"I speak my mind!"

"I believe her!" Midnight screamed as she poked at Kelemvor's armored chest. "You might never have regained full use of your arm if not for Mystra!"

Kelemvor seemed shaken. He thought of his father, retired from adventuring because of *his* wounds, prowling Lyonsbane Keep, making young Kelemvor's life a living hell.

"You're right," Kelemvor said. "I should be grateful. But . . . Caitlan, a god? You must admit, it stretches the imagination."

Midnight looked back to Mystra. The goddess, cloaked in the form of the girl they had traveled with the previous day, was not an impressive sight.

"Yes," Midnight said. "But I know it's true."

Behind Midnight and Kelemvor, unnoticed, Adon listened to their words, then turned away.

We have fought a god, he thought. And now we serve one, although the others haven't fully accepted it yet. Even as he experienced this revelation, Adon wondered why he was not filled with excitement and reverence. These were the gods themselves that walked the Realms!

Adon looked at the scrawny child kneeling in the dirt and felt a mild discomfort at the sight. Then he recalled the brief glimpse he had had of the abomination Mystra had identified as Bane, the Black Lord.

These are the gods themselves?

Across from the waiting adventurers, Mystra rose to her feet. She stood before the stairway, preparing herself for ascension. A slight smile inched its way across her avatar's face, and she realized the importance of this moment as she turned to address her rescuers.

"Before you, invisible to your human senses, is a Celestial Stairway," Mystra said. "The stairway is a means of traveling between the kingdoms of the gods and the humans. I am about to undertake a dangerous task. If I succeed, the four of you will be my witnesses as I return to the Planes. If I fail, at least one of you must carry my words to the world. This is a sacred task that I may only charge to one whose faith is unquestioning."

Midnight stepped forward. "Anything," Midnight said. "Tell me what must be done!"

Kelemvor shook his head and stood beside Midnight as he spoke to her. "Haven't we done enough? We have risked our lives to save your goddess. Let's quit while we're ahead. There's an entire world to explore and a thousand ways to spend our reward. We should leave."

"I'm staying," Midnight said.

Adon stepped forward. "I stand with Midnight."

Kelemvor looked to Cyric, who merely shrugged. "My curiosity roots me to the spot," Cyric said in a half mocking tone.

Kelemvor gave up. "What is it you have to say, goddess?"

"The Realms are in chaos," Mystra said.

"That much we know."

"Kel!" Midnight said.

"But do you know why?" Mystra said sternly. Kelemvor was silent.

Mystra continued. "There is a power greater than even the gods. This force, which humans are not meant to know about, has cast the gods out of the heavens. Lord Helm, God of Guardians, blocks the gateway to the Planes, keeping us in the Realms. While we are here, we must take human hosts, avatars, or else we are little more than wandering spirits.

"We are paying the penalty for the crimes of two of our number. Lord Bane and Lord Myrkul stole the Tablets of Fate. At least one of these tablets has been hidden in the Realms, although I do not know where. We have been charged with the duty of finding these tablets and returning them to their rightful place in the heavens."

Cyric seemed confused. "But you don't have the tablets," he said. "What do you intend to do?"

"Barter the identities of the thieves for leniency toward those gods who are innocent of this crime," Mystra said.

Kelemvor folded his arms over his chest and laughed as he leaned against his horse. "This is absurd. She's making all this up as she goes along."

Suddenly Mystra's words bore into the privacy of the fighter's mind.

I could have cured you, she said. *Since you do not believe me, I will not.*

Kelemvor's laughter stopped and his flesh became pale.

"Goddess! I would accompany you!" Midnight said, and Kelemvor looked to the magic-user in alarm.

Mystra weighed the offer carefully. A human witnessing sights only a god could comprehend? The woman would be driven mad. Caitlan's mind would be protected, but there was nothing she could do to protect Midnight.

"Only gods may follow," Mystra said. The power that had been secreted in the pendant, along with the stolen energies Mystra had taken from Lord Bane, coiled within her, as if waiting for release. Then Mystra felt the wellspring of magic within her threaten to overflow. There was a moment of purely human panic for the goddess as she lost control of the forces within her. Gently swaying grass crackled as blue-white fires enveloped every blade.

Cyric felt a pleasant warmth beneath his feet. The air was charged with blue-white sparks, and the winds became visible as great glowing streaks of light, delivered with the passionate brush strokes of a mad genius, seared the air, then faded away.

For just an instant, the stairway became visible to Midnight, and she saw that it was a stairway in name only. An endless amount of delicate white hands lay palm up, some standing alone, others in strange clusters where their flesh seemed to have merged. They rose and fell in irregular patterns and their steely fingers constantly flicked back and forth, anxious to receive their next guest. A network of crystalline bones attached the clusters of hands. Oddly, the stumps of the disembodied hands could never be seen. Soft, flowing mist floated down from cluster to cluster.

Then the stairway was gone and Midnight returned her attentions to Mystra.

Caitlan's form was becoming less distinct, and as it shimmered, the heroes saw the child transformed into the woman she had been destined to become. Her body was lush and beautiful, her face delicate and sensual, but her eyes were very old, revealing a millennium of private concerns.

The goddess was shaken as she turned from the heroes and moved away. She seemed to be walking up into the air, and wherever the goddess's feet touched, tiny bolts of bluish white lightning were loosed.

Mystra saw that her perceptions of the stairway and of the gateway to the Planes were constantly shifting. One moment she saw a beautiful cathedral carved from the clouds, with a broad, ornate stair leading up to it. The next moment the area surrounding the gateway seemed to be made of vast, living runes that danced an unknowable dance as they changed positions with their fellows to spell out secrets of the art Mystra had long pondered and never discovered, until now.

Only the gate itself remained constant: it was a large steel door, forged in the image of a giant fist, the symbol of Helm.

Halfway up the stairs, the clouds parted and the God of Guardians materialized before Mystra.

"Well met, Lord Helm," Mystra said cordially.

Helm simply watched Mystra. "Go back, goddess. This way is not for you."

"I would return to my home," Mystra said, angered by the guardian.

"Do you bring the Tablets of Fate?"

Mystra smiled. "I bring *word* of the tablets. I know who stole them, and why."

"That is not enough. You must turn back. The Planes are

no longer ours."

Mystra seemed confused. "But Lord Ao would wish to have this information."

Helm was unmoving. "Give it to me, and I will pass it along."

"I must deliver this information personally."

"I cannot allow that," Helm said. "Turn back before it is too late."

Mystra continued to climb the Celestial Stairway, the primal forces of magic gathering tightly around Faerun as she willed them to be ready for her call.

"I have no desire to harm you, good Helm. Stand away."

"It is my duty to stop you," Helm said. "I was lax in my duties once. Never again."

Helm descended further.

"Stand away," Mystra said, her voice as loud as a thunderclap.

Helm stood his ground. "Do not force me to harm you, Mystra. I am still a god. You are not."

Mystra froze. "Not a god, you say? I will prove you wrong!"

Helm lowered his eyes, then looked back to her. "So be it."

Mystra called upon all the energy she had gathered as she advanced upon the God of Guardians. She shuddered with power as she prepared her first spell.

On the ground below, Midnight watched as the gods moved toward one another. Helm reached out even as Mystra loosed bolts of fire against him. Helm recoiled from the magic and gritted his teeth as the tiny white fires seared his skin. The guardian swung a fist in Mystra's direction and the goddess moved back to avoid the blow, nearly falling from the stairway in the process.

Helm advanced forward. He was not armed in any way, yet flames seemed to leap from his hands as he moved toward the goddess. Mystra knew instinctively that she must not allow his hands to touch her. She moved back, and primal magic cleaved the air around the guardian. Mystra attempted to summon Bigby's Crushing Hand, but the spell went awry and a countless number of razor-sharp claws sailed toward Helm. The guardian shrugged them off without effort.

Helm's hand came down in an arc, and Mystra felt an incredible pain pierce the core of her being as his fingers ripped across her chest. A spray of blood reached into the air, painting tiny flickering sparks of magic a deep crimson and forcing them out of existence.

Mystra felt her blood turn cold as Helm's hand grazed her shoulder. In retaliation, the Goddess of Magic released a spell meant to attack Helm's psyche, exploiting his fears and forcing him to bow before her as he quaked in terror. The guardian gritted his teeth and struck again, ignoring Mystra's attack. The guardian's greatest fear had been to fail Ao. As he had already confronted this fear, there was nothing left to frighten him.

Mystra realized she had lost even as Helm's hand moved across her midsection, opening a gash in her flesh that released a torrent of bluish white fires along with a splatter of blood. Then the goddess felt a cold breeze beside her neck as Helm came within inches of taking her throat.

Cyric stood and watched as the gods attempted to slay one another, fascinated by the spectacle. He felt a rush of excitement every time Helm delivered a blow. The sight of a god's blood falling from the sky filled him with an inexplicable bliss.

Mystra avoided another of Helm's thrusts and delivered an advanced spell of binding, causing shackles formed from primal magic to descend on the guardian. Helm shrugged them off without effort, but Mystra used the momentary distraction to stumble past the guardian. It was difficult to concentrate beyond the incredible agonies her body had endured, but she clawed her way up the stairway, her mind reeling as the gateway rose up before her and the true majesty of the Planes presented itself. For an instant, the goddess caught a glimpse of the beauty and perfection of her home in Nirvana.

All this was mine, Mystra thought. She reached the summit, her legs trembling beneath her. Then the Goddess of Magic grabbed for the gate, and a hand grasped her arm, spinning her around. There was a look of sadness in Helm's eyes.

"Farewell, goddess," Helm said.

Then he drove his hand through her chest.

Midnight looked at the sky and wondered if she was going mad. Kelemvor was beside her, barking commands at Adon to help Cyric with the horses and their supplies.

Midnight had watched as Helm had been stunned for a moment, and Mystra crawled up past him, then rose to her feet. The goddess spread her arms wide, and the chaos of the arcane bolts of magic and the nebulous forms the elements of the air had been molded into suddenly revealed a gateway in the form of a huge fist. Then Helm was upon Mystra, turning her to face his wrath.

"No!" Midnight screamed, and both Kelemvor and Adon looked to the sky just in time to see Helm run Mystra through with his hand.

Mystra's head was thrown back in unknowable agony as her essence fled from her avatar and her fragile human flesh exploded. Midnight felt an intense heat rush toward her, as if a searing, invisible wall of energy was approaching. The bluish white fires that had set the grass ablaze with their gentle magics now became black flames that scoured the earth and left the soil barren in their wake. The devastation began in the area directly below the goddess, and branched out in every direction.

Midnight attempted to summon a wall of force to protect her comrades. Streaks of light began to swirl around the group of adventurers, and in moments they were surrounded by a prismatic sphere. Despite the whirlwind of colors that made up the walls of the protective globe, the adventurers were able to catch glimpses of the chaos that reigned around them.

The horizon seemed to blur and the earth and sky became one as huge black glass pillars formed from the air and rooted themselves to the ground in a wide circle around the adventurers and the Celestial Stairway, similar to the colonnade where they'd spent the night. The clouds turned black as the pillars rose up to greet them, and beautiful gossamer beams of soft pastel-colored light broke from between the black clouds. The beams swept back and forth, searing the surface of the earth and creating fissures big enough to swallow a man.

Rivers of flaming blood filled the cracks in the ground, and the heat that radiated from the boiling rivers of blood was terrible. The black columns were shattered by the beams, and immense pieces of debris crashed to the ground as the beams lost their form and became wisps that sliced through the air, destroying all they touched.

Castle Kilgrave fell before the onslaught, its walls exploding like chalk. The massive towers at each corner collapsed inward and the walls connecting them sank into rubble.

In the sky, Helm stood at the apex of the disaster, his body a silhouette against the blinding light of the sun behind him. Midnight saw Helm bring down his hand once more, cleaving a swirling mass that hung in the air before him.

Was this Mystra's essence? Midnight wondered.

The bluish white fires that escaped Helm's hands wove themselves into an intricate design, similar to Midnight's vision of the magical weave in her illusion. Then a shaft of brilliant light erupted from the center of the weave and penetrated the protective sphere where Midnight and her companions huddled. Against the pure white tapestry of her perceptions, Midnight saw an even brighter light, in the shape of a woman, moving toward her.

"Goddess!" she cried.

I was wrong. Other gods may attempt what I have tried. . . . The Realms may be destroyed. There is another Celestial Stairway in Shadowdale. If Bane lives, he will try to take control of it. You must go there, warn Elminster. Then find the Tablets of Fate and end this madness!

Suddenly an object fell from the sky and passed through the protective sphere. Midnight reached out, and the pendant fell directly into her grasp. Then the light from the weave seemed to pass through the magic-user, as if drawn by the blue-white pendant. Every nerve in Midnight's body rebelled as white-hot fires coursed through her and the last words of the goddess burned into her brain.

Take the pendant to Elminster . . . Elminster will help you.

"Help me?" Midnight cried. "Help me to do what!?"

An image of the Tablets of Fate burned itself into Midnight's memory. Formed from clay, the ancient tablets were less than two feet high, small enough to be carried and easily concealed from prying eyes. Runes were carved into them, reporting the names and duties of all the gods. Each rune sparkled with a blue-white glow.

The image of the tablets vanished as the shaft of light withdrew into the weave, taking Mystra's shimmering form with it.

"Goddess," Midnight whispered. "Don't leave me."

There was no reply, but through the prismatic sphere, Midnight could see the magical weave disappear. Then the chaos stopped around them, and the heroes saw Helm stand before his gate, cross his arms, and disappear. It was as if he was never there at all.

❧ 8 ❧

Not Always Human

Tempus Blackthorne cleared the main chamber of Bane's new temple in Zhentil Keep whenever his Black Lord was not in attendance. Blackthorne was responsible for overseeing the day-to-day operations of the Dark Temple, and he had personally supervised the construction of the second, smaller chamber to the rear of the temple. Then, once the workers had completed the room, the mage had slain them as well. "No one must know," Bane had said, and Blackthorne would give his life to protect the secrets of Bane's "Chamber of Meditation." In truth, it was a filthy place, but it served its purpose well.

Bane had been careful to hide certain facts from his worshipers; the Black Lord feared that if they knew about his human limitations, his need for sleep and nutrients, their worship might not be so fervent and their willingness to sacrifice themselves to his cause might be impaired. So Bane had Blackthorne bring all his food and drink to him through a secret tunnel, and whenever the Black Lord had to sleep, he did so in the chamber's small bed, with his emissary on guard by his side.

Piled up in the corners of this room were arcane texts that Bane had spent every available moment pouring over. Upon a nearby table lay a collection of sharp, tiny blades that looked like the tools of a sculptor. Bane had used these to perform horrible experiments upon the flesh of a handful of his followers, staring for hours at a time at the flow of blood he had caused, listening intently to the cries of agony from the weaker of his subjects. Blackthorne knew these studies were important to his lord, but he did not know why. Still, Bane was his god, and Blackthorne knew enough not to question the motives of a deity. After a time, Bane had grown tired of the experiments, as if they had not yielded the results he had desired. But the blades had been left in plain sight, a reminder that he had not yet found the answers he sought.

When Bane occupied Castle Kilgrave, the chamber had been empty, but now a swirling vortex came into being, and the Black Lord fell from the rip in space to the hard floor, his breathing shallow, tears dripping from his eyes. He attempted to remember even the simplest of spells, something to levitate his shattered form from the floor to the hard mattress of the bed that sat just out of reach, but his efforts were futile. Then Blackthorne appeared out of the vortex and dragged Bane toward the bed. The emissary grunted as he lifted the Black Lord's avatar and placed him on the bed.

"There, my lord. You will rest. You will heal."

Bane was comforted by the voice of his faithful emissary. Blackthorne had saved him. He had seen Bane weakened, near the point of death, and still he came. It made no sense to the Black Lord. Had their positions been reversed, he would have allowed the emissary to perish rather than put himself at risk.

Perhaps he feels indebted to me for the life of his friend, Knightsbridge, Bane thought. That must be the reason for his service. Now that he's paid the debt, though, I suppose I'll have to watch my back with him.

Bane saw a pool of his blood on the floor: crimson, with amber streaks floating through it. Though one of his lungs was ruptured and he should not have tried to speak, the god gasped as he reached out and touched the scarlet pool.

"My blood," Bane cried. "My blood!"

"You will be well, lord," Blackthorne said. "You can grant healing magics to your clerics. Use those same magics to heal yourself."

Bane did as Blackthorne urged, but he knew that the healing process would be slow and painful. He tried to take his mind from the discomfort by concentrating on the memories of his rescue from Castle Kilgrave. Blackthorne's magic had been strong enough to bring the mage to the castle, and to teleport Bane and himself away. But they had only escaped as far as the colonnade beyond the castle.

Bane had watched as Mystra took the pendant from the dark-haired magic-user. Then, an instant later, the Goddess of Magic was challenging Helm, both gods standing upon a Celestial Stairway.

The Tablets of Fate! Helm asked for the tablets!

Bane watched in complete horror as Helm destroyed the Goddess of Magic. He witnessed the last vestige of Mystra's essence approach the magic-user and heard the warning of the goddess as the pendant was returned to the dark-haired human. Incredible magics had been released during Mystra's battle with Helm, and Bane had seized upon them to finish the task Blackthorne had started, and gated them back to Zhentil Keep.

Bane laughed when he thought that he never would have used the stairway in Shadowdale as part of his plans had it not been for Mystra's warning. If she had accepted her fate quietly, the events she was so worried about might never have been set into motion. So as Bane lay upon his bed, seeking to recover from the grievous injuries inflicted on him by Mystra; he began to make plans, until finally, he settled into a deep, healing trance.

*   *   *   *   *

The sky was a deep lavender, with streaks of royal blue and gold. The clouds were still black, reflecting the dead, charred earth below them, and the huge pillars had become trees with wilting stone branches that snaked across the ground for miles. The mantle of the earth was slick as glass in places, torn apart and filled with debris in others. The red rivers were cooling, becoming solid. Ice no longer fell from above.

The walls of the prismatic sphere that enshrouded the adventurers and their mounts vanished as Midnight rescinded the spell. Touching the blue-white star pendant that once again hung from her neck, Midnight found that there were no signs of the powers that had once resided in the item. Now it was merely a symbol of the strange, apocalyptic encounter between Midnight and her goddess.

Midnight climbed upon her horse and surveyed the shattered countryside. "Mystra asked me to go to Shadowdale to contact Elminster the sage. I don't expect any of you to go along, but if you're coming, we're leaving right now."

Kelemvor dropped the sack of gold he was loading onto his horse. "What?" he screamed. "And when did the goddess tell you this? We never heard it."

"I expect you to understand least of all, Kel, but I have to go." Midnight turned to Adon. "Are you coming?"

The cleric looked from the magic-user to Kelemvor to Cyric, but no one said a word. Adon mounted his horse and moved to Midnight's side. "You are truly blessed to be given a mission like this. Thank you for asking me to aid you. I will most certainly accompany you."

Cyric laughed as he finished packing the party's supplies and grabbed the reigns of the packhorses. "There isn't much left for me here. I might as well go with you. Coming, Kel?"

Kelemvor stood by his horse, his mouth hanging open with shock. "You're all going off to follow a fever dream," he said. "You're making a terrible mistake!"

"Follow us if you will," Midnight said, then turned from Kelemvor and rode off, Adon and Cyric trailing behind her.

The way was treacherous and unpredictable, and by the time the trio had begun to make headway on their journey toward the mountains in the far distance, the unmistakable sound of Kelemvor's mount approaching grew louder, until the fighter caught up to Midnight. No one spoke for a mile or so.

"We haven't even split our shares of the booty," Kelemvor said at last.

"I see," Midnight said, a slight smile playing across her face. "Quite so. I am in your debt."

"Aye," Kelemvor said as he reminded her of her words in the castle. "That you are."

As they made their way across the nightmarish landscape left in the wake of Mystra's destruction, the heroes saw that the devastation grew worse. The roads were gone, and huge craters filled with smoking black tar barred their path, forcing them to double back and circle around to pass some areas. But by nightfall, the mountains came into view, and they made camp overlooking Gnoll Pass.

A caravan of merchants with wagons loaded with wares appeared on the road below the adventurers' camp. The caravan was heavily guarded, and when Adon sprang from cover and attempted to warn the travelers of what lay ahead, he was met with a volley of arrows. The cleric leaped to the ground.

The caravan passed, and soon faded from view. Adon returned to the campsite only to find a roaring fire and Midnight preparing something that appeared to be meat, but smelled quite awful. She seemed intent on the task before her, ordering Kelemvor to turn the meats at certain times as she sliced vegetables with her dagger.

The meal was not turning out well, and it seemed that the party would go hungry that night when Cyric held up a small pouch he had found with Mystra's gifts and motioned for quiet. He reached into the bag and pulled out entire loaves of sweetbread, armloads of dried meats, tankards of ale, blocks of cheese, and more. And yet the pouch seemed empty at all times, even as more food was taken from it.

"We won't hunger or thirst again!" Kelemvor said as he drank his fill of the mead before him.

Later, as they ate a meal taken from the pouch, Kelemvor felt a tightness in the pit of his stomach. The food was dreadful, and he seriously questioned the wisdom of eating any food taken from a magical source during this time of instability in the art. The heroes finished their meal without conversation, but the looks on their faces conveyed their thoughts quite well. Then Midnight broke the silence in the camp with a wish that Adon's healing spells would return at the earliest opportunity to settle their upset stomachs. The comment met with a hearty round of approval from both Kelemvor and Cyric.

As the meal was ended, Kelemvor and Adon stopped to examine the gifts that Mystra had given them, while across the camp, Midnight was helping Cyric clean up after their meal.

"Will you ride all the way to Shadowdale with me?" the magic-user asked Cyric as they gathered the leftovers.

Cyric hesitated.

"We have supplies, healthy mounts, and enough gold to make us wealthy for the rest of our lives," Midnight said. "Why not come along?"

Cyric struggled with his words. "I was born in Zhentil Keep, and when I left, I vowed never to return. Shadowdale is far too close for my liking." He paused and looked at the magic-user. "Still, my path seems to lead in that direction, no matter how much I desire it to be otherwise."

"I wouldn't want you to do something you didn't want to," Midnight said. "The decision is your own."

Cyric let out a deep breath. "Then I will go. Perhaps from Shadowdale I'll buy a boat and travel the Ashaba River for a time. It would be peaceful, I think."

Midnight smiled and nodded. "You've earned the chance to rest, Cyric. You have also earned my gratitude."

The magic-user heard noises from the other side of the campsite, where Kelemvor and Adon were still taking an inventory of Mystra's gifts. Adon had promised to keep Kelemvor honest, which met with a laugh and a powerful slap on the back from the fighter.

Midnight and Cyric continued their conversations about far-away lands, exchanging knowledge of customs, rituals, and languages. They discussed their past adventures, though Midnight spoke more on this subject than Cyric.

"Mystra," he said at last. "Your goddess . . ."

Midnight wiped her dagger clean and returned it to its sheath. "What of her?"

Cyric seemed surprised by Midnight's response. "She's dead, isn't she?"

"Perhaps," Midnight said. She thought about it for a moment, then went back to the small pit Cyric helped her dig to bury their refuse. "I'm not a child, not like poor Adon. I am saddened by Mystra's passing, but there are other gods to give thanks to, should the need arise."

"You don't need to hold back with me—"

Midnight stood up. "Finish this," the magic-user said as she gestured to the pit and walked off. Cyric watched her back as she left, then turned to the job before him. He remembered looking up at the warring gods and the childish glee that filled him as their blood was spilled. Ashamed of his reaction to Mystra's death, Cyric then turned his thoughts aside and concentrated on cleaning up.

Down the path, away from the campfire and Cyric, Midnight felt a coldness that had nothing to do with the thin mountain air. There's no point in grieving over Caitlan's and Mystra's passing, Midnight thought. She silently cursed Cyric for mentioning the goddess and scolded herself. There was no malice in the man that she could judge, only a lifetime of hardship that made him uncomfortable with any form of communication except the exact science of words.

Kelemvor, on the other hand, was Cyric's opposite in this regard. His actions and his unspoken declarations excited Midnight. Only when he tried to hide his feelings behind his curtain of ill-conceived and ill-timed banter did he assume the appearance of an infuriating lummox, betraying his many strengths. Perhaps they had a future together.

Only time would tell.

She approached Kelemvor and Adon, and the two were still bickering.

"We split it up equal!" Kelemvor snarled.

"But this is equal! You, me, Midnight, Cyric, and Sune, without whom—"

"You're not going to start about Sune again!"

"But—"

"Four ways," Midnight said coolly, and both men turned. "Do what you like with your share, Adon. Give it to your church if you will."

Adon's shoulders slumped. "I wasn't being greedy. . . ."

Kelemvor seemed ready to question this.

"Perhaps you need some rest," Midnight said, and the young cleric nodded.

"Aye, perhaps this is so."

Adon walked away, the flickering light of his torch showing him the trail that led to the campfire beyond. Sliding on one of the rocks, then righting himself, Adon mumbled something else about Sune and was gone.

"How do you feel?" Midnight asked. "Were the tender

mercies of this woman's cooking to your fancy?"

"Shall I speak plainly?" Kelemvor said.

Midnight smiled. "Perhaps not."

"Then I feel fit to carve a kingdom from these rocks."

She nodded. "I feel that way myself." She motioned to the riches before them. "Shall we?"

"Aye. It's always a pleasure to work with a keen mind and a level head when it comes to such matters."

Midnight stared at him, but he did not take his gaze from the treasure. Before them the gold lay in piles on the stump of a huge tree. There were rubies, bits of jewelry, and a single, strange artifact that Midnight bent low to examine. She cried out in joy, picked up the magical item, and grinned at Kelemvor.

"We *will* be splitting this five ways it seems!"

Kelemvor sat back. "What do you mean?"

"This is a harp of Myth Drannor. Elminster is a known collector of these. If all else fails, we may use it to gain his audience."

Kelemvor thought about it. "But what's it worth?"

Midnight refused to be discouraged. "We won't know until someone makes an offer, now will we?"

"Oh. Aye, good thinking."

"Each of the harps is said to possess magical properties," Midnight said as she handled the object. The harp was aged, although it had once been a thing of shining beauty. The finely wrought ivory and gold inlays had been realized by a true artisan, and the dark red wood reflected the fire from the torches as if it still retained its original polish. Midnight plucked at the strings without skill, and the sound that issued forth was a strange, discordant flow of reverberating notes that grew louder and caused Kelemvor's armor to shake as if an unseen force was attacking him.

"MID—"

Suddenly each and every tiny clasp that held it in place popped open, and Kelemvor's armor fell to the ground.

"—NIGHT!"

Kelemvor sat, covered in nothing but a chain mail tunic, his armor spread around him in a heap. Midnight's mouth was open wide as she worked her jaws soundlessly, then she fell over in a fit of laughter.

"See here!" Kelemvor frowned.

"Please!" Midnight said, discouragingly.

"No, I meant. . . ." The fighter looked down at the armor and sighed.

Midnight sat up and took a deep breath. "This must be Methild's Harp. It is, as I remember, known to part all webs, open all locks, break all bonds . . . all of that."

"I see," Kelemvor said, his mild agitation giving way to Midnight's infectious grin. "Perhaps *now* is the time for the reward we discussed. What say you?"

Midnight stood up and backed off. "I think not," she said, her heart suddenly pounding like a trip hammer.

Midnight turned around. She heard Kelemvor stand and felt his hand touch her shoulder. The mage bit her lip as she stared at the torch in front of them. His other hand gently encircled her waist and she trembled, fighting her own desire.

"We're only talking about a kiss," he said. "One kiss. Where is the harm in that?"

The mage leaned back into Kelemvor's arms. He brushed the hair away from her neck as he blew gently upon her tingling flesh and tightened his hold around her waist. Midnight's hand covered his.

"You promised you would tell me . . . ," she said.

"Tell you what?"

"You were stricken in the castle. You made me swear to give you a reward to carry on. It made no sense."

"It made sense," Kelemvor said, slipping away behind her. "But some things *must* be kept secret."

Midnight turned. "Why? Tell me that much, at least."

Kelemvor was backing into the shadows. "Perhaps I should release you from your pledge. The consequences would be suffered only by me. You do not need to concern yourself. Perhaps it would be—"

Midnight didn't know if it was a trick of the light, or if Kelemvor's flesh really was turning darker, his skin seeming to ripple beneath the mail.

"—better," the fighter said, his voice low and guttural. Kelemvor's entire body began to quake, and it seemed as if he were about to double over in pain.

"No!"

Midnight ran toward him, placed her hands on either side of his face, and brought her lips to his. His eyebrows had seemed thicker, his hair wild and dark, as if the gray were vanishing, and his piercing green eyes were like emerald flames. As they kissed, his body seemed to relax and he pulled away, as if he were about to speak.

She studied his face. It was as she had always remembered it. "Don't talk," she said. "We need not talk."

She kissed him again, and this time he took control of the kiss, his iron grip pressing her to him.

Unnoticed by either Kelemvor or Midnight, Cyric approached soundlessly. He watched as they kissed again and Kelemvor lifted the mage from her feet. Midnight had her arms around the fighter's neck as he gently lowered her to a bed of gold pieces. She began to laugh and tug at the clasps of her clothing.

Cyric retraced his steps, his head hung low, a slow tide of anger rising within him as the laughter of the couple followed him, taunting him even as he made his way to the campfire and ordered Adon to go to sleep.

"I will take the watch," Cyric said and stared at the flames.

* * * * *

After his watch, Cyric lay down to get some rest, but he dreamed he was once again in the back alleys of Zhentil Keep. This time he was only a child, and a faceless couple led him through the streets, taking offers from passers-by as they attempted to auction him off to anyone with enough money.

Cyric woke with a start, and when he tried to remember the dream, he could not. He lay awake for a few moments, thinking that there was a time when his dreams had been his only form of escape. But that was a long time ago, and for now, he was safe. He rolled over and fell into a deep, restful slumber.

Adon paced nervously, anxious to leave the wilderness. Midnight suggested he use the time to give thanks to Sune.

The cleric stopped, wide-eyed, muttered "of course," and found a spot to make a small shrine. Midnight and Kelemvor did not speak. They simply lay against a great black boulder, their arms around one another, watching the flames of a fire they had started. Midnight leaned close and kissed the fighter. The gesture seemed uncomfortable and strange, although only a few hours before it had seemed perfectly natural.

The heroes woke Cyric at the first light of morning and led their horses from the mountain. By highsun they had established a healthy pace, although their morning repast— taken from the pouch—left each the gift of a bitter taste and an upset stomach.

The road was damaged in places, and huge silver fish with sharp teeth leaped from one of the lava pits the adventurers encountered. At times the sun appeared to be in the wrong position, and the heroes feared they were traveling in circles again, but they went on, and soon the skies returned to normal.

As they made their way across the twisted land, the adventurers encountered many strange things. Huge boulders, carved to resemble the faces of frogs by the bizarre forces that had been unleashed during Mystra's fight with Helm, alternately cursed and praised the travelers, then told them risque jokes that they laughed at, but did not slow down for.

Farther down the road, a war seemed to be in progress between opposing hills, as boulders and bits of rock were tossed back and forth, striking thunderous blows. The hostilities ceased as the travelers approached and resumed once they had passed. As the party moved farther from the site of Mystra's death, the strange occurrences became less and less, and the heroes relaxed just a bit.

They stopped and made camp for the night in a clearing at the foot of a huge mountain that seemed unaffected by the chaos Mystra's passing had brought about. Cyric was shocked to find the self-replenishing pouch of food and drink completely empty. When he reached inside, he felt the pull of something cold and damp that licked at his hand until he withdrew it in haste and tossed the pouch away.

They were forced to rely on the separate food that was left, but the heroes felt confident these would be enough for the long journey ahead. When Midnight and Cyric prepared the meal, however, the meat seemed to be spoiling, the breads becoming stale, and the fruits gone to rotting. They ate what they could and drank heavily of the mead and ale. But that, too, seemed to have lost its taste, going down more like bitter water than nectar.

Cyric was very quiet. Only when a topic that truly fascinated him arose did he bring his opinions to bear, and then he was vehement in his assertions. Then Cyric would lapse into one of his meditative silences, staring at the flames of the campfire as night wrapped itself around the weary travelers.

That night, Midnight went to Kelemvor, and he took her in his arms without uttering a word. Afterward, she watched him as he slept, excited by the quiet rhythms of his body. Midnight smiled; there was such strength and ferocity in his movements when they touched, such wonderful passion, that she wondered why she doubted her feelings for the man. She was amazed that he had never married, one of the few facts she was able to draw from him as they lay side by side just before sleep took hold of the fighter.

Midnight quietly dressed and made her way to Adon, who had taken first watch. She found the cleric trying to hold a small mirror between his bare feet, moving the angle slightly as he plucked at any unseemly facial hairs with one of Cyric's daggers. Then he tended to his hair, running a silver comb through it as he quietly counted off one hundred strokes. Midnight relieved him of the watch, and he carefully made his bunk, then settled into a deep sleep with a contented smile. Once during her watch, Midnight heard Adon whisper, "No, my dear, of course I'm not shocked," then the voice faded.

When Midnight attempted to rouse Kelemvor to relieve her of the watch, the fighter swatted at her playfully and attempted to drag her back to his bed. "Tend to your duty," she told him as he rose, stretching his arms wide. He turned, grinned, then walked away before he could say something that would have caused Midnight to stone him on the spot.

Just before morning, Kelemvor became hungry. The packhorses had been roped nearby, and he decided not to wait until morningfeast. He left the campfire and made his way to the horses and supplies. Even in the dim light of dawn, he could see that the horses were dead. Beyond the packhorses, the mounts that had been provided by Mystra for Cyric and Adon were on their sides, trembling.

Kelemvor called out to the others, bringing them to his side in moments. Cyric fetched a torch, lighting it in the flames of the campfire. They found no reason for the condition of the animals. There were no marks upon the beasts, nor tracks that would indicate a wild animal or saboteur in their midst.

When they checked their provisions, the heroes found that their food had become completely foul. The meats bubbled with green, cancerous growths. Strange, black insects crawled from the fruits. The breads were stale and moldy. The ales and meads had evaporated. Only the water they had taken from the colonnade outside Castle Kilgrave was unaffected.

Kelemvor searched through the pouches containing their gold and treasures and let out a cry as he found nothing but yellow and black ash. The harp of Myth Drannor had been rotted through, and it broke apart as Midnight tried to pick it up. She found a bag that had once contained diamonds. Now it held only their dust. The mage set it aside for use as spell components.

"No," Kelemvor said softly, pulling away from Midnight's comforting hand as she attempted to console him. He glared at her. "Now all we have is your miserable quest!"

"Kel, don't—"

"It's all been for nothing!" he screamed as he turned his back on the magic-user.

Adon moved forward. "What will we eat?"

Kelemvor looked over his shoulder. His eyes and teeth seemed unusually bright, as if they were catching the first rays of sun and holding them. His skin seemed darker. "I'll find something," Kelemvor said. "I'll be the provider for us all."

Cyric offered to help, but Kelemvor waved him away as he ran toward the mountains. "At least take the bow!" Cyric called, but Kelemvor ignored him, becoming a dark blur against the shadow-filled foothills.

"'The gods giveth, the gods taketh away,'" Adon said philosophically, shrugging.

Cyric let out a bitter little laugh. "Your gods—"

Midnight raised her hand, and Cyric didn't finish his sentence. "Take what you will from your mounts," the mage said. "Then we should make them as comfortable as possible until the end."

"Is there nothing we can do?" Adon said, taking pity on the suffering animals.

"There is one thing," Cyric said, and drew his blade.

Midnight exhaled a ragged breath and nodded. Cyric offered to wait until after Midnight and Adon were out of view of the dying mounts, but they each agreed to remain and offer some degree of comfort and compassion to the animals as Cyric mercifully ended their pain.

*   *   *   *   *

Hours passed, and Kelemvor did not return. Finally, Adon volunteered to look for the fighter.

Adon found deep shadows and tiny, unseen creatures that made odd sounds. The cleric wondered if Kelemvor had been injured, or if perhaps he had deserted them. The fighter would have taken his mount, Adon reminded himself, though the thought brought little comfort as the cleric allowed himself to be swallowed up by the darkness.

Something scampered by his boot, and Adon was pleasantly surprised to see a soft, gray squirrel suddenly stop, look at him, then bolt as the cleric crouched down to look into its deep, blue eyes. He moved through a thicket of trees, forcing branches away carefully so that his face would not be scratched. As he climbed higher, Adon found a clearly marked trail before him.

Kelemvor had come this way.

Adon was congratulating himself for finding the trail when he stumbled over Kelemvor's breastplate. The armor was covered with blood. Adon cautiously untied his war hammer from his belt.

Farther up the trail, the cleric found the rest of Kelemvor's armor, bloody like the breastplate. He considered Kelemvor's fighting prowess, and wondered what manner of beast could have brought the fighter down.

There was movement in the trees. Adon caught a glimpse of black fur and snarling teeth, and he bit back a call for help, afraid he would reveal his position. The cleric remained still for a few minutes, then heard a roar from behind him.

Adon didn't bother to look back as he ran, following the trail of broken branches and disturbed patches of earth, and he didn't look down long enough to realize that the tracks leading away from the armor had begun as the imprints of human feet and become the pawprints of some huge animal.

The cleric didn't know how far he had run when he broke through a web of branches and the earth suddenly disappeared from beneath his feet, sending him tumbling through the air. An instant later his body made a splash as he plunged into water.

Rising to the surface of the water, Adon shook the mire from his hair and surveyed the area. A swamp? he thought. Here? This is madness!

Madness or no, the fact remained that Adon found himself paddling to the marshy shore of a beautiful, ghostly land, lit by a soft, bluish white glow. The sunlight was absorbed by elegant strands of Spanish moss that hung from the tall black cypress trees and glowed to reveal the wiry intricacies of its design. The moss seemed to be straining as it reached downward, an occasional strand gently touching the surface of the swamp. Huge lotus pads floated toward Adon, and as he climbed to the shore, he saw a beautiful butterfly with orange and silver wings burst from its cocoon before his eyes. A lone heron started as it watched Adon approach, then fled, making tiny splashing sounds as its feet broke the water.

Adon rose from the bog, disgusted at the mess he had made of his fine clothing. Suddenly he froze as he heard a roar and the sounds of some beast crashing through the forest above him. But, the sounds stopped as suddenly as they had begun, and Adon looked around in vain for someplace to hide. Clusters of bright yellow and red leaves capped the spindly gray trees close by, but little cover was afforded the cleric as he slowly made his way up the hill toward the tiny clearing from which he had fallen.

As he climbed, Adon found his war hammer, where it had landed when his fall jolted it from his grasp. Good, he thought. At least I'll go down fighting.

Like Kelemvor.

The creature in the woods howled once more, and Adon broke into a run, reminding himself not to scream for help with every passing step. Finally, the clearing rose up before him, but a huge black shape padded back and forth, barring the way.

Adon stopped.

It was a panther, and at its feet lay a deer, savaged almost beyond recognition. How very natural, the cleric thought. And here I thought it was some horrible troll.

The panther's head swung back and forth, as if it were dazed. Adon prayed to Sune that the beast would be content with its feast, and just before he took his first step backward, the beast began to shudder. It threw back its head, and Adon caught a glimpse of its shining green eyes as the beast roared in pain, a human hand bursting from its throat.

Adon dropped his hammer. It fell to the earth and landed with a thud. The creature didn't notice. A second gore-drenched hand burst from the flank of the beast, and there was a sickening sound as the rib cage exploded and Kelemvor's head emerged from the opening. One of the beast's legs tore open, and a pale, shriveled, child-sized leg emerged. The leg grew until it was the proper length for a man's limb, and its twisted foot straightened, its bones crackling as they popped into place.

A second leg emerged, repeating the process, as the thing that was somehow becoming Kelemvor sprang from the shell of the beast. The fighter gave an exhausted grunt as he fell to the ground, a sleek network of hair already forming on his naked and smooth flesh.

Adon felt himself bending low to retrieve his hammer. He moved forward, shuddering as he approached the fighter. "Kelemvor?" he said, but the fighter's eyes, wide and staring, registered nothing. Kelemvor's breathing was shallow, and a current ran beneath his skin as blood vessels burst and his flesh aged to it proper years.

"Kelemvor," Adon said again, and issued a blessing over the man, then passed through the clearing without looking back. He found the trail without difficulty, and soon he was moving down through the thicket of trees until he reached the campsite. Midnight and Cyric were waiting.

"Did you find him?" Midnight asked.

Adon shook his head. "I wouldn't worry," he said. "Game and solitude are plentiful in the valley over the first ridge. I'm sure he has found both. He will return soon."

Adon told them of the odd swamp nature had created over the ridge, and soon the sounds of a man awkwardly making his way through the brush drifted to their ears. Midnight and Cyric met Kelemvor at the base of the foothills. The blood covering his armor looked to have come from the bloodied deer swung over his shoulder. Cyric helped the fighter with his freshly slain burden. They butchered the animal and quickly prepared it over a small fire.

Adon watched the fighter, who seemed oblivious to everything except the meal before him. Kelemvor looked up sharply at one point, catching the cleric's gaze. "What? Did you forget to bless the meal?" Kelemvor asked bitterly.

"No," Adon said. "I was—" he waved his hand in the air. "—lost in thought."

Kelemvor nodded and returned to the feast. When they were done, Adon and Cyric went to work saving what meat they could from the animal, wrapping it tightly for their dinner.

"I must speak with you," Kelemvor said, and Midnight nodded, following him as they made their way to the road. Midnight had already sensed his intent, and was not surprised when Kelemvor made his request. "There must be a reward, or I cannot go with you."

Midnight's frustration was evident. "Kel, this makes no sense! At some point you're going to have to tell me what this is all about!"

Kelemvor said nothing.

Midnight sighed. "What shall I ply you with this time, Kel, more of the same?"

Kelemvor hung his head. "It must be different every time."

"What else can I give you?" Midnight put her hand up to the fighter's cheek.

Kelemvor grabbed Midnight's hand roughly, forcing it away from him as he broke from her embrace. "It is not what I desire that matters, only what you are willing to give! The reward must be something of value to you, but worth what I must go through to earn it."

Midnight could barely hold back her anger. "What we have together is of value to me."

Kelemvor nodded slowly as he turned to face her. "Aye. And to me."

Midnight moved forward, stopping before she came close enough to touch the fighter. "Please tell me what's wrong. I can help you—"

"No one can help me!"

Midnight looked at Kelemvor. The same violent desperation she had seen in his eyes at Castle Kilgrave was there now. "I have conditions," Midnight said.

"Name them."

"You will ride with us. You will defend Cyric, Adon, and me from attack. You will help in the preparation of meals and setting up camp. You will impart any information you have that is relative to our safety and well being, even if it is only your opinion." Midnight drew a breath. "And you will follow any direct orders I give you."

"My reward?" Kelemvor said.

"My *true name*. I will tell you my *true name* after we have spoken to Elminster of Shadowdale."

Kelemvor nodded. "It will suffice."

The adventurers traveled the rest of the day, returning to their earlier practice of sharing two mounts. That night, after they set up camp and feasted, Midnight did not go to Kelemvor. Instead, she sat beside Cyric, keeping him company on the watch. They spoke of the places they had seen, with neither ever telling what they had done in those strange lands.

Soon, though, Midnight grew tired and left Cyric, settling into a deep, restful sleep that was shattered by an image of a horrible black beast with glowing green eyes and a slavering, fanged mouth. She woke with a start, and for a moment she thought she saw tiny blue-white fires playing over the surface of the amulet. But that was impossible. Mystra's power had been returned to the goddess, and the goddess had been slain.

The magic-user heard movement and reached for her knife. Kelemvor stood above her.

"Time for your watch," he said and vanished into the night.

As Midnight sat by the fire, she watched the darkness for signs of Kelemvor, but there were none. A few feet away from her, Cyric tossed and turned in his sleep, plagued by some personal nightmare.

Adon found he could not sleep at all. He was disturbed by the secret he had inadvertently uncovered. Kelemvor seemed to have no memory of Adon's presence during his metamorphosis from panther to human. Or was Kelemvor merely pretending not to remember? Adon wanted desperately to confide in someone about what he had seen, but he felt honor-bound as a cleric to respect the privacy of the fighter. It seemed clear that he should let Kelemvor's secret remain just that until the fighter either chose to confide in his comrades or became a threat to the party due to his affliction.

Adon stared into the night and prayed that he had made the right decision.

* * * * *

Tempus Blackthorne lit a torch before he entered the tunnel, then he wrestled with the supplies he had purchased. The tunnel had been expertly constructed. The walls and ceiling were perfectly cylindrical, and the floor was a long two-foot wide plank. The walls had been polished then sealed with a substance that resembled marble when it dried. Blackthorne still regretted killing the craftsmen and fabricating the story of their accidental death. He wondered if anyone believed him.

In the chamber above, Bane was bellowing incoherently in a tongue Blackthorne had never heard before. The emissary listened as he climbed the stone steps carefully and practiced the routine he had helped Lord Bane install as a fail-safe against intruders: right foot on the first step, left on the third. Right foot joining left on the third step. Left up one, right up two, then retracing the steps in reverse, and returning upward once more in a different sequence. Any who varied from this routine would be sliced to ribbons by the traps Bane had created.

Blackthorne teetered on one foot as he struggled to keep hold of the packages. He touched the lever on the wall, pulling it back three clicks, forward nine, back two. The wall before him vanished, and Blackthorne stepped through into Bane's secret chamber.

The mage turned away from the sight of Bane's dark, bubbling flesh and the froth of blood at his mouth. There was a new hole in the wall beside the Black Lord, and Blackthorne saw that one of the restraints had been torn from the wall. The bed frame had been shattered long ago, and the mattress torn to ribbons. Bane screamed, his body convulsing as the fit grew worse.

Blackthorne was attempting to devise a new excuse for the Black Lord's absence when the noises behind him abruptly ceased. He turned and saw that Bane was absolutely still. As the emissary moved close to his god, he feared that Bane's heart had stopped. There was an odor of death in the room.

"Lord Bane," Blackthorne called, and Bane's eyes shot open. A taloned hand moved toward Blackthorne's throat, but the emissary fell back and out of the way of the blow, saving himself. Bane sat up slowly.

"How long?" Bane said simply.

"I am pleased to see you well!" Blackthorne fell to his knees.

Bane tore the remaining restraints from the wall and

snapped the bonds at his ankles and wrists. "I asked you a question."

Blackthorne told Bane everything about the dark times after Bane had been rescued from Castle Kilgrave. The Black Lord sat on the floor, leaning against the wall as he listened, nodding occasionally.

"I see my wounds have healed," Bane said.

Blackthorne smiled enthusiastically.

"My physical wounds, anyway. There is always the matter of my pride."

Blackthorne's smile faded.

"Aye. My pathetic *human* pride . . ." Bane held up his talons before his eyes. "But I am not human," he said, and looked to Blackthorne. "I am a god."

Blackthorne nodded, slowly.

"Now help me dress," Bane said, and Blackthorne rushed forward. As they struggled with Bane's black armor, the god inquired about specific followers and the progress that had been made on his temple.

"The humans that came to Mystra's rescue in Castle Kilgrave," Bane said at last. "What of them?"

Blackthorne shook his head. "I do not know."

One of the ruby red eyes of Bane's gauntlet opened wide, and the Black Lord grimaced. Memories of Mystra's final moments and of her warning to the dark-haired magic-user filled the mind of the dark god.

"We will find them," he said. "They will journey to Shadowdale, to seek out the assistance of the mage, Elminster."

"You wish them detained?" Blackthorne said.

Bane looked up, startled. "I wish them dead." Bane's attentions returned to the gauntlet. "Then I want the pendant from the woman brought to me. Now leave. I will call for you when I am ready." The emissary nodded and left the chamber.

The Black Lord fell back against the wall, his body trembling. He was very weak. Bane corrected himself. The body had been weakened. Bane, the god, was immortal and immune to such petty concerns, despite his situation. Bane reveled in his first moments of true clarity since awakening from his healing sleep, then he considered his options.

Helm had asked Mystra if she bore the Tablets of Fate. When she offered the identities of the thieves instead of the actual tablets, Helm destroyed her. The secret he shared with Lord Myrkul was still safe.

"You are not omniscient after all, Lord Ao," Bane whispered. "The loss of the tablets has made you weak, as Myrkul and I suspected it would."

Bane realized he had said these words aloud in an empty room and felt a coldness in his essence. There were still a few traces of his avatar's humanity to exorcise, but he would accomplish this in time. At least his search for power had not been a strictly human conceit. The quest had begun with the theft of the tablets and would end with the murder of Lord Ao himself.

Yet there were obstacles Bane would have to overcome before he could achieve his final victory.

"Elminster," Bane said softly. "Perhaps we should meet."

In the darkest hours of morning, Bane stood before an assembly of his followers. Only those who had been awarded the highest ranks or privileges were in attendance as Bane sat upon his throne and addressed his followers. He linked the minds of all present so they could share in his fevered dream of incredible power and glory. Without uttering a word, Bane had whipped the humans into a frenzy.

Fzoul Chembryl had the loudest voice and the most intense passion for Bane's cause. Though the God of Strife knew Fzoul had opposed his will in the past, he felt a growing admiration for the handsome, red-haired priest, as Fzoul argued for the eventual dissolution of the Zhentarim—of which Fzoul was second in command—and the reformation of the Black Network under the strict authority of Bane himself. Naturally Fzoul requested to be considered for the position of leader of these forces, but the decision would be Bane's alone, Fzoul cried, and Bane's wisdom was beyond criticism.

The Black Lord smiled. There was nothing like a good war to motivate humans. They would march on Shadowdale, Bane leading the troops personally. In the frenzy of battle, Bane would slip away and dispatch the troublesome Elminster. In the meantime, assassins would be sent to intercept Mystra's magic-user before she could deliver the pendant to the sage of Shadowdale. Another group would be sent to occupy the tiresome Knights of Myth Drannor. Satisfied with the plans, Bane went back to his secret chamber in the rear of the temple.

That night the God of Strife did not dream, and that was good.

🌻 9 🌻

The Ambush

Whenever the bald man attempted to sleep, his dreams would inevitably return to the same shocking nightmare. He would wake almost the instant it began, but then he would see that his dream only reflected reality: his nightmare was only a memory of the widespread destruction he and his men had faced on their journey from Arabel to the place where Castle Kilgrave had once stood.

And somehow the bald man knew that he was now camped near the place that had been the eye of whatever supernatural storm had taken place. The effects had reached almost as far as Arabel, then stopped. The denizens of the walled city were relieved that their home had been spared, although one only had to look from the watchtowers to view the startlingly altered landscape and see how close the city had come to destruction.

The goddess Tymora had suffered an agonizing attack the day the sky had been filled with the odd lights from the north. Then the goddess had gone into a deep shock from which she had not yet risen when the bald man and his Company of Dawn left the walled city in pursuit of Kelemvor and his accomplices. Constant vigils had been held by Tymora's followers, but the goddess merely sat upon her throne, unresponsive to their calls, staring at something beyond the limited range of human senses.

Dismissing the nightmares and memories, the bald man attempted to get back to sleep. In the morning he and his men would set out from the untouched place of beauty they had found, a lovely colonnade that once may have been a shrine to the gods. The cool, sparkling water of the glorious pool had served to refresh his men, but they had not washed away the memories of the vast destruction they had witnessed.

Although he was not a worshiper, the bald man uttered a small prayer to Shar, Goddess of Forgetfulness. Just as it seemed his prayer might be rewarded, a scream sounded in the night. The bald man sprang into action.

"There!" one of his men shouted, pointing at the fair-haired fighter who had been lifted from the ground by his neck. The flesh of the man's assailant appeared to be white as chalk, the moonlight casting an unearthly glow upon the headless creature.

"The statues," another man called. "They live!"

The bald man heard the soft crush of earth behind him and turned to face the statue of two lovers, still connected, the stone flesh of the man's hand and arm bonded to the woman's back. The stone lovers moved as one as they surged forward with a speed the bald man was not prepared for.

There were screams in the night.

*　*　*　*　*

The mountains of Gnoll Pass were visible behind Kelemvor and his companions, but the riders did not look back at them very often. If they had, they would have seen the mountains shimmer against the soft blue of the sky, as if the brave peaks held the consistency of little more than illusion.

The decision to follow the road north and travel on to Tilverton instead of braving the open countryside had been a unanimous one. Even Kelemvor raised no objection to the change in plans, despite his hurry to ride on to Shadowdale and put this job behind him. Before the packhorses died and their food and supplies turned to dust he might have argued, but it was clear now that they had to stop and get new supplies before crossing through the Shadow Gap and moving on to Shadowdale.

Kelemvor and Adon still shared a horse, as did Midnight and Cyric, through most of the journey. After the lack of supplies, this seemed to be the biggest annoyance for the heroes, and soon the tempers of the mounts and their riders were flaring regularly.

The heroes were at the end of a long day in the pale gray expanses of the treacherous Stonelands when they spotted travelers a quarter mile off the road. One moment the area appeared flat and safe, an inviting alternative to the plodding, twisting road before them. But upon approach, the carefully disguised ridges and falls of this area became apparent.

The travelers seemed to have journeyed from the road in an attempt to cut time from their trip, but instead blundered into a gap in the land's surface. Their wagon had been overturned, their horses crushed beneath the weight of the cart. There were bodies lying on the flat, gray lands beside the wagon, and the sobs of a woman were carried by the wind to the ears of the adventurers. Adon was the first to badger Kelemvor as the fighter turned away from the sight.

"There is nothing we can do. The authorities in Tilverton can send someone." Kelemvor said.

"We can't just leave them," Midnight said, shocked at Kelemvor's attitude.

Kelemvor shook his head. "I can."

"That should surprise me," Midnight said. "Yet somehow it doesn't. Does everything have a price for you, Kel?"

Kelemvor glared at the dark-haired magic-user.

"We can't turn our backs on them," Adon said frantically. "Some may be injured and require the attentions of a cleric."

"What good can you do them?" Cyric said sharply. "You can't even heal."

Adon looked down. "I'm aware of that."

Midnight turned to Kelemvor. "What do you say, Kel?"

Kelemvor's eyes were cold. "There is nothing to say. If you wish to indulge in such foolishness, you'll do so without me!" He looked at Midnight. "Unless of course, you wish to *order* me to go."

Midnight looked away from the fighter and turned to Cyric, who shared her horse. The thief nodded and they galloped off in the direction of the fallen travelers.

Adon's pleas fell on deaf ears, until at last Kelemvor leaped from the mount and waved the cleric on.

"Go if you must," Kelemvor said. "I'll wait here."

Adon looked at the angry fighter, a mixture of pity and confusion in his eyes.

"Go, I said!" Kelemvor shouted and slapped the horse, sending it into a frantic race to catch up with Midnight and Cyric.

Midnight's horse covered the distance quickly, but the sobbing woman did not seem to take notice of the approaching riders. As Cyric and Midnight got close to her, they saw that the blood on her pale blue skirt had turned an ugly brown. The woman's bare legs were deeply tanned, and her hands, even as they moved across the body of a fallen man, seemed hard and calloused. Her hair was blond and thickly matted to her face. She cradled the man to her breast, rocking him gently.

"Are you hurt?" Midnight said as she climbed down from her mount and approached the woman. The magic-user realized that the woman before her was younger than she first believed. In fact, she seemed barely old enough to deserve the honor of the wedding ring that graced her hand.

The man had been dressed in tight leather trousers, and the soles of his boots were nearly worn out. He wore a pale blue ruffled shirt, which was covered with a brownish red stain. The magic-user saw no weapons near the dead man.

Even as Adon caught up with the others, Cyric realized there was no wedding ring on the hand of the dead man.

"Turn back!" the thief screamed, and six men suddenly burst from the gray sands surrounding the heroes. The dead man grinned, gave his "wife" a quick kiss, and reached for a broadsword that had been half-buried in the darkened sands beneath him. The woman withdrew a pair of daggers from under her legs. She gracefully leaped to her feet and settled into a slight crouch as she joined the others who moved about their prey in an ever-tightening circle.

Standing by the road, Kelemvor cursed as he saw the trap sprung. *Midnight's conditions say I must defend them,* the fighter realized, and he rushed toward the figures in the distance. Just as his sword was leaving its sheath, though, something rushed past the fighter's ear. There was a cold breeze, and the object passed with a hiss. Kelemvor saw a steel-tipped arrow sail by him and end its flight in the sands.

Behind him, Kelemvor heard the sound of men shouting. He focused past their angry voices and concentrated on the tiny sound of bowstrings being drawn tight, then released. The fighter turned and fell to his knees, his sword flashing as it cut through two of the three arrows that would have surely brought him down.

Kelemvor faced three archers who had risen from the filthy sands at the other side of the road. Already they were notching another round of arrows. The sound of steel striking steel rang out in the distance behind him, and Kelemvor knew that Midnight, Cyric, and Adon were fighting for their lives, too.

"We have nothing!" Kelemvor shouted as the archers loosed their volley, and he rolled to avoid the missiles. The sight of a single arrow passing just over his face revealed the hopelessness of the situation to the fighter. No matter where he turned, one of the three archers would eventually anticipate his movements. His armor offered little protection against the archers' longbows, and the added vulnerability of his unprotected head presented a target the highly skilled bowmen already sought.

The archers scrambled forward, crossing the road. They dug in at new, closer positions. Then they tried a new tactic: rotating their assault. In moments Kelemvor faced a constant volley of arrows as the third archer released his arrow even as the first took aim.

Across the field of stone and sand, by the overturned wagon, the fighting had become desperate. Midnight caught a glimpse of a crossbow trained on Cyric's back. Her first thought was to throw a spell to save the thief, but there was no time to cast and there was no way of knowing if her spell would fail or succeed. She dropped to a crouch, sending one of her daggers into the throat of the assailant. The steel bolt went wild as it was loosed and flew harmlessly over Cyric's head.

Unaware of the attempt made against him by the man with the crossbow, Cyric fought on against the leader of the brigands. His hand axe had proven to be an awkward defense against his opponent's broadsword, so the thief feinted to the left to draw the man in close, hoping to disarm him. But the swordsman wasn't taken in by the ruse, and his blade came within inches of Cyric's throat. The thief rolled and drew first blood as his axe bit deeply into the brigand's ankle, nearly severing his foot. The swordsman fell, his blade thrust out to gut Cyric, but the dark, lean man rolled out of the way of the blade and brought his axe up with all his strength. The brigand made no sound as the axe was buried in his throat.

Cyric removed his bloodied axe from the swordsman, and a sharp, biting pain flushed through his system as one of the blades of the brigand's "wife" hit home.

At the periphery of the circle formed around Midnight and Cyric, Adon was dragged from Kelemvor's mount. His war hammer broke free of the bonds that held it at his side and fell to the ground as Adon fell beside it. He snatched up the weapon as a filthy boot moved to cover his hand. Adon grasped the boot and pulled hard. A moment later the owner of the boot fell to the ground, and Adon clubbed him with the hammer. Then Adon sprang forward, barely avoiding a knife thrust that would have relieved him of a portion of his beautiful, well-combed hair, as well as his scalp. Adon clubbed that attacker, too.

Adon heard movement behind him. He turned and saw a filthy man running toward him with a short sword aimed at his heart. Before the cleric even had time to react, the body of another of the brigands crashed into the man with the short sword, knocking him to the ground. Adon looked up and saw Midnight engaged in a hand-to-hand duel with a burly fighter. The man brought his knee up into Midnight's stomach and clasped his steel-gloved hands together as he brought them high over his head, preparing to crack open the skull of the magic-user with his mighty fists.

Adon remembered his long hours of study, got a running start, and delivered a blow to the small of the man's back that shattered his spine instantly. The brigand fell back, eyes wide, and Adon stepped out of the way. He helped Midnight to her feet, and she stared at him in disbelief.

"A follower of Sune must be trained to protect the gifts his goddess gave so freely!" Adon said and smiled.

Midnight almost laughed, then shoved the cleric out of the way as she released a spell that caused a new assailant to stop dead in his tracks, dropping his weapons. He shook as if something horrible were growing within him, then his eyes rolled back in his head as his flesh darkened and became stone. A single tear ran from his eye.

Midnight froze. It was a child she had struck down, no more than fifteen summers in age. She had only meant to erect a shield to ward off the blow he was about to deliver. How could she have turned him to stone?

The statue exploded, sending bits of dark stone in every direction.

Close enough to hear the explosion, Cyric fell away from the wild-eyed girl as she thrust at him again and again. He felt a warm flow of blood dripping down to his legs from the wound at his side, and the pain became worse as he moved. He fell over the corpse of the swordsman, the soft blue ruffled shirt now stained a bright crimson. The girl's slashes moved closer to his chest, so Cyric took his chance and grabbed the girl's wrist with one hand, her throat with the other.

Only a child, the thief thought, and her free hand raked across his unprotected face, her nails biting into his flesh. Cyric twisted the hand with the dagger until he heard the sound of bones snapping, and pushed the girl away, forcing her against the hard ground. Her skull made a high, cracking sound, and her eyes suddenly glazed over as the fight went out of them. A tiny trickle of blood swam from her mouth, cascading down the length of her neck until it touched the top of her breast.

She was dead.

Something dark and horrible within Cyric rejoiced at the knowledge, but a brighter part of his soul pushed the thoughts away.

Cyric heard a noise beside him and turned. The pain from his wound suddenly flared, and the thief tumbled to the ground, falling upon the corpse of the girl. Although he could not move, he saw Midnight and Adon as they challenged the remaining two members of the band of brigands.

There were less than forty summers in age between the two remaining attackers, so it wasn't surprising when they turned and ran to the other side of the overturned wagon. They barked out commands for their supposedly injured mounts to rise as they pulled the gently laid debris from the flanks of the beasts.

Cyric watched as Midnight scanned the area, her gaze suddenly locking on him. He reached out as Midnight and Adon rushed to his side. A moment later he was staring up at Midnight's face. His head was in her lap, and her hand was gently caressing his chest. The thief's head fell back in relief, and Midnight's hand caressed his brow. Then her expression changed.

"Kel," she said softly, and Cyric realized she was staring toward the road. He turned his head in the direction of the road and watched as Kelemvor was besieged by a small band of archers. Midnight called to Adon, and the cleric took Cyric as the magic-user stood and started to run toward the road.

"Midnight, wait!" Adon shouted. "You'll only get yourself killed!"

Midnight hesitated. She knew Adon was right. Kelemvor was too far away. Even if she had been by his side, her daggers would be useless against arrows. The only way she could save the fighter was with her magic. She thought of the child she had inadvertently slain, images of the exploding stone body etched in her mind.

When Mystra's gifts had crumbled into dust, Midnight had taken a small pouch of diamonds that had been reduced to powder. Reciting the spell to create a wall of force, Midnight reached into the bag and took a pinch of the diamond dust between her fingers. She released the dust at the correct moment, and there was a blinding flash of blue-white light. Midnight was thrown from her feet as a complex pattern of light formed in the air where she had stood. Feeling as if a part of her soul had been wrenched from her, Midnight looked to the road as the pattern of light vanished.

The wall had not appeared.

Midnight threw her head back in frustration. She was just about to loose a scream of rage when something appeared in the sky.

It was a huge rift in the air, a swirling mass, with lights of every color of the spectrum visible within it. The rift appeared in the form of a coin set on its end and thrust at the sky, and as the rift grew, it began to block out the sun.

By the road, Kelemvor stood his ground as the archers closed in. There was a roar in his ears, but he assumed it was an effect of the wounds he had sustained. Two arrows had already gotten past his defenses, but Kelemvor turned a blind eye to the pain that surged up from his right calf and his left arm.

The archers were advancing, ready to finish the fighter off, when suddenly they stopped.

Kelemvor wondered if the brigands had finally run out of shafts as they backed away, pointing at the sky. Two of the archers dropped their weapons just as Kelemvor noticed that his shadow seemed to be deepening. Then a vast, dark veil fell upon the earth, and the archers screamed in a language Kelemvor did not understand and ran in the direction of Arabel.

Kelemvor looked up. The archers, all else, was instantly forgotten. The rift was growing larger now, and Kelemvor stumbled back as something that appeared to be an incredibly huge eye looked out of the vast hole in the sky, then vanished.

Kelemvor turned and looked across the battlefield for Midnight, Cyric, and Adon. Their shapes were hard to distinguish because of the darkness that fell over the entire area, but the fighter could see that two figures were still on their feet. They seemed to be carrying someone.

Adon, Kelemvor thought. The thieves murdered poor, defenseless Adon!

Despite the blood he had lost and the pain he had suffered, Kelemvor ran to the figures in the distance.

Across the field, Cyric, too, had seen the eye. His head had lolled back as Midnight and Adon carried him to the relative safety of the overturned wagon, then set him down.

The earth shuddered.

"Don't leave me," Cyric said.

Midnight looked down at him, confused. She caressed the

side of his face. "No," she said simply.

Then, just before he lost consciousness, he saw a figure approaching from the road through the blinding whirlwinds of sand and dust.

Midnight ran toward the fighter as he struggled across the sand, and with her help, Kelemvor reached the overturned wagon. Just then, a huge part of it was sheared off by the wind. The oak planks creaked horribly, then snapped and sailed off into the air. "We've got to get out of here!" the fighter screamed, but he was barely able to hear his own voice of the whine of the wind.

"Cyric's been wounded. We can't leave him," Midnight cried.

"Cyric!" Kelemvor yelled in surprise, and a wall of dust rushed toward him. The fighter turned his face away from the winds. "Can he be moved?"

"No!" Midnight shouted. "Adon is tending to his wounds as best he can!"

There was a slight hiss as the ground beside the couple turned into vapor. The air beside them crackled with a rim of tiny white stars, and a hole the size of a man tore through the air just as Midnight raised her hands and prepared to release another spell.

An old man exited from the portal, a large staff in his left hand. His face, although lined with wrinkles, held a sharpness that spoke volumes on his barely contained annoyance. Beneath his frown, the man's pure white beard reached down to play against his chest. The man wore a large hat and a simple gray cloak. He looked to Midnight.

"Why have ye summoned me?" he said.

Midnight's eyes widened. "I didn't summon you!"

The old man looked up at the growing rift in the sky. Strange lights had begun to play across the opening. Eyes narrowing, he pointed to the rift. "Are ye responsible for this?"

"I didn't mean to—"

Raising his hand to indicate silence, the old man shook his head and turned from Midnight. "There are far easier ways of getting my attention, ye should know. Ye could have come to Shadowdale, for example."

"Elminster!" Midnight cried, and suddenly the winds cut her off from the old sage. The dust cleared, and she caught a glimpse of movement from Elminster's direction. The gray mist parted and revealed the seemingly frantic movement of hands, coupled with the sage's unmistakable voice rising to levels that cut through the winds. Then the mist engulfed Elminster once more. A moment later a section of the mist faded and the sage stood before her.

"Do ye know what that is!?" Elminster said, his impatience all too evident as he gestured at the growing rift in the sky. He did not wait for a reply. "*That* is the direct effect of Geryon's Death Spell. Spells of this sort are directly forbidden, although it is difficult to punish transgressors as they are usually dead before the spell reaches this stage!" Elminster let out a deep breath. "Besides that, Geryon himself died over fifty summers ago."

The roar from above became worse.

"Can you stop it?" Kelemvor shouted.

"Of course I can stop it!" the old sage shouted. "I'm *Elminster*, aren't I?" Elminster looked back to Midnight. "Is this spell written some place?"

"No," Midnight said.

"Can ye recall it again, through any other means?"

Midnight shook her head. "No," she said. "I summoned it by accident."

"Very well," Elminster said. "Consider thyself warned. A spell of this type is very dangerous."

The rift seemed to be lowering. Elminster looked up and stood away from Midnight and Kelemvor, concentrating his attentions on the hole in the sky.

The fighter and the magic-user found themselves staring at the old man, speechless.

The aged hands of the great mage moved with surprising speed, and he chanted in a deep, resonant voice. A field of sparkling energies surrounded him, a flood of stars that pierced the heavy veil of grayish winds. Sweat was beginning to form on Elminster's brow as he worked his spell, then a web of tiny, glowing eyes began to form in the space between his fingers. Just before it reached completion, the web collapsed inward and a silver, spinning disc hung in the air.

Elminster issued a command, and the spinning disc shot up into the air, growing in size. It shattered in a blinding display, and the rift in the sky slowly tilted down. The hole descended like a kite with its strings cut, floating to the ground at a leisurely pace, moving back and forth on the winds erratically.

"Goddess!" Midnight screamed as the rift engulfed the entire area, robbing her of her senses. When sight and sensation returned, she found that she was still standing in the same spot, but night had fallen.

Elminster let out a deep sigh.

The rift was gone. The only source of light came from the glowing blue-white portal behind Elminster. The mage looked at Midnight.

"No more of this," he said solemnly.

Midnight shook her head frantically. She heard a groan and saw Kelemvor sitting on the ground, holding his head.

Elminster stepped into the portal, and Midnight screamed at the top of her lungs for him to stop. He poked his head from the glowing rift. "What is it!?"

"The goddess Mystra," Midnight said.

Elminster looked at her sadly.

"The goddess is dead," she finished.

Elminster tilted his head. "So I've heard." Then he darted back inside the portal, and the opening burst apart in a shower of spiraling flames.

Midnight stood in the darkness. "But she had a message," she said, alone and in shock. "A message for you." The mage walked forward, to the spot where the portal had been.

"Elminster!" she cried, but her desperate call remained unanswered.

*　　*　　*　　*　　*

Lighting torches to pierce the absolute pitch-black of the night sky, Midnight and Kelemvor went in search of Cyric and Adon. Twice they had ventured south, to the road, the stars misleading them, and their calls had fallen upon deaf ears. But now they stood before their fallen comrades.

Adon's back was turned to Midnight and Kelemvor as they approached, and the cleric jumped as Midnight touched his shoulder. Turning to address his comrades, Adon nearly screamed his welcome. When Midnight inquired about Cyric's condition, the cleric stared at her in surprise. As she continued to speak, his expression changed to one of panic.

In moments it became clear that Adon was deaf. Most of his attempts to read his friends' lips met with failure, adding to the cleric's panic, but Midnight managed to calm Adon by holding his palm open and tracing her words, letter by letter, with the gentle touch of her index finger.

It was easy enough for Midnight to figure out that the rift's collapse had somehow caused Adon to lose his hearing. Adon was left in the middle of the storm, protected only by the disintegrating wagon, while she was near Elminster, who must have been protected from the effects of the storm somehow.

When Midnight examined Cyric, she found that, although his breathing had become regular, she could not wake him. As the magic-user had no means of examining the extent of the damage the brigand's blade had caused, she covered the wound and hoped for the best.

While Midnight tended to Adon and Cyric, Kelemvor searched for any horses, either their own or the brigands', that might have survived the sandstorm. The fighter found Midnight's horse and one of the brigands' mounts still alive. He brought them back to Adon. The cleric knew what to do with the animals without Kelemvor having to mouth one word at him.

As Adon tended the horses by torchlight, Kelemvor and Midnight sat in the darkness with Cyric. "Your debt must be paid," Kelemvor said.

Midnight turned on the man. "What? We have far to travel before we reach Shadowdale."

"That was not our agreement," Kelemvor said quietly. "I was to accompany you until you spoke with Elminster of Shadowdale. You've already done that."

"He wouldn't listen!" the magic-user cried.

"Nor will I," Kelemvor said harshly. "Every debt must

be paid."

"Very well," Midnight said. "My . . . *true name* . . ."

Kelemvor waited.

"My *true name* is Ariel Manx."

There was a cough, and Midnight and Kelemvor both turned to see Adon help Cyric raise his head. "Cyric," Midnight said as she went to the man's side.

Cyric cried out when he tried to sit up, but his body slowly relaxed as Midnight eased him back to the ground. Kelemvor stood watching, a sharp uneasiness biting through him.

"How will we move him, Kel? His wound is serious," the mage said.

Kelemvor looked away. "I had not considered . . ."

"Surely you didn't mean to leave him—"

"Of course not!" Kelemvor said. "But . . ."

"Another reward?" she said. "Doesn't what we've been through together make any difference to you? Do you really care about any of us, or is it only the reward you care about?"

Kelemvor said nothing.

"I need your help getting Cyric to Tilverton and seeing that he is well enough to ride on to Shadowdale. After that, I don't care what you do." Midnight took out the purse of money she had earned with the Company of the Lynx. "I'll give you all the gold I have left."

After a few moments, Kelemvor lifted his head and spoke. "We can make a wooden frame from the wreckage of the thieves' wagon, wrap the canvas of our tent around it, and make a stretcher. The wheels are intact, and we can pull Cyric behind us as we ride."

Midnight handed the bag of gold to Kelemvor. "Take this now. I want to be certain that you honor your promise."

Kelemvor took the gold and waded into the pile of wreckage that was strewn about the plain, where he found a small lantern that was still in one piece. Once the lantern was lit, Kelemvor looked at Midnight's face and noticed the tears running down her face.

* * * * *

In Zhentil Keep, a criminal had been dragged through the streets, hands and feet bound. His body bounced against the pavement of the torch-lit streets, and his screams echoed for all to hear. The mangled body had been deposited at Bane's feet and the Black Lord was surprised to find the human still clinging to life, though by a gossamer thread at best.

The man was Thurbal, captain of arms and warden of Shadowdale. He had somehow entered the city undetected, then tried to join the Black Network under an assumed name. Fzoul had caught on to the man instantly, and although he advised Bane to feed the man false information then allow him to return to Shadowdale, the god could not suffer the affront so casually.

Thurbal had been subjected to endless sessions of interrogation, and he claimed he knew nothing of Bane's plans. The Black Lord did not wish to take chances, and so he ordered his men to drag the spy through the streets and then bring him to the temple to be executed. Invitations had been sent by messenger to Bane's elite, and the execution had become a standing room only event.

As the time of execution arrived, Bane left his throne to stand over Thurbal, then attempted to torment the aging, half-dead warrior at his feet. The man's eyes were sharp and alert, and Bane suspected they would continue to look that way, even after the spy had passed into Lord Myrkul's domain.

The throne room was crowded with officials and their wives. They raised a toast to their dark lord and chanted his name as his taloned hands reached down toward Thurbal. Just before the tip of a single nail from Bane's gauntlet could reach the eye of the dying man, there was a flash of blue-white light and Thurbal vanished. Bane was stunned for a moment. Someone had teleported Thurbal away, presumably to a place of safety.

The chanting ceased.

Bane studied the eyes of his worshipers. He noticed surprise and confusion in their expressions. Until this moment, the loyalty of Bane's worshipers had been unswerving. He did not want them to know that his will could be thwarted this easily.

"And now only a memory remains," Bane said as he rose and allowed his talons to unfurl with practiced grace. "I have sent the interloper into Myrkul's Realm, where he will pay for his crimes with an eternity of suffering!"

Then the chanting started once more. The Black Lord was relieved that the lie had been accepted. Still, he was troubled for the rest of the evening by the victory that had been snatched from him.

Hours later, when Bane was alone in the chamber, he sat and brooded.

"Elminster," Bane said aloud. "No one but you would dare interfere with my plans." Bane's goblet was crushed in his grip. "You will take Thurbal's place soon enough, and your agonies will be legend throughout my kingdom! For this I will not only see you dead, but after I secure the Celestial Stairway, I will reduce your precious Shadowdale to a smoking pit. I swear it!"

The Black Lord felt the wine that had escaped the ruined goblet stain his leg. He stared at the goblet and cursed at it, but it did not regain its shape. He threw it across the room and called out for Blackthorne to bring him another.

"Milord," Blackthorne said, lowering his head.

"The assassins?"

"They have departed, Lord Bane. We await word of their success."

Bane nodded and became silent as he stared off into space. Blackthorne didn't move, as he had not yet been dismissed. Bane and his emissary stayed like this for close to thirty minutes before Blackthorne's leg cramped and he involuntarily shifted his weight. Bane looked up slowly.

"Blackthorne," Bane said, as if he had forgotten about the other man's presence. "Ronglath Knightsbridge."

"Yes, milord?"

"I wish to have Knightsbridge lead one of the contingents from the Citadel of the Raven in the attack on Shadowdale. He has much to atone for, and he may be willing to do what others are not and without hesitation," Bane said.

"There may be some resentment on the part of his troops, Lord Bane. He is seen as having failed the city—"

"But he hasn't failed me!" Bane said. "Not yet, anyway. Go about your duty and do not question me again."

Blackthorne lowered his eyes.

"Deliver my word on this matter personally," Bane said. "While you are there, survey the readiness of our troops and the hiring of mercenaries."

"How should I travel, Lord Bane?"

"Use the emissary spell, you fool. That is why I taught it to you."

Blackthorne waited.

"You may go," Bane said.

Blackthorne frowned as he spread his arms wide and recited the emissary spell. The mage knew that, with the instability of magic in the Realms, it was only a matter of time before the spell failed. He might be struck in the form of a raven or changed into something far worse. It could even kill him. But as the magic-user finished the spell, he was transformed into a large raven that sailed at the wall then vanished. This time the spell worked as planned.

Alone in the chamber, Bane found that he had much to think about.

* * * * *

Ronglath Knightsbridge thrust his sword into the floor, then knelt down on one knee before it. He lowered his head and gripped the hilt of the sword with both hands. He had been given private quarters in the Citadel of the Raven, despite the recent overcrowding. When he ate his meals, no one else sat at his table. When he trained with his sword or mace, only his trainer arrived for the sessions. At most times, he was left completely alone.

Knightsbridge was just past forty winters, with close-cropped, salt-and-pepper hair, azure eyes, a moustache, and deeply pitted, sunburned skin. His features were strong and distinctive. He was almost six feet tall, with a very impressive build.

All of his life he had served Zhentil Keep, but now he was in disgrace, and would have gladly taken his own life, but for the interference of Tempus Blackthorne.

Blackthorne, because of his well-meaning sentiments of friendship and loyalty, had damned Knightsbridge to a far greater punishment than death would have afforded him. Knightsbridge turned those thoughts away.

He had others to direct his hate against. There was the wizard Sememmon, for instance, who addressed Knightsbridge as "the chosen" and laughed at the spy, taunting him before the others whenever possible. Knightsbridge knew that the wizard resented the tie he had to Bane through Blackthorne. If only the wizard knew how greatly Knightsbridge desired to sever the bond himself, he would have laughed at the irony.

Then there was the man who was truly responsible for all that Knightsbridge faced: Kelemvor Lyonsbane.

If it had not been for the interference of the fighter, Knightsbridge would not have been found out, and the torments he had undergone would never have occurred. If not for Kelemvor, his plan to disgrace the city of Arabel might have succeeded.

Knightsbridge clutched the hilt of the sword tightly, until his knuckles became white. Suddenly he threw his head back and released a scream of rage that echoed through the passageways of the fortress he had been assigned to serve in. The scream had been the first sound Knightsbridge had uttered since he came to the citadel.

No one knocked upon the door to see if he was hurt. No one came running, as they should at an officer's cry.

The echoes of the scream faded away, and Knightsbridge heard a sound behind him.

"Ronglath," Tempus Blackthorne said. "I bring word from Lord Bane."

Knightsbridge stood and yanked the sword from the floor. He said nothing as Blackthorne relayed the Black Lord's message.

"Come with me, and we will make the announcement together!" Blackthorne said, oblivious to the searing hatred in the eyes of his childhood friend. "You will march from the citadel to the ruins of Teshwave, where mercenaries wait to join our ranks. The armies will gather at Voonlar, to await the signal to attack the dale. Of course, there are other troops being sent in different directions, but you will not have to concern yourself with that."

Knightsbridge felt his hand shake. The sword had not yet found its sheath.

"Kelemvor," Knightsbridge said, testing the sound of his own voice as he sheathed his sword and followed the emissary out of the room.

Blackthorne turned. "What did you say?"

Knightsbridge cleared his throat. "A debt I must settle," he said. "I pray I get the chance."

Blackthorne nodded, and he led the spy to the assembly hall, where a crowd had already begun to gather. Knightsbridge looked out into the sea of faces, and hope began to flicker in his heart.

I can redeem myself in this battle, Knightsbridge thought. And then I will have my revenge.

❧ 10 ❧

Tilverton

Kelemvor worked long into the night to finish the cart for transporting Cyric. And though he was in pain, the fighter ignored the pain of his own wounds. They were not serious enough to keep him from his task, and he wanted to leave for Tilverton at first light. When he was certain that the modified wagon would perform satisfactorily, Kelemvor lay beside it and fell into a deep sleep.

Midnight sat with Cyric, keeping watch as Kelemvor and Adon slept.

"You stayed with me," Cyric said. "I didn't believe you would."

"Why do you think I'd abandon you?" Midnight asked with genuine concern.

A moment passed before Cyric spoke, as if he were attempting to gather his words and arrange them in just the right order. "You're the first person who hasn't abandoned me," he said. "In one way or another. It's what I expect."

"I can't believe that," Midnight said. "Your family—"

"I have none," Cyric said.

"None that are living?" Midnight asked gently.

"None at all," Cyric said with a degree of bitterness that surprised Midnight. "I was orphaned in Zhentil Keep as a baby. Slavers found me in the street, and a wealthy family from Sembia bought me and raised me as their own until I was ten. I heard them arguing one night, as parents often do. But the subject of this fight was not their dissatisfaction with one another, but their shame over me.

"One of our neighbors had learned the truth about me, and my 'parents' felt nothing but humiliation over their

❧ 197 ❧

dark secret. I confronted them, threatened to leave if I was such an embarrassment." Cyric's eyes narrowed as his lips pulled back in a cruel, wicked smile. "They didn't stop me. It was a long journey back to Zhentil Keep. I almost died several times. But I learned."

Midnight brushed the hair from his brow. "I'm sorry. You don't have to go on."

"But I want to!" Cyric said savagely. "I learned that you do what you must to survive, even if it means taking from others. I arrived in that black pit known as Zhentil Keep, where I attempted to learn something of my past. But of course there were no answers to be found. I became a thief, and my actions soon gained me the attentions of the Thieves' Guild. Marek, the leader, took me in and taught me all the skills of the trade. I was a quick study.

"For a long time I did whatever Marek told me to do. I was anxious to please that black-hearted rogue. It took me many years to realize that it was taking more and more to get that treasured, tiny nod of approval from him.

"Then, when I was sixteen and Marek's attentions turned to a new recruit, who was the same age as I had been when he first took me from the streets, I realized that I had been used yet again and planned to leave. When my plans became known, the Guild put a price on my head. No one would help me as I attempted to escape Zhentil Keep. I suppose I shouldn't have been surprised; the people I had regarded as allies no longer had a use for me. I wouldn't have made it out of the city at all if it weren't for my talent with a blade. It was quite refined, even then. The streets ran red with blood the night I left."

Midnight lowered her head. "Then what happened?"

"I spent eight years on the road, using my skills to indulge the one passion I had cultivated since I had been a boy: travel. But wherever I would go, people were the same. Poverty and inequality were as widespread as luxury and splendor. I had hoped to find fellowship and equality; instead I found pettiness and exploitation. Somehow I thought I would escape the betrayals of my youth and find a place where honesty and decency prevailed, but no such place exists. Not in this life."

Midnight hung her head. "I'm sorry for your pain."

Cyric shrugged. "Life is pain. I've come to accept that. But don't pity me just because my vision is clearer than yours. Pity yourself. You'll wake to the truth soon enough."

"You're wrong. It's just that there's so much you haven't seen, Cyric. You've been cheated out of so many of the joys life has to offer."

"Really?" the thief said. "Love and laughter, you mean? A good woman, perhaps?" Cyric laughed. "Romance is a lie, too."

Midnight brushed the hair from her face. "And why do you say that?"

"I was twenty-four when I realized that my life had no direction, no real meaning. I returned to Zhentil Keep, and this time my efforts to find my roots met with some limited success. I was told that my mother had been young and madly in love with an officer in the Zhentilar. When she became pregnant, he cast her out, claiming the child was not his. She fell in with the poor and homeless, who cared for her until I was born. Then my father returned and murdered her and sold me for a healthy profit. Quite a fairy tale romance, wouldn't you say?"

Midnight said nothing as she sat, staring at the fire.

"I heard other versions of the story, but that's the one I believe to be true. It was a beggar women who claimed to have befriended my mother who told me this tale, but she could not give me the name of the man who had sired me, nor could she tell me what had befallen him. A shame, really. I was looking forward to having a nice long talk with the man before I slit his throat.

"Eventually, Marek and the Guild offered to take me in again, but I refused. The refusal was not accepted, and I was forced to flee the city once more. When I was gone from Zhentil Keep, though, I felt as if I was leaving the past behind. I attempted to start over, and I adopted the life of a fighter. But my past always catches up to me and forces me to move on. With Mystra's reward I had hoped to travel far, perhaps across the desert. I don't really know where—just someplace where I could find some peace."

Midnight let out a deep breath.

Cyric laughed. "Now we know each others secrets, and you no longer have reason to be afraid."

"I don't know what you mean," Midnight said, attempting to hide her concern. "What secrets of mine do you know?"

"Only one, Ariel," Cyric said.

"You heard my *true name*—"

"I didn't try to find it out," he said. "If I could forget it, I would, although it *is* a beautiful name." Cyric swallowed hard. "No one alive knows all that I have told you. If you wished to ruin me, I couldn't stop you. Inform the Guild of my whereabouts and I'm a dead man."

Midnight caressed his face. "I wouldn't think of it," she said. "Secrets are always safe between friends."

Cyric tilted his head. "Is that what we are, friends?"

Midnight nodded.

"How interesting," Cyric said. "Friends."

Cyric and Midnight talked long into the night, and when it came Adon's turn to take the watch, Midnight didn't wake him.

By morning, after Kelemvor relieved Midnight of the watch and Cyric had a chance to sleep, the pain from the thief's wound had lessened enough for him to sit up. Cyric even had the strength to eat with the others, although there was nothing more than a few sweetbreads to be had.

After morningfeast, Cyric asked Midnight to bring his bow, and he instructed her on its proper use. Midnight took aim at a large bird that had hovered over the party since morningfeast began. Cyric's instincts combined with Midnight's great strength brought the black bird down, and they roasted its carcass after Adon retrieved the fallen creature.

After a night's rest, Adon's hearing returned to some degree. The first sign of progress came when the cleric no longer required a slight blow from Kelemvor's steel-plated elbow to realize that he was shouting in the fighter's ear instead of speaking at a normal level. And Adon's loss of hearing in no way stopped him from talking, Now, though, he strained to hear himself when he voiced his flowery opinions, as if he could not risk the utter damnation that would certainly follow if his important statements about the righteous path of Sune were not said with the proper timbre and volume.

After the adventurers finished off the roast bird, they packed their belongings and mounted the two remaining horses. Kelemvor was again subjected to Adon's company, and the cart the fighter had built was lashed to Midnight's mount.

The ride was surprisingly comfortable for the wounded thief, despite the sweaty, leathery embrace of the stretcher. Cyric met with only an occasionally bump, until late morning, when one of the cart's wheels was shattered on a huge stone in the road and couldn't be repaired. Kelemvor was forced to cut the assembly free and toss it to the side of the road. Cyric rode with Midnight for the remainder of the journey.

A storm had been on the horizon when the heroes first spotted the gates of Tilverton, and the threat of bad weather had hung above their heads ever since. Steel-gray skies stood behind ominous black clouds. Tiny flashes of lightning were visible in the distance all morning, and the roar of far-off thunder drifted across the plains.

A few hours later, they reached the town of Tilverton and were promptly stopped by a group of men wearing white tunics with the insignia of the Purple Dragon. The men seemed tired but alert, and they were filthy. Six crossbows had been readied and aimed at the adventurers even before the leader of the Cormyrian patrol asked to see their charter. Kelemvor found the false charter Adon had bought back in Arabel and offered it to the captain. The patrol leader examined the charter, handed it back, and waived them on. They rode past the patrol, and entered the town without incident.

The adventurers rode into Tilverton tired and without humor. The hour of highsun was upon them, and their stomachs growled like beasts searching for release. Cyric was exhausted from the trip, and as the heroes stopped in front of an inn, the thief tried to get down from Midnight's horse. He got to the ground, but fell back into the red-maned beast with a grunt. His second attempt to walk was only slightly more successful, and he got two steps from the mount, but could go no further.

Midnight dismounted and threw one of the thief's arms around her neck. The magic-user was taller than the thin, dark-haired man, and she had to crouch slightly as she helped Cyric stumble into the inn. Kelemvor and Adon rode in behind Midnight. The cleric, whose hearing had returned to normal, immediately rushed to help Midnight, but the fighter dismounted and led both horses to the stables behind the gray stone inn.

The sign above the door identified the inn as the Flagon Held High. As Midnight and Adon struggled to reach the door handle, they noticed a young man with pale gray eyes sitting in the shadows beside the door.

"Your assistance if you would," Midnight said as she tried to get a better grip on the sagging thief.

The young man continued to stare directly ahead, ignoring the magic-user's request.

Now, a dirty brown rain started to fall on the city. Midnight struggled with the door, and with Adon's help, the mage dragged Cyric inside. Kicking the door of the inn shut behind her, Midnight helped Cyric to a wooden chair beside the door. At first she thought the inn was deserted, and then she saw a flickering light and heard voices in one of the dining rooms. She called out, but her requests for assistance went unanswered.

"Damn," she hissed. "Adon, you stay here with Cyric." Midnight went off in search of the innkeeper.

As she entered the common room, Midnight saw that it was crowded. Men were scattered throughout the room. Some appeared to be soldiers, bearing the coat of arms of the Purple Dragons. A few had been wounded, although their wounds had been bound. Others appeared to be only civilians. All seemed sullen and withdrawn.

"Where is the innkeep and his help?" Midnight asked the closest soldier.

"Off to pray, I suppose," the man said. "It's about that time."

"It's always about that time," another men said, nursing his drink.

"I don't understand," Midnight said. "No one is here to tend the inn?"

The soldier shrugged. "There may be a guest or two upstairs. I don't know." Midnight turned away, but the soldier continued to speak. "You can just take what you need. No one will care."

Midnight walked away from the common room, shaking her head. She returned to the foyer of the inn, where Adon was standing beside Cyric.

"Where's Kel?" she said. Adon shrugged and looked back to the door, holding his hands up in confusion.

Midnight cursed again and ran from the inn. She saw Kelemvor's back at the far end of the street, and she called to him. "Where are you going? You owe me!"

The fighter stopped and lowered his head. What I owe you is to get out of your life, Kelemvor thought. There are too many secrets between us, too many questions that you would not like the answers to.

But he chose not to tell Midnight any of this. Instead, the fighter barked, "The debt will be paid!" then continued on his way.

Midnight stood trembling for a moment, then she returned to the inn and sat beside Cyric.

"Perhaps he needs time," Adon said, slightly louder than he should have.

"He can have a lifetime," Midnight said, her harsh expression falling away as the door opened and she rose to her feet. A white-haired man who had seen more than fifty winters stood in the doorway, his expression cold as he looked to the travelers. He walked by them to a small antechamber and vanished, ignoring Midnight's attempts to get his attention. When he emerged from the room, stinking of some foul liquor, he was surprised that the travelers were still there.

"What do you want?" he asked at last.

"Food, lodgings, perhaps some information—"

The old man waved her away. "You can *take* the first two. No one will stop you. Information comes at a price."

Midnight wondered if the man was mad. "We have no coin to pay for our lodgings, but perhaps we can provide protection from those who seek to rob you of your valuable services—"

"Rob me!?" the man said, alarmed. "You misunderstand." He leaned in close, and the smell of the cheap liquor made Midnight recoil. "You can't rob what someone no longer cares to keep! Take what you like!"

The man returned to the antechamber. "I no longer care," he cried from the dark room.

Midnight looked to the others, then leaned against the wall, defeated. "Perhaps we should get our things," she said at last. "We may be here awhile."

They brought their gear to the first available room, then Adon took the keys which were hanging behind the counter in the small room where the innkeep lay drunk. The room the heroes took was quite pleasant and came with two beds. Adon settled his things on one bed and went about changing his clothes, indifferent to the magic-user's presence.

It was still raining outside and the room was dark, so Midnight lit a small lantern beside the bed. Adon checked on Cyric with a cursory examination, then set off to explore the city.

Midnight helped Cyric out of his clothes, laughing as the thief actually blushed. "Have no worry," Midnight said at one point. "I'm a complete amateur."

Cyric winced. "You're doing fine," he said as he pulled the covers back up to his chest.

"I'll sleep on the floor," Midnight said at last. "I prefer it for my back. You remember to keep covered and warm."

Cyric frowned. "I'm too old to be mothered. You should worry about yourself, not about me—"

Midnight held out her hand, motioning for him to stop. "We must make you well," she said softly. "You must be strong for your journey."

Cyric seemed confused. "What journey?"

"Your search for that better place," the mage said. "You don't have to accompany me any farther. The way between Tilverton and Shadowdale should be clear. I can make it there alone."

Cyric shook his head and tried to sit up. Midnight gently pushed him back on the bed. "There is no need," he said. "No need to go on alone."

"But, Cyric, I can't ask you to come with me. You need to

rest, to heal—"

Cyric had already made up his mind. "There must be heal-ing potions in this place. Medications, salves. Everything in town seems to be here for the taking. Find something to heal me, and I'll be by your side for as long as you need me."

"I wouldn't have left until you were well," she said.

"Your mission is urgent. You can't afford to wait."

"I know that," Midnight said. "But I would have stayed just the same. After all, you're my friend."

For the first time in a long time, Cyric smiled.

* * * * *

Kelemvor was alone on the streets. The storm was hang-ing directly overhead, and the drops of rain, now orange, fell on him as he searched for the smithy. Eventually, he found the blacksmith hard at work in the shelter of his shop, and he ducked inside as the rain started to fall harder.

The smith was a burly man with a build similar to Kelem-vor's. He had curly black hair, and the flesh of his bare arms was bruised in places and seared black in others. The smith did not look up from his work as the fighter approached. The bright metal shoes he created for the nearby horse were almost ready, and he turned to test the pair he had set aside to cool.

"A moment of your time," Kelemvor said.

The blacksmith ignored the fighter, training his gaze on the job before him. Kelemvor cleared his throat noisily, but that, too, was ignored. However, Kelemvor was cold and tired and in no mood to be insulted.

The fighter peeled off the armor where the brigands' arrows had struck him. He threw the steel plates at the smith, knocking the red-hot tools from his hands. The man bent low to retrieve the instrument before the hay at his feet could catch fire, and he examined the armor plating. Then he looked up to see the ravaged flesh of the fighter's arm, where fragments of the brigands' arrows had lodged themselves.

"I can mend this," the smith said without emotion. "But I can do nothing for your wounds."

"Are there no healers in Tilverton?" Kelemvor asked. "I saw a large temple over the roofs of the shops down the street."

The man turned away. "The Temple of Gond."

"All right, I saw the Temple of Gond. There must be clerics who could—"

"Remove the rest of your armor so I can get to work," the smith interrupted. "Then you can go to the temple yourself. I only heal metals."

Kelemvor gave the smith his armor and put on some clothes he had taken from the party's supplies. The smith worked silently, ignoring the fighter's questions no matter if he screamed them or couched them in all the politeness he could muster. When he was done hammering out the damaged armor, the blacksmith refused to take any payment.

"It's my duty to Gond," the smith said as Kelemvor wandered back into the street.

Kelemvor found the Temple of Gond without difficulty, despite the rain. Occasionally he passed a commoner wandering the streets or lying on the walk outside a shop, but the people he met were indifferent to his presence, their eyes vacant, staring at something only they could see. He also found the greatest concentration of smith shops he had ever seen in one area, though they were generally deserted.

When Kelemvor finally reached the temple, he saw that it had an entrance constructed in the form of a great anvil. The building itself was made of stark, powerful shapes that rose up to dwarf the hovels and shops around it. There were fires burning within the temple, and an unending chorus of worship sounded from the doorway.

As he entered the Temple of Gond, the fighter was surprised by the vast expanse of the main chamber. If there were quarters for the high priests in the temple, they must surely have been underground, since every square foot of the ground floor had been devoted to the chamber.

In the chamber, worshipers crowded around a hooded high priest who stood atop a huge stone anvil. Giant stone hands were visible at either side of the altar; a gigantic hammer was poised in one of them. Fires had been lit in the four corners surrounding the hooded man.

The support pillars that rose up to the arched ceiling were carved in the form of swords, and the windows were framed with an interlocking series of hammers. It was hard to understand the exact words of the high priest, as the continuous shouting from the audience drowned out all but a few key phrases, but it was clear that the high priest was issuing an endless series of praises to his god and an equal number of condemnations to the commoners of Tilverton.

"The gods walk the Realms!" a man beside Kelemvor shouted. "Why has Lord Gond forsaken us?"

But the man's words were swallowed up in the endless flow of chants and screams. Kelemvor judged that nearly the entire population of the small town was crowded into the temple, though occasionally, a few worshipers would wander out.

"Wait!" the priest would cry as people tried to leave. "Lord Gond has not abandoned us. He has given me the gift of healing to keep the faithful well until he arrives!" Few seemed to be swayed by this, but some of the people were persuaded to stay.

Listening to the Tilvertonians, Kelemvor learned that they had devoted themselves exclusively to the worship of Gond, God of Blacksmiths and Artificers. When tales of the gods walking the Realms reached the city, the people began to prepare for the arrival of their deity. They stood at readiness, waiting for some sign, some communication.

They waited in vain. Gond had risen in Lantan and did not make any attempt to contact his devoted worshipers in Tilverton. When a small group from the town reached Lantan and requested an audience with the god, they were turned away. When they persisted, two of them were slain and the others forced to flee for their lives. When this story was related to the townsfolk, it broke their spirit. Now they spent almost every waking hour in the temple, attempting to contact their god, attempting to disprove what they already knew in their hearts.

Gond didn't care about Tilverton.

Kelemvor was about to leave the temple when he noticed the silver-haired man standing to the rear of the chamber. A short, dark-haired girl stood beside him, her attentions riv eted on his beautiful, unearthly face. No one else seemed to notice the man, and he turned away from the girl without acknowledging her presence. She turned and ran behind him as he walked to the place where Kelemvor stood and looked into the eyes of the fighter, a slight grin playing over his face. The eyes of the silver-haired man were bluish gray, with tiny red flecks floating through them. His skin was pale, although fine silver hairs were growing on his face and arms.

"Brother," the man said simply, then walked away.

Kelemvor turned and tried to catch the man or the girl, but when the fighter got to the street, the silver-haired man was nowhere to be seen.

After standing for a moment in the purple and green hail that was now falling on Tilverton, the fighter returned to the temple. As Kelemvor again stood at the rear of the main chamber, a young woman, a priestess, caught his eye. The fires of belief had not dimmed in her eyes: they burned bright enough to set the night sky aflame. She was very beautiful and wore a white gown tied at the waist by a leather belt. Intricate patterns had been woven into the fabric of her gown, and steel plates covered her shoulders. The odd mixture of delicate silks and hard steel somehow lent even more power to her appearance.

The fighter pushed his way through the crowd and was soon talking to the priestess, whose name was Phylanna.

"I need a place to stay," Kelemvor said.

"You'll need more than that," the priestess said, "judging from your injuries. Are you a follower of Gond?"

Kelemvor shook his head.

"Then we have something to talk about as our healer tends to your wounds." Phylanna turned and beckoned for him to follow. "I sense you have suffered greatly these past few days." She did not wait for his reply.

Phylanna brought him to a small stairway, which led down to a cramped chamber. There they waited until the high priest, now finished with his tirade against the town's wavering faith, entered the room. Phylanna closed and locked the door as the priest entered.

"You must never tell anyone about what you are going to

witness," Phylanna said as she helped Kelemvor lay back upon the room's single cot.

"I am Rull of Gond," the priest said, his voice harsh and cracking from his prolonged sermon. "Are you a worshiper of the Wonderbringer?"

Before Kelemvor could answer, Phylanna held her hand to the fighter's lips and said, "It does not matter if he worships Lord Gond in this time of trouble. He needs our help, and we must give it."

Rull frowned, but then nodded in agreement. The priest closed his eyes and took a large, red crystal from a chain around his neck. He waved it over the fighter.

"It is a miracle you find yourself walking and of clear mind. A lesser man might have died from the infections you carry," Rull said as he examined Kelemvor. The fighter looked at the crystal and noticed a strange, burning glow in its interior.

"Kelemvor is proud," Phylanna said. "He bears his injuries without complaint."

"Not entirely true," Kelemvor grunted as the high priest went to work.

Phylanna seemed concerned as Rull performed the ritual to heal the fighter, but the priest's skills as a healer became obvious as his deft fingers worked in the air and the black welts that surrounded the fighter's wounds were slowly flushed with blood. The priest was sweating, his voice raised in supplication to Gond. Phylanna cut anxious glances to the door, fearing others might blunder in and interrupt the priest's efforts.

The splinters left by the arrow points rose to the surface of Kelemvor's skin, and Phylanna assisted Rull in removing them with her bare hands. Kelemvor cursed himself as he winced at the pain.

Then it was over. Rull's body relaxed, almost as if he had been completely drained of energy, and Kelemvor slumped forward on the cot. The fighter's wounds were no longer tender, and he knew that his fever had lessened.

"Rull's belief is strong, and so he has been rewarded by the gods," Phylanna said. "Your belief must be strong, too, to survive that kind of wounding."

Kelemvor nodded. He saw that the light within the crystal had become a slight flicker.

"Foolish and stubborn, perhaps, but still very strong," Phylanna said.

Kelemvor laughed. "You're lucky I'm flat on my back, woman."

Phylanna smiled and looked away. "Perhaps."

Though both Phylanna and Rull asked Kelemvor about his business in Tilverton and his religious beliefs, he told them very little about himself. But when the fighter spoke of payment for the priest's efforts, Rull said nothing and departed.

"I meant no offense," Kelemvor said. "In most places it is customary—"

"Material concerns are the least of our worries," the priestess said. "Now about your lodgings . . ."

Kelemvor glanced around the tiny, windowless cell. "I have an aversion to closed-in spaces."

Phylanna smiled. "The Flagon Held High may have an open room."

Kelemvor swallowed. "I have . . . an aversion . . . to that particular inn."

Phylanna folded her arms across her chest. "Then you'll have to stay with me."

There was a loud crash and angry voices erupted from the stairway leading to the cell. Kelemvor sat up quickly and reached for his sword. Phylanna put her hand on his shoulder and shook her head.

"There is no need for that in the Wonderbringer's temple. Now, lay back and rest until I return."

"Wait!" Kelemvor called.

Phylanna turned.

"When Rull is finished, please ask him to return," the fighter said. "I would like to apologize."

"I will bring him at the end of his next sermon," she said.

"Alone," Kelemvor said. "I need to speak to him alone."

Phylanna seemed puzzled. "As you wish," she said and hurried from the small room.

Kelemvor rested in the cell for an hour, growing more uncomfortable in the small room as his condition got better. The crowd of commoners in the Temple of Gond were noisy, and the fighter entertained himself by listening to their cries, which mixed in with Rull's sermon.

"Tilverton will perish!" someone screamed.

"We should all go to Arabel or Eveningstar," another voice cried.

"Yes! Gond doesn't care about us, and Azoun will protect Cormyr before he protects us!"

Rull's voice rose over the shouting, and he launched into another tirade against the people who had fallen away from their worship of the Wonderbringer. "Tilverton will certainly be cursed if we give up hope! Lord Gond has left me with healing spell, hasn't he?" the priest cried, and Rull continued to yell over the crowd for a few minutes. Then the sermon was over, and Kelemvor heard footsteps upon the stairs again. He reached for his sword.

The fighter put his weapon down as Rull entered the room, obviously exhausted from his shouting matches with the people in the temple. "You wished to see me," the priest said as he slumped to the floor.

Without sitting up on the cot, Kelemvor turned toward the priest and sighed. "I am grateful for what you've done for me."

Rull smiled. "Phylanna was right. It really doesn't matter that you do not worship Gond. It is my responsibility as his cleric to use the spells he gives me to cure anyone who needs my help."

"And the good people of Tilverton really seem to need your help badly," Kelemvor added.

"Yes," Rull said. "They are losing faith in Lord Gond. I am the only one who can bring them back to his flock."

"If you fail?"

"Then the town will perish," the priest said. "But that won't happen. Eventually they will listen to me."

"Of course," Kelemvor said, "if the people of Tilverton knew that Gond had forsaken you, too, and your healing magic was taken only from the stone you carry, they would listen to you even less than they do now. They would all turn away from Lord Gond for good."

The high priest stood up. "The healing magic is mine. It is a gift from the Wonderbringer to show the good people of

Tilverton that he still cares. I will—"

"You will do what I ask of you, Rull," Kelemvor growled. "Or I will expose you to the people of Tilverton. Even if I'm wrong, they'll believe me."

Rull hung his head. "What do you want of me?"

Kelemvor sat up on the cot. "I need you to help someone who is injured far worse than I was. I made a promise to keep him safe, and I have to uphold it."

"I don't suppose he worships the Wonderbringer by chance," Rull said. "But then, that really doesn't matter, does it?"

Kelemvor gave Rull a description of Cyric and sent him to the Flagon Held High. The priest was just leaving the temple when Phylanna returned to the cell. "I'm here to take you to your accommodations for the evening, brave warrior," she said, grasping Kelemvor's hand and leading him from the room.

*　*　*　*　*

Adon wandered the streets, trying to find someone to talk to. The heavy storms had abated, and the thought that perhaps he was unsafe on the streets at night, that he might fall victim to robbers or cutthroats, did not occur to him. Even after the cleric learned that there had been a number of bloody murders in the last week, he continued to roam Tilverton. He had important matters to attend to.

Beginning with the young man who had lain outside the inn, oblivious to the heavy rain and hail that had fallen, the reactions to the cleric's inquiries about the town's problems were uniformly apathetic. The eyes of the Tilvertonians had been closed to all but their own inner suffering.

The worship of the gods was meant to uplift the soul, Adon thought as he walked through the streets. And worship was a higher calling than any other the cleric could think of. Still, that same calling had been turned into a fountain of pain and bitterness from which the people of Tilverton had drunk freely, and it cost them all sense of joy and reason.

As Adon stalked the streets of Tilverton, talking to anyone

he could find, the words that had been spoken in the darkened chambers of Castle Kilgrave returned to him.

Truth is beauty, beauty truth. Embrace me, and the answers to all your unspoken questions will be made clear.

There was beauty in truth, Adon knew, and he worshiped the Goddess of Beauty. So he spent the night desperately trying to return the light of truth to the eyes of the poor wretches he found. Just before dawn, a woman had looked up into his eyes, a faint glimmer sparking in her eyes as he spoke his sermon, and Adon's heart filled with hope.

"Good woman, the gods have not deserted us. Now more than ever they need our support, our worship, our love. It is in our hands to bring about the golden age of beauty and truth in which the gods will again grant us their favor. Now, in this dark time when our faith is put to the test, we must not falter. We must find solace in our belief and forge ahead with our lives. For in so doing we will pay a greater tribute to the gods than even the strongest prayer can achieve!

"Sune hasn't sought me out, but I haven't given up the hope of one day standing in her presence," the cleric told the woman. As Adon held her by the shoulders, he was tempted to shake her, just to see if it would help her to understand his words.

The old woman stared at the cleric, a wellspring of tears threatening to flood from her eyes. Adon was pleased that his words had touched the old woman, that she seemed to understand.

And then she spoke.

"It sounds as if you're trying to convince yourself," she said bitterly. "Go away. You're not wanted here." Then she turned from the young cleric and covered her face with her hands as she lay in the street, sobbing.

A single tear ran down Adon's cheek as he walked from the woman and lost himself in the darkness.

* * * * *

Kelemvor awoke and found Phylanna gone. The side of the bed where she had slept was now ice cold. He thought of her gentle kisses and the strength he had found in her embrace, but the thoughts soon became clouded as his mind returned to the same topic again and again.

Midnight.

Ariel.

His debt to her had been fulfilled, but he could not forget her.

Kelemvor knew that Rull would have visited Cyric by this time, and he hoped Cyric would be ready to ride from Tilverton with Midnight come morning, even though he would not be accompanying them.

There was a noise at the end of the corridor outside the bedroom. Kelemvor slipped his mail frock over his head, lifted his sword from its sheath, and rose from the perfumed bed of the priestess. She had brought him to her rooms on the top floor above her brother's shop, leading him up a winding back stairway. No words were passed between them; no words were necessary. Meetings like this had their own subtle language, and Kelemvor knew that in the morning he would leave Tilverton and not think of the woman again.

He was fairly certain she would view their night of passion in much the same way.

Kelemvor opened the bedroom door and drew back as he saw Phylanna standing at the end of the corridor. The huge window had been opened, and the moonlight bathed her naked form, lighting an aura around her as she spread wide her arms and allowed the billowing curtains to caress her as she danced in the cool night wind.

The fighter was about to close the door and return to bed when he heard the voice of a man from the hallway, singing in some strange tongue. Kelemvor stepped out in the hallway and stopped as he saw the silver-haired man from the temple standing near Phylanna.

The man who had called him "brother," then vanished.

Phylanna danced with a lilting, graceful quality. Her eyes were open, but she did not seem to see Kelemvor as he approached. The silver-haired man continued to sing to her, although his gaze was now fixed on the fighter. The silver-haired man's blue-gray eyes blazed despite the darkness that shrouded his features, his form a silhouette against the bright moonlight.

The man stopped singing as the fighter got close to Phylanna. "Take her," he said "I mean her no harm."

Phylanna collapsed in Kelemvor's arms, and he gently laid her down in the hallway.

"Who are you?" Kelemvor said.

"I am known by many names. Who would you like me to be?"

"It's a simple question," the fighter snapped.

"With no simple answers," the man sighed. "You may call me Torrence. It's as good a name as any."

"Why are you here?" Kelemvor gripped his sword tightly as he felt something dark and heavy churn within his gut.

"I wished to draw you out, that you might join in my banquet. Come. Look."

Kelemvor stood at the window and looked down to the street. The girl who had been at the silver-haired man's side in the temple lay in the alley below, her clothes shredded, although she did not appear to have been harmed.

Yet.

Torrence shuddered, and the fine white hairs that covered his flesh grew thick. His clothes fell away, gently floating to the ground, as his spine crackled and lengthened. His face became bestial, his jaws extending outward as he emitted a guttural moan of pleasure. His entire body changed. He bent his limbs back and forth, the bones creaking. Huge fangs lined his open snout. His fingers ended in razor-sharp claws.

"A jackalwere," Kelemvor gasped in astonishment.

Phylanna awoke. She looked up at Kelemvor, confused. She did not see the monster standing next to the window. Kelemvor looked back to Torrence.

"Come, my brother. I will share with you."

Kelemvor fought against the rising tide within his breast. Abruptly Phylanna saw the jackalwere and rushed to Kelemvor's side. "Gond help us!" she screamed.

"Yes, bring her closer," Torrence said. "We may feast on them both."

"Get away!" Kelemvor shouted as he slammed the priestess against the far wall and raised his sword. The look of fear in her eyes was almost more then he could bear. "Now!" he screamed as he felt the familiar agonies begin to play upon his soul.

He was saving Phylanna from the jackalwere, but he was receiving nothing for the heroic act.

"I have erred. You are not one of my kind. You are accursed." Torrence glanced at Phylanna, then returned his gaze to Kelemvor. "You cannot save her, cursed one. She will pay for your trickery with her life!"

Kelemvor slowly turned, his skin dark and crawling with black, twisting hairs. He dropped his sword and stripped off the mail frock. His arms were still caught above his head when his flesh exploded and the great beast he held within him leaped at the jackalwere, pushing it out the window. The silver-haired creature howled as the beasts met in midair and plummeted to the ground.

*   *   *   *   *

Dawn was breaking, and Adon was shocked from his introspection by the screams of the dying.

The cleric approached the source of the screeches with growing apprehension; the screams he heard were not the sounds a human would make. And as he drew closer, he saw that many townsfolk had been drawn by the noise, as if the sounds had pierced the veil of lethargy that hung over them, allowing awareness to sear across their minds. The commoners stood staring at a nightmare.

The watchers were at either end of the alley, and Adon could only glimpse an occasional blur of movement from the area beyond—a flash of glaring white; a huge black form darting forward, then retreating as it let out an inhuman roar. There were two figures locked in some obscene dance of death.

Adon pushed forward, past the onlookers. Neither of the combatants was human, although one stood on its crooked hind legs. Its face was that of a jackal, but there was human intelligence in the gray-blue eyes, which registered alarm at the crowd that had gathered and at the warm sunlight breaking from above. The creature was covered in soft, matted hair, and it bled profusely from the score of wounds that had been opened in its hide.

The other beast was all too familiar to Adon: the sleek, black, rippling body; the piercing green eyes; the savage, bloodied maw; and the manner in which it stalked its prey. They all served to remind Adon of the impossible scene he had witnessed not so long ago in the mountains beyond Gnoll Pass.

The creature was Kelemvor.

At the feet of the dueling horrors was the prize for which they fought: a dark-haired girl who lay unmoving, her clothes shredded. Adon saw that she was still breathing and her eyelids fluttered from time to time.

The panther rose up on its hind legs as it engaged the jackalwere. They fell away from one another, sliding on the slick reservoir of blood that covered the street beneath them. Blood splattered in the face of the sleeping girl.

Adon turned and addressed the people. "We must bring low the jackal and save the girl!"

But the people merely stared.

"One of you must have a weapon of some sort—anything!"

Adon cursed himself for having left his war hammer behind, and took a step toward the creatures. The animals suddenly stopped and stared at him. Then the panther that had been Kelemvor took a swipe at the jackal and the hostilities were renewed. Adon backed away, through the indifferent crowd that viewed the spectacle with mild interest, and bolted toward the street.

He shouted two names as he ran down the street toward the Flagon Held High.

❦ 11 ❦

The Shadow Gap

"He's been attacked?" Midnight said. "By some kind of beast?"

"Yes! A silver-furred jackal that walks like a man!" the young cleric screamed.

"And the townspeople merely watched?"

"You've seen the way they are. We must hurry. Kelemvor's a beast, too."

"Kelemvor's a *what*?" Midnight cried.

Adon's explanation of the events he had witnessed made little sense to either Midnight or Cyric. His panic had ruined his usual adroit handling of descriptive passages in his narrative, and only nightmarish fragments of the entire story were at all clear when the cleric attempted repeatedly to convey what he had seen.

The heroes ran for the stairs and fled the inn. Cyric, who had received a strange, but successful visit from Rull of Gond, cut their mount's tethers with his blade, and they rode from the stables in haste, Cyric upon Kelemvor's mount, Adon riding with Midnight. The cleric's directions were hardly necessary. The entire population of Tilverton seemed to have been awakened by the battle. Men, women, and children flocked to the alley.

Midnight ordered Adon to tend to the horses, and Cyric took his bow and a good supply of arrows from one of the pouches slung over Kelemvor's mount. They broke through the crowd, shoving people aside. Just before an elderly couple parted and revealed what lay in the alley, Cyric looked down and saw a puddle of blood spreading outward on the gray stone pavement. Then he looked up and was startled by the bizarre scene that lay before him.

The jackalwere lay gutted in the middle of the alley. It shuddered and clung to life, though death would obviously soon be upon it. A huge black panther padded noiselessly back and forth, occasionally stopping to lick at one of the many pools of blood that radiated out from the dead creature. The woman Adon had attempted to describe was there as well, splattered with blood. She shrank against the wall, sobbing as she drew her knees up to her chest and only peeked over them to catch sight of the wounded panther that came closer with every orbit it made around its savaged prey.

Cyric notched an arrow, oblivious to Midnight's cry. All sound appeared to die away as Cyric drew back the bow, and the tiny vibrating sound the arrow made as it scraped along its sight filled the dark-haired man's ears. He felt a slight strain in his lower back from his recently healed wound as he held the arrow ready for release.

The panther stopped and looked directly at Cyric. The intensity of its perfect, green eyes caused the thief's arm to relax slightly. The beast roared, which also brought the sounds of the commoners crashing to Cyric's ears as he realized they were cheering him on, asking him to do what they could not.

Midnight dared not make a move, afraid that Cyric might release the arrow in surprise. She knew the truth the instant her gaze had met with the panther's. Adon had appeared beside her, then slipped past her and made his way along the wall to the girl, whom he dragged to the far side of the crowd. The panther ignored the young cleric's movements.

I want to understand, Midnight thought. Look at me, damn you! But the beast had eyes only for its potential executioner.

Unnoticed by all, the jackalwere breathed its last.

Suddenly the panther averted its eyes and trembled as if Cyric's arrow had left the bow and found its mark. The creature roared in pain, then fell to its side. The ribs of the beast were forced apart as the head and arms of a man burst from its gut. Moments later, all that remained of the panther were bits of matted fur and gore that deteriorated rapidly.

Kelemvor lay in the alley, naked and covered with blood. His hair was full and black, and it fell across his face as he attempted to rise, then collapsed flat on his stomach with a groan.

"Kill it!" someone was shouting. Through a haze of pain, Kelemvor looked up and saw Phylanna, one of the women he had saved, standing over him. Her red hair seemed to be aflame in the sunlight. "Kill it!"

Kelemvor looked up at her face and found only hatred.

Yes, he thought. Kill it.

A few of the commoners surged forward, emboldened by Phlyanna's cries. One found a brick that had been dislodged in the battle between Kelemvor and Torrence, and raised it high over his head.

Cyric rushed forward, his bow still at the ready. "Hold!" he cried. The commoners stopped. "Who dies first?"

Phylanna was unmoved by Cyric's threats. "Kill it!" she screamed.

Adon rose from the wounded girl's side. "It was not this man who took the lives of your people! This girl would be dead—slain by that *abomination*, were it not for this man!"

Midnight stood beside Phylanna. "The cleric is right. Leave him alone. He's suffered enough." The mage paused. "Besides, those of you who want to harm him will have to go through us to do it. Now go home!"

The commoners hesitated. "Go!" Midnight screamed, and the people dropped their bricks, turned their backs on the alley, and walked away. Still, Kelemvor had seen their faces and the utter revulsion they held for him.

Phylanna stared at the fighter and watched as the gray returned to his hair, the small wrinkles to his face.

"You are unclean," she said, her hatred radiating from her like a blinding sun at midday. "You are accursed. Leave Tilverton. Your presence is foul and unwanted."

Then the priestess turned and went to the frightened child, the "feast" Torrence had desired. "Join your fellow," she said to Adon as she lifted the girl up into her arms. "You're not welcome here either."

Kelemvor caught a glimpse of the girl's face as Phylanna carried her away. He hoped there might be a trace of understanding in the girl's eyes, but there was only fear. The fighter sunk to the ground once more, his face only inches from the pool of blood he'd spilled. He closed his eyes and waited for the last of the spectators, his former allies, to leave the alley.

"Is he alright?" Cyric asked.

Kelemvor was confused. The sounds of the man's boots became louder.

"I don't know," Midnight said as she crouched beside the fighter and touched his back. "Kel."

Kelemvor squeezed his eyes tightly shut. He could not bear to see the disgust and fear of the commoners in the eyes of his friends.

"Kel, look at me," Midnight said sternly. "You owe me a debt for saving you. Look at me."

Kelemvor started as a sheet unfurled in the air above him and gently settled on top of him. He looked up and saw Adon's face as the cleric pulled the sheet over his back. Kelemvor gathered the sheet to him and rose to a crouch. Midnight and Cyric were beside him.

There was concern in their eyes. Nothing else.

"My . . . armors and mails are upstairs."

"I'll get them," Cyric offered. He took the steps slowly, his side still sore from holding the bow drawn for so long.

Kelemvor studied Midnight's face. "Are you not . . . revolted by what you've seen?"

Midnight touched his face. "Why didn't you tell us?"

"I've never told anyone."

Cyric returned with Kelemvor's gear. He set it beside the fighter, then motioned at Adon. "We'll ensure your privacy as you ready yourself. There is a long road ahead of us, and we'd best meet it with the sun above our heads, not at our backs."

Adon stood watch at the far end of the alley, while Cyric went back the way they came and stood beside the mounts. Kelemvor bowed his head, and Midnight ran her hand through his hair.

"Ariel," he said quietly.

"I'm here," Midnight said, and she held the fighter tightly until he spoke. Once he began the tale, Kelemvor found that he could not stop until the debt of trust he owed to Midnight was fulfilled.

*   *   *   *   *

The curse of the Lyonsbanes had been passed down through Kelemvor's family for generations. Kyle Lyonsbane was the first and only of the Lyonsbanes to receive the curse due to his own actions. All those who followed received it from his tainted blood and through no fault of their own. Kyle was known as the quintessential mercenary: every service had its price and he was utterly ruthless in extracting payment, even from grieving widows if they held the gold that he was entitled to.

Kyle's actions caught up to him in a great battle, when he was given the choice of defending a fallen sorceress or continuing to cut through the enemy to reach their stronghold and be the first to plunder the vast riches within.

With Kyle's help, the sorceress might have gathered her strength, but the mercenary knew she would object to the plundering and could see no clear gain in helping her. He left her to die at the hands of the enemy. Before she died, she spat out one last intricate work of magic and cursed him to pursue his fortunes in a form more suitable to his true nature than a human shell could ever be.

When Kyle arrived at the stronghold and attempted to take his share of the gold, he felt a sudden weakness. He dragged himself away to a secluded chamber where he changed into a near-mindless, snarling panther. Instinctively, the beast knew it had to escape the stronghold. Only after half a day's flight from the castle, when the beast had killed a traveler, did Kyle suffer the painful transformation and become human once again.

For the rest of his days, Kyle Lyonsbane suffered the curse of the sorceress: whenever he attempted to perform an act for any type of reward, he became the beast. And even though only selfless, heroic acts were permissible for the mercenary under the curse, he had sworn he would never devote his life to such activities. He was forced to retire from the mercenary life he loved the most and live off the gains he had made from his previous adventures. When his gold ran out and the only avenue open to him was to live off the charity of his wife's family, he took his own life rather than live with the humiliation of poverty or perform any good deeds.

Before Kyle died, he sired an heir to his misfortune. Strangely, when the curse finally revealed itself in Kyle's son, the effects were reversed. Kyle's son could not perform any act, unless it was to protect his own life, without the promise of some type of reward. If he performed an act and did not receive his reward or he dared to perform a charitable act for no reward at all, he became a panther and was forced to take a life.

A roaming mage had a theory that as the original curse was meant as a punishment for evil and greed, and as all babes were born into the world as innocents, the curse found no evil to punish, and instead altered itself to punish the innocence and good in Kyle's son.

The intent of the sorceress' curse had been undone, and a long line of mercenaries with histories as bloody and unscrupulous as Kyle Lyonsbane's were born. It was Lukyan, Kyle's grandson, who discovered an inherent danger in his father's condition as his sire grew old and senile: the aged mercenary could no longer remember when a reward had been offered or warranted, or even when or if it had been paid. Because of this, the old man changed into the beast without provocation, and became a menace to all he came near. It became the responsibility of every child in the Lyonsbane clan to slay their father when they reached fifty summers.

The family survived for many generations, but the ritualistic killing of sires by their offspring was not always necessary: the curse did not strike every generation. Kelemvor's father and uncle had, for example, been exempt from the effects of the curse, free to live their lives the way they pleased. Like Kelemvor, all of the sons of Kendrel Lyonsbane were not as fortunate as their father.

Kelemvor was a seventh generation descendant of Kyle,

and he had tried all his life to free himself of the curse. He longed to perform acts of kindness, of charity and right. But the years had passed for the fighter, and there had been no hope of a cure, no hope for redemption. Only the bloody path of service and payment as a mercenary lay before him.

Kelemvor finished the tale and waited for Midnight to respond. She was quiet and caressed the fighter gently as he spoke.

"We'll find a way to cure you," she said at last.

Kelemvor looked into her eyes. There was compassion, mixed with regret.

"Will you come with me to Shadowdale?" Midnight asked, her hands caressing Kelemvor's face. "I offer a handsome reward."

The fighter could not look away. "I must know what you offer."

"I offer my love."

Kelemvor touched her hands. "Then I will come with you," he said and held her close.

*　*　*　*　*

As Kelemvor and his companions rode back to the Flagon Held High, Cyric stopped a number of times to gather the supplies they would need for their journey to Shadowdale. He found fresh mounts for Adon and himself, and meats and breads for the party. When they reached the inn, Midnight accompanied Kelemvor inside so they might retrieve their few possessions. Cyric and Adon waited outside, near the inn's front door.

The young man with pale gray eyes sat unnoticed in the shadows beside the door. There was an uncomfortable silence between Cyric and Adon. Looking out at the main street of Tilverton, Cyric saw a group of riders approaching from the direction of the temple. A floorboard creaked, and Cyric turned just in time to see the gray-eyed man rise up from the shadows behind Adon, wielding a knife. Cyric was already moving as the cleric turned, but the blade sliced through the air, too quick for even the thief to stop. A spray of blood blossomed onto the wall as the knife struck Adon in the face.

Cyric pulled the unconscious cleric back with one hand as the gray-eyed man prepared to strike again. The thief already had his dagger in his free hand, and he thrust forward, impaling their attacker.

"I die for the glory of Gond," the gray-eyed man said and fell back into his chair.

Kelemvor and Midnight appeared in the doorway. "Take him," Cyric said as he shoved Adon toward Kelemvor. The cleric's face was covered with blood. Midnight moved to help Kelemvor with their wounded, unconscious friend, and Cyric ran for the horses.

The gray-eyed man clutched at his stomach as he leaned back in his chair. "Phylanna warned us," he said and pointed at Kelemvor. "She told us that Lord Gond had sent a monster into our midst to test us. Only by killing it can we prove ourselves worthy of the presence of Lord Gond, the Wonderbringer. . . ."

The gray-eyed man fell out of the chair and sank to his knees, his back scraping against the wall.

Cyric looked to the road. The riders from the temple were approaching and would be upon them in moments. "We have to leave now, Kel," he said and turned his mount away from the Temple of Gond, toward the road to the north and Shadowdale.

With a swiftness born of desperation, Kelemvor heaved Adon over his shoulder and climbed to his mount. Midnight grabbed the cleric's belongings as she ran to her horse. The townsfolk were still on their heels when the heroes reached the road and headed out across the Stonelands.

The heroes rode long into the night, their pursuers never far behind. Kelemvor's plan was simple: the riders were not prepared for a lengthy journey, so they would have to stop or turn back at some point. Losing the pursuers was simply a matter of endurance.

It was dawn, and the riders from Tilverton were falling behind by a considerable distance, when the heroes came across a small lake near the mountains of the Shadow Gap. The water was surrounded by a scattering of trees, tired sentinels that longed to reach down and cool themselves in

the sparkling water. Kelemvor knew that the party couldn't
afford to stop, though he almost fell to the temptation of the
cool water. As they rode by the lake, the fighter hoped that
their pursuers' willpower was not as strong as his own.

A few minutes later, the heroes let out a cheer when they
saw that Phylanna and the Gond worshipers had stopped by
the lake. And though they were now far ahead of the Tilvertonians and were all very tired, the heroes pushed on until
highsun. By then, there had been no sign of their pursuers
for almost two hours. They stopped long enough to eat and
drink, but sleep was out of the question.

As Cyric and Kelemvor ate and tended to the horses, Midnight checked on Adon and took the time to cover his
wound. He had lost a great deal of blood during the ride and
was still unconscious, but the magic-user thought that he'd
live to see the Twisted Tower in Shadowdale. However, as
the heroes got ready to leave and Adon was hoisted onto
Kelemvor's horse, Midnight wondered if the cleric would be
better off not waking up at all.

As the day wore on, the heroes got closer and closer to the
Shadow Gap. At highsun, the huge granite slabs that made
up the steel-gray ranges of the gap appeared ghostly, as light
bathed the valley between the opposing ridges and made
the heroes wonder how the place got its name. But as afternoon wore on and the heroes got closer to the mountains,
they quickly learned that the gap's name was really quite
appropriate.

As the sun moved to the west, a veil of darkness fell upon
the road as the massive peaks of the Shadow Gap blocked
the sunlight at every turn. Long before nightfall, the heroes
felt as if they had been traveling with a blanket of cool thin
air over them, even though the sun baked the Stonelands to
the south of the gap, as well as the Desertmouth Mountains
to the west.

Still, the heroes pushed on, until in the half-light just
before night fell upon the Stonelands, the ground started to
make odd noises. Kelemvor dismissed the sounds at first,
believing them to be nothing more than underground rock-
slides, or perhaps the earth settling after the rain that had
drenched the area recently. But then the mountains around

the Shadow Gap started to move.

At first, Midnight thought a lack of sleep was causing her senses to betray her, but then she saw the ridge to the west slowly turning to face her. To the east, massive boulders were falling from the cliffs, crashing through the trees, crushing or uprooting them.

The earth quaked beneath the heroes, frightening the horses. The sounds quickly became deafening, and soon the boulders were coming closer, crashing against the trees that flanked the road. The road through the Shadow Gap was closing, and to the northeast, the heroes could see new mountains pushing up from the ground.

"We have to make it through," Kelemvor yelled, and dug his heels into his mount's side. "Come on!"

As the fighter raced down the narrowing road, Cyric and Midnight behind him, it became clear that both ridges were moving, closing the distance between them, closing off the gap. Rocks and other debris crashed down around them, uprooting trees and raising huge clouds of dust and dirt as the chaos continued. Soon it was impossible for the adventurers to see more than a few feet ahead, but they had to ride on as fast as they could. Though they might be hit by a boulder as they dashed for the other side of the gap, they would certainly be crushed when the mountains came together if they slowed down and rode cautiously.

Then, as the heroes raced through the falling debris, the chaos in nature struck again. Midnight's mount sensed it first and abruptly drew back, despite the magic-user's efforts to force the horse on. The color of the clouds that suddenly engulfed them was burnt amber, and they had to cover their noses and mouths to keep from inhaling the foul gases that made up the mist. When they had no choice but to breathe, the billowing, heavy clots of air the heroes inhaled burned horribly. No matter which direction they turned, the mist was there.

Their horses found breathing difficult, too, but they continued to move, gasping and wheezing. In the thick, filthy air the heroes could barely see where they were going. Luckily, when the mists came, the mountains seemed to stop moving so quickly.

Cyric knew it was a miracle that they had survived this long. And if the peaks started to shift again, the adventurers would be buried in a river of displaced earth, rocks, and trees long before they could get out of the Shadow Gap.

"We'd better stop for a minute," Midnight said, hacking and coughing. "We can get our bearings and make sure we're going in the right direction."

"Aye," Kelemvor wheezed. "It seems safe enough at the moment."

The heroes stopped and let their horses rest for a moment. They searched the mist for some recognizable landmark, something to guide them north through the destruction. The mist was too thick, though, and it was already getting dark, so they had to settle for Cyric's best guess.

"I think we're heading in the right direction," the thief said as the heroes mounted and got ready to move. "We have no choice but to follow what we think is the road through the gap."

Midnight laughed. "That certainly worked in that bizarre forest outside of Arabel."

As Cyric and Kelemvor scowled and kicked their horses into motion, Midnight screamed. A rat with glaring red eyes and a huge bloated body shot at her out of the mist. The magic-user struck the creature, which was as big as a man's forearm, and it squealed loudly. The rat fell to the ground with a thump and ran away.

Then the heroes heard a sound that made even Kelemvor shake. All around them were loud, high-pitched squeals. The cries echoed in the rocks and sent shivers down the adventurers' spines. There must be at least two hundred of them, Cyric thought as the first of the horde of giant rats broke through the mist.

Kelemvor's horse reared and nearly dumped Adon to the ground. "Get behind me!" Midnight screamed. Suddenly, a blue-white shield appeared all around the heroes, deflecting the bodies of the giant rats.

Kelemvor tried to steady his horse within the shield. "Don't you think throwing a spell is a little risky? I mean, you could have turned all the rats into charging elephants or something."

"If you're so unhappy about it, Kel, she could let the shield down," Cyric said.

The fighter said nothing, and Midnight smiled, though she didn't turn to look at her companions. Instead, she concentrated on holding the shield up as rat after rat bounced off the magical barrier.

Cyric looked out at the rodents running by them. "They don't seem to be particularly interested in attacking us," he said. "I wonder if they're running away from something or if the earthquake destroyed their nests."

Once the last of the rats had scampered by, the shield shattered as if it were a mirror struck with a hammer, and the broken shards faded from existence. "I think we should go right now," Kelemvor said, and the heroes navigated a passage through the fallen trees and boulders.

They rode for hours that night, but the mist showed no sign of lessening. Kelemvor felt a sickness growing in the pit of his stomach, caused no doubt by the sour air. He felt weak and tired, and from time to time he was certain he was going to be ill, though he never was. Occasionally, the rocks ahead seemed to shift slightly, but Kelemvor was so used to the sounds, he had grown deaf to the noise of the mountains as they shifted and drew closer.

Eventually, though, the mist got thinner, and the heroes' spirits rose as they found it easier to breathe. The road, too, was clearing. After walking their mounts for over a mile through a broken terrain of rocks and shifting ground, the adventurers found that they could again ride. Adon was moved to Midnight's horse, and Kelemvor pushed his horse to a gallop and rushed ahead to scout.

The fighter found that the mist soon parted and he could breathe in fresh, clean air again. The mountains hadn't tossed debris in the road this far north, and it looked like they were out of danger. Still, the land to the north of what used to be the Shadow Gap had changed, too. It was now strange and beautiful.

The road glowed white as it wound its way north for a few miles. Then it disappeared into the jagged foothills of a beautiful mountain range, which looked as if it were made entirely of glass.

Cyric and Midnight rode up beside Kelemvor as he stood, staring at the strange mountains to the northeast.

"Where are we?" Cyric said as he stopped and dismounted. "I don't remember any glass mountains in the Realms."

"I think they're new," Kelemvor said. "We went in the right direction. Now we're just north of Shadow Gap. See," the fighter said, pointing to the west. "Those are the Desertmouth Mountains, and that's the Spiderhaunt Woods right in front of us to the north."

"Then we're trapped," Midnight said and hung her head. "We can't go through those mountains, and they're right in our path."

The heroes were silent for a moment. "Then we'll have to go through the woods," Cyric said at last. "We certainly can't go back the way we came. So that's our only choice unless, of course, Midnight wants to fly us over the mountains on her broom."

"If she had one, it probably wouldn't work right anyway," Kelemvor said and started for the woods.

As the heroes got closer to the woods, something moved in the trees, something the size of a horse, with eight spindly legs and icy blue eyes.

As Midnight and Kelemvor stared at the glowing eyes in the woods, Cyric turned to get one last look at the Shadow Gap. Emerging from the mist were a group of riders. "The riders from Tilverton!" the thief cried. Cyric wheeled his horse around and drew his bow.

Kelemvor drew his sword and rode up next to Cyric. Midnight looked for a way out. The shapes in the woods were moving quicker now, patrolling the shadowy perimeter of Spiderhaunt Woods.

Midnight dismounted and stood in the path of the advancing riders. Despite her exhaustion, she drew her dagger and prepared to fight. The unearthly glow from the road illuminated the scene, and the heroes could see the riders clearly as they got close. Midnight recognized the bald-headed man in the lead.

Dragon Eyes.

"Thurbrand," Kelemvor and Midnight said together, their

mouths hanging open.

The bald-headed man stopped and dismounted. "Well met," he said to Kelemvor and Cyric. Then the fighter turned to Midnight. "We meet again, fair daffodil."

"How did you get through Shadow Gap?" Kelemvor said as he sheathed his sword.

"The same way you did. I've seen worse disasters," the bald man said. "The mountains had pretty much stopped moving by the time we got to them anyway. It wasn't so tough."

One of Thurbrand's men cleared his throat noisily. "We did lose one man in there," Thurbrand added. "He was crushed by a boulder."

"The people of Tilverton," Midnight said with concern. "The ones who were chasing us."

"They needed a bit of persuading to turn back. We lost two of our men doing so, but they lost a dozen of theirs," Thurbrand said. "That persuaded them."

Cyric shook his head. The fools, he thought. Dying for a god who doesn't care about them.

"By the way," Thurbrand said. "Along the road we learned that a squad of assassins is on the way from Zhentil Keep to dispatch the lot of you. They are Bane's elite force, trained practically from birth."

Cyric drew a sharp breath. "They wear bone-white armors, and their skin is bleached. The symbol of Bane is painted in black upon their faces." The thief shuddered. "I was almost sold into their order as a child. If they find us, we'll all be corpses soon."

"So now what?" Midnight said.

Thurbrand surveyed the travelers. "You have wounded. He should be taken care of first. And I imagine you haven't eaten or slept for quite some time."

"But what about the assassins?" Kelemvor asked, anxiously cutting glances back to the gap.

"We might as well wait for them," Thurbrand said as he turned and signaled his men to approach. "No use in running away if they are that highly trained. It'll be best to fight them on our own terms right here."

Midnight touched the bald man on the arm. "Why did you

follow us?"

Thurbrand turned, but didn't say anything.

"Why are you here?" Midnight said quietly.

"My men will tend to the cleric, then we can talk," Thurbrand said.

"Damn you!" Kelemvor yelled. "What do you want with us?" Thurbrand's men all drew their swords.

Thurbrand frowned. "Did I forget to mention? You're all wanted for questioning in Arabel. The charge is treason. Technically, you're all under arrest."

The bald man motioned for his men to sheathe their weapons and walked away.

* * * * *

Bane was alone in the throne room with Blackthorne, who stood beside the room's huge doors. An amber cloud filled the center of the room, and the image of a huge, mottled skull hung in the mist.

"I am intrigued, Myrkul," the Black Lord said as he paced back and forth. "As you have delighted in reminding me, our last collaboration was hardly a crashing success. Still, after my battle with Mystra, when I asked for your assistance, you all but laughed. I, on the other hand, am polite enough to answer your summons in the middle of the night."

"What is time to you or me?" Myrkul said. "Will you listen to my proposal?"

"Yes, yes. Get on with it!" Bane shouted impatiently, curling his hands into fists.

Myrkul cleared his throat. "I believe we should unite once again. Your plan of bringing together the power of the gods has merit that I am only now able to fully appreciate."

"And why is that?" Bane asked wearily as he dragged himself to his throne and sat down, a yawn escaping from him. The amber cloud followed him. "Have you grown as tired as I have of spending your time in these hated bonds of flesh?"

"That is one consideration," Myrkul said. "I also know where you can find another Celestial Stairway. You need it to gain access to the Planes, do you not?"

"Go on," the Black Lord said, drumming his fingers on the arm of his throne.

"You've told me of plans to invade the Dales. Did you know that a stairway lies just outside of the Temple of Lanthander in Shadowdale?"

"Yes, Myrkul, I knew of the stairway," Bane said. "But I appreciate your effort."

The Black Lord smiled. Though Myrkul's news of the stairway's presence in Shadowdale wasn't new to Bane, its exact location in the town was. Of course, Bane never even considered letting the Lord of Bones know that he had uncovered information of some value.

The ghostly skull closed its eyes. "How can I make up for my failings as an ally, Bane? I wish to help you in any way I can."

Bane raised one eyebrow and stood up. "You still refuse to take part in battle directly, so what help can you be?"

"I still have some control over the dead. I can . . . draw off the power of a human's soul when he dies."

Bane walked closer to the floating skull. "And could you give me that power?"

The skull nodded slowly.

Bane thought it over. Finally he spoke. "These are my conditions. You will collect the souls of all who die in battle and funnel their energies through me."

"And then?" Myrkul said.

"You will stand ready to join me in the assault on the Planes. When the time comes to climb the stairway, you will be at my side. We will first send my followers who survive the battle to attack the God of Guardians. When Helm slays the humans, he will only feed my power, weaken himself, and hasten his own destruction."

The skull in the mist was expressionless. Finally Myrkul nodded. "Aye. Together we shall retake the Planes, and then, perhaps, usurp mighty Ao's throne."

Bane raised his fist. "Not *perhaps*, Myrkul. We *will* destroy Lord Ao!"

Then the amber cloud dissipated and Lord Myrkul was gone. Bane walked to the spot where last the skull had hovered. "As for you, Myrkul, we will be allies for as long as it proves convenient."

Bane laughed. The ceremonies Myrkul would have to perform to invest Bane with the power he had requested would exhaust the Lord of Bones and most of his high priests. When the time came to climb the stairway, Myrkul would be relying on Bane's strength. He would not be expecting the betrayal Bane had planned.

"Blackthorne!" Bane said. "Prepare my chambers."

The emissary hurried past the Black Lord.

"I believe I'll sleep quite well tonight."

❧ 12 ❧

Spiderhaunt Woods

"Kindly remove your foot from my face," Thurbrand said and reached for his sword.

It was just before morningfeast, and the bald man found himself being roused from a short nap by a series of kicks to the back. He was then greeted by the sight of Kelemvor's boot looming over his skull.

"Traitors? What's this about the four of us, of all the beings who walk these Realms, being traitors?" Kelemvor shouted.

"*Suspected* traitors," Thurbrand said. "Now please remove your foot before I hack it off at the ankle!"

Kelemvor stood back from the bald man. Thurbrand rose, and a symphony of moans and crackles sounded as he ironed the kinks from his back, neck, and shoulders. The adventurers and Thurbrand's party were camped at the outskirts of Spiderhaunt Woods.

"How are your companions, Kel?" Thurbrand said as he got up to get some food.

"They live."

Thurbrand nodded. "And Midnight? Is she well? We have the matter of an outstanding debt—"

Kelemvor's sword left its sheath before Thurbrand could utter another word. "Consider it cancelled."

Thurbrand frowned. "I just want my hair back."

Kelemvor looked around the camp. The telltale skitter of his sword leaving its sheath had caught the attention of at least six men, who now stood with weapons to the fore, waiting for a word from their leader.

"Oh," Kelemvor said, and replaced the sword. "Is that all?"

Thurbrand scratched his bald pate. "It's enough," he said. "Although my mistresses seem to like this look."

Kelemvor laughed, and sat beside Thurbrand as he ate. Cyric, who had been wakened by the argument, made his way to the fighters. He walked slowly, and his arms gleamed in the bright morning sunlight with dark bruises from the treacherous ride through Shadow Gap.

"You look—" Kelemvor said as the thief approached.

"Don't say it," Cyric said, and took a plate of food. "If you looked or felt the way I did, you'd be dead."

"You're not," Kelemvor said absently.

"I'm not convinced," Cyric said, running his hand through his matted hair. "Midnight? Adon?"

"Adon's still unconscious," Kelemvor said.

"Then he doesn't know," Cyric said, his voice low as he made a gesture with his hand across his face.

Kelemvor shook his head.

Cyric nodded, then turned and barked a command at one of Thurbrand's men. The man looked to Thurbrand, who closed his eyes slowly and nodded. The man brought a warm mug of ale to Cyric, who downed the contents in one swift motion, then handed the mug back.

"That's better," Cyric said, turning to Thurbrand. "Now, what's this talk about traitors?"

Thurbrand related the tale of Myrmeen Lhal's battle with the attacker who had identified himself as Mikel, and Cyric laughed. "Marek never could come up with a decent alias," he said.

The bald man frowned and went on with his story. He told them of his meeting with Lhal and Evon Stralana, and the party he'd been asked to arrange. "Naturally I insisted on leading the company myself," Thurbrand said. "For a long time it's been common knowledge that the Knightsbridge conspiracy originated in Zhentil Keep. When we learned of the band of Zhentish assassins who are tracking you, your innocence became somewhat obvious."

"You had doubts?" Kelemvor said.

"You paid for false identification and a false charter, then left the city in disguise, running out on your contracts to serve and protect Arabel. Then this Mikel—or Marek—

implicates you in the conspiracy. I believe you can see the obvious conclusions that were drawn." Thurbrand grinned. "But of course, I had no doubts."

"So why didn't you just turn around and go right back to Arabel?" Cyric said.

Thurbrand frowned. "Once we learned what lay ahead for you, the only lawful decision was to blaze our way through the Shadow Gap and come to the aid of a former ally."

Kelemvor rolled his eyes.

"Oh, *please*," Cyric said. "There must be something you wanted."

"Now that you mention it," Thurbrand said. "Besides the prompt return of my hair, there is a little job I could use a few good men for, back in Arabel . . ."

"We have business in Shadowdale," Kelemvor said.

"And after that?"

"Wherever the wind takes us, I suppose," Cyric added.

Thurbrand laughed. "There's a hearty wind blowing in our direction. Perhaps we can arrange something at that!"

"We'll see what Midnight has to say," Kelemvor said quietly.

Cyric and Thurbrand stared at the fighter, then began to laugh as he rose and went to scavenge more food from the company's cook. He didn't notice that Adon was awake.

The cleric had awoke at the sound of Myrmeen Lhal's name, though it had been spoken all the way across camp. "By Sune, I'm cooked!" he said out loud. Adon realized he wasn't alone when he heard a young girl's laugh.

A girl of no more than sixteen summers sat beside him, making indelicate slurping noises as she made her way through the huge bowl of gruel that rested in her lap. Her name, Adon soon discovered, was Gillian, and she had stringy brown hair and deeply tanned skin that was hard and dry. Her eyes were a deep blue, and her features were ordinary but not unattractive.

"Ah!" she said. "You're awake!" She set the bowl down, then lifted it and held it out to Adon. "Care for any?"

Adon rubbed his forehead and suddenly remembered the attack of the gray-eyed man in Tilverton. He knew he'd been hit by the man's dagger, then passed out. Still, he now felt rested and only a little weak.

"I knew Sune would protect me," he said, contented.

The girl stared at him. "Care for any stew or not?"

"Yes, please!" Adon said, any concerns he might have had about Myrmeen Lhal and her lackeys now vanquished by his hunger. As the cleric sat up, though, he felt a sharp tug along the left side of his face and a deep burning sensation. Something warm and wet rolled down his cheek. Odd, Adon thought. It isn't unusually warm this early in the morning. I wonder why I'm should be sweating so. Then he looked at the girl.

Gillian's shoulders were drawn up tight, and her knees had ground together as she looked away from Adon.

"What's wrong?" the cleric said.

"I'll get the healer," Gillian said and rose to her feet.

Adon ran his hand across his face. The sweat was even worse. "I'm a healer. I'm a cleric in the service of Sune. Am I feverish?"

Gillian glanced back at the cleric, then quickly looked away.

"Please, what's wrong?" Adon said, and reached for the girl. Then he saw that there was blood on his hand. It wasn't sweat he had wiped from his face at all.

Adon's breathing slowed, and he felt as if a huge weight were pressing down on his chest. His skin grew cold. His head began to swim.

"Give me your bowl," he said.

Gillian looked to the others in the camp and called out to one of them. Midnight saw that Adon was awake and jumped to her feet.

"Give it to me!" Adon cried, and wrenched the bowl from her hands, spilling the contents to the ground. His hands were trembling as he shined the metal bowl with his sleeve, then raised it to his face and looked into the curved mirror.

"No."

Gillian was no longer by his side. There were crashing footsteps. Midnight and a cleric wearing the symbol of Tymora stood before Adon.

"It cannot be," Adon said.

The cleric of Tymora had been grinning from ear to ear when he approached, thankful that the young Sunite had risen from his sleep with no ill effects. Once he saw the expression on Adon's face, though, his smile quickly faded.

"Sune, please . . . ," Adon said.

The muscles in the healer's face tensed. He suddenly understood. "We did what we could," he said somberly.

Midnight put her hand on Adon's shoulder and looked at Cyric and Kelemvor, who were sitting together across the camp.

Adon said nothing. He simply stared at his reflection.

"We are too far from Arabel and the goddess Tymora for healing magic to work," the cleric continued. "There were no potions. We had to rely on the salves and natural medications I could create."

The rim of the thin metal bowl began to curl in Adon's grip.

"What's important is that you're alive, and perhaps one of your own faith will be able to help you where we could not."

The metal twisted.

"You must let me examine you. You're bleeding again. You've torn the stitches."

Midnight reached down and took the bowl from Adon's hand. "I'm sorry," she whispered.

The healer bent low, toweling away the blood from Adon's face. The damage was not as bad as he had feared, though, as only a few of the stitches had been torn. As the cleric looked at the scar, he wished they'd been in a city when he found the Sunite. At least he could have made a cleaner job of the stitching with the proper tools.

Adon's fingers traced the darkening scar, following it from his left eye, down over his cheekbone, and through the center of his cheek. The ragged cut ended at the base of the cleric's jaw.

* * * * *

Later that morning, as the adventurers broke camp, Cyric got into an argument with Brion, a young thief in Thurbrand's company.

RICHARD AWLINSON

"Of course I understand what you're saying!" Cyric shouted at the albino. "But how can you deny the evidence of your own senses?"

"I gazed upon the face of the goddess Tymora herself," Brion said. "That's all the evidence I need. The gods are now visiting the Realms to spread their sacred word first hand."

"Aye, pay your money and step right up," Cyric said. "Perhaps your goddess will start telling fortunes next."

"All I'm saying—"

"Dullard! I heard you the first time," Cyric yelled.

"Contributions are always necessary—"

"A necessary evil, you mean." Cyric shook his head and looked away from Brion.

"It must be terribly lonely not believing in anything but yourself," Brion said. "My belief makes me whole."

Cyric trembled with rage, then gained control of his emotions. He knew that Brion had not intentionally provoked him, but the dark-haired, lean fighter had been unusually edgy since he woke that morning. Perhaps it was the sadness that hung over the camp because of Adon's wound, but a part of him wanted to charge into the mountains once more and let fate throw any monstrosity it could imagine at him. Even Spiderhaunt Woods felt vaguely tempting, although Cyric knew that the only catharsis he would likely find in that place was death.

There was a sound in the distance, and the earth beneath the adventurers shuddered. Cyric saw huge crystalline shards sliding from the face of the glass ridges that had positioned themselves across the road to Shadowdale.

"Merciful Tymora," Brion said as the massive glass boulders shattered and sent rainbows across the land as they reflected the sunlight.

Then, without warning, a glossy black spear, the size of a small tree, shot out of the earth next to Cyric. The thief was knocked to the ground, but quickly got up and grabbed his horse. All around the plain, similar jagged ebon spears thrust up through the dirt and towered a dozen feet into the morning sky.

"Time to leave," Kelemvor said to Thurbrand, and the two men ran for their mounts. "It looks like we're going through the woods after all."

Thurbrand surged through his company, rallying his people and hurrying them toward the woods. Before they could get away, though, two of his men were impaled by the spikes, and three horses were gutted. The only remaining members of the company bolted into the darkness of the Spiderhaunt Woods. Spears continued to shatter the plain, and huge avalanches of glass fell from the mountains to the northeast.

As she got close to the woods, Midnight discovered that Adon was missing. As she scanned the plain from the edge of the woods, she saw the cleric's riderless mount racing amidst the spears. Midnight charged toward the renegade animal and caught up with it in the center of the plain.

A figure was moving slowly through the clouds of dirt, approaching the horse.

"Adon, is that you?" Midnight called.

The cleric took his time as he mounted the horse and led it away from the deadly plain at a leisurely pace. He reigned the animal in when it tried to bolt, and if he heard Midnight's words or saw her frantic gestures, he ignored them. But when Adon didn't react, even as a spike shot from the ground a few feet away from him, Midnight moved beside the cleric and slapped the hind quarters of his mount with all her strength. The horse galloped toward the woods and relative safety. Adon didn't cry out or even lurch forward as the horse ran. He merely dug his fingers into the horse's mane, his legs into its flank, and hung on.

Kelemvor waited at the perimeter of the woods. All but a few of Thurbrand's people had vanished within, and the last of the riders joined their allies in the darkened recesses of Spiderhaunt Woods.

There was no movement from the creatures they had spied the previous night. "Perhaps they sleep by day," Kelemvor said. The sounds of shattering glass and exploding ground had lessened, though the adventurers could still hear an occasional crash as a huge wall of glass slid off the mountains.

"If the creatures sleep during the day," Midnight said. "We'd best be in Shadowdale by night."

Kelemvor, Cyric, and the Company of Dawn all mumbled in agreement. Adon silently rode off into the woods.

Throughout the day, the adventurers rode through the woods, starting at every sound, their swords always at the ready. Adon rode ahead of Kelemvor and Midnight, and Cyric rode with Brion, who had lost his horse to one of the ebon spears. As they got deeper into the forest, the flora grew thick and unmanageable, and soon Thurbrand signaled for everyone to stop and dismount. The horses would have to be lead.

Adon ignored the signal, and Kelemvor ran to his side. "Have you lost your sight this time, Adon?" he said. When the cleric ignored him and continued to force his horse to plow through the undergrowth, the fighter slapped him on the arm to get his attention. Adon looked down at Kelemvor, nodded, and got off his horse.

"There's death in this place," Adon said, no life in his voice. "We've walked into a charnel house."

"It wouldn't be the first time," Kelemvor said and returned to Midnight.

Farther ahead, Cyric walked with Brion. Although he had been alternately amused and frustrated by the young thief, Cyric sensed an innocence in him that was refreshing. Surely Brion had not been an adventurer very long, although his proficiency with a dagger rivaled Cyric's.

After morningfeast, Brion had challenged Cyric to a test of skill with the dagger, and Cyric nearly lost to the albino. After the challenge was over, Cyric and Brion did a trick using six daggers each, which they first gathered from their friends, then tossed at each other with blinding speed. Each knife Cyric threw was deflected by one of Brion's, then each one Brion threw was deflected in midair by one of Cyric's tosses.

Still, for all his skill with knives, the albino did not reek of blood and madness as so many adventurers did. Even Brion's companions, like the girl who sat with Adon, reveled in the idea of taking a life. Cyric could see it in their eyes.

Cyric could see, too, that the number of times Brion had willingly shed blood could be counted on a single one of his gloved hands, and that the albino had never taken a man's life without regret.

As the adventurers walked along, the woods themselves were misleadingly beautiful, at least at the start. The trees were thick and healthy, covered with rich green leaves. Bright sunlight pierced the openings in the ceiling of the forest, and warm shafts of light fell here and there, occasionally caressing the faces of the heroes who navigated through the thick foliage.

Then, as they moved across a thick bed of gnarly roots, which covered the ground completely in many places, Kelemvor heard twigs snapping in the trees. He turned sharply and motioned to Zelanz and Welch, the mercenaries who brought up the rear, but they hadn't heard the sounds. They looked at Kelemvor and shrugged. Kelemvor saw no hint of movement around the party, so he turned and walked on.

The noises came again and again, and finally the entire company had been alerted. Weapons were drawn, but no one could spot any signs of the creatures in the trees. In the lead, Thurbrand carefully navigated through a small path in the woods. Rounding a tree, the bald man stopped quite suddenly, his body tensing as he prepared for an attack.

A man wearing bone-white armor stood before Thurbrand, stuck to a tree by long, ropy strands of webbing. His helmet had been removed, and the bleached white skin of his face was marked with the symbol of Bane, black over his white features. Sword drawn, the assassin stared at Thurbrand, his face frozen in a wild-eyed grimace.

A few yards away, Thurbrand saw five other men wearing the armor of Bane's elite assassins, stuck to other trees in a large clearing.

"They're dead," Thurbrand said. "But whatever killed them is close by."

The adventurers stood still for a moment as Kelemvor and Thurbrand examined a huge web that was strung in the trees around the assassins. The rest of the party, with the exception of Adon, gathered closer together and watched the trees. The Sunite, on the other hand, simply stood by his horse, staring up at the dark canopy of leaves that blotted out the sun.

As the party stood, listening for something to move in the trees, they noticed that there was no sounds at all coming from the woods. The leaves didn't rustle in the wind. No insects chirped. The woods were completely silent.

Without a single word, Gillian handed the reigns of her mount to the cleric of Tymora, then took to the trees like a monkey. She made no sound as she rose to the highest branch, then surveyed the woods with her practiced eye. The adventurers waited for five minutes as she leaped from branch to branch, carefully taking in the area from every possible vantage, and finally she signaled all clear.

The girl motioned for Thurbrand to come close, even before she leaped down to the ground. "Not even the strongest winds could move these branches. This place is dead, frozen in this state." She made a motion with her fingers to indicate an odd texture. "There is a light film covering everything. That's what causes the stillness."

Thurbrand nodded, and reached out to help her down. She frowned and leaped over and past him, landing in a graceful crouch. But as her feet struck the earth, directly in the center of a tangle of roots that radiated from the spot, there was a harsh, wet sound and the ground gave way just a bit. Before the girl could utter a word of warning, the roots burst from the ground in a shower of displaced earth.

Eight limbs in all burst up to grab Gillian, all of them tall, spindly, and pitch-black. Each limb had four joints, and they culminated in a razor-sharp tip the size of a large sword. The vast underbelly of the creature that the girl stood upon moved from the earth, pitching her off balance before she could leap from the trap. Then the creature's head burst from the ground, and she saw its blazing red eyes and four jagged pincers.

The legs of the giant spider collapsed inward, impaling Gillian from eight different directions. Then the spider flipped over, and the woods came alive. All around the travelers, the knotted roots revealed themselves. Another man had been standing on the belly of one of the spiders and met the same fate as the girl.

Cyric and Brion stood back to back, daggers drawn. One of the spiders attacked Cyric's mount, injecting it with a poison from its mandibles that paralyzed the horse. The spider dropped the animal and waited for the poison to act before it carted the horse off to its web. Cyric cursed as he realized most of his supplies, including his hand axes, were on the horse, but he wasn't about to try and rescue his clothes from the spider that stood guard over his dying mount.

The spiders were everywhere, and the smallest of them was the size of a large dog. Cyric stared into the eyes of one of the creatures as it advanced. Its legs were a pale green, and its body was black with huge orange blotches on its side. The predatory gaze of the spider brought a smile to Cyric's face as he launched a dagger into one of the creature's unblinking eyes.

Cyric's blade found its mark and was enveloped in the quivering mass of the spider's eye. The eye collapsed inward, following the blade, but the spider continued to advance.

"Gods!" Cyric cried, and leaped to a low-hanging branch. The giant spider surged forward, snapping at the air where the thief had stood only moments before. As he climbed higher into the tree, Cyric heard a scream and looked down.

The wounded spider had pierced Brion's side with one of its legs; the daggers he held were little defense against the horror. The spider lifted a second leg, preparing to run its victim through again. Brion's head fell back as he struggled, and he looked up at Cyric.

Cyric could see that Brion's lips were moving, begging him for help.

Cyric hesitated, weighing his options. He knew the man was already dying from the creature's poisons. There was little he could do but die beside him.

The spider struck with its second leg. Life faded from Brion's eyes as Cyric watched.

At the other end of the clearing, Midnight watched as three spiders charged. Kelemvor, Zelanz, and Welch stood beside her, and Adon stood motionless behind them, seemingly oblivious to the threat that was barreling down on them.

Two of the spiders were huge and fat, with black and red

bodies and bloated crimson legs. The third was completely black, with sleek sharp legs and a greater agility than the others. The narrow gaps between the trees did little to slow this one, as it pitched at an angle, climbing across the sides of the trees to get at its prey.

The sleek spider jumped at the heroes, and Kelemvor snapped off three of its limbs with a single swing of his sword. The fighter struck again and cut a channel in the body of the beast, narrowly avoiding its pincers. Then Kelemvor turned, and the spider was directly over him, rising up on its back legs. He thrust his sword into its exposed underbelly and forced it up and back. The creature slashed at the fighter with a leg, and Kelemvor was knocked off his feet. His sword pulled free as he sailed through the air and crashed into a tree.

Midnight watched as the remaining pair of spiders advanced on them. Looking down at her dagger, she realized that it was going to be useless against the monsters, so she tried to remember her decastave spell. Midnight grabbed a branch from a nearby tree and recited the incantation. Suddenly a glowing blue-white staff materialized in Midnight's hands. As Midnight attacked the spider, she was startled to find that the staff took on the properties of a scythe. She slashed open the first spider she saw, but the other went for easier prey.

It pounced on Zelanz and Welch, who fought it side by side. Their sweeping swords dispatched it quickly, but others approached. The drip of a milky white substance was all that alerted them to the spider that had been busy forming a web above them. Zelanz looked up, just in time to see the reddish mass of the spider as it descended upon them.

At the edge of the clearing, the cleric of Tymora moved forward. He touched the edge of a tree and saw Thurbrand fighting for his life against the spider that killed Gillian. He took another step and came face to face with Bohaim, a young mage from Suzail. He stumbled back to clear the way for Bohaim, but a spider's leg burst through the mage's chest. The man screamed as the spider pulled him up into the air and lowered him toward its hungry mandibles.

The Company of Dawn is dying, the cleric of Tymora

thought. There was a slight crunch behind him. He brought up his mace and turned to face a purple and white spider. One of the spider's legs impaled the cleric with blinding speed. The cleric formed a silent prayer to Tymora, and the world became darkness.

Not far from where the cleric fell, Thurbrand's sword flashed and the head of the spider that killed Gillian was caved in, spilling its poisons even as the fighter turned away to avoid being soaked. Five more spiders advanced on the bald man. Just ahead of him, the other two living members of the Company of Dawn were fighting for their lives. Thurbrand ran toward the two men, ignoring the pack of spiders closing in behind him.

High above in the trees, Cyric watched with a growing fascination as the spiders climbed in the woods around him and worked their intricate art. Cyric knew he should be revulsed or angered by the sight: the sole purpose of the spider's work was to ensnare and kill him and his friends. But the patterns of this waiting death were quite lovely to Cyric. There was such simplicity and such order in its design.

There was a sound beside him, and Cyric leaped from the tree even as a jagged set of pincers ground together in the air where he had been. The ground rushed up at him as he fell, and the thief twisted in midair, then rolled to absorb the fall's impact as he struck the ground.

Cyric heard the telltale snapping sound of a spider breaking from the earth just before its legs rose up, snaring him in its trap.

Fifty yards away, Kelemvor rose to his feet. The sounds of the spiders engulfed his senses. Their limbs crackled, and the petrified trees shifted slightly beneath their weight. The monsters surrounded him, but they were not rushing in for the kill. Then, a huge white spider moved toward him very slowly, and all the other spiders cleared the way for its approach. It was the largest spider Kelemvor had ever seen.

A small circle was formed around Kelemvor, so that the white spider might have room to maneuver. The fighter looked up and saw a host of spiders waiting in the trees above. There was no escape for him; the other were probably all dead. Then the huge white spider rushed forward, and Kelemvor severed one of its legs just as another pierced the air beside his face. Then a third leg moved along his armor, opening the tempered breastplate and making a shallow gash across his chest.

With horrible clarity, Kelemvor saw the fourth leg sailing at him. In an instant, the leg would pierce his chest, and the spider would drag his twitching body to its hungry mandibles. Then, a piercing blue-white pain shot through the fighter's head.

As Cyric jumped from the tree and Kelemvor started his battle with the white spider, Midnight moved against a blood-red spider as Adon stood behind her, making no move to protect himself. Midnight ran between the grasping legs and planted her magical scythe in the creature's eyes.

As the blood-red spider lay twitching on the ground, Midnight looked around her and saw that both Cyric and Kelemvor were in terrible danger. Then, a white, milky substance struck her boot. She looked up just in time to see the huge, yellow underbelly of a spider as it plunged down at her, its legs working the air with hungry anticipation.

Midnight cast a spell to create a shield in front of the spider. As she finished reciting the incantation, her pendant suddenly crackled with energy. Bolts of energy shot from the star and struck Adon, Kelemvor, Cyric, and the three remaining members of the Company of Dawn.

Then, just at the white spider brought its leg down on Kelemvor, just as Cyric landed on the trap, just as Adon stared uncaring as a gray spider descended toward him, they all disappeared.

Midnight felt as if the air were being ripped from her lungs. A brilliant flash of blue-white light blinded her for an instant, and when her vision cleared, she found herself standing on a long road. For a moment she thought she had gone mad, then the mage realized that she had teleported from the woods.

Kelemvor lay on the ground in front of her, holding his head. "What did you do?" the fighter groaned, then he tried to stand up, but couldn't. He looked down and saw that the cut on his chest was still bleeding slightly. "Not that I mind, whatever it was."

Cyric and Thurbrand helped the fighter to his feet. "Yes. *Whatever* you did, we owe you our lives," the bald man said. "And that certainly fulfills your debt to me, fair daffodil."

Midnight opened her mouth to speak, but couldn't think of a thing to say. She just looked around, wide-eyed.

"Gillian, Brion, they're all gone," one of the remaining members of the Company of Dawn said as he helped cover his friend's wounds.

"I'm sorry," Midnight said at last. "I don't even know how I got us here, even *if* I got us here."

"Wherever 'here' is," Cyric said as he looked around.

Adon, who was standing a few yards away, staring up the road to the north, turned around and said quietly, "We're a half day's ride south of Shadowdale."

* * * * *

The doors leading to Bane's throne room burst open wide and Tempus Blackthorne rushed inside to answer the call of his god. Bane gripped the edge of his throne, his talons scratching the surface.

"Close the door." Bane's voice was cold and measured. Despite the latitude that Bane had granted his emissary, Blackthorne felt a momentary flicker of fear.

"You wished to see me, Lord Bane?" Blackthorne said, his voice deceptively steady.

The Black Lord rose from his throne and gestured for the mage to come closer. The taloned hand of the fallen god flashed before the eyes of the emissary. Blackthorne made no move to defend himself as the God of Strife grabbed his shoulder roughly.

"The time has come," Bane said.

Blackthorne's heart skipped a beat as he saw that Bane's lips were pulled back in what he could only call a smile. It was a horrible thing to see.

"The time to unite the gods is upon us," the Black Lord cried. "I want you to take a message to Loviatar, the Goddess of Pain. I believe she is in Waterdeep. Tell her I wish to see her . . . immediately."

Blackthorne's body tensed. The taloned grip upon the

emissary's shoulder tightened as Bane registered the change in Blackthorne's stance.

"You have a problem with this order, emissary?" the God of Strife growled.

"Waterdeep is halfway across the Realms, Lord Bane. By the time I return, your campaign against the Dales will be a part of history."

The Black Lord's smile vanished. "Aye, if you travel as a normal man would travel," Bane said. "But with the spell I've given you, you will be in Waterdeep within a few days."

Blackthorne lowered his eyes, and the Black Lord removed his hand from his shoulder. "What if the goddess does not wish to accompany me on the journey back to Zhentil Keep?"

Bane turned his back on the emissary and folding his arms. "I will trust you to convince her otherwise. That is all."

"But—"

"That is all!" Bane screamed as he whirled on his emissary, his dark eyes flashing.

Blackthorne took a step back.

The eyes of the Black Lord blazed as the seething anger Bane felt intensified. "You disappoint me," Bane said, although his tone suggested disgust rather than anger. "Do as I say and win back my favor."

Bowing before his lord, Blackthorne murmured the first prayer he had ever learned—a prayer to Bane. Then the mage stood up and raised his arms as he began to chant the emissary spell. He visualized his destination, remembering a visit he had paid to Waterdeep in his youth. A moment later, Blackthorne's body began to shimmer and change as he tried to assume his raven form. But something was wrong. His flesh was being pulled in every direction as it turned charcoal-black. The emissary's clothing shredded and fell to the floor.

Blackthorne screamed and held out one partially transformed arm to his god. "Help me," was all the mage had time to say before he imploded in a shower of black sparks. Where Blackthorne had stood only a moment before, a small black gem dropped to the floor next to his breastplate and shattered.

Bane watched in complete shock. "The spell," he said absently as he stumbled back into the shadows near the entrance to his private chamber.

The guards who rushed into the room didn't see their god as he stood in the shadows. They looked down at the tattered remains of Tempus Blackthorne and shook their heads.

"I suppose that had to happen sooner or later," one of the guards said.

"Aye," the other guard said. "Any idiot knows that magic is unstable."

Bane rushed forward and killed both guards before they even knew he was there. Then Bane turned and stripped off his bloodied armor. A moment later, he was sitting upon his throne, staring at Blackthorne's ruined breastplate on the floor.

I will not grieve, the god decided coolly. Blackthorne was merely a human. A pawn. His loss is regrettable, but he can be replaced.

Then Bane thought of his endless talks with Blackthorne. He remembered the strange emotions that coursed through him when he had realized that Blackthorne had saved him, and aided in his recovery.

The Black Lord looked at his hands and noticed he was trembling. Then the God of Strife screamed a cry of grief, loud and long. All over Bane's Dark Temple, people covered their ears and shivered at the sound of the Black Lord's pain.

When his scream ended, the God of Strife looked down through tear-clouded eyes and saw a figure standing before his throne.

"Blackthorne?" Bane said, his voice harsh and rasping.

"No, Lord Bane."

Bane wiped his eyes and looked down at the red-haired man who stood before him. "Fzoul," he said. "All is well."

"Milord, there are dead men surrounding you in the temple—"

Bane raised his taloned hand.

The red-haired man hung his head. "Yes, milord." Then Fzoul picked up his god's scattered armor and helped Bane to his feet.

"All is in readiness," Fzoul said as the Black Lord finally put on his bloody armor again. "When shall we begin to prepare for the battle?"

A fire crackled in the eyes of the Black Lord and Fzoul stepped back from the angry god. Then Bane's lips curled back in a frightful grimace. There was fire behind the God of Strife's pointed teeth, too, as his eyes narrowed and he said, "Now."

❦ 13 ❦

Shadowdale

The time for eveningfeast had passed, but the travelers walked on, determined to reach Shadowdale before the night was through. The spell that had spirited them from certain death in Spiderhaunt Woods had deposited the adventurers almost two days' journey ahead on their route.

Midnight, Kelemvor, and Thurbrand walked together, as did Cyric and the other surviving members of the Company of Dawn, Isaac and Vogt. Adon walked alone, thinking of everything he had lost.

"They died bravely," Kelemvor said to Thurbrand at one point.

"That is little comfort," Thurbrand said, memories of the last quest he had shared with Kelemvor edging into his thoughts. It had been many years ago, but the results had been much the same: Thurbrand and Kelemvor had lived. Everyone else had died.

Cyric had a confused, haggard look as he walked through the dale. It was as if he'd been forced to confront some great truth, and the knowledge had left him weak and trembling. When he spoke, it was in a soft, almost quavering voice.

Adon, on the other hand, didn't speak at all. There was nothing for him to do as he walked, nothing to fill his head but his own unwelcome thoughts. And as he walked on through the night, the cleric's relentless fears drove him down into a white-faced, trembling shadow of the man he'd once been.

But not all of the adventurers were grim-faced and mournful as they walked toward Shadowdale. Midnight and Kelemvor behaved as if the worst was behind them.

They laughed and exchanged taunts as they had earlier in their journey. Every time they smiled or laughed, though, one of their companions would frown at them, as if they were interrupting a funeral with their mirth.

Eventually, however, most of the heroes relaxed as they trekked through the countryside south of Shadowdale. The green, flowing hills and rich, soft earth of the dale's outlying districts were wondrous to behold. Even the air was sweet, and the harsh winds that had plagued the heroes ever since they entered the Stonelands became light breezes that caressed the travelers, enticing them to walk ever faster in their pursuit of sanctuary.

It was very late when they reached the bridge that spanned the Ashaba and led into Shadowdale. The tiny, sparkling lights they had seen in the distance now revealed themselves to be glowing fires set at the far end of the bridge. Guards armed with crossbows and wearing bright silver armor walked back and forth on the bridge and warmed their hands by the fires from time to time.

Kelemvor and Midnight walked beside Thurbrand as the party approached the bridge. As they got close to the river, however, something moved in the bushes. The heroes turned and reached for their weapons, but stood still when they saw six carefully aimed crossbows sticking from the bushes on both sides of the bridge. The steel-tipped arrows gleamed in the moonlight.

Thurbrand frowned. "I believe this is where we hold and state our business." He turned to the men who crawled out of the bushes. "Isn't that so?"

"A fair beginning," one of them said.

"I am Thurbrand of Arabel, leader of the Company of Dawn. We have come to gain audience with Mourngrym on matters most pressing."

The guards shifted nervously and whispered to each other. "What matters?" a guard said after a moment.

Midnight's face got red, and she moved closer to the guard. "On matters pertaining to the safety of the Realms!" she cried. "Is that not urgent enough?"

"All well and good to say, but are you able to prove it?" The guard moved toward Thurbrand and held out his hand.

"Your charter?"

"Certainly," Thurbrand said and handed the guard a rolled up parchment. "Signed by Myrmeen Lhal."

The guard examined the parchment.

"We have suffered many casualties in Spiderhaunt Woods," Thurbrand said.

"These are your survivors? What are their names?" The guard said.

Thurbrand turned to the two actual survivors of his company. "Vogt and Isaac," Thurbrand said.

Kelemvor and Midnight exchanged glances.

"And the others?" The guard said.

Thurbrand pointed at Midnight. "She is Gillian. The rest are Bohaim, Zelanz, and Welch."

The guard passed the charter back to Thurbrand. "Very well, you may pass," he said, then backed away. The guards all disappeared into the shadows once more.

The travelers crossed the bridge carefully, and when they reached the other shore, Thurbrand looked to Kelemvor.

"Quite an interesting place already," Thurbrand said.

An armed contingent, patrolling by the bridge, stopped when they saw the adventurers, and the ritual of questions, answers, and documentation was repeated. This time the soldiers "offered" to escort the tired travelers to the Twisted Tower, despite Midnight's anxious cries about Elminster.

"Protocol," Cyric whispered. "Think of your last meeting with the mage. Would it not go easier if the path were laid down for you by the local lord?"

Midnight said nothing.

As they approached the Twisted Tower, Cyric noted that the small shops and houses that lined the path seemed deserted. However, there were lights in the distance, and the sounds of activity from a few streets over. A wagon loaded with bales of hay moved across the road. Another wagon, filled with livestock, came behind it. Soldiers escorted both wagons.

"If they are moving livestock at this time of night," Cyric said to Midnight, "they are probably preparing the town for war. I fear your warning from Mystra about Bane's plans comes too late."

As they got closer to the Twisted Tower, the heroes could see that torches lined the stone walls of the square, squat building. The torches were patterned oddly, though, and they followed the odd curvatures of the tower as they spiraled up one side of the building, vanished, then reappeared higher and higher until the lights gave way to shadowy mist that even the unusually bright moon could not penetrate.

More guards waited at the entrance to the tower. The guards spoke for moment with the heroes' armed escort. Then one guard, probably a captain of the watch, whistled long and loud. As the heroes and the guards waited for whatever or whoever it was that the captain had summoned, Adon turned and started to wander off down the street. A guard rushed to intercept the cleric, then steered him back with the others. Adon sullenly complied.

A young man dressed in the livery of a herald appeared at the door. He was still bleary eyed with sleep, but he listened to the guardsman as politely as he could, hiding his yawns behind a ruffled sleeve when possible.

The herald led Kelemvor, Thurbrand, and the others through a long corridor, and soon they stood before a heavy wooden door with three separate locking systems. Cyric casually studied the locks as Kelemvor grumbled impatiently. Finally the door was opened and the herald, a tall, lean man with salty brown hair and a thick mustache and beard, turned to address the travelers.

"Lord Mourngrym will see you in here," he said simply. Kelemvor caught a glimpse of the poorly lit interior of the room. As he had feared, it was some type of cell with bare floors and chains hanging from the walls. The fighter's eyes became slits as he turned to the herald.

"We desire an audience with Lord Mourngrym, not the rats of Shadowdale. If he cannot see us tonight, then we will return in the morning."

The herald did not flinch. "Please wait inside," he said.

Midnight brushed past Kelemvor and entered the chamber. The moment she crossed the threshold, there was a rippling in the shadows and she disappeared.

"No!" Kelemvor shouted, and leaped through the door after her, only to find himself in the throne room of the

Twisted Tower.

Torches had been lit within the throne room, and Midnight could see that the finely crafted plasterwork on the otherwise bare walls spoke of many battles and paid homage to those who had died in the service of the dale. Red velvet curtains covered the one wall devoid of plasterwork. The curtains rested behind the two black marble thrones that stood across the room from the entrance. In all, the hall was large enough to entertain visiting emissaries, but it wasn't huge and overly ornate like the halls of Arabel's palace.

At the far end of the chamber stood an older man whose physique did not reveal his advancing years. His build was similar to Kelemvor's, but the heavy lines marking his face revealed him to be at least twenty years older than the fighter. He was dressed in shining silver armor and a jewel-encrusted sword hung at his side. The man looked up from a long planning table that was strewn with maps and smiled warmly at the heroes as they entered the hall.

There was a noise at the outer wall of the chamber, a thump followed by a curse. "And I say he *did* move the bloody door!" A series of taps were heard, then a hand emerged from the seemingly solid wall, fingers extended tentatively. A face followed, then vanished. "I want an envoy sent to Elminster come first light. I will not be held captive by his magic!" Silence. "No, I am not just being cranky!" A sigh. "Yes, Shaerl. I will be up shortly, my wife."

A figure emerged from the wall just as the rest of the adventurers, accompanied by two guards, appeared behind Kelemvor and Midnight. The figure turned, looked at his guests, and froze. He was extremely handsome, with thick black hair, deep azure eyes, and a square-set jaw. His clothing was a glaring testament to the lateness of the hour. He wore a frock that revealed his bare arms, hairy bare legs, and bare feet ending in nervously twitching toes. His arms were thick and strong, his muscles well-tended. A crimson band encircled his right upper arm. He cut a glance to the older warrior, who merely shrugged.

"I wasn't expecting guests," the black-haired man said. Then he straightened up, cleared his throat, and flashed a smile. He approached the travelers. "I am Mourngrym, lord of this place. How can I help you?"

Kelemvor was about to speak, but a guard leaned toward the fighter, his axe held in a threatening manner. Mourngrym scratched the side of his face as he motioned for the travelers to hold for but a moment, then he took the guard aside.

"Good Yarbro," Mourngrym said. "Do you remember our little discussion concerning the down side of over-zealous behavior?"

Yarbro swallowed. "But, milord, they have the look of vagrants! They have no gold, no supplies, they walked into town, and their only form of identification is a charter which is almost certainly stolen!"

"And how was it that my men found you on the outskirts of Myth Drannor all of two winters ago?"

"That's different," Yarbro said.

Mourngrym sighed. "We will talk again."

Yarbro nodded, then turned to leave the chamber with the other guard. Kelemvor was relieved to see the guards go. It would have been difficult explaining why they had given the guards names other than their own to gain access to the tower, and they might have been forced to keep the adopted names so as not to arouse suspicion.

The older warrior stood at Mourngrym's side. A look passed between Kelemvor and the old man as Yarbro brushed past the fighter on his way out. They both grinned. "This is Mayheir Hawksguard, acting captain of arms."

Thurbrand winced. "*Acting* captain of arms? What happened to the old one?"

"I would rather not discuss that until I understand your purpose for being here," Mourngrym said as he turned away. "What happened to the lot of you?"

All but Adon surged forward, and six versions of what they had witnessed erupted simultaneously. Mourngrym rubbed his tired eyes and glanced at Hawksguard.

"Enough!" Hawksguard shouted, and there was silence in the chamber.

"You there," Mourngrym said to the sullen, scar-faced man. "I would hear your version of the tale."

Adon stepped forward, then told all he knew of the events that plagued the Realms in the least amount of words possible. Mourngrym leaned against his throne and frowned.

"You might have noticed a few of the precautions that have already been put into effect around here," Mourngrym said. "It is feared that Shadowdale will be under siege in a matter of days." Mourngrym looked to Thurbrand. "To answer your earlier questions, the old captain of arms infiltrated Zhentil Keep and nearly died getting us this information. He is in his quarters, recovering from his injuries.

"Hawksguard will lead your delegation to Elminster after morningfeast. Tonight you are my guests." Mourngrym yawned. "Now if you will excuse us, I believe there were other reasons I was woken from the tender embrace of sorely needed sleep. We will speak further come morning."

Each of the adventurers were then led to private chambers, where steaming baths and soft beds lay in wait. Midnight went out to get some air, and after walking around near the tower, she returned to her room to study her spells. But as she opened her door, she heard a a slight splash. Someone was in her room, waiting for her to return.

She thrust open the door and flashed her lantern into the bedroom. There was a startled yelp as the lantern illuminated a large man leaping out of the room's bathtub. He ran for his clothes and weapons, which lay in a heap nearby.

"By the gods," Kelemvor muttered as he saw who the intruder was. "Midnight."

Kelemvor shook himself off like a cat, then picked up a towel. He gingerly dried his chest, where the cut he received fighting the white spider had healed, but was still slightly tender. Midnight set her lantern on a small table across from the bed. She held open her arms. "Come here, Kel. I'll help you with that."

Even in the dimly lit room, she could see his grin.

In the other chambers of the Twisted Tower, the night did not pass so peacefully. Cyric was haunted by nightmarish visions of Brion's death, which played over and over in his head as he slept. A number of times Cyric cried out and woke up, sweating. And each time he went back to sleep, the nightmare returned.

In another room, Adon stood at the window and looked out on the rooftops of Shadowdale. All around the town, he saw the spires of temples, although he could not discern what gods they were a tribute to. Come morning, when a rather plain serving girl named Neena knocked on his door, he was still standing at the window. She entered and lay down the clothes he had given the servants for cleaning.

"Morningfeast is due to commence shortly, good sir," she said.

Adon ignored the girl. Brushing the bangs out of her eye, she touched Adon's shoulder then drew back as he spun on her, his hands set to deliver a killing blow. When he saw it was only a servant, he faltered and stood silently. Neena looked at the cleric's face, then turned away respectfully.

To Adon's failing heart, the gesture was worse than any physical blow.

"Leave me," he said, then he prepared himself for morningfeast.

Kelemvor was standing across the hall from Adon's door as Neena left. He heard the cleric dismiss her and shook his head. Adon won't be healed inside from that scar for a long time, the fighter thought as he turned to knock on Thurbrand's door.

"They're about to serve morningfeast," Kelemvor said when Thurbrand finally opened the door.

"I've already been informed," the bald man said. "You may leave now."

Kelemvor pushed past the fighter and shut the door behind him. "We should talk . . . about you and your men."

"Men die," Thurbrand said and sat down on the bed. "Those are the fortunes of war." The bald man kicked his sword across the room and looked up at Kelemvor. "I'm leaving, Kel. Vogt and Isaac are coming with me."

"Aye. I expected as much."

Thurbrand ran his hand over his bald head. "I'll go back to Arabel and tell Myrmeen Lhal what I've seen. I'm certain she'll drop the charges."

"Charges? I thought we were wanted for questioning!"

Thurbrand shrugged. "I didn't want to alarm you," he said. "Perhaps I should just tell her you're all dead. Would you prefer that?"

"Do as you will. But that's not what I came here to talk to you about." Kelemvor looked at Thurbrand's sword, now laying in the corner. "You blame yourself for what happened in Spiderhaunt Woods."

"It doesn't matter, Kel. It's over. The blood of my entire company is on my hands. Can you wash it away with your consoling words?" Thurbrand stood, walked to the corner, and picked up his sword. "I might as well have killed them myself." The bald man swung the sword halfheartedly in the air, as if to chase his thoughts away. "Besides," he said quietly, "there are many more deaths than theirs on my conscience. You know that."

Kelemvor said nothing.

Thurbrand grimaced. "I still see the faces of the men who died in my stead—in *our* stead, so many years ago, Kel. I still hear their screams." Thurbrand paused and looked up at Kelemvor. "Do you?"

"Sometimes," Kelemvor said. "We chose to survive, Thurbrand, and that's a difficult decision to live with. But what happened to our friends has nothing to do with the Company of Dawn. The company had no choice but to follow us into the woods. If they'd stayed on the plain, they'd all have died with no chance to fight back."

Thurbrand turned his back on Kelemvor. "Why are you so concerned about this?"

Kelemvor leaned against the door and sighed. "There was a girl—about the same as Gillian was—who started with us on our journey. Her name was Caitlan."

Thurbrand turned to look at Kelemvor, but the fighter was staring off into space, reliving Caitlan's death.

"She insisted on coming with us, and she died when I was supposed to be protecting her."

"And you feel that you're to blame," Thurbrand said.

Kelemvor let out a deep sigh. "I merely thought you might like to talk about the company."

"Gillian," Thurbrand said after a moment. "She seemed rather young to be an adventurer, didn't she?"

Kelemvor shook his head. "I've seen younger on the road."

Thurbrand closed his eyes. "She was filled with enthusi-

asm. Her youth . . . gave me back some of my own. I wanted—
no, I needed her around. I was certain I could protect her."

A long silence hung over the room as both fighters
thought about companions, some long dead, some dead
only a few days. "It was her choice to come with you,"
Kelemvor said at last and turned to leave.

"And it's my choice to get out of Shadowdale before I end
up dead, too," Thurbrand said softly. "I'll be away from here
by highsun."

Kelemvor left the room without saying anything.

* * * * *

Hawksguard smiled and shook his head in disbelief.
"What do you mean 'this is not a good time?' I haven't led
these good people to Elminster's tower just to have them
turned away."

"I'm sorry you bothered. You'll have to come back later.
Elminster is conducting an experiment. You know how little
it takes to arouse his anger if he is interrupted in such
moments. Now I suggest you people move on, unless you
wish to find yourselves transformed into horseflies, or
receive some similar, unpleasant fate."

Lhaeo attempted to shut the door only to find an unusual
doorjamb blocking the way. Hawksguard winced as the
heavy door pressed against his foot with greater force than
Elminster's scribe could ever apply. More of the sage's
enchantments, he thought, then forced the door back a bit.

"Look here," Hawksguard said as Kelemvor appeared at
his side and shoved at the front door with him. "I have an
unhappy liege. If I have an unhappy liege, then *you* have an
unhappy liege. And if we have an unhappy liege, then—"

Suddenly the door swung open wide, and Lhaeo moved
out of its way. Hawksguard and Kelemvor were both tossed
forward and fell in a tangle at the scribe's feet.

"Oh, let them in, lest he begin the sordid tale of woe all
over again!" a familiar voice called out.

Midnight felt flushed with awe at the sound of Elminster's
voice. She heard the sound of footsteps on rickety stairs
growing louder. Then, a white-bearded sage appeared at

the foot of the steps and fixed Midnight with his gaze. The number of lines surrounding his eyes seemed to double as he squinted, as if he doubted his senses.

"What? Ye again! I thought I had seen the last of ye in the Stonelands!" Elminster said. "Mourngrym sent word that someone with a message of *importance* would visit me. That's supposed to be ye?"

Cyric helped Kelemvor to his feet. Adon stood back and watched.

Midnight refused to allow her anger to get the better of her. "I carry the last words of Mystra, Goddess of Magic, as well as a symbol of her trust; it is an item she told me to give to you, along with her message."

Elminster frowned. "Why didn't ye tell me this when we first met?"

"I tried!" Midnight said.

"Obviously, ye didn't try hard enough," Elminster said as he turned back to the stairs and motioned for her to follow. "I don't suppose ye would consider leaving that troublesome entourage with Lhaeo while ye relate this *vitally important* information?"

Midnight drew a deep breath. "I don't suppose I would," she said. "They have seen what I have seen, and more."

The sage cocked his head to the side as he climbed the stairs. "Very well," he said. "But if they touch anything, they do so at their own risk."

"There are dangerous objects here?" Midnight said as she climbed the winding staircase behind the sage.

"Aye," Elminster said as he looked over his shoulder. "And I am the most dangerous of them all."

Then the sage of Shadowdale looked away and did not speak again until the heroes had left the stairs and entered his chamber.

Midnight was certain something would fall on her if she dared another step into the sanctum of the wizened sage. There was a window directly ahead, and the beams of sunlight that pierced the air beside her revealed a small army of dust particles floating in the air. There were parchments and scrolls, ancient texts and magical artifacts strewn about the modest quarters of the sage.

"Now," Elminster said. "Give me the details of thy involvement with the goddess Mystra. Then tell me her exact message, word for word."

Midnight related all that she had seen, starting with her brush with death on the road to Arabel and her salvation by Mystra, and finishing with the seeming destruction of the goddess at the hands of Helm.

"Hand me the pendant," Elminster said.

Midnight pulled the pendant over her head and gave it to the sage. Elminster passed the pendant over a beautiful glass orb that glowed with an amber cast and waited a moment. When nothing happened, the sage brought the pendant even closer to the orb, touching the cold metal of the star against the sphere, while holding the item as far from his body as possible. The globe had been designed to shatter if any powerful object was brought within its range, but nothing happened as the pendant touched it.

Elminster's eyes narrowed as he looked up. "Worthless," he said and dropped the pendant to the floor.

"There is no magic within this trinket." Elminster kicked the pendant across the floor. It landed in the corner and a cloud of dust rose. "Ye've been given my time and my patience," Elminster said. "Neither is to be trifled with, especially not in these trying times for the Dales."

"But there is powerful magic in the pendant!" Midnight said. "I've seen it. We all have!"

And soon the stories began to flow from both Cyric and Kelemvor. Elminster looked to Hawksguard wearily.

"That's all," Elminster said finally. "Ye may leave now, and rest assured that the protection of the Dales lays in the hands of those who think better than to waste the precious time of its defenders with tall tales and fantasies that ye cannot even substantiate."

Midnight stood, staring in shock at the old sage.

"Come on," Kelemvor said. "We've done all that we can here."

"Aye," Elminster said. "Begone!"

Suddenly the pendant shot from the corner and hung in the air beside the old sage. Elminster's gaze fixed on Midnight once more. She felt a cold wave of panic pass through her mind.

"A minor display of your magic does not interest me," Elminster said in a low and measured voice. "In fact, these days it's rather dangerous."

The pendant started to spin in the air. Sharp streaks of lightning played across its surface and began to radiate out from the star.

"What's this, then?" Elminster said.

There was a blinding flash of light, and a cocoon of blue-white lightning formed around the old sage, cutting him off from view. Something that looked like an amber whirlwind erupted within the cocoon, searing its edges. Seconds later, the cocoon dissolved in a puff of smoke and the amber streaks of light vanished.

"Perhaps we *should* talk further," Elminster said to Midnight as he snatched the pendant from the air.

Hawksguard moved forward.

"A word, great sage," he said, respectfully.

"Is it one that immediately comes to mind or must I guess?" the sage muttered. Hawksguard stopped for a moment, then laughed heartily. Elminster looked to the ceiling. "What? Can't ye see I'm busy?"

Hawksguard drew himself to attention. "Elminster, Lord Mourngrym would have a word or two with you about the defenses you have cluttered the Twisted Tower with."

"Would he now?" Elminster said. "Where is he? Show him in."

The muscles in Hawksguard's face twitched. "He's not here."

"That does present a problem, does it not?"

Hawksguard's face was turning red. "He sent me to fetch you, good sir."

"Fetch!? Am I a dog, then! And after all the help I've given that man!"

"Good Elminster, you turn my words against me!"

The sage thought about it for a moment. "I suppose I do at that. But I cannot leave here today. There are elements at work that I must watch carefully." Elminster gestured at Hawksguard. "Come close," he said. "I have a message for our liege."

The edges of Hawksguard's mouth twitched as he approached. "You're not going to tattoo it on my flesh, are you?"

"Of course not," Elminster said.

"Or change me into some unearthly beast, then set me to the winds that I may repeat the message to all I may find until I am at last brought before Lord Mourngrym?"

Elminster rubbed at his forehead and cursed. "Where did I get this reputation?" he said absently. Hawksguard was about to answer, but the mage's wrinkled finger pierced the air before him, entreating him for silence. Elminster gazed into Hawksguard's eyes.

"Tell him that I am terribly busy preparing the mystical defense of his kingdom. The wards I have placed in the Twisted Tower are for his own good, and he should accept them as such."

Hawksguard was sweating in his armor. "That is all?"

Elminster nodded. "The three of ye, come forward."

Kelemvor, Cyric, and Adon carefully navigated the length of the room.

"Each of ye has witnessed sights that very few will ever know. Where do ye stand on the defense of the Dales?"

The trio stood in place. Kelemvor looked to Midnight, who averted her eyes.

"Are ye deaf? Are you with the dale or not?"

Adon moved forward. "I wish to fight," he said. Elminster looked at the young cleric, intrigued.

"Do ye, now?"

Kelemvor looked to Midnight. Her gaze told him that she had no intention of leaving, even though she had fulfilled her agreement with the goddess. Anger coursed through him. He did not want to stay, but he could not bring himself to leave Midnight behind. "We've come this far. Bane tried to kill us all. I will fight if there is a reward in it for me," the fighter said at last.

"Ye will be rewarded," Elminster said coldly.

A cold hand clutched Cyric's heart as the silence in the small room grew to epic proportions. Midnight looked up at him. There was something in her eyes. Cyric throught of Tilverton, of how close they had become on their journey.

"I will fight," he said. Midnight looked away. "I have nothing better to do anyway."

Elminster glared at Cyric, then turned away. "All of ye have faced the gods and survived. Ye have seen their weaknesses first hand, as well as their strengths. That will be important in this battle. Those who fight must know that the enemy can be conquered, that even the gods may die."

Adon flinched.

Elminster spoke softly now. "Ye see, there are forces greater than man or god, just as there are worlds within, and worlds without. . . ."

* * * * *

It was just after highsun that Hawksguard, Kelemvor, and Cyric left Elminster. Adon wanted to go with them, but even Kelemvor agreed that the cleric was in no condition for combat. Cyric had been amused by Adon's desire to spill blood, but he kept his amusement to himself. He knew that the cleric could not be trusted in a battle such as the one they faced; Adon seemed to care less and less for his own survival, and he would be the last man any soldier would want guarding his back.

Halfway to the Twisted Tower, Cyric started to question his own reasons for aiding the defense of the town. There was nothing for him here, except perhaps a quick death. If that were all he desired, there were easier ways to find it. A stroll down the streets of Zhentil Keep in the middle of the night was sure to reward him with such a fate. Or perhaps he wished to test his mettle against the god who attempted to slay him once already.

We four faced a god and survived—even without Mystra's assistance, Cyric thought. Imagine if we were successful in slaying a god! Our names would be sung in ballads that minstrels would recite for hundreds of years.

Elminster's words haunted Cyric even as they approached the Twisted Towers and sat waiting for Lord Mourngrym to make his appearance. Without the presence of the gods in the Planes, magical and physical laws were breaking down. All of the Realms might fall. What then might rise from the ashes? Cyric thought. And who would be the gods of that dark future?

Mourngrym appeared, and Hawksguard recited Elminster's words. Kelemvor and Cyric pledged their assistance, and by nightfall they had been given their parts to play in the battle. Kelemvor would be stationed with Hawksguard and the majority of Mourngrym's forces at the eastern border, where Bane's troops were expected to attack. Cyric was called to help defend the bridge at the Ashaba and to assist the refugees leaving via the river to seek sanctuary in Mistledale. Archers were already taking up positions in the forest between Voonlar and Shadowdale and traps were being laid for Bane's troops.

And though Mourngrym believed he had organized his forces in the most efficient way to counter the larger Zhentish army, the dalelord was concerned about Elminster's place in the battle to come.

"I suppose Elminster still believes the true battle will take place at the Temple of Lathander," Mourngrym said ruefully. "We need his help at the borders! By Tymora we've got to talk some sense into that man!"

"We would be the first to ever do so, I'm afraid," Hawksguard said, smiling broadly.

Mourngrym laughed. "Perhaps you're right. Elminster has always stood in defense of the Dales. But to catch just a glimmer of the man's reasoning before he chose to reveal it would be a prize I would cherish for the rest of my life!"

Both Kelemvor and Hawksguard broke into braying laughter at the dalelord's comments. Cyric just shook his head. At least Kelemvor wasn't being morose anymore. In fact, the fighter's camaraderie with Hawksguard almost made him pleasant to be around.

But Cyric wasn't much in the mood for the fighters' jokes, so he left the throne room quietly. The halls of the Twisted Tower rang with activity as the thief made his way back to his room to prepare for eveningfeast.

After he changed his clothes, the thief turned to leave his room. As he walked toward the door, his boot slid across a slick patch of wood on the floor. He regained his balance, then looked down. Had one of the clumsy cows they called 'serving girls' in the tower made a mess she was too dainty to clean up? Cyric wondered. There, in the center of the room, was a stain that looked like blood.

Cyric's fingers trembled as he reached down and touched the red stain. He smeared his finger in the liquid, then touched his finger to his tongue, just to see what the liquid was.

Something exploded in his skull, and Cyric felt his body fall backward into the far wall, then land on the bed. He was dimly aware of the damage he had caused to the wall and to himself, but his perceptions swam in a fantastic haze of sights and sounds. The thief was finding it hard to tell his delusions from reality.

He was only certain that someone else was entering the room, closing the door, and locking it.

And before he passed out, Cyric realized that the man was laughing.

The next thing the thief was aware of was an odd taste in his mouth, like bitter almonds. His throat was dry, and sweat poured into his eyes. The sound of his own breathing came to him: raspy and without steady rhythm. His skin felt as if it had been flayed. Sight and sound returned suddenly, and he found himself lying upon his bed. A gray-haired man sat on the edge of the bed, facing away from Cyric.

"Don't try to move yet," the man said. "You've had quite a shock."

Cyric attempted to speak, but his throat was raw and he began to cough, which only caused a greater pain.

"Settle back," the man said. Cyric felt as if something were pressing him back against the bed. "We have much to discuss. You won't be able to raise your voice above a whisper, but don't worry. My senses are quite acute."

"Marek," Cyric croaked. The voice was unmistakable. "It can't be! You were arrested in Arabel."

Marek turned to face Cyric. He shrugged. "I escaped. Have you ever heard of a dungeon that could hold me?"

"What are you doing here?" Cyric said, ignoring the man's boasts.

"Well . . . ," Marek said, and rose from the bed. "I was on my way back to Zhentil Keep. I grew tired on the road. My documentation—the same documentation that gave me access to Arabel—was taken from a soldier outside Hillsfar. A professional mercenary, actually. He won't be missed.

"I claimed that I was on my way back to rejoin the conflict between Hillsfar and Zhentil Keep, which I assumed the people of Shadowdale would see as a worthwhile enterprise. My cover, I was certain, was assured. I didn't know that Shadowdale was preparing for a war of their own with Zhentil Keep, and the guards demanded I join their damned army!"

"What happened to your cache of magical items that you bragged about in Arabel? Couldn't you have used them to escape the guard?" Cyric said.

"I was forced to leave almost all of them behind in Arabel," Marek said. "Are you expecting me to attack you? Don't be foolish. I'm here to talk."

"How did you get into the Tower?"

"I walked in through the front door. Remember, I'm a member of the guard now."

"But how did you know I was here?"

"I didn't. This is all chance, as all of life really is. As the guards tried to convince me that joining their army, even if it wasn't my own idea, would be beneficial for me, they described a small adventuring troop that came to the dale and was welcomed into the Twisted Tower itself for their aid to the town. Amazingly enough, part of the party sounded very much like the band you left Arabel with. It really wasn't hard to find you after that.

"By the way, I apologize for the effects of the potion that laid you out. Actually, there was one magical item I had managed to retain—this locket," Marek said, and produced a solid gold locket that had been opened. A drop of red liquid that resembled blood fell from it and hit the floor. The liquid hissed as it touched the boards.

"I was shown to your room earlier today and told that I could wait for a few moments. When you didn't arrive, I became bored. I noticed that the catch on the locket seemed as if it might break. When I examined it, it did break and the potion spilled to the floor. And that's when you came in. Actually, I wasn't sure that it was you at first, so I hid in the closet. Then you tasted the potion, and, well, here you are."

"What do you intend to do?" Cyric said. "Will you expose me, as you did in Arabel?"

"Certainly not," Marek said. "If I do that, what's to stop you from exposing me? That, you see, is the reason for my visit. I merely wished for you to maintain your silence until after the battle."

"Why?"

"During the battle, I'll make my escape. Switch sides. Return to Zhentil Keep with the victors."

"The victors," Cyric said absently.

Marek laughed. "Look around you, Cyric. Do you have any idea how many men Zhentil Keep has mustered? Despite the preparations, and despite the advantage of the woods between here and Voonlar, Shadowdale doesn't have a chance. If you had any intelligence, you'd follow me out of here, follow right in my footsteps."

"So you have told me," Cyric said.

"I offer you salvation," Marek said. "I offer you a chance to return to the life that you were born for."

"No," Cyric said. "I'll never go back."

Marek shook his head sadly. "Then you will die on this battlefield. And for what? Is this your fight? What is your stake in all of this?"

"Something you wouldn't understand," Cyric said. "My honor."

Marek couldn't contain his laughter. "Honor? What honor is there in being a nameless, faceless corpse left to rot on a battlefield? Your days away from the Guild have left you a fool. I'm ashamed that I ever thought of you as a son!"

Cyric turned white. "What do you mean?"

"Just what I said! Nothing more. I took you in as a boy. Raised you. Taught you all you know." Marek sneered. "This is pointless. You're too old to change. So am I."

Marek turned to leave. "You were right, Cyric."

"About what?"

"In Arabel, when you said I acted on my own. You were right. The Guild doesn't care whether or not you ever return. It was only me that wanted you back. They'd have forgotten long ago that you ever existed had it not been for my insistence that we try to draw you back."

"And now?"

"Now I no longer care," Marek said. "You are nothing to me. No matter what the outcome of this battle, I never want to see you again. Your life is your own. Do as you will."

Cyric said nothing.

"The effects of the potion are disorienting. You might experience some delirium before your fever breaks." Marek took the locket and left it beside Cyric on the bed. "I wouldn't want you to dismiss our conversation as a fever dream in the morning."

Marek's hand had just closed over the doorknob when he heard movement from Cyric's bed. "Lay back down, Cyric. You'll hurt yourself," he said, just as Cyric's dagger entered his back.

The thief watched as his former mentor fell to the floor. Moments later Mourngrym and Hawksguard appeared at Cyric's door, along with a pair of guards.

"A spy," Cyric said hoarsely. "Tried to poison me . . . Came back to question me in return for the antidote. I killed him and took it."

Mourngrym nodded. "You have served me well already, it seems."

The body was removed, and Cyric climbed back into bed. For a time, he was poised on the brink of fantasy as the poison from the locket coursed through his system. He seemed to be trapped, half awake, half asleep, and visions ran through his head.

He was a child on the streets of Zhentil Keep, alone, running from his parents as they sought to sell him into slavery to pay off their debts. Then he was standing before Marek and the Thieves' Guild as they passed judgement on him, a ragged, bloodied youth they had found on the streets, robbing to survive; their judgement made him a part of the Guild.

But of course Marek turned away when Cyric needed him the most—when he was marked for execution by the Guild and forced to flee Zhentil Keep.

Turning away.

Always turning away.

Hours passed and Cyric rose from the bed. The red haze lifted from before his eyes. His blood had cooled, his breathing became regular. He was too exhausted to stay awake, so he simply collapsed on the bed again and surrendered to the tender embrace of deep, dreamless sleep.

"I'm free," he whispered in the darkness. "Free. . . ."

* * * * *

Adon left Elminster's abode late at night, at the same time as the scribe, Lhaeo. The old man had actually shown concern over Lhaeo's well-being as he sent the man off to contact the Knights of Myth Drannor. Magical communication with the east had been blocked, and armed with Elminster's wards, the scribe would have to travel by horse to deliver the message to the Knights.

"Till we meet again," Elminster said, and watched his scribe ride off.

On the other hand, Adon simply walked away, without raising a single word or gesture from the sage. He was halfway down the walk before Midnight caught up to him, and gave him a small purse of gold.

"What is this for?" Adon said.

Midnight smiled. "Your fine silks have been ruined during our journey," she said. "You should replace them."

She pressed the gold into the cleric's cold hands and attempted to warm them between hers. The breathless excitement she had felt all day was painfully apparent to the cleric. Besides attempting to fathom the answers to some of the mysteries that had plagued her all during the journey, Elminster had allowed Midnight to participate in some minor rites of conjuring. There were many instances however, when even Midnight had been shut out of Elminster's private ceremonies that evening.

The darkness had already enveloped Adon when Midnight called out, reminding him to return in the morning.

Adon almost laughed. They had set him in a tiny room and given him volume after volume of ancient lore to read so he might attempt to find some reference to the pendant Midnight had been given. It was a gift of the goddess, Adon

argued. Forged from the fires of her imagination. It had no
existed before she called it into being!

"But what if it had?" Elminster said, eyes gleaming. Bu
Adon was not blind. Interspersed in the lore he had bee
given were tales about clerics who had lost their faith, the
regained it.

They would never understand, Adon thought. His finger
touched the scar that lined his face and he spent the evenin
reliving their journey, attempting to spot exactly where h
had committed such an affront against his goddess to war
rant her desertion in his greatest time of need.

By the time he noticed where he was, Adon was startle
find how far he had traveled. He was long past the Twiste
Tower, and the sign for the Old Skull Inn was just overhead
The gold Midnight had given him was still clutched in hi
palm, and he slipped it into one of his pockets before h
entered the three-story building.

The taproom was crowded and filled with smoke. Ado
had worried that he would find dancing and merriment
but he was relieved to find the people of Shadowdale as pre
occupied with their thoughts as he was. Most of the inn'
customers were soldiers or mercenaries, come to the Ol
Skull to kill time before the battle. Adon noticed a youn
couple who stood off to the far end of the bar, laughing a
some private joke.

Adon sat with one elbow on the bar, resting his face in hi
open hand, trying to cover the scar.

"What spirits will you be wrestling with tonight?"

Adon looked up and saw a woman in her mid-fifties, wit
a pleasant, robust glow in her cheeks. She stood behind th
bar and waited patiently for the cleric to respond. When hi
sole communication was a wounded, dying flicker from hi
once fiery eyes, she grinned and vanished behind the ba
When she returned, she carried a glass filled with a ric
violet brew that sparkled and sputtered in the light. Bits o
red and amber ice whirled around in the drink, refusing t
come to the surface.

"Try this," she said. "It's the house special."

Adon lifted the drink, and a sweet aroma drifted to hi
nose. He squinted at the drink, and the woman gesture

encouragingly. Adon took a swallow, and felt every drop of blood in his body turn to ice. His skin pulled taut against his bones and a raging fire burned its way through his chest. With trembling fingers he attempted to set the drink down, and the woman grinned as she helped him in the task.

Adon's breathing was heavy, his head spinning, when he asked, "What in Sune's name is in that!?"

The woman shrugged. "A little of this, a little of that. A lot of something else."

Adon rubbed his chest and tried to catch his breath.

"I'm Jhaele Silvermane," the woman said. "And who are—"

Adon heard a slight hiss from the bar. One of the ice cubes was dissolving, and amber bands drifted through the liquid. "Adon of Sune," Adon heard himself say, then wished he could take it back.

"Nasty cut there, Adon of Sune. There are powerful healers in the Temple of Tymora who may be able to help you. They have quite a collection of healing potions. Have you visited them yet?"

Adon shook his head.

"How did you come by such a mark? Accident or design?"

Adon's flesh tingled. "Design?" he said.

"Many a warrior would wear such a mark as a badge of courage, of lawful service." Her eyes were bright and clear. She meant every word of what she said.

"Aye," the cleric said sarcastically. "It was something like that."

Adon gripped the glass once more and took another drink. This time his head became slightly numb, and there was a buzz in his ears. Then that sensation passed, too.

"A toast!" someone shouted. The voice was dangerously close. Adon turned to see a complete stranger raising a flagon above his head. The stranger wore a grizzled mane of stringy hair, and he seemed to be the veteran of many conflicts. His huge hand reached out and clasped Adon's shoulder.

"A toast to a warrior who has faced the forces of evil and brought them low in the service of the Dales!"

Adon tried to intervene, but a huge roar went up as every man and woman in the inn saluted him. Afterward, many came forward and slapped him on the back. Not one shied away from the ragged scar that marked his face. They shared tales of battles, and Adon felt strangely at home. After about an hour, the stool beside him scraped against the floor and a lovely crimson-haired serving girl sat down beside him.

"Please," Adon said as he hung his head, "I want to be alone." But when he looked up, the woman had not left. "What is it?" he said, then realized she was staring at the scar. He turned away and covered the side of his face with his hand.

"Fair one, you need not hide from me," she said.

Adon looked around to see who she was talking to. The woman was staring at him.

Adon found himself staring back. The woman's hair was full and wild, with thick curls that reached to her shoulder and framed the soft contours of her face. Her eyes were a soft, piercing blue, and her elegantly chiseled features supported the mischievous grin she wore. Her clothes were plain, but she carried herself with the manners of royalty set at ease.

"What do you want?" Adon said softly.

Her eyes brightened. "To dance."

"There is no music," Adon said, shaking his head.

She shrugged and held out her hand.

Adon turned away and stared into the depths of his newly replenished drink. The woman dropped her hand to her side, then sat down next to Adon once more. Finally, he looked over to her.

"Surely you have a name, at least?" she said.

Adon's expression grew dark as he turned to her. "There is no place for you here. Go about your duties and leave me alone."

"Alone to suffer?" she said. "Alone to drown yourself in a sea of self-pity? Such actions hardly befit a hero."

Adon almost choked. "Is that what you think I am?" A nasty sneer fixed upon his face.

"My name is Renee," she said, and held out her hand once more.

Adon tried to hold his hand steady as he took her hand in

greeting. "I am Adon," he said. "Adon of Sune. And I am anything but a hero."

"Let me be the judge of that, darling one," she said and caressed the side of his face as if the scar did not exist. Her hand trailed down across his neck, chest, and arm, until she took his hand in hers and asked him to tell his tale to her.

Reluctantly, Adon told the story of his journey from Arabel again, with little emotion in his voice. He told her everything, except for the secrets of the gods he'd learned. Those he saved for himself to ponder.

"You are a hero," she said, and kissed him full on the lips. "Your faith in the face of such adversity should be known, and held as an inspiration."

A soldier nearby laughed, and Adon was sure that he was the subject of the joke. He pulled away from the girl and slammed a few gold pieces to the bar. "I did not come here to be mocked!" he said in a rage.

"I did not—"

But Adon was gone, making his way through the adventurers and soldiers who crowded the inn. He reached the street and wandered almost a block before he fell against the wall of a tiny shop. There was a metal sign on the door with a name engraved upon it, and the moonlight allowed Adon to see his reflection in the metal. For an instant, the scar seemed barely noticeable. But as he raised his fingers to the ragged flesh, he saw his image distort, his face elongating so that the scar appeared to be even worse than it really was. Turning away from the sign, Adon cursed his weary eyes for betraying him.

As he walked through town, Adon thought of the woman, Renee, and her fiery hair that was so like Sune's. His treatment of the woman had been shameful. He knew he must apologize. On the way back to the inn a patrol stopped him, then let him go. "I remember the scar," one of them said.

Adon's spirits fell. He reached the Old Skull Inn, and after a few minutes of wandering the taproom, he sat back on his original stool and motioned for the attentions of Jhaele Silvermane. He related the story of the red-haired woman named Renee, the serving wench, and Jhaele merely nodded toward a darkened corner of the room.

Renee was there, sitting close to another man. The enticing gestures she made toward him were similar to those she had used on Adon. She looked up, saw Adon staring, then looked away.

"She must have smelled the gold on you," Jhaele said, and Adon suddenly understood Renee's true purpose in the bar. Moments later, he was on the street once more, his anger threatening to consume him. In the distance he saw the spires of a temple, and he made his way to it, passing the same patrol again.

The healers of the temple, he thought. Perhaps their potions would be powerful enough to remove the scar.

Tymora's temple in Shadowdale was far different from her temple in Arabel. Adon passed between a mighty set of pillars that burned with small watchfires set atop them. The vast double doors of the temple had been left unattended, and a large, polished gong lay on its side before the doors. Adon moved to the doors themselves when a voice rang out of the darkness behind him.

"You there!"

Adon turned and faced the same patrol he had spoken to outside the Old Skull.

"Something is amiss," Adon called. "The temple is silent, and the guard is nowhere to be found."

The riders left their mounts. There were four men, and their armor had been dulled to allow them the full cover of the night.

"Move aside," a burly man said as he brushed past Adon. The soldier pulled the heavy doors apart and turned his face away as the stench of death welled out of the temple.

Adon took a torn silk handkerchief and placed it before his face as he walked into the temple with one of the guards. Then the two men surveyed the bloody scene before them.

There were almost a dozen people in the temple, and all of them had been savagely murdered. The main altar had been overturned, and the symbol of Bane had been painted upon the walls with the blood of the murdered clerics. By the fires that still raged in the braziers and the smell that lingered in the temple, Adon knew the desecration had not taken place more than an hour earlier.

No children, Adon noted thankfully. The guard beside Adon became ill, and fell to his knees. When he rose, he found the young cleric moving through the rows of benches and the tiers of the platformed altar. Adon was removing the dead from the horrible positions their attackers had left them in, and was laying them out upon the floor. Then he tore the silk curtains from behind the altar and covered the bodies as best he could. The guard moved to his side, knees trembling. There was movement from without, then a cry as the other guards saw the horrors within the temple.

"There may be others," Adon warned as he pointed at the stairway leading into the heart of the temple.

"Alive?" the guard said. "Others . . . alive?"

The cleric said nothing, somehow sensing what they would find. The one thing he was certain they would not find were the precious healing potions he had been told about.

Adon remained in the temple even after the stench became unbearable for the others. He attempted to say a prayer for the dead, but the words would not come.

* * * * *

Kelemvor turned from the window. He had checked Midnight's room and found that she had not yet returned from Elminster's house. He went back to his own room, but he could not sleep. For a moment, he toyed with the idea of riding to Elminster's tower and confronting Midnight, but he knew that his efforts would be wasted.

Then, as he was once again watching out the window of the tower, he saw the mage approaching. The fighter watched as she passed the guards and entered the Twisted Tower. A few moments later, there was a knock at his door. Kelemvor sat on the edge of the bed and ran his hands over his face.

"Kel?"

"Aye," he called. "Enter."

Midnight entered the room and closed the door. "Shall I light a lantern?" she said.

"You forget what I am," Kelemvor said. "By the moonlight

your features are as plain as if I beheld them at highsun."

"I forget nothing," she said.

Midnight was wearing a long, flowing cape, a more than adequate replacement for the one she had lost. Tiny flames leaped across the surface of the pendant. Kelemvor was surprised to see that she had taken it back, but he did not bother to question her about it.

Midnight removed the cape, then stood before the fighter. "I think we should talk," she said.

Kelemvor nodded slowly. "Aye. What about?"

Midnight ran her hands through her long hair. "If you're tired. . . ."

Kelemvor rose to his feet. "I am tired, Ariel."

"Don't call me that."

Kelemvor flinched. "Midnight," he said and let out a deep sigh. "I assumed we would leave this place together. You would deliver the warning Mystra entrusted you with, then we would put this business behind us and be free for once!"

Midnight laughed a small, cruel laugh. "Free? What do either of us know of freedom, Kel? Your entire life has been ruled by a curse you can do nothing about, and I've been played for a fool by the very gods!"

She turned away from him and leaned against a dresser. "I can't walk away from this, Kel. I have a responsibility."

Kelemvor moved forward and turned her around to face him. He held her roughly by the shoulders. "A responsibility to whom? To strangers who would spit in your face even as you lay down your life to save them?"

"To the Realms, Kelemvor! My responsibility is to the Realms!"

Kelemvor released her. "Then we have little to discuss, it seems."

Midnight picked up the cloak. "It's more than just the curse with you, isn't it? Everything and everyone has their price. Your conditions are too much for me to bear, Kel. I can't give myself to someone who isn't willing to do the same for me."

"What are you talking about? Have I run from this place? Have I run from you? On the morrow we begin preparations for war. There's a good chance I won't see you again until this battle is over. If we survive, that is."

There was silence for a time.

"You would leave this place, wouldn't you?" Midnight said. "If I agreed to come away with you, you'd leave this very night."

"Aye."

Midnight let out a deep breath. "I was right, then. We have *nothing* to discuss."

She reached for the door, but Kelemvor called to her. "My reward," he said. "Elminster promised there would be a reward, but he didn't say what it would be."

Midnight's lips trembled in the darkness. "I told him about the curse, Kel. He believes it can be lifted."

"The curse . . . ," Kelemvor said absently. "Then it was a good decision to stay."

Midnight's hair fell before her face.

"He'd have done it anyway, damn you. . . ."

She opened the door. "Midnight!" Kelemvor called.

"Aye," she said.

"You still love me," Kelemvor said. "I'd know if you didn't. That's my reward for coming this far with you, remember?"

Midnight's whole body stiffened. "Yes," she said softly. "Is that all?"

"All that matters."

Midnight closed the door behind her and left Kelemvor to stare into the darkness.

☙ 14 ☙

Rumors of War

Mourngrym learned of the vicious attack against the Temple of Tymora in the hours before dawn. Elminster had been summoned, and met his liege at the gateway to the temple. Adon was still there when the sage arrived.

The bard, Storm Silverhand, soon showed up, too. She wore the symbol of the Harpers, a silver moon and a silver harp against a backdrop of royal blue. The night winds caught her wild silver hair, blowing it high into the air, giving her the appearance of a vengeful apparition rather than a human woman. Her armor was the bright silver of the Dales, and she moved past her liege and the sage without a word of greeting.

Mourngrym did not attempt to stop her. Instead he joined her in the desecrated temple, and they surveyed the destruction and the carnage in respectful silence. The symbol of Bane, painted in the blood of the victims, caught their attention instantly. Later, as Storm spoke to the guards who had found the destruction, Adon put forth the theory that it was the theft of the healing potions that had prompted the attack; the debilitating effects such an assault would have on the morale of Shadowdale's faithful was probably also a consideration. Storm Silverhand regarded the cleric very suspiciously, as she would any outsider present during such a tragedy.

"The blood upon his hands he came by in honest service, laying out the dead," Elminster said. "There is no malice in this one. He's innocent."

Storm turned to Mourngrym, seething with fury over the attack. "The Harpers shall ride with you, Lord. Together we will avenge this cowardly act."

Then she was gone, her grief at the tragedy threatening to overwhelm her steely continence. Mourngrym set his men to the grisly task of identification and burial of the dead. The old sage stood at the dalelord's side and spoke in hushed tones.

"Bane is the God of Strife. It is not surprising that he seeks to distract us, to strike at our hearts and leave us grief-stricken and vulnerable to his attack," Elminster said. "We must not allow his plan to succeed."

Mourngrym trembled with rage. "We won't," he said.

Hours later, after returning to the Twisted Tower, Mourngrym stood at the side of his friend and ally, Thurbal, as the man lay in a deep, healing sleep. Thurbal had not spoken since the night Elminster's magic retrieved him from Zhentil Keep, when he warned Mourngrym of the planned attack against the Dales.

"The horrors I have seen, Thurbal. Men of worship slain like dogs. There is a rage that burns in my heart, old friend. It threatens to sear away the frail bonds of reason." Mourngrym hung his head low. "I want their blood. I want revenge."

Such rage leaves you a mad dog, incapable of victory and easily disposed of, Thurbal had said in the past. Cool the fires in your heart, and let reason guide you to the halls of vengeance.

Mourngrym stood watch at Thurbal's side until the first light of morning broke and he received a summons to join Hawksguard in the war room.

* * * * *

The work details had been organized in the early hours of morning, and Kelemvor was amazed at the progress that had already been made during the past few days. He had stood at Hawksguard's side as the older warrior rallied the hundreds of soldiers who had volunteered to serve in Shadowdale's defense. Many had passed through the nightmare vistas of Gnoll Pass and the Shadow Gap to make it to the dale. They knew the fate that would befall the Dales should they fail to repel Bane and his armies. A cry of unity had resounded, and Kelemvor found himself swept up in the momentum, raising his fist in the air with the others.

Then came the drudgery, though few complained. Merchants and builders toiled side by side with soldiers as highsun approached and the lines of defense began to take shape in the area of Krag Pool, on the road to Voonlar. Wagonloads of rock and debris from the ruins of Castle Krag were brought to the edge of the main road northeast out of the dale. There the materials were used to build large fortifications.

Around the workers, on the ground and in the trees, the archers prepared to defend the road and lay siege to the Zhentish troops that would advance from the northeast. The battle might not come for days, but the archers knew they had to prepare, too.

And after their work was completed, they waited patiently. The sky above was a clear blue, and there were very few clouds. The trees around them were alive with the sounds that one could only fully appreciate after spending endless hours chopping wood, cutting down trees, sharpening spikes, digging holes and covering them up again. The woodsmen did this and more as they set traps and prepared their hiding places.

The archers were not alone in this task, though. There were work crews from the town to help, lead by a pair of city planners from Suzail Key. The planners had been visiting relatives in Shadowdale when news of the imminent invasion arrived. They helped to place the various obstacles the men of Shadowdale would put in the way of Bane's armies, and stayed to make detailed charts of escape routes through the forest. Of course, the maps would be memorized and destroyed long before the first of Bane's armies arrived.

The work proceeded at a brisk pace throughout the morning, but as the day wore on and the dalesmen worked the defenses back toward the town, they were forced to leave more and more men behind to guard their elaborate traps and ensure their proper deployment. With each man lost to man a trap or watch for advance scouts, the construction of new traps slowed down. But even the dalesmen left in the woods tried to be useful as they waited for the battle to begin. The archers, especially, took the time to learn the small part of the forest they would defend.

These archers, the first who would engage the enemy, spent hours learning every sound of the forest, becoming completely attuned to the intricate flow of nature. Any sound or scent that was out of the ordinary would be instantly detected. They rarely spoke, and instead practiced hand signals that would be used to relay word of the enemy approach, if the attack came during the day. Other measures, like signal lanterns, had been taken on the chance that the armies would arrive at night.

For now there was nothing to do but experience the elegance of nature as they waited.

Patiently.

As the day wore on, Kelemvor was sent to rally the many smiths who had been working for days hammering out shields, swords, daggers, and armor for those who would fight with nothing but their bare chests and their resolve if it were necessary. With the help of two assistants, the fighter supervised the loading of the weapons onto wagons. Then Kelemvor checked on the fletchers and wood carvers who were busy making arrows and bows for the archers.

At the crossroads outside of the Old Skull Inn, other preparations were being made. At Jhaele Silvermane's farm and on the opposite side of the road slightly further east, at Sulcar Reedo's farm, movable walls made of straw were being constructed to take the brunt of the attack from the Zhentish archers when they reached the town. The warehouse of Weregrund the Trader had been emptied. A small force of men would emerge from the warehouse when the Zhentilar began to fight at the crossroads, hopefully taking the enemy by surprise.

Mourngrym hand-picked the lookouts who would lay signal fires on Harper's Hill and the Old Skull to herald the arrival of the enemy. Only men who had no families to mourn them, no wives to be made widows, were chosen for this task. Before he sent them to their posts, the dalelord checked to be sure they were properly outfitted and supplied should their wait be a long one.

The disbursement of supplies had started in the early hours of the day, but it was an endless task. Jhaele Silvermane and her workers had delivered rations of meat, sweetbreads, and fresh water to each group of men. They gathered tents and bedrolls, too, but these were distributed sporadically.

At the other side of the township, Cyric arrived at the Ashaba bridge and discovered the two-fold resentment of "his" men almost immediately. First, not one of the men had volunteered his assignment; each had desired to see the glory of battle at the front lines instead of guarding the bridge on the chance that a second force of soldiers would be sent to take Shadowdale from the west. Second, and most importantly, they resented taking orders from an outsider. It was a well-matched union, as Cyric despised having to give orders to what he considered a group of ill-mannered, loud-mouthed cretins.

But before Cyric could even consider getting his troops organized, he had a large number of refugees to deal with.

The refugees had gathered by the river. The boats that would take them down to Mistledale had not yet arrived and Cyric ordered a handful of soldiers to see to the well-being of the old people and children as he tried to organize the work details. In time, he walked among the families and was struck by the wellspring of strength he found in their eyes.

Imbeciles, Cyric thought. Didn't they understand that they would probably be leaving their homes forever? The thief found that he couldn't help but toy with the idea Marek had placed in his head: turning and joining the enemy if there was no other option but death. After all, what did he owe these people? If it were not for Midnight, he would have left long ago.

The majority of the refugees were children, or those too infirm either by age or by disability to fight. They all stood and stared as the soldiers dug trenches at either end of the bridge. They knew that these men would likely die to defend homes they no longer lived in, but they knew, too, that running away would have killed most of the soldiers quicker than any Zhentish arrow or sword could.

But as the refugees watched, the men working at the bridge slowed their digging. Most of the men complained loudly, criticizing the dark-haired man who moved among them, barking orders with an ever-shortening temper.

Then a dozen men suddenly threw down their shovels and rose from the half-formed ditch they had toiled in for hours. The leader of the men, a giant of a man named Forester, called out to Cyric, who was busy digging with the soldiers at the other end of the bridge.

"Enough!" Forester screamed, the sweat matting his long, stringy hair to his face. "Our brothers stand ready to lay down their lives at the eastern border to protect the dale! I say we join them! How many are with me?"

The majority of the soldiers on Forester's side of the bridge threw down their shovels at once and rallied behind the wild-haired fighter. Some of the soldiers on Cyric's side of the bridge had yelled out their support for Forester's plan, and threw down their shovels, too.

Cyric gripped the handle of his shovel and gritted his teeth. "Damn!" he hissed, and when he turned to rise from the ditch, he saw that all of the refugees were staring at him. His gaze locked on that of a young mother, who stood no more than twenty paces from Cyric, her eyes filled with concern not for her children, but for herself.

Thoughts of his own parents abandoning him as a baby came to Cyric as he averted his gaze and climbed out of the ditch. Forester and his men were already coming across the bridge, weapons drawn, when Cyric barred their way on the other side of the bridge. Although he would have been happy to let these men rush off to their deaths, he would not allow his authority to be questioned.

"Stand aside!" Forester called. "Else you'll be entering the river without benefit of a ship beneath you!"

"Go back to work," Cyric said coldly. "We have orders from Lord Mourngrym to secure this bridge."

Forester laughed. "Secure it against what—the setting sun? The wind at our backs? The battle will be to the east. Move aside."

Forester was closer now, and still Cyric did not move.

"You coward," Cyric said.

Forester stopped suddenly. "Brave words from a corpse," he said as he raised his sword. The blade glinted in the sunlight, but still, Cyric did not move or draw a weapon.

Cyric's lips drew back. He pointed at the refugees. "Look there."

The refugees stood huddled on the bank of the Ashaba. Fear glittered in the eyes of every one of them.

"You wish glory? You wish to lay down your worthless lives? Alright. But will you seek it at the cost of their lives?"

Forester's blade wavered. The murmur of voices began to rise.

"Leave this place and who will protect them? Daggerdale is infested with Bane's Zhentilar! Allow this bridge to fall and you deliver them and Shadowdale into the hands of the enemy!"

Cyric turned his back on Forester. "Stand with me and you stand with Shadowdale! How say you? How say all of you?"

Silence. Cyric waited for the blade of the giant to pierce his back.

"For Shadowdale," a voice called.

"For Shadowdale!" more voices cried. Then a chorus of loud, angry voices picked up the call. Even the refugees joined in.

"For Shadowdale!" a voice called directly behind Cyric. He turned, and Forester raised his weapon high overhead as he chanted with the others.

"Aye," Cyric said at last, and all fell silent. "For Shadowdale. Now get back to work."

The efforts of the soldiers redoubled, and in the far distance Cyric saw the first of the ships that would carry the refugees to safety.

"For Shadowdale," a woman said to the thief as she headed for a boat, her eyes positively aflame with Cyric's words, tears streaming down her face. Cyric nodded, although he felt nothing but contempt for these weak-willed sheep who sought to hide behind their belief in their gods or their country to justify their actions rather than confront life head on. He turned from her as he took his place in the ditch, his patience for dreamers and cowards at an end.

He had convinced the others that staying behind was the correct choice.

Now all he had to do was convince himself.

As Cyric got the refugees loaded onto boats and on their way down the Ashaba, and drove his men on as they dug their trench at the bridge, Adon was cloistered in Elminster's tower. After the cleric and the sage had returned from the Temple of Tymora early in the morning, Elminster set Adon to work in the cluttered antechamber that Lhaeo normally occupied.

"You are to find all references to the following names," Elminster said. "Then study and learn the spells set forth by each of them in their lifetime. They are all contained in these volumes. Make lists that we might access them again."

"But my spells fail me," Adon said. "I don't know—"

"Nor do I, but as the Realms depend on us all, I think now's the time to find out, do you not agree?" Then the sage was gone, and the cleric poured over the tomes until Midnight arrived and they left for the temple.

By the time Adon, Midnight, and Elminster reached the Temple of Lathander, a purple haze was drifting across the evening sky, and it was already time for eveningfeast. The sage, the cleric, and the magic-user passed through a nearly empty town, though they could hear Cyric's men digging to the west and the soldiers building fortifications to the east.

As they approached the building, Adon and Midnight could see that Lathander's temple had been constructed in the form of a Phoenix, with huge stone wings rising up on either side of its gate. The wings curved and became turrets. In the center of the building there were huge double doors that had been left unattended, and Elminster rapped at them impatiently. A window opened three stories up, and a handsome, square-jawed man with wavy hair looked out.

"Elminster!" the cleric said in awe.

"I might still be by the time ye get thyself down here and open this door!"

The window snapped shut, and Elminster wandered away from the heavy doors. Midnight continued to harangue him about the temple, and the role she and Adon were to play in the battle.

"Simply remember what I taught ye and do as I've said!" Elminster said wearily.

"You're treating us like children!" Midnight snapped. "After all we've been through, a simple explanation should not be out the question."

Elminster sighed. "Ye wouldn't mind if an old man rests his sorry frame while ye pound at him, would ye?"

Elminster sat down. It wasn't until Midnight was halfway through her argument about the Tablets of Fate that she noticed he was sitting in midair and the air about him crackled with mystical energies.

Midnight stopped.

"A Celestial Stairway," she said.

"Aye, like the one your lady Mystra used in her bid to regain the Planes."

Midnight backed away in horror. "Then Bane. . . ."

"He doesn't want the dale," Elminster said. "He wants the Planes."

"But Helm will stop him, possibly slay him—"

"And Shadowdale will be reduced to a smoking pit, a black mark on the maps of travelers for all time."

Adon ran his hands over his face. "Just like Castle Kilgrave. But what can we do?"

Elminster tapped at the air beside him. "Destroy the Celestial Stairway, of course!" He reached out to Midnight. "Help me up!"

Midnight assisted the sage to his feet. "How can we destroy that which the gods created?"

"Perhaps ye will tell me," Elminster said. The door to the temple opened and the blond-haired man appeared. He was dressed in bright red robes with thick bands of gold trim.

"Elminster!" the man said. "I had not realized the time. You are expected, of course."

Rhaymon gestured for the old sage to come inside. "Would you like me to give your assistants a tour before I go?"

"That will not be necessary," Elminster said.

Rhaymon was halfway to the door when Adon stopped the priest.

"I don't understand," Adon said. "Where are you going?"

"To join my fellow priests and the faithful who worshiped here," Rhaymon said. "To the last man they will be joining forces with the army of Shadowdale, preparing to lay down their lives in defense of the Dales."

Adon took the man's hand. "Make them pay for what they did to the worshipers of Tymora."

Rhaymon nodded and was gone.

"Let's get inside," Midnight said as she gently touched Adon's arm and guided him from the doorway, then closed and locked the doors to the temple behind her.

* * * * *

It was night, and memories plagued Ronglath Knightsbridge. The soldier had not learned of the death of Tempus Blackthorne until after his arrival at Voonlar. The wizard Sememmon had laughed as he informed Knightsbridge of the emissary's fate.

"Have no worries," Sememmon said. "You will be joining him soon enough. You will lead the first battalion against the dalesmen."

Knightsbridge had said nothing.

The journey from the Citadel of the Raven to Teshwave had been trying. The soldiers he had commanded were openly hostile and rebellious. The mercenaries who had joined them in the ruins of Teshwave knew nothing of the failure of Knightsbridge in Arabel, and cared only about the gold they had been given to report on time and prepared for the march. Knightsbridge had not been in Voonlar for more than a few days before the order came from Lord Bane to gather the men and ride out.

There had been no attacks on their supply wagons on either the first or second day of their journey, and this made Knightsbridge particularly suspicious. Either the defenders of Shadowdale had not perceived the greatest weakness of Bane's five-thousand-man army, or they did not have the manpower to spare to even make the attempt on the food supply. For every ten miles of road they conquered, almost fifty men had been left behind to protect the road against attackers. Though Bane might not approve, Knightsbridge would not leave their rear unguarded, even if it used up a quarter of his troops to do so.

Knightsbridge was surprised again when the army reached the forest northeast of the dale. He expected the woods to have been set ablaze. It seemed the people of Shadowdale would not die quietly after all. They wanted to fight.

As night fell, Knightsbridge expected to camp at the outskirts of the forest, but Lord Bane sent up orders to the contrary. They would march into the forest under the cover of night, where presumably they would have the advantage of surprise if they were to meet any resistance.

They would not be allowed torches.

Bane's magic-users had been given strict orders not to use magic under any circumstances, as the art had become unstable and could easily backfire upon them. That meant there would be no spells cast to enhance the night vision of the soldiers as they stomped noisily through the woods.

As Knightsbridge led his frightened men into the forest, it became clear that at least a few shared his opinion of Bane's strategy. The oldest and most experienced, Mordant DeCruew, rode beside Knightsbridge. Leetym and Rusch rode beside him.

"This is suicide," Leetym said.

Much to the shock of the other officers, Knightsbridge nodded.

Rusch raised his sword. "Our lord and god has given us a commandment."

"Which he has made impossible for us to keep!" Leetym protested. "He has driven us like livestock before the slaughter house. I am among those who has seen our 'god' eat and drink like a human. As a temple guardian, I have seen him cry like a simpering child. He has lied to us from the beginning!"

"We shall win this day," Rusch said, gesturing with his weapon.

"Stay your sword," Mordant said. "Our enemies will not expect us to move against the forest until the morning. They will not expect us in Shadowdale until late the following day. We will take them by surprise."

"Mordant is correct," Knightsbridge said. "Our fight is not with each other. The true battle lies ahead. If death is our destiny we will meet it like men, not like cowering animals. If the pair of you cannot accept that, I'll gut you right now."

The troops were silent as they rode deeper into the woods.

*　*　*　*　*

Connel Greylore, the first of Shadowdale's archers to hear the approach of the soldiers, took a moment to question his senses. He had climbed into position in the trees to take the watch for his fellows. Five hundred yards behind him, another archer had done the same. The pattern continued all the way back to Krag Pool. Each of the sentry archers had chosen a position where a clear beam from their signal lanterns could be seen by the next sentry, closer to the town. This way, they could signal the sentry behind them without revealing their position to the approaching enemy.

The noises came again. This time it was accompanied by an unmistakable cry of pain.

Connel raised his lantern so quickly that it slipped from his sweaty hands. He nearly fell from the heavy branch that supported him as he grabbed at the lantern. His heart was thundering as he felt the surface of the cold metal and forced his hand to relax.

The archer looked ahead. He could see the Zhentilar now as they struggled in the net of twisted branches that covered the width of the road. The trees had been made to fall in three directions, allowing the aggressors to walk or ride into the trap. Yet even if they tried to go through the forest, around the tangle of branches, the Zhentilar would find the flanking woods similarly set.

Connel gave the signal. A single flash from the other direction told him that it had been received. He climbed down from the tree and quickly woke three other archers who stealthily assumed their positions in the trees somewhat closer to the road. The sound of men hacking away and attempting to crawl under or push through the branches filled the night, covering any sounds the archers might have made as they readied themselves, moving to their blinds and readying the quivers of arrows that had been left at each position.

Someone sent these men like cattle to the slaughter, Connel thought. Then the leader of the four archers gave the order to fire on the Zhentilar.

Suddenly the shouts of annoyance and fury became the screams of the dying as a hail of arrows erupted from the trees, skewering Bane's troops. More archers arrived from the contingents behind the first group, taking up temporary positions in the trees beside the road.

A few of the Zhentilar pressed through the barriers, some using the corpses of their fellow soldiers as shields from the rain of arrows from above. They yelled curses as they rushed forward and did not see the huge wooden stakes that had been planted in the road, aimed chest high, until they impaled themselves.

Connel and the first group of Shadowdale archers began to fall back, climbing from their positions to the safe route through the woods that would put them behind the next line of defense, a series of pits in the road that had been carefully camouflaged. The pits were three feet deep, with a single stake rising up from their center.

The second group of archers was climbing down behind the first, preparing to follow them back toward town, when Connel Greylore thanked the gods that none of the Shadowdale archers had yet been killed by the Zhentilar. He didn't hear the notching of arrows from behind on the road as the Zhentish archers loosed a volley of arrows over the wall of branches. Suddenly there were hundreds of arrows sailing through the air. Almost all of them struck trees or became imbedded in branches or fell harmlessly to the road.

Connel Greylore didn't even feel the arrow that pierced his back and split his heart, killing him instantly.

Bane's men fought for hours in the darkness as they hacked through the myriad defenses of the road. Each time they found a stretch that seemed to have been left defenseless, Bane insisted on his troops reforming their line. The foot soldiers would march out in front, and inevitably be the first to fall back and break the line as they discovered new traps hidden in the road. The soldiers died as they fell into the pits or were pressed into caltrops by the press of the troops behind them.

Bane was ecstatic. With each death his power grew, just as Myrkul had promised. The body of the Black Lord glowed with a red aura, a visible result of the soul energies he absorbed. The intensity of the aura increased as more men—both Zhentilar and dalesmen—died, and the Black Lord had difficulty suppressing his delight.

Nevertheless, Bane feigned anger at the incompetence of his troops for not being able to overcome such simple defenses as he drove them on to their deaths.

* * * * *

"Not a speck of dust should be left in this temple that we don't know about," Elminster said. He was quite serious, though he knew he was asking the impossible. "Any items of a personal nature must be removed from this hall, as well. There's no telling what may prove useful to our enemy."

After the horrors Adon had encountered in the desecrated Temple of Tymora, he was reluctant to participate in Elminster's plans for the Temple of Lathander. Ultimately, though, the cleric was forced to think of the temple in the most base terms. It was brick and mortar, stone and steel, glass and dripping wax. A different configuration of these elements and he might have been standing in a stable or an inn.

If it had been Sune's temple, Adon wondered, could he have been so cold and calculating? He touched the scar that lined his face.

He didn't know.

And so he busied himself with the tasks that had been laid out for him. The windows facing the invisible stairway on every floor of the temple were opened, their shutters removed. The windows that faced in all other directions were nailed shut. However, as he moved around the temple, Adon couldn't keep himself from noticing the small items that had been left behind in every room he visited. This was a place of fierce devotion and belief, and yet it was also a place where men and woman laughed and cried over the joys and sorrows life had brought to them.

One of the beds was unmade. Adon stopped his work and set about the task of making it before he realized what he was doing. He drew back from the bed, as if the power of the priest who had lay there that morning would reach up and destroy him.

As Adon stepped back from the bed, he noticed a black leather journal hidden beneath a pillow. The journal lay face down and open. Adon turned it over and read the final entry. It read:

Today I died to save Shadowdale. Tomorrow I shall be reborn in the kingdom of Lathander.

The journal fell from his hands and Adon ran from the small room, the window he was supposed to nail shut still open, its curtains blowing gently in the gathering winds that caressed the temple as if they were alive.

The cleric returned to the main chamber, and Midnight was surprised by the pale, worn look on the cleric's face as he approached. She knew that he had been struggling to maintain his resolve, even in the face of his grief and confusion, but there was little she could do to help him.

Or herself, for that matter.

But as the magic-user thought about the battle that was to come, she could not help but think of Kelemvor. And although Midnight regretted the harshness of her final exchange with the fighter, she knew that Kelemvor had found her out. No matter what she might say, she loved him. Perhaps, she thought, he loves me, too.

Midnight had long ago discovered that Kelemvor had a vulnerable side; his posturing was meant to draw attention away from the dark secret of his curse. He was more intelligent and caring than he would ever be willing to admit. And that gave Midnight hope.

Perhaps, she thought.

The sound of Adon yelling grabbed Midnight's attention, and she let the possibilities of her relationship with Kelemvor slip away. The cleric was standing next to the old sage, repeating the same phrase over and over, but Elminster was ignoring him.

"It's done!" the cleric screamed.

The sage of Shadowdale turned a page in the book he was studying.

"It's done!" Adon yelled again. Elminster finally looked up, nodded, mumbled, and went back to the crumbling tome he poured over, gingerly turning the pages so they would not become dust and cheat him of some secret bit of knowledge that might turn the tide in the battle with Bane.

Adon walked off to sulk in a corner.

Midnight watched the old man, and absently fingered the pendant. The great hall of the temple had been cleared, the pews moved off to the sides of the room. The dark-haired magic-user had given up her efforts to fathom the sage's reasoning. All would be made clear, he had promised. There was little she could do but place her trust in the wizened sage.

"Do you wish to use the pendant now, good Elminster?" Midnight said as she walked to the sage's side.

Elminster's face was suddenly plagued with a half-dozen new wrinkles. His beard seemed to draw up slightly. "That trinket? What use have I for that? Ye may keep it. Perhaps it will fetch a pretty penny at the fair in Tantras."

Midnight bit her lip. "Then what would you have me do here?" she asked.

Elminster shrugged. "Fortify this place, perhaps."

Midnight shook her head. "But how? You didn't—"

Elminster leaned over and whispered in her ear. "Do ye not remember the rite of Chiah, Warden of Darkness?"

"Of Elki, of Apenimon, draw from thy power—"

Elminster grinned. "The dream dance of Lukyan Lutherum?"

Midnight felt her lips tremble. She recited the incantation perfectly, yet Elminster stopped her before she could finish.

"Read for me now, from the sacred scrolls of Knotum, Seif, Seker. . . ."

The words erupted from Midnight and suddenly a blinding flash of light filled the room. Then, a beautiful, intricate pattern of blue-white light raced across the walls, floor, and ceiling. It burst through the partially opened doorway leading to the antechamber. In an instant, the temple was ablaze with eldritch fires. Then the pattern sank into the walls of the temple and was absorbed.

Midnight was stunned.

"That wasn't so difficult, now, was it?" Elminster said and turned away.

"Wait!" Midnight cried. "How can I remember what I've never learned?"

Elminster raised his hands. "You cannot. It is time to prepare for the final ceremony. Go and ready yourself."

As Midnight turned and walked away, Elminster felt a wave of trepidation pass through him. From the night of Arrival, he had been preparing for this moment. His *sight* had revealed that he would be met by two allies in this battle, but the identities of his champions had startled him at first, filling him with a dread he would have to be a madman or a fool to ignore.

Of course, Elminster had not survived more than five hundred winters in the Realms by being either a madman or a fool, though many claimed he was both. Still, though, he would soon place his very existence in the hands of an inexperienced magic-user and a cleric whose faltering belief not only in the gods he worshiped but in himself might bring about the downfall of the temple's only defenders.

Midnight had quite accurately identified her plight as that of a pawn of the gods, and Elminster sensed that the magic-user was intrigued by the attention, as if she believed she had been singled out for some purpose. Such vanity, Elminster thought. Unless, of course, it was true. He had no way of telling.

How he longed for the assistance of Sylune, who had had the sense to leave the Realms before they could fall into such a horrid state, or even the Simbul, who had not responded to any of his communications.

"Elminster, we are ready," Midnight said.

The sage turned and faced the dark-haired magic-user and the cleric. The main doors of the temple had been propped open, waiting to release the energies that might consume them all.

"Perhaps ye are at that," Elminster said as he studied

Midnight's face. There was not a trace of doubt to be found in the magic-user; her primary interest was the safety of the Realms. Elminster knew that he had no choice but to trust her. "Before we begin, there is something ye must know. Mystra told ye of the Tablets of Fate, but she did not tell ye where ye can find them."

Understanding dawned on Midnight. "But you can. The spells I helped you perform in your study, to locate intense sources of magic in the Realms—"

"One of the tablets is in Tantras, although I cannot give ye the precise location," Elminster said. "The other eludes me completely. Although, given time, I could certainly find it."

"Now let us begin," Elminster said. "This ceremony will take many hours. . . ."

* * * * *

The signal fires had been lit. Bane's armies were breaking through the defenses of the eastern woods. They would arrive at Krag Pool within hours.

It was nearly dawn, and like most of the troops, Kelemvor had been asleep when the fires had been spotted. The blaring horns that accompanied the signal fires woke him up instantly, however.

"Those fools must have ridden all night," Hawksguard said, shaking the effects of sleep from him.

"Madness," Kelemvor said, refusing to believe any general would try so foolish a trick.

"Aye," Hawksguard said. "But we are dealing with the Zhentilar, after all." The fighter smiled and patted Kelemvor on the back.

In the days spent preparing the defenses near Krag Pool, Kelemvor and Hawksguard had become virtually inseparable. They had come from similar backgrounds, and Hawksguard had known stories of Lyonsbane Keep and of Kelemvor's father in the man's glory days, long before he had degenerated into the soulless monster Kelemvor had known as a child. Hawksguard also knew of Burne Lyonsbane, Kelemvor's beloved uncle.

But knowledge of the past was not all that bound the two

fighters together. They shared similar interests in sword-play, and dueled each other nightly to keep their skills as finely honed as their blades. Hawksguard introduced Kelemvor to many of the men on the detail, and soon they all spoke as long-lost friends. Hawksguard often deferred some of his authority to Kelemvor, and the men followed the fighter's orders without hesitation.

In fact, as Hawksguard's place was defending Lord Mourngrym in the battle, Kelemvor was given command of the defenses at Krag Pool. Hawksguard's men accepted the change of command readily, and were glad to know that Kelemvor would be at their front during the battle.

The defensive position Kelemvor commanded was impressive, considering the small amount of time the dales-men had to prepare it. The road leading to the east from Shadowdale was now completely blocked off just west of Krag Pool. The final load of rocks and debris had been laid along the road, and then the wagons had been overturned to help block the way. Trees had been cut down and laid across the road before the barricade, adding to the inaccessibility of the road. In addition, archers lined the trees to the north of the obstacle.

The final piece of inspired tactics came from the city planners from Suzail Key, and it centered on the trees that stood sentinel along the road to the west of Krag Pool. Though Kelemvor found both of the planners unlikely military minds—being slight of build, very refined, and having no experience at all with weapons—he had to admit that their trap was nothing short of brilliant. Even Elminster had been pursuaded by the plan's originality to help in setting the trap. Kelemvor could hardly wait until the Zhentish troops stumbled into it.

However, there was nothing for Kelemvor to do now but wait. More fighters were responding to the horns, leaving their homes for perhaps the last time, and rushing to fill out the lines. But once they arrived, they just sat behind the barricade, nervously leaning on drawn swords or plucking bow strings in anticipation.

Nearly a quarter of an hour passed before anyone spoke. Many of the men had to fight to push their fears away. They were brave men, but none of them wanted to die, and the size of Bane's army was suspected to be ten thousand men strong, although other estimates cut that number in half.

As the soldiers sat waiting for the sound of battle to get close, Hawksguard stood up and yelled, "Morningfeast, men!" His words cut through the nervous silence like arrows, startling everyone from their morose thoughts. And even Kelemvor was surprised when Hawksguard began to beat on his metal bowl. "Bane be damned!" the fighter shouted. "If I'm going to die this day, it certainly isn't going to be on an empty stomach!"

The men began to voice similar sentiments, and soon that which had been unthinkable just moments before consumed the attentions of the entire company of fighters.

Only one man in Kelemvor's company didn't follow Hawksguard's lead. He was a very thin man, with an odd gleam in his eye. He sat beside Kelemvor and Hawksguard as they ate. His name was Mawser.

The defenders of Shadowdale needed a volunteer for the final trick they would play on Bane's forces before engaging them one on one. The thin man, a devout worshiper of Tymora, had leaped at the chance to set off the trap, even though his own death was practically assured. Mawser believed that his goddess would protect him by endowing him with enough good luck to escape with his life.

The thin man looked at the clearing to the west of Krag Pool and grinned.

"I don't understand Bane's strategy," Hawksguard confessed. "He's given us time to get a full night's rest and a meal in our guts. In the meantime, he's run his own troops the entire night. They'll be exhausted and starved by the time they reach us."

Kelemvor shook his head. "I wish Midnight were here," he said as he pointed to Krag Pool. "Her sorcery could change that water into steaming acid. I'm sure of it. Then we'd only have to force the Zhentilar back and victory would be assured."

Hawksguard smiled. "Actually, Kel. I was thinking you could just run out over the barricade and chase Bane's troops away all by yourself. We all might as well go home."

The fighters ate the hastily prepared meal, gave thanks to the gods they worshiped, then settled back to wait for Bane's army. Hawksguard moved among the men, saying his farewells, wishing them victory.

Kelemvor thought of Midnight. His initial reaction to the dark-haired magic-user had been anger. There she was, a woman attempting to make a name for herself in a man's game, but she didn't seem willing to make the sacrifices necessary to play by the rules. After all, Kelemvor had met warrior-women before. They subverted their sexuality and behaved in a repressed, masculine manner to fit in. They were usually quite loud and quite boring. Midnight, on the other hand, expected to be accepted for what she was—a woman.

And even Kelemvor's myopic vision allowed him to see that she really was worthy of respect as a warrior. She proved again and again on the trip that she was capable and dependable. And perhaps she didn't need to give up her femininity to achieve her goals, Kelemvor thought. She was attractive and strong, and her generosity, warmth, and humor made her irresistible.

If they both survived the battle, Kelemvor wondered, would it be different between them, or would there always be some excuse for them not to be together?

Kelemvor heard a shout, and he turned just in time to see Mawser running down the road to his battle station. Kelemvor smiled as he imagined what the Zhentilar would see as they approached from the northeast: As had been the case for the last few miles of their trek, trees would line the right side of the road—with the exception of the small path to Castle Krag. The trees stretched for a little way down the road, then the forest opened onto the town. On the Zhentilar's left, Krag Pool bordered the road for a while. One hundred yards past the pool, also on the left of the road, they would see what appeared to be a clearing. Covering the entire road right in front of the pool was a large barricade, the last major obstacle on the road before Shadowdale.

At least, that's the way it seemed.

Kelemvor could barely contain his excitement as the first Zhentilar appeared on the road.

❧ 15 ❧

The Battle

As the Zhentilar approached the barricade blocking the road at Krag Pool, Bane's archers were sent forward in the ranks. Before the army even tried to cross the ten-foot-tall, twenty-foot-wide wall of stone, dirt, debris, and overturned wagons, the dalesmen would have to be routed from the trees, from where they had harassed the Zhentilar all along the road east of Shadowdale. However, Kelemvor had most of his men positioned far back in the woods, so that the Zhentish archers couldn't strike at them effectively. Only when Bane's troops tried to cross the barricade, when the Zhentilar would be disorganized, would the fighter order a full-scale attack. For now, striking at the enemy with arrows from the trees across from Krag Pool would have to do.

Bane, who was riding in the rear of the line, was furious when the army ground to a halt at the wall. "Why aren't we simply going over that pile of rock?" Bane screamed as a young officer reported on the situation. "I want my troops to be in Shadowdale within the hour, so you'd best order them to breach that wall or climb over it."

The officer was shaking as he said, "But-but, Lord Bane, the dalesmen are waiting for us to try to cross the barricade before they attack. Our troops will be easy targets for them as we climb over the wall."

"Then why not go around it?" another officer said.

The Black Lord frowned. "If we go around it, our forces will have to scatter to make it through the woods. That would be fighting the dalesmen on their own terms."

The young officer from the front lines stammered for a

moment. "We will lose a large number of men—"

"That's enough!" Bane screamed and lashed out with his gauntleted hand. He struck the officer in the face, knocking him from his horse. As the man staggered to his feet, Bane looked down at him, a cruel grin etched on his face. "I am your *god*. My word is law. We will cross the barricade now, in force."

The officer mounted his horse. "Yes, Lord Bane."

"And you will lead the first group over the top," the Black Lord added. "Now, you may go."

The officer turned and headed back to the barricade. At the wall, the archers were showering the trees with arrows, but the dalesmen still refused to show themselves. "I want a work detail to start breaking up our supply wagons and begin building a ramp so we can cross this damn thing," the young man screamed when he reached his troops.

Within thirty minutes, the Zhentilar were ready to charge over the barricade. Bane waited anxiously for his men to storm the wall and the killing to begin again. The power of the hundreds of souls Myrkul had channeled to him coursed through his veins, but the God of Strife wanted more. He wanted the power to crush Shadowdale with his own hands, as he could have done before Ao's wrath robbed him of his godhood. He wanted to kill the sage Elminster, for his meddling ways and because he fought for justice and peace.

But most of all, Bane wanted the Planes.

The Black Lord heard the shouts of his troops as they prepared to charge over the wall, and a chill ran up his spine. Soon, Bane thought. Soon I will have the power of a god again.

At the front, Kelemvor saw that the Zhentilar were ready to cross, so he readied the dalesmen for the attack. If everything went according to Hawksguard's plan, as the first of Bane's troops reached the top of the wall, the archers from Shadowdale would hit as many of the soldiers as possible. The bodies of the men and horses killed by the archers would then slow the troops behind them down, making them even easier targets for the bowmen from the Dales.

Kelemvor and his men would take care of any Zhentish that made it over the wall. The fighter had organized the defenders into small groups, so that as more and more of Bane's troops stormed over the barricade, the dalesmen could fall back in small units and retreat through the woods back toward town.

And as soon as any Zhentilar crossed the wall and were on their way to Shadowdale, Kelemvor would signal the foot soldiers and cavalry that waited to cut the Zhentish troops down. The fighter had no illusions that the dalesmen could hold the Zhentilar back for long, as they were outnumbered by at least three-to-one, but he knew that they could cut those odds down considerably, even before Mawser sprung the trap in the clearing.

Only one hundred yards away, the young Zhentish officer mounted his horse and led his troops onto the barricade. A thick rain of arrows fell from the trees on the north side of the road, killing most of the soldiers before they'd even taken three steps on the wall. The officer made it across with only an arrow shot through his leg and into his horse's flank.

As soon as his horse jumped to the ground on the side of the wall closest to Shadowdale, however, a squad of dalesmen dispatched the Zhentish officer with little trouble. The young man died cursing Lord Bane for his stupidity and arrogance.

The battle at the barricade raged for almost an hour before the Zhentilar got enough troops to the western side of the wall to drive the dalesmen back down the road. Kelemvor ordered a retreat, and the archers and soldiers ran through the forest to their final positions in the woods, just west of the clearing next to Krag Pool.

By this time, Bane was himself at the barricade. As he looked out on the retreating dalesmen and the hundreds of corpses that littered the wall, he smiled. Victory was his; he could feel the stolen power writhing within the frail form of his avatar.

The Black Lord turned and addressed his troops. "We have passed through the gauntlet our enemies prepared for us and faced the worst they have to offer. I must leave you for a time, to go to the other front. The wizard Sememmon will lead you on to Shadowdale. Your god has spoken."

A shimmering vortex of light enveloped the Black Lord, then the God of Strife vanished.

Safely hidden in the woods to the west of the clearing, Kelemvor could hardly believe his eyes. He watched as Bane's army moved right into their trap. As the soldiers massed before the clearing, the fighter gave the signal and Mawser set off the trap.

Almost fifty trees suddenly appeared in the clearing next to Krag Pool. Then all of them started to fall toward the road and the Zhentish army.

The city planners had pointed out that the best kind of trap was one you couldn't see, at least until it was too late, so Mourngrym had a work detail cut the trees west of Krag Pool so that they could easily be toppled on troops using the road. Then the trees were linked by strong ropes so that, once a single tree was knocked over, the entire road would be covered by falling timber.

The most difficult task was convincing Elminster to complete the plan. The dalelord pleaded with Elminster to throw one spell, a powerful mass invisibility spell on the trees, so they would be hidden from Bane's troops. The old sage was not happy about being dragged away from his experiments, but he agreed to help after the plan had been explained to him.

"I just hope one of the oaks knocks Bane's avatar on the skull," Elminster said. Then he threw the spell and headed back to his work.

But after the trap was set, someone had to be found that was brave enough—or foolish enough, depending upon one's philosophy—to set that first tree in motion without giving away the trap's location. Even though it was a suicide mission, someone volunteered.

Mawser.

When Kelemvor gave the signal, the worshiper of the Goddess of Luck jumped from the tree nearest to the road. Mawser had been hidden by the invisibility spell as he sat at the top of the tree, tied to it by a short rope. And when he jumped, his weight set the first tree in motion. But he also appeared in midair, as the invisibility spell was negated by the fact the trees were now weapons on the attack.

As Mawser plumetted toward the Zhentilar, fifty huge trees falling behind him, he said a prayer to the Goddess of Luck to protect him, to somehow let him survive the fall and the crush of the trap.

Kelemvor didn't see the Zhentish arrow pierce Mawser's throat. The thin man was dead before he hit the ground.

But the trap worked. The trees crashed down on the Zhentish soldiers, killing or injuring at least a third of them. Kelemvor let out a yell, and the dalesmen followed his lead. Though the plan had been carefully orchestrated, no one was ever really positive that it would work. But, now, as the fighters and archers from the Dales watched Bane's men scramble to save themselves from the incredible network of falling trees, they had no other option but to believe their senses.

Luck is with us this morning, Kelemvor thought, as he broke from his blind and signaled for the next phase of the attack to begin.

Hawksguard had stationed a group of archers in the forest behind the falling trees, and any of the bowmen who had retreated from positions farther east on the road to Voonlar also knew to fall back to the trees behind the trap. Now that the trap was sprung, the archers fired down into the tangled maze of fallen trees that lined the road. They loosed their arrows at any hint of movement in the trap, and hundreds of Zhentish soldiers who had escaped being crushed were killed or wounded by the archers. Despite the efforts of the archers, despite the fall of the gargantuan trees, Bane's troop still pressed on.

From his position in the trees west of the trap, Kelemvor caught a glimpse of the remainder of the Zhentilar. Already they were attempting to advance, even though they could do little more than crawl beneath the fallen trees or climb over them. The Zhentish cavalry that was not crushed in the attack had been rendered useless. Kelemvor's ground forces waited near the edge of the forest. He had hoped that even if the traps didn't rout the Zhentilar, the dalesmen's layered defense would at least slow the God of Strife's troops down.

If Bane's troops pushed past the tree trap, Kelemvor's men would rush out and attack. Then, if things went badly, they would pull back and the archers would provide covering fire for them. If things went well, the Zhentilar might be forced back to the wall made by the fallen trees, where the archers from the dale could continue to cut them down with little fear of return fire. If Bane's men were foolish enough to enter the forest to get at the archers, they'd be wiped out by Kelemvor's troops, who knew how to fight in the forest far more effectively than the Zhentish.

Kelemvor had not planned for the power of the wizard Sememmon, however. The information Mourngrym had received from Thurbal indicated that Bane had placed a prohibition on the use of magic, as magic was unstable and thus unreliable in so important a conflict. Few magic-users would even be allowed to march against the Dales, and those powerful mages that were allowed to fight, like Sememmon, were made officers.

Now, Sememmon stood in the easternmost section of the road hit by the tree trap. One of the trees hung just over his head, as if it had been stopped by a wall of force. The top section of the tree, past the magic-user's defenses, had fallen to the ground, its trunk shattered. Then the wizard walked out from under the tree and released his spell. The oak crashed to the ground, and Sememmon turned and called out to his men.

"We must use magic to push through this trap or we'll be slaughtered," he cried. "Bane be damned!" Then the mage quickly spoke an incantation and threw another spell.

Ten massive fireballs blasted a path through the tangle of trees before Sememmon, killing the Zhentish soldiers trapped beneath them and setting the tangle of trees ablaze. "No!" the wizard screeched. "That isn't the spell I called!" He attempted another spell. The ground seemed to shake, as if an earthquake had been called into existence. A symphony of cries erupted from the frightened soldiers surrounding the magic-user.

"You'll kill us all, you fool!" someone shouted.

Sememmon recognized the voice, despite the cacophony

of sound from the road. "Knightsbridge," he said in hoarse wonder. "You survived—"

Before the shocked wizard could finish his sentence, Knightsbridge struck him with the flat of his sword. The tremors stopped as Sememmon fell.

"Onward for Bane!" Knightsbridge yelled. "Onward for glory!"

A cadre of archers from Bane's army fired flaming arrows into the trees where the archers of Shadowdale had been stationed. Some of the dalesmen fell, others managed to make their pre-arranged retreats. Waiting with his men, Kelemvor felt a moment of panic as he watched the fire the Zhentish had created. If the flames spread in the forest, a blaze of unimaginable proportions could begin. If the woods burned, it would only be a matter of time before the fields of the dale were caught in the inferno, and all of Shadowdale would be destroyed.

A young lieutenant named Drizhal, a boy less than twenty winters old, stood at Kelemvor's side, sharing the fighter's concerns. The gangly youth was running a hand nervously through his bright yellow hair as he listened to the veteran warrior.

"If only there was a magic-user at our side," Kelemvor said. "I finally understand Mourngrym's frustration at Elminster's decision not to join the battle at the front. We're faced with this blaze while that old relic is off preparing some 'arcane defense' of his own."

"It isn't fair," Drizhal said, his voice cracking.

Kelemvor looked to the younger man. "Are you afraid?"

Drizhal said nothing, his expression telling all.

"Good!" Kelemvor said. "Fear keeps you sharp. Just don't let it get in the way."

The youth nodded, his terror seeming to lessen.

On the besieged road, Knightsbridge led the Zhentilar through the smoldering gauntlet of fallen trees. As the troops passed him, the wizard Sememmon rose on uncertain legs and attempted yet another spell. The men on every side of the wizard scattered as best they could, fearful of the unpredictable effects of magic.

Bolts of flaming red energy left the wizard's hands, then

went wild as an arrow from one of the archers of Shadow-dale pierced the mage's shoulder. Sememmon fell, and the bolts of energy flew over Knightsbridge's head and carved a path into the trees near Kelemvor. The wizard screamed in pain as a pair of soldiers dragged him to safety.

Knightsbridge saw the dalesmen scattering from where Sememmon's bolt had cut through the trees and ordered the Zhentilar to attack while the enemy was still in confusion. If Bane's army was fatigued from the night of marching through enemy territory, facing death with every step, it didn't show as they charged toward Kelemvor's men. The Zhentish seemed renewed, hungry to finally pay back some of the agonies that had been inflicted upon them during the trek from Voonlar.

Near the western edge of the forest, Kelemvor quickly gathered the leaders of his assault teams. Drizhal remained at the fighter's side.

"There's no chance of dragging them into the woods," Kelemvor said. "All we can do is face the enemy directly and try to keep them from breaking through to Shadowdale too quickly. We'll implement a layered defense right here and try to slow them down."

The leaders hurried to their men and informed them of the plans as Kelemvor watched Bane's army emerge from the opening the wizard had created in the fallen trees.

*　*　*　*　*

The last of the refugees had left down the Ashaba, and none of the soldiers had left their posts at the bridge to join their brothers at the eastern front. Nevertheless, Cyric skirted the length of the bridge every hour, checking and rechecking its defenses and keeping the men alert.

The thief was on Forester's side of the bridge, opposite from Shadowdale, when the sounds of the battle in the west reached him. The men on the other shore started talking loudly. Cyric turned to Forester.

"Keep to your position," the thief said. "I'd better go warn the others to settle down."

Cyric climbed up onto the bridge. He was almost to the

gateposts when he heard the sound from the road to the west—riders approaching at a gallop. The thief scrambled back to the ditch and signaled the fighters at the other bank. Then he readied his long bow.

"You wished for death and glory, you might get it yet!" Cyric whispered, and Forester smiled as he drew his sword. Then the thief turned to the other men near him. "Follow the plan. Wait until the last of them is upon the bridge, then move on my signal."

It seemed an eternity before the Zhentilar arrived. But at last the sounds of the riders crossing the bridge filled the dalesmen's ears, and Cyric watched as two dozen armored warriors passed overhead, nervously looking over their shoulders. No other troops were in sight on the road, so Cyric signaled the attack.

The Zhentilar had no chance. Cyric's bow laid out two of the soldiers, and a squad of men surged up from the trenches on either side of the river and attacked. Forester hacked away at the Zhentilar with glee, and as the last of the enemy fell, Cyric heard his men shout "For Shadowdale! For Shadowdale!"

There were sounds from the road to the west, and Cyric turned in time to see horsemen breaking from the trees in the distance. An army of riders led by a red-haired man on a beautiful warhorse was charging toward the bridge. Cyric saw that there were at least two hundred men heading their way.

"Ride on!" Fzoul shouted, and the wall of attackers closed on the bridge.

As Cyric ran, the eastern end of the Ashaba Bridge seemed to be moving away from him, not getting closer. The bridge was a little more than a thousand feet long, but it seemed like miles to the thief as he ran across it, an army closing in from behind. Forester and a handful of men were at Cyric's side as he ran.

The eastern bank was ahead of them when they heard the sound of Bane's army moving onto the other end of the bridge. Cyric saw that none of the Zhentilar were stopping on the western bank of the river, so the men that were hidden at the base of the bridge, right beneath the Zhentish troops, were safe. Everything was going according to their plan. That frightened Cyric. Nothing ever went exactly according to plan.

"Do you think it will work?" Forester said as they reached the eastern bank.

How should I know? Cyric wanted to say. Instead, he said, "Of course" and jumped for the bank.

Fully expecting an arrow to pierce his back just as he left the stone bridge, Cyric suddenly felt moist earth beneath his feet and realized he had made it across. Forester and the others were still beside him.

"Now for the hard part," Cyric said, almost out of breath. The thief turned and faced the oncoming horde and heard the telltale sounds of metal pulleys creaking beneath the bridge.

"At least two hundred are on the bridge. Mostly cavalry," Forester whispered.

There were more sounds. Men grunted as they pushed away the stones concealing their hiding niches in the pillar supports. Cyric hoped the splashes as the heavy stones hit the water wouldn't alert the Zhentilar on the bride to the trap.

"They're more than halfway across!" someone screamed.

"Do it, Cyric!" Forester hissed.

"Retreat!" Cyric screamed at the top of his lungs. Then Cyric and Forester ran as if Bane himself were chasing them, and they split up as they ran to the Twisted Tower so as not to present an easy target.

"Any time now," Cyric whispered.

Nothing happened.

Forester stopped before he reached the tower. Cyric stopped as well. "They didn't hear you," Forester cried.

"They must have heard me!" Cyric snapped.

They both turned toward the bridge. The main body of the army was approaching the eastern bank, and a few horsemen had already made it across. Cyric and Forester ran for the bridge.

"Retreat!" they screamed.

Still nothing happened.

Cyric cursed himself. If he had not listened to the men

from Suzail Key, this situation would not exist. He wanted to set more reliable traps, but they wouldn't listen.

"Retreat!" Cyric cried again.

Either the men under the bridge heard him this time or they got tired of waiting for the command and took matters into their own hands. Whatever the reason, though, they started to remove the flat-hewed logs that had been placed inside the holes where the keystone supports had once been. Then the men at the center of the bridge swung out from under the bridge on ropes, and their weight exerted the force necessary to break the weakened center support. Finally, the other supports for the bridge shattered and collapsed, too. The Zhentish soldiers shouted in surprise as the bridge fell away and the wildly churning Ashaba loomed up toward them.

Even Fzoul was stunned by the sight of the massive bridge falling. The red-haired man, who had already reached the eastern bank, turned in his saddle and stared. In seconds, there was nothing left of the bridge. Less than twenty of Fzoul's men had made it to the eastern bank. On the western bank, many were attempting to slow their mounts before they were pushed into the gaping hole left by the collapse of the bridge. Over three-quarters of the force had been tossed into the Ashaba and drowned in their heavy armor.

There were less than twenty archers in the Twisted Tower, but the soldiers who rode or stood beside Fzoul didn't know this. Even when the arrows began to fly and the soldiers at the front were slain, there was no realization that so few could have brought down so many. There were only the cries of the wounded and the frightened as Fzoul slid from his horse and fell to the ground, taking cover from the archers as his men died around him. Some of the soldiers were backing away, falling into the river. Fzoul realized that the corpses of his men and their mounts would block the edge of the bridge, and their movement would be slowed until they were killed one by one from the tower. The Zhentilar had lost the battle before they'd even met sword to sword with one dalesman.

On his hands and knees, Fzoul crawled back through the

ranks of his dead and dying troops and started to strip off his armor.

The men who had sapped the bridge climbed up onto the western bank and attacked the remaining Zhentilar. The archers from the tower also moved out toward the road and began to move forward.

Cyric took his bow from his back and grabbed an arrow from the quiver of a nearby archer. The thief had not taken his gaze from the red-haired commander who was attempting to make his escape from the shattered bridge. The man was crawling away and taking off his armor. Obviously the coward was going to try to leap into the river.

Cyric notched a single arrow and braced himself. As the commander stood up and prepared to dive off the edge of the bridge, the thief screamed "Red hair!"

Fzoul locked eyes with Cyric for a moment, then tried to jump. At the same instant, Cyric loosed the single shaft with unerring accuracy. The arrow pierced Fzoul's side as he fell into the river.

The slaughter of Bane's men continued, but the battle at the western front was over. Cyric gathered most of the men together and headed for the eastern front. As they approached the center of town, though, they heard the sounds of a battle in progress—steel clashed against steel, and commanders screamed out orders. Cyric and his men charged into the nearest group of Zhentish soldiers. When they had driven them off, Cyric quickly asked a commander what had happened.

"The Zhents came from the north, too. Just as we'd expected. We slowed them down a bit with the traps and ramparts we'd set up in the farms they had to pass, but they got here anyway."

Then another group of Zhentilar charged Cyric and he was once more lost in the battle.

In the furious fighting that covered the crossroads of Shadowdale, few noticed the squad of Zhentilar cavalry break off and head down the road to the east.

* * * * *

Kelemvor knew they would face impossible odds. Still, he gave the order to advance without hesitation. As commander of the entire movement, Kelemvor's place was in the third line of defense. Those who charged out in the first line would account for the heaviest percentage of casualties in the attack on Bane's armies, but there wasn't a soldier that had not volunteered for their position. Kelemvor had been spared the duty of selecting those who would rush off to die.

Bane's soldiers emerged, six at a time, from the path Sememmon had blazed. Most of the horses had been killed in the trap, so most of the troops were infantry.

"Why not use our cavalry?" Drizhal said to Kelemvor. "We might be able to force them back that way."

"We'll need the mounts later," Kelemvor said. "Their speed will allow our survivors to fall back and regroup long before Bane's army can reach them." The fighter turned away from the younger man and deployed the foot soldiers to cut down Bane's forces as they left the narrow opening through the fallen trees in the road.

The dalesmen had some success in slowing down the Zhentish charge. Soon, however, they were forced back by the sheer number of Zhentilar still advancing. Kelemvor used the archers to provide covering fire as the survivors of the first group fell back and joined with Kelemvor and his men. At the same time, another band of dalesmen moved forward.

"Whoever their commander is, he's good," Kelemvor said. "My own tactics don't seem to be fazing him at all."

"It's almost as if he knows you," Drizhal said.

Kelemvor shook his head. "Or he knows what to expect."

Bishop, the commander of the first group of dalesmen to attack, approached Kelemvor. He was slightly older than Kelemvor, with dirty blond hair and a fair complexion.

"They're fighting like desperate men. If this was a holy crusade, like you said, they wouldn't be. It's more like fighting for survival, now," Bishop said. "They're not so anxious to die anymore."

"But they keep coming," Kelemvor said. "Do you think we can force a retreat?"

Bishop shook his head. "The Zhentilar in front have some madman driving them on, but they're scared and they want to turn back. Those in the rear are hungry for revenge, and they're pushing forward. That's what it seems like from all the shouting. I wouldn't be surprised if a lot of them are deserting into the forest."

Suddenly there were shouts from the rear of Kelemvor's troops. The fighter turned and saw a squadron of men approaching from the west. They wore the colors of Bane's army.

"Where did *they* come from?" Bishop said.

"The north road," Kelemvor said with growing alarm. "A battalion must have come through the north road. That means Hawksguard and Mourngrym have already been attacked, and these men were forced to retreat from them."

"Or the dalelord is already dead," Bishop said quietly.

"Don't even think it," Kelemvor shouted as he sent a group to stop the Zhentish cavalry in the rear before they caused too much havok in the ranks. It was already too late for that, though, as the horsemen charged into the dalesmen's lines.

"Kelemvor!" Drizhal shouted. "More of Bane's soldiers are breaking through from the east!"

"We'll have to fight them, hold them here, and cut down their numbers as best we can until help arrives." Kelemvor said.

"What about the bog? Can't we still draw them into the bog and fight them there?" Drizhal said.

"You might as well forget that idea," Kelemvor said, smiling weakly at the boy. "I've spent enough time with dalesmen to know they would never retreat from anyone . . . especially the Zhentish."

Drizhal watched as Bane's soldiers poured through the opening.

"Prepare cavalry!" Kelemvor shouted as he drew his sword. "We fight to the last man!"

Soon all of Kelemvor's finely drawn battle plans turned to dust as the dalesmen faced the enemy in a chaotic melee. Kelemvor knew that they would be hopelessly overwhelmed when the full weight of Bane's army was brought against them. He knew that the only real hope was an organized retreat through the remaining, small stone barricades on the way to Shadowdale. But as the situation rapidly deteriorated strategically, Kelemvor saw that the defenders of Shadowdale were more than happy to go to their deaths fighting the Zhentish man-to-man.

The fighter watched half-a-dozen men whom he had stood beside rush into battle, then fall before the dark army of the evil god. When he faced an enemy soldier himself, however, Kelemvor drew little satisfaction in the man's death. He wasn't fighting for the same thing the dalesmen were fighting for; all Kelemvor was doing was delaying what he saw now as the inevitable fall of Shadowdale. Then Drizhal fell before an enemy soldier, and Kelemvor turned to face the boy's attacker.

The Zhentish soldier lashed out with his mace and Kelemvor drew back and away from the weapon. The fighter then swung blindly with his sword, and he realized with disgust that he had only impaled the mount of the mace-wielding Zhentilar. The wounded horse pitched forward and its rider flew to the ground without losing his grip on his bloodied weapon.

Kelemvor advanced on the downed soldier, then froze as the man turned over and Kelemvor saw his face:

It was Ronglath Knightsbridge, the traitor to Arabel.

Seizing upon his enemy's momentary surprise, Knightsbridge swung his mace once more. The heavy club grazed Kelemvor's leg and knocked him from his feet. Drawing his sword with his free hand as he scrambled to his feet, Knightsbridge waited until Kelemvor had half-risen before slashing at the fighter's ribs with the sword, then swinging his mace again. Even as he fell to dodge the sword, Kelemvor brought his sword up in a block, stopping the mace before it met his neck.

Kelemvor got to his feet at once, and the two fighters slowly circled one another, looking for an opening. Suddenly, Knightsbridge shouted "No!"

Kelemvor ducked and the horseman's sword swished just over his head. The fighter leaped to his left, then brought the pommel of his sword down hard on the rider's hand. There was a crack as something in the Zhentilar's hand broke, and the horseman dropped his weapon.

Before Kelemvor could react, Knightsbridge charged at him again and slashed viciously at his head. "You die by my hand alone!" Knightsbridge hissed and raised his mace again.

Kelemvor rushed at the Zhentilar, and the fighter's sword ripped through the traitor's side as the mace swung toward him. Avoiding the blow, Kelemvor brought his armored fist into Knightsbridge's jaw, sending him stumbling back.

Knightsbridge was exposed for an instant, and Kelemvor rushed at him again and and tackled him, giving the Zhentilar no chance to use his weapons. They struck the ground and Knightsbridge kicked Kelemvor in the chest, forcing him to tumble to his side.

"You cost me my life!" Knightsbridge screamed. "Everything I cared about is gone because of you!"

Knightsbridge raised his sword high over his head, but the swing exposed his chest and Kelemvor drove his sword through Knightsbridge's breastplate before he could deliver his final blow. The traitor's eyes gave no quarter, even as life fled from them. His face fixed in an eternal grimace of hatred and pain, Knightsbridge fell into the dirt and died.

As Kelemvor pulled his sword from Knightsbridge's chest, he saw a glint of bright, shining metal as a Zhentish dagger flew toward him. A sword flashed before the fighter and the dagger was deflected. Another flash and the Zhentilar fell.

"That's the problem with these jackals," a familiar voice said flatly, "there's always more than one of them."

Kelemvor's savior turned to face the fighter. It was Bishop, commander of the first group.

"Behind you!" Bishop shouted, and Kelemvor spun and dispatched another Zhentish soldier.

Two more riders approached, swords drawn. Bishop dragged the first of the riders from his mount and ran him through, as Kelemvor faced the soldier's fellow and killed him. Then another wave of Bane's soldiers approached on foot, and the warriors fought back to back until they were knee-deep in the bodies of the dead and dying. Their swords flashed as the endless parade of dark soldiers closed in on the dalesmen.

As Kelemvor looked to the road to the west, his heart sank; Bane's army was getting through the men and the barricades, and moving toward Shadowdale.

* * * * *

With each death, Bane's power grew until his vision was glazed over by an amber haze of power. He felt his frail mortal shell blistering from his stolen energy, but he endured the discomfort gladly.

Teleporting from the barricade had been a simple matter. He found himself at the outskirts of the dale and quickly cast a spell of invisibility upon himself, then used the power of the soul energies to take to the air.

A small band of Zhentilar had been deployed to travel the north road into Shadowdale and engage the soldiers at the crossroads of the town, where Bane had assumed the defenders would make their last stand. There were no more than five hundred men in this detail, and many would be stopped by the defenses Mourngrym's men had certainly placed in their way along the road and in the farms to the north.

As he flew toward the crossroads, Bane was delighted to find that at least a few hundred of his men from the north had made it through, yet it seemed they had been expected. Bane descended to the center of the fighting while maintaining his invisibility. In the distance he could see the Celestial Stairway, its changing aspects a beacon in the sky that drove him onward, and would eventually take him home. Beside the stairway he could see the brightly lit Temple of Lathander. One combatant had been notoriously absent throughout the battle and Bane suddenly realized the logical place for his adversary to hide.

"Elminster," Bane said and laughed. "I would have given you more credit."

A human approached, wielding a sword.

Mourngrym.

How delightful it would be to carry the head of the lord of Shadowdale upon his belt as he opened his arms in greeting to the hated sage. Bane dropped his invisibility and laughed as Mourngrym stopped just before the Black Lord, startled by Bane's sudden appearance. Bane crushed Mourngrym's sword in his taloned hand as Mourngrym swung at him, then reached down to claim his prize.

Suddenly another man appeared and pulled Mourngrym from the Black Lord's grasp. Bane ripped open the second man's chest.

"Hawksguard!" Mourngrym shouted as the older man fell to the ground.

Bane was about to kill the stunned dalelord when he caught sight of the Celestial Stairway.

It was burning, set ablaze by blue-white eldritch fires.

The humans all but forgotten, Bane used the power of the dead to take to the cold night air. Bane drew close to the Temple of Lathander. The temple, molded in the form of a phoenix, was releasing a flow of bluish white fires that assaulted the stairway like a dragon spewing forth its fiery breath. The stairway crackled with the eldritch flames, and Bane watched with horror as the changing aspects became a heated blur that the eyes of his avatar could no longer bear to look upon.

The flesh of the Black Lord was engulfed in an amber haze as the continuous flow of souls ripped through his form, strengthening the god until his power reached levels he had only tasted for fleeting instants in the dungeons of Castle Kilgrave. Knowledge of countless spells and the power to cast them at will, without the physical components usually necessary, coursed through the Black Lord. He was almost a god again.

I can destroy this place, Bane thought. I can raze it to its foundations and slay all who dare stand against me.

He looked back to the Celestial Stairway and flew as close as he dared, then hovered in midair and watched as his way back to the Planes melted away. There was nothing he could do to stop the destruction of the stairway; his plans to retake the Planes had been thwarted. Elminster had dared to stand against the Black Lord and now the old sage would pay.

Bane descended to the temple and studied it for a

moment. He did not dare to enter through the passages that released the mystical fires. That would certainly destroy his avatar. And when he checked the doors and windows, Bane found they had been fortified by a spell of some sort. To break the magical ward would certainly alert Elminster to his presence.

Then Bane saw a window that had been left unguarded, and he rose to it tentatively, expecting Elminster's gaze to meet his when he looked into it. But no one was there. Bane passed through the bright stream of light that flowed from the window without harm, and he found himself standing in the bedroom of a high priest of Lathander. At his feet, Bane noticed a book with the words "Diary of Faith" embroidered on its cover. The Black Lord crouched and picked up the leather-bound journal.

When Bane read the words on the final page, he could not stop laughing. Only when he heard the sound of voices directly below did he drop the book and stop laughing. Casting a glassee spell, Bane looked at floor, then through the wood planks and supports that separated him from the sage.

He saw Elminster casting a spell. The mage looked exhausted, as if he had been working on this spell for the entire night. Swirling mist whirled in all directions. The magic-user and the cleric who had interfered with Bane's plans in Castle Kilgrave were here; the failure of his assassins to report had steeled him for this knowledge, and somehow he was made quite happy by this turn of events. To the Black Lord, there was nothing sweeter than taking the lives of his enemies with his own hands.

The cleric was busy rifling through ancient tomes, locating spells for the dark-haired magic-user to study. Occasionally Elminster would address the magic-user, and she would recite one of the spells she had learned.

And when the woman mage repeated the spells, they worked, even without components! Bane stared at the woman, then saw the star pendant, the symbol of Mystra, around here neck. Each time she cast a spell, tiny strands of energy played across the pendant and disappeared when the spell was finished.

RICHARD AWLINSON

She must have some of Mystra's power in that trinket, Bane thought. I must have it for my assault on Helm and Ao.

Bane considered how best to take the old sage by surprise, but there was no spell he could think of to accomplish his goal. Refusing to be daunted, Bane lay face-down upon the floor and used his stolen power to make his form insubstantial. Then he slowly drifted into the floor until his face protruded from the other side very slightly, and followed the ceiling until it met with the wall nearest Elminster. The Black Lord then drifted down the wall, keeping his prey in view at all times. Finally, when he stood no more than six paces behind Elminster, Bane pushed away from the cover of the wall and advanced on the sage, talons extended.

By the time the dark-haired magic-user noticed Bane's presence, the Black Lord's talons were only inches away from Elminster's throat.

The sage of Shadowdale was lost in the private world of the spells he was casting. He felt the great powers he was releasing flow from the magical weave around Faerun, and when he opened his eyes, he saw that a section of the temple's floor had vanished as planned. A rift had been opened by his conjurings—a rift that was lined by a swirling mist that flashed with a power he had summoned only once before, and then when he was much younger. In those days, when he was only one hundred and forty, he believed himself to be immortal. Now, as Elminster looked down into the rift, he was frightened just a bit by the forces that he had brought into the Realms to combat the Black Lord.

The old sage was shocked from his conjuring by Midnight's cry. He looked over his shoulder and caught a glimpse of the fiery eyes of the God of Strife as his talons descended toward him. Elminster spoke a word of power, and Bane was thrown back by an incredible force. The Black Lord struck the wall he had emerged from.

A horrible screech came from the rift in the floor, and Elminster turned to see that his spell of summoning had gone awry when Bane attacked. The thing that had come to him instead of the eye of eternity was unknown to the old sage, and that frightened him very much.

"Midnight!" Elminster cried. "You must try a spell of

containment!" There was no time to wait for a reply, as Bane moved forward against the aged sage again. Elminster released a blinding flash of blue-white lightning that ensnared the dark god in a nearly endless series of traps. The Black Lord screamed in rage and used his power to cut away at the eldritch bonds.

Elminster recoiled as a searing bolt of amber flame tore through him. He countered the spell, but he could sense the dark god growing in power, his spells replenished almost as quickly as they were cast. The great sage could afford no such luxury. Every incantation took its toll, until finally the God of Strife began to drive him back into the swirling mist of the rift.

Bane pressed the advantage, calling into play the forces he had reserved to unleash on Helm. Unspeakable energies flowed through the dark god, and he felt incredible pain as his mortal avatar struggled to maintain its form and focus the great powers. Bane would feed the sage to the creature that had been summoned, then he would use the creature to devour the God of Guardians and great Ao himself. Bane would have to remind himself to ask Myrkul to deliver his thanks to the sage in the land of the dead.

Suddenly a blue-white bolt unlike anything Bane had ever felt before cut through him, sending him flying back and away from the sage. He looked up and saw the dark-haired magic-user standing at the other side of the room, her hands moving as she intoned another spell.

Bane laughed. "You may have part of Mystra's power, girl, but you are not a goddess." Then the God of Strife lashed out with a bolt of energy that knocked Midnight across the room. Bane stood up and prepared to kill the mage. Then he heard the horrible rumbling from the rift, and knew that whatever Elminster had summoned had arrived.

When the God of Strife turned and saw the thing from the rift, his avatar's heart nearly stopped beating.

"Mystra," Bane said slowly.

But the being before him shared little with the ethereal goddess he had enslaved and tortured in Castle Kilgrave. This was a creature that had no place in the world of men or gods. Mystra was no longer a creature of flesh and blood or a god of the Planes. She had become a primal essence, a part of the phantasmagoric wonderland of the weave of magic surrounding the world. She could only be called a magic elemental.

Rational thought came only with the greatest of efforts to her now; Mystra was barely conscious and powerless to act. Only the power of Elminster's summoning had been great enough to allow her essence to reform and give her access to the Realms—and a chance to face Lord Bane once again.

Huge threads of primal magic burst from Mystra's eyes and encircled the room. A single, impossible hand clawed from her ectoplasmic flesh, and Mystra reached out toward Bane.

Adon covered Midnight with his body as the bolts of energy raced around the room, scorching the walls and scattering Elminster's books. Then Midnight stirred and looked up at Mystra in horror. "Goddess," was all she could say.

Then Elminster released another spell at Bane, but a steady flow of green eggs shot from the old sage's hand and struck the dark god. Elminster cursed and started another incantation. Bane turned from Mystra and released a single bolt of amber light. Just before the amber light struck Elminster, he created a shield to hold the bolt off, but he was knocked, screaming, into the rift anyway. Then blinding bolts of blue-white energy leaped from the hand of Mystra as it fell on the God of Strife.

Bane fell to his knees as the force of his stolen power was turned on him, and his frail human avatar slowly ripped apart. Flesh and blood and bone collapsed into a steaming mass that was now only remotely human.

"I'll not—die—alone!" Bane hissed, and the bloodied avatar crawled forward, reaching out as he saw the dark-haired magic-user huddled with the cleric. Her hands were on the pendant, as if she were about to use the magic against the Black Lord again. Then the pendant snapped from her neck and flew to Lord Bane. The god laughed as his talons closed over it.

"Your power is mine again, Mystra," the God of Strife said through blistered lips.

Midnight heard the cracking, maniacal voice of Mystra inside her head as the mage got up and walked toward the God of Strife. *Strike him* the voice said. *Use the power I gave you.*

A bolt of blue-white power surged from Midnight as she completed her spell. It struck Bane and knocked him closer to Mystra. The Black Lord looked up at Midnight for a moment, confusion in his eyes. "But I have the—"

Then the God of Strife screamed as Mystra covered him. *Here, Lord Bane*, Mystra said as she engulfed him. *Have all the power you want.* There was a flash of blue-white fire and Bane's avatar exploded violently. Mystra's amorphous body stiffened for a second as the avatar died, as she absorbed the power from the blast. Then she, too, disappeared in a flash of brilliant white light.

"Goddess!" Midnight cried, but even as she spoke the word, the mage knew this time that Mystra was dead. Then she remembered that Elminster had been knocked into the rift. When she looked up, Adon was at the rift's edge, staring into the mist that was pouring from it, his arms in front of him as if the cleric were reaching out for someone inside the mist.

"Elminster," she said slowly. Then Midnight saw a blur of motion inside the rift. The mist parted for only a moment, and she saw the old sage locked in a desperate battle to seal the rift that he had opened.

Midnight ran to Adon's side. The cleric was holding his hands out in front of him, as he would if he were casting a spell. "Please, Sune," he said softly, and tears started to run down his cheeks.

Elminster didn't seem to see Midnight and Adon as they stood at the edge of the rift. He was too busy moving his hands in complex patterns and chanting long incantations. Then, the old sage screamed, and a dark violet light poured from the rift. Midnight prepared a spell, but as she raised her hands to throw it, there was a flash, and Elminster and the rift were gone. The temple started to shake, and Midnight fell to her knees.

Adon dragged her to her feet and pulled her forward. She felt the warm air and sunlight rush at her face as they

RICHARD AWLINSON

passed through the blinding blue-white lightning that filled the corridor. When they got outside, Midnight looked to the sky and gasped as she saw the massive flames that engulfed the Celestial Stairway blazing into the heavens. For an instant, the charred, black fragments of the stairway itself were visible to her, its aspects frozen in a dizzying array of images. In places she saw the myriad hands she had glimpsed once before; they were trembling and clutching at the air. Then the stairway was gone, and she could only see the flames.

Midnight and Adon fell to the ground and behind them an ear-splitting sound erupted as the walls of the temple splintered, and the wings of the turrets crashed to the ground.

All of Shadowdale trembled as the Temple of Lathander exploded.

To the east of the explosion, there was a moment when almost all fighting on the road near Krag Pool stopped; a moment in which the combatants had stared at the sky in stunned silence. The fires seemed to cascade down from the heavens, cutting through the sky to engulf the area near Lathander's temple.

Kelemvor stared at the flames in shock. His first thought was to abandon his post and ride to Midnight's side, but he knew that Elminster had to be alive. He was legendary for his powers, and he could protect Midnight better than a fighter ever could. Besides, Kelemvor knew he couldn't leave his men without a leader. Midnight's fate was in her own hands, just as she had desired.

The respite caused by the explosion lasted no more than a few seconds, then the fighting resumed. Bane's forces were clearly exhausted, and the loss of their key commanders from the battlefield had reduced the ranks of the Zhentilar to an undisciplined rabble fighting for their lives. Bane had not returned, Sememmon was wounded and unconscious, and Knightsbridge was dead. Most importantly, the defenders of Shadowdale showed no sign of buckling before the dwindling, but still superior numbers of Bane's army.

Commander Bishop stood beside Kelemvor. "They come from all directions," Bishop said, barely able to catch his

330

breath. "By the gods, this is a young man's game!"

"It's a sad and gruesome game, then," Kelemvor said as he guarded the Bishop's back and they slowly moved forward through the pockets of carnage. Bodies were everywhere. The dead numbered in the thousands, and the fighting had become more desperate than ever. Kelemvor heard one of the Zhentilar call out for Lord Bane. Others responded that he had fled.

"Did you hear that?" Kelemvor said, but Bishop was already busy with a swordswoman who matched his every blow and showed no sign of the exhaustion that had over-taken the dalesman.

Before Kelemvor could turn and help Bishop, another Zhentish horseman rode at him, slicing down with his sword. Kelemvor dragged the soldier off his horse and ran him through. Pulling himself onto the ebon mount, Kelem-vor held out his hand to Bishop, who had just killed the swordswoman. The commander reached up, then cried out as an arrow pierced his leg. He faltered and Kelemvor grabbed his hand and dragged him to the mount.

Another arrow sailed past them, and Kelemvor kicked the horse into motion. They found a small contingent of dales-men fighting for their lives against the Zhentilar, and Kelem-vor forced the horse to charge into the skirmish.

Kelemvor and Bishop waded into the sea of dark armor, their blades cutting a wide arc in the forces of the Zhentilar. But their efforts weren't enough to even the odds. They were dragged down from opposite sides of the horse, and forced to fight on foot. Then, there was a mad chant from the west, and another troop of ebon-armored riders burst into the battle. But they were not Zhentilar; they wore the symbol of the white horse upon their helmets.

The Riders of Mistledale.

Kelemvor let out a wild scream and gutted the Zhentilar he was fighting. The Riders were the best cavalry in the Dales. Though they only numbered twenty men, they were each a match for five Zhentish soldiers.

Another dalesman let out a cheer and pointed to the west again. "Look there!"

Kelemvor saw another group of fighters, who could only

be the Knights of Myth Drannor, charging down the road. They were leading the majority of Shadowdale's defenders from the town, Lord Mourngrym in their lead.

Before another hour was up, Bane's army started to retreat. The presence of the Riders of Mistledale and the Knights of Myth Drannor had broken the resolve of most of the Zhentilar. Nearly all of the soldiers from Bane's army that managed to break through the gray stone barricade had been killed by the defenders in town. The dalesmen at the bridge had driven off Fzoul and his troops. The Zhentish riders who had attacked from the north had been killed or forced to retreat. Now, the Zhentish forces in the east were running, too.

At the barricades leading to Shadowdale, Kelemvor and Bishop met up with Mourngrym and two of the Knights.

"They are retreating!" Mourngrym cried out. "We've won!"

Kelemvor could not believe the words so easily. Many of the Zhentilar would stay and fight until their last breath had been taken from them. The skirmishes had led into the forest, and small fires burned there already, threatening to grow out of control. If nothing else, Shadowdale had lost far too many men to deal with even a small forest fire well.

Kelemvor looked around the battlefield, but didn't see any of his friends. "Lord Mourngrym, where are Cyric and Hawksguard?"

Mourngrym's triumphant expression vanished. "They are at the crossroads," the dalelord said softly. "Cyric is fine save for a few scratches. Hawksguard. . . ."

Kelemvor looked into the eyes of the lord of Shadowdale.

"It was Bane," Mourngrym said at last. "He had me within his grasp and Hawksguard saved me."

Kelemvor turned and spurred the horse into a gallop as he rode to the crossroads. The fighter passed Cyric and a handful of his men as they rode into the woods to chase down retreating Zhentish soldiers, but he didn't even hear Cyric's cries of greeting.

When Kelemvor finally reached the center of Shadowdale, he found the dead being carted away and the injured being tended where they fell. He saw Hawksguard almost immediately, layed out with the other officers.

Kelemvor made his way to the side of the older warrior. Hawksguard was not dead, but there could be no doubt that he would not survive the day. Bane's taloned hands had cut deeply into his chest, and it was a miracle that he was not dead already. Kelemvor took Hawksguard's hand and looked into his eyes.

"They'll pay for this," Kelemvor growled. "I will hunt them down and slay them all!"

Hawksguard grasped Kelemvor's arm, smiled weakly, and shook his head. "Don't be melodramatic," he said. "This life . . . is too short. . . ."

"This isn't fair," Kelemvor said.

Hawksguard coughed, and a deep spasm shook his body. "Closer," Hawksguard said. "Something you must know."

His voice had become a whisper.

"Important," Hawksguard said.

Kelemvor leaned close.

And Hawksguard told him a joke.

Kelemvor felt his lower lip tremble, but finally, he laughed. Hawksguard had driven out the thoughts of death and blood that Kelemvor felt welling up inside of him by reminding him of something he had almost lost:

Hope.

* * * * *

The Battle of Shadowdale was over. Bane's forces had retreated into the forest, although many found only a fiery death instead of the escape they hoped for. The blaze was spreading, but there was little the tired dalesmen could do to contain the fire.

Sharantyr, a ranger with the Knights of Myth Drannor, rode to the Temple of Lathander, along with the Harper bard Storm Silverhand, to investigate the explosion and fire there, and to check on Elminster and the two strangers to Shadowdale he had with him.

As they approached, Sharantyr and Storm saw Midnight and Adon stumble from the wreckage of the temple. Then a fireball erupted from within the ruins and shot into the air.

Sharantyr had to leap from her mount and drag Storm to the ground to prevent her from riding into the inferno.

"Elminster," Storm cried, her gaze fixed on the destruction. A bubble of blue-white energy enshrouded the cleric and the mage who had escaped, and the Knights watched as a wall of debris was vaporized when it hit the shield. Finally, when the earth settled and all that remained of the Temple of Lathander was a shattered ruin, the Knights ran to the strangers, who lay untouched by the destruction.

After seeing if the cleric and mage were alive, Storm ran past into the temple. Within the flaming ruins, navigating past the debris-filled antechamber, Storm forced a fallen support beam out of her way and entered what was left of the main room of worship. The silver-haired bard felt her heart beat faster as she searched through the wreckage for some sign that Elminster had survived. At the far side of the room, she found fragments of his ancient spell books and even tattered pieces of his robe.

Blood and bits of bone were splattered on the walls that still stood in the temple.

Storm screamed from the depths of her heart. Her rage consumed her and she ran from the flaming temple to face the strangers.

When the silver-haired bard got outside, she saw that Sharantyr was talking to the cleric and mage who had fled from the temple. The ranger was about to question the dark-haired woman when Storm appeared before them, sword in hand.

"Elminster," she said, her voice low and tinged with hatred. "Elminster is dead. Murdered."

Storm lunged forward, and Sharantyr had to hold her back and disarm her before she could let Storm go again. Then, a great shadow passed over the temple, and the air grew thin and cold. In seconds, the perfect blue of the sky became a steel-gray, and storm clouds converged at the head of the blazing Celestial Stairway. A huge eye appeared at the apex of the clouds, and a single tear left the eye as it blinked and vanished. The tear became a flood of unnatural rain that burst from the heavens, drenching the entire dale. Bluish white wisps of smoke rose from the stairway as the flames that had destroyed it were extinguished, and far from the temple, in the forest near Krag Pool, the fires died away beneath the torrents of rain.

Storm Silverhand had seemed to calm as the wall of rain fell, but then she saw the face of the young, scarred cleric.

"He was—he was at the Temple of Tymora," the bard whispered, breathlessly. "He was there right after the murders!"

Sharantyr moved forward, and this time she had her sword drawn. "I am Sharantyr of the Knights of Myth Drannor," she said. "It is my solemn duty to place you both under arrest for the murder of Elminster the Sage. . . ."

ABOUT THE AUTHOR

The Avatar project, which consists of both game and book releases, is the combined effort of a number of TSR staff members and talented free-lance authors. Richard Awlinson is the pseudonym of *Shadowdale*'s author, Scott Ciencin.

New Characters, New Adventure

The Avatar Trilogy

Richard Awlinson

Tantras
Book Two

Convicted for the murder of Elminster, the heroes flee in search of evidence to clear themselves, and to find the missing Tablets of Fate, needed for the gods to return to their planes . . . or for others to take their places. . . .

Waterdeep
Book Three

The search continues to the largest city in the Realms, where the characters believe the last tablet is hidden. However, one of the heroes has cast his lot with the evil gods, and his denizens await the others at every turn.

EMPIRES TRILOGY

HORSELORDS
David Cook

Between the western Realms and Kara-Tur lies a vast, unexplored domain. The "civilized" people of the Realms have given little notice to these nomadic barbarians. Now, a mighty leader has united these wild horsemen into an army powerful enough to challenge the world. First, they turn to Kara-Tur.

DRAGONWALL
Troy Denning

The barbarian horsemen have breached the Dragonwall and now threaten the oriental lands of Kara-Tur. Shou Lung's only hope lies with a general descended from the barbarians, and whose wife must fight the imperial court if her husband is to retain his command.

CRUSADE
James Lowder

The barbarian army has turned its sights on the western Realms. Only King Azoun has the strength to forge an army to challenge the horsemen. But Azoun had not reckoned that the price of winning might be the life of his beloved daughter.

THE MAZTICA TRILOGY

Douglas Niles

IRONHELM

A slave girl learns of a great destiny laid upon her by the gods themselves. And across the sea, a legion of skilled mercenaries sails west to discover a land of primitive savagery mixed with high culture. Under the banner of its vigilant god the legion claims these lands for itself. And only as Erix sees her land invaded is her destiny revealed.

VIPERHAND

The God of War feasts upon chaos while the desperate lovers, Erix and Halloran, strive to escape the waves of catastrophe sweeping Maztica. Each is forced into a choice of historical proportion and deeply personal emotion. The destruction of the fabulously wealthy continent of Maztica looms on the horizon. Available now.

FEATHERED DRAGON

Forces of terror rack Maztica, destroying cities and forcing whole populations to flee for their lives. The one hope for survival is the promised return of Qotal, the Feathered Dragon. Erixitl of Palul holds the key to that return, but only if she succeeds in her final and most difficult quest.

OFFICIAL
Advanced Dungeons & Dragons
COMPUTER PRODUCT

SECRET OF THE SILVER BLADES

A FORGOTTEN REALMS
Fantasy Role-Playing Epic, Vol. III

STRATEGIC SIMULATIONS, INC.

LONG-AWAITED SEQUEL TO POOL OF RADIANCE AND CURSE OF THE AZURE BONDS COMPUTER GAMES!

Available for: IBM, C-64/128.
Visit your retailer or call 1-800-245-4525 for VISA/MC
orders. To receive SSI's complete catalog, send $1.00 to:

STRATEGIC SIMULATIONS, INC.®
675 Almanor Ave. Suite 201
Sunnyvale, CA 94086

 ADVANCED DUNGEONS & DRAGONS, AD&D, FORGOTTEN REALMS, and the TSR logo are trademarks owned
by and used under license from TSR, Inc. ©1990 TSR, Inc. All rights reserved.

DRAGONLANCE Sag

Meetings Sextet

Dragonlance
KINDRED SPIRITS
Mark Anthony

The Meetings Sextet
Volume One

Dragonlance
WANDERLUST
Mary Kirchoff & Steve Winter

The Meetings Sextet
Volume Two

Dragonlance
DARK HEART
Tina Daniell

The Meetings Sextet
Volume Three

Kindred Spirits

Mark Anthony and Ellen Pora

The reluctant paternal dwarven hero, Flint Fireforge, is invited to the
elven kingdom of Qualinesti, where he meets a young, unhappy half-e
named Tanis. But when Laurana, the beauteous daughter of the elves
ruler, declares her love for Tanis, a deadly rival for her affections con-
cocts a scenario fraught with risk and scandal for both the half-elf and
his dwarven ally. On Sale April 1991.

Wanderlust

Mary Kirchoff and Steve Wint

Tasslehoff Burrfoot accidentally pockets one of Flint's copper bracele
and Tanis good-naturedly defends the top-knotted newcomer to
Solace—triggering a thoroughly unpredictable tale, which includes a
sinister stranger who has evil on his mind for the three new friends.
On Sale September 1991.

Dark Heart

Tina Dani

At long last, the story of the beautiful, dark-hearted Kitiara Uth Matar
from the birth of her twin brothers, the frail mage Raistlin and the
warrior Caramon. Kitiara's increasing fascination with evil throws her
into the company of a roguish stranger and an eerie mage whose fate
are intermingled with her own. On Sale January 1992.